BEAST OF SHADOWS

Copyright © 2020 by Krista Street
All rights reserved.
Published in the United States.

Paperback ISBN-13: 979-8697534489
Hardcover ISBN: 979-8838403940
Large Print ISBN: 979-8551784333
ASIN: B086SCHDNQ

All rights reserved. No part of this publication may be reproduced, scanned, transmitted or distributed in any printed or electronic form, or stored in a database or retrieval system for any commercial or non-commercial use, without the author's written permission.

This book is a work of fiction. Names, characters, places and plot are either products of the author's imagination or used fictitiously. Any resemblance to any person, living or dead, or any places, business establishments, events or occurrences, are purely coincidental.

The author expressly prohibits any entity from using any part of this publication, including text and graphics, for purposes of training artificial intelligence (AI) technologies to generate text or graphics, including without limitation technologies that are capable of generating works in the same style or genre as this publication.

5841021080806849
www.kristastreet.com

All books written by Krista Street are written entirely by her. No AI is used in the creation of Krista Street's books.

Cover art created by Maria Spada: www.mariaspada.com

BOOKS BY KRISTA STREET
SUPERNATURAL WORLD NOVELS

Fae of Snow & Ice
Court of Winter
Thorns of Frost
Wings of Snow
Crowns of Ice

Supernatural Curse
Wolf of Fire
Bound of Blood
Cursed of Moon
Forged of Bone

Supernatural Institute
Fated by Starlight
Born by Moonlight
Hunted by Firelight
Kissed by Shadowlight

Supernatural Community
Magic in Light
Power in Darkness
Dragons in Fire
Angel in Embers

Supernatural Standalone Novels
Beast of Shadows

Links to all of Krista's books may be found on her website:
www.kristastreet.com

BEAST
OF
SHADOWS

wolf shifter romance
SUPERNATURAL WORLD

KRISTA STREET

PREFACE

Beast of Shadows is a wolf shifter paranormal romance standalone novel set within the same world as *Supernatural Community*. The recommended reading age is 18+.

CHAPTER ONE
COLLIN

Her scent drifts to me on the hot Arizona breeze. She smells of warm caramel and sunshine.

An apron cinches her narrow waist, and the flare of her hips draws my attention, but she works quickly and efficiently, not allowing me time to admire her curves.

She scoops up dishes from the café table while speaking to the couple dining in the outdoor seating area. They both beam at her, their napkins tossed to the side as potted plants of rosemary and thyme jut up around them partially obstructing my view.

"I'll be right back with your bill," she says.

Even though she's forty feet away, I easily hear her. I watch avidly as she glides to the cash register, drops the dishes in a tub, and then grabs the diners' receipt. She tilts her head, giving me a clear view of her long arching neck and defined jaw bone.

The beast stirs inside me.

Images of a huge tawny wolf crunching that jaw bone

between his teeth fill my mind. My mouth salivates. No, not *my* mouth. The beast's mouth. He wants her.

Now.

I scoff. *Hell, he'll take any human since it's been ten days since his last meal.*

"Quit filling my head with images you sick fucker," I mutter to him.

Even though he can't speak, I talk to him often, considering he's a part of me. His emotions and impulses constantly invade my mind. Images of what he wants then follow. Those images convey his desires better than any words could.

I hunker down lower in the alleyway. A dumpster hides me from view so if a human peers in here they won't see the ragged man with glowing eyes watching the young waitress working in the café across the road.

The sun's bright light filters onto the city street, and the fact that I'm out during the *day* says everything.

Since when do wolves stalk during the day?

Desperate motherfuckers that's who.

Even though I stand six-three, and my shoulders are as broad as the dumpster, nobody detects me. Couples and groups of people have passed by and not even sensed me.

My large form is still—deathly still. If there's one thing I've become very good at in the past eighteen months it's stalking.

So the humans remain oblivious to the hunter hiding in the shadows while the tall, fit-looking waitress across the street glides around the café.

My interest in her is growing, and I'm aware that it's . . . unnatural. As for why I have this interest—I don't know.

I've never felt this intense need to watch a woman before. Of course, approaching her in my current state isn't an option, so I've been stalking her every day for the past week, sometimes for multiple times per day, hoping *that* will satiate my interest in her.

But it hasn't.

My fascination with her has only increased.

I can't even blame the beast for this obsession. Because even though a pile of murder victims lie in my wake, none of those kills were due to my interest. Those deaths were a result of the beast's appetite.

But with the waitress . . .

I want her.

And that makes me realize that my human mind may finally be giving into the darkness, but the crazy thing is that I don't want to hurt her.

I just want her.

It's fucked up and I know it, but I can't help myself.

I shift slightly in my crouched position. The waitress has moved back to the table and is speaking to the diners again. My gaze trails up and down her frame as she finishes with the couple.

Firm, round breasts strain against her shirt. If I cupped one of those globes in the palm of my hand, her tit would fill it.

The waitress whisks the diners' drinks from the table as they get ready to leave. Her long dark hair drapes down her back, highlighting her strong shoulders. She can probably bench press more than most men.

A flutter of admiration runs through me, but the beast has a different reaction. His mouth waters, which makes *my* mouth moist, since the beast is fantasizing again.

Sick bastard.

I try to shake his interest off, but it's no use.

As I watch her retreat inside the café, I wonder if it's her banging body that's captured my interest. Her butt looks round and toned. She works out and plays sports regularly. Strong thighs, toned calves, and slim ankles form her lower half.

My cock hardens at the thought of taking her. It's been so long since I've been with a woman. It's amazing that my nuts haven't turned into shriveled-up raisins.

But I haven't been with a woman like *that* in a very long time for good reason. It's too dangerous now since the beast is so strong, which means sex isn't an option.

So why are you watching her if nothing can come from this?

I ignore that little voice in the back of my mind, even though my conscience poses a very good question.

The beast churns in my belly again, and his interest shifts from her throat to what's between her legs, which makes *my* attention shift there too. I feel him goading me, encouraging me to take *that* from her.

"Shut the fuck up!" I hiss. Anger stirs in my gut. I've been battling him over this all week. Since the beast has realized that my obsession with her isn't waning, and because I've managed to stop him from shifting and killing during the past week, he's turning desperate.

His addiction to human flesh is pulling at him like a drug, but even though I was a prick to a lot of women before the beast turned me rogue I've never raped a woman.

Never.

And I don't intend to start now despite his suggestions.

Saliva pools into my mouth again when the beast's appetite gnaws at me. He howls inside my belly, flailing against his restraints.

A shudder wracks my body, then another.

"Shit!" I whisper.

It's the third time today he's shaken my control. He's testing me—always testing me.

I clench my teeth, but hairs sprout on the backs of my hands. My jaw crunches as bones realign, elongating as the shift sets in.

I slam my back against the dumpster, the cold concrete wall in the alley pressing against my side.

But I can't stop him. I fall onto all fours.

"No!" I whisper, but the word sounds guttural and gravely.

I drag in a breath and concentrate as a drop of sweat falls onto the black grimy asphalt under my hands. Another groan stifles my chest.

No!

I wrestle the growing darkness. Already, the beast is invading my mind, cutting off my thoughts that are still human as his bloodlust and the need to hunt takes over. Veins sprout on my forearms as my hands ball into fists.

Stop him, Collin! You have to stop him!

I clench my partially shifted teeth together so tightly I fear my jaw will crack. Trembles shake my frame as the beast and I fight. Another bead of sweat drops to the ground, but the hair slowly recedes from my arms.

I just barely rein him in, and I breathe a sigh of relief.

Still, it was close. Too close. And it's daytime nonetheless.

Get out of here before it happens again.

I take off at a run down the alleyway. Despite my heavy boots, my footsteps are silent.

When I reach the end of the alley, I vault over the ten-foot wall like I'm hopping a puddle on the sidewalk. On the other side, I land silently before launching into another run, skirting the shadows like Death himself.

It takes me fifteen minutes to get back to the manhole leading into the sewer. None of the humans above have detected me in the three weeks I've called this place home, but the rats do. More than a few of the repulsive rodents have become a midnight snack when the beast gets hungry.

Humid, stank air surrounds me when I jump off the bottom of the ladder into a narrow tunnel.

I don't let the putrid smells bother me, though. I've slept in worst, and fuck knows, I'll sleep in worse again. Inhabiting places like city sewers are the only way to exist in my current situation. Not only is the beast unstable, but I can't afford anything else.

How my life has changed.

When I first left my pack, I had an apartment, a job, and I still had ties to the Ward money. But I was determined to leave the Wyoming pack behind me and make my own life, which meant saying goodbye to my family's assets.

My first job in the human world had gone fine initially, but after a year without my pack, my wolf began to change.

I grind my teeth, remembering my arrogance and stupidity. The beginning changes were subtle—subtle enough that I didn't appreciate what was happening, and by the time I did, it was too late. My wolf had already begun his irreversible metamorphosis into the beast.

And now, there's no stopping him.

My eyes adjust to the dim lighting in the sewer, and after a few minutes, the stench filters to the back of my senses. I let the beast out more but am careful to keep a tight hold on him. His eyes make my vision better and sharper, allowing me to see easily as I maneuver the tunnels.

I duck under a narrow channel and approach the small area that I've made my dwelling.

The fact that I even have a place that I consider mine means that I've been in this city too long. Three women and one man have gone missing since I arrived, and while questions haven't been asked yet, I know it's only a matter of time before the human police figure out that their disappearances are linked.

But the Supernatural Forces already know.

The beast doesn't care about recklessness, though. He doesn't care that only yesterday I spotted two SF members prowling the street right above us, searching for me—*hunting* for me.

As one of the few rogue werewolves terrorizing the land, I pose a huge threat to the supernatural community's secret existence, and the SF is determined to take me out.

I scoff.

Me.

After eighteen months on the run, I've become one of the most hunted rogue werewolves in history, and even though I'm one of the greatest hunters to walk the earth *I'm* being hunted by the motherfucking Supernatural Forces.

But even those two SF members would be no match for me if I unleashed my beast. He's grown so strong since I left Hidden Creek. Strong enough that I can no longer deny him.

A memory of the prostitute's scream—the beast's last kill—filters to the front of my mind. A moment of self-loathing steals my breath. The beast killed her only ten days ago, and her scream hadn't lasted long. He'd sunk his teeth into her neck, crushing her windpipe, before tearing her throat out and wolfing it down. The only sound left after that was her blood pooling on the ground.

Bile rises in the back of my throat, as it does every time I think about what I've allowed my wolf to become.

I know there's an easy way out of this. I can let the SF catch me. They'll stop the beast, but they'll also execute me.

Some days I consider it, when my self-hatred becomes

too great to bear, but each time I've almost turned myself in, a survival instinct has roared to life inside me.

So I've stayed on the run, even though each day I hate myself a little bit more.

I sink down onto the damp cold concrete. The sound of trickling water reaches my ears along with the ever-present skitter of galloping rats. I know the time has come to venture to a new location since the SF has tracked me here, but then I remember the waitress.

I close my eyes and picture her again. I don't want to leave her.

So take her.

My hands ball into tight fists. I can't take her. She'll be missed. Her disappearance will most definitely draw questions and attention from the human police *and* the SF, which is reckless, and I know it.

Yet...

From the first moment I laid eyes on her, something about her beckoned me, and it's not something I can ignore. I've tried so hard to push this throbbing impulse away, but I've realized I can no more do that than I can stop the pull of the moon.

A shudder of anticipation runs through me, then fear. I can't leave her, yet if I take her...

The beast growls in approval.

I can only hope that I can protect her from the beast, protect her from *me*. But that will take careful orchestration—a strategic plan is the only way I can pull it off.

Nausea churns my stomach, because even with meticulous planning there's no guarantee she'll stay safe.

Because what the beast wants, the beast always gets.

CHAPTER TWO
BRIANNA

The hairs on the back of my neck stand on end again. I stop mid-run, my cleats digging into the grass as I twist my head in all directions. The strange sensations of being watched have been happening for two weeks.

But the area around the sports field looks as it always does—pebbled landscaping, the campus gymnasium toward the west, a few dormitories off in the north, and desert trees and cactuses scattered about.

Nothing looks amiss, yet, I can feel that something's . . . off.

"Brianna!" one of my teammates yells.

Crap. The Frisbee comes from out of nowhere. I grab it just as an opponent barrels toward me. She stops a foot away and flanks me, her arms out as I search for a teammate to throw to.

Kate's open near the end field. Faking a pivot to the left, my opponent falls for it and lunges. I pivot the other way and dip low, then hurtle the Frisbee toward Kate.

The second the Frisbee is out of my hand, I take off running. Kate grabs the disc in midair before landing, and my hand flies up as I near the end field.

I leap into the end zone just as the Frisbee descends. When my feet hit the grass, the Frisbee is in my grasp.

"Score!" Kate whoops.

The opponents chasing me grumble, their faces shiny with sweat as their ponytails whip around their faces.

"Nice one!" another teammate yells in my direction.

When our game finally finishes, the sun is descending toward the western horizon. Across the field, a maintenance man is pruning bushes. His large belly hangs over his pants every time he bends over.

"We kicked ass." Kate takes a drink from her water bottle and nudges me. "And we wouldn't have if you hadn't scored so many points. For someone new to this sport, you got serious game, girl."

I wipe at sweat running past my ear as another teammate gives me a high-five. "It was a team effort."

Carly laughs. "Always so modest."

I chuckle, then Kate and I say goodbye to our teammates before we begin walking toward the apartments off campus. We chat easily the entire way.

A mile later, Kate stops outside my building. Bright petunias and marigolds fill the standing pots that flank the main entrance. They bring much needed color to the drab gray building.

"See ya at practice tomorrow?" Kate asks.

"Yeah, wouldn't miss it."

She gives me a quick hug then carries on down the sidewalk since her building is on the next block, while I dash inside and run up the stairs to my modest one-bedroom apartment. I shower in record time, then wolf down a cold dinner of leftover pizza and a banana before slipping into my black shorts and signature white polo top for my waitressing gig.

A quick look in the mirror shows my dark hair is still damp, but when I slick it up into a ponytail it's hard to tell that I just showered.

"It'll do," I mutter before dabbing on some lip gloss and twirling a mascara wand through my thick lashes.

Once done, I hightail it outta there for the fifteen minute walk to Café Trois Soeurs. I check my phone along the way. A few texts from Jill pop up, and there's one from the guy I went on a date with last week.

I reply immediately to Jill but don't bother with the guy. It's the third text he's sent today despite me telling him yesterday that I'm not interested.

After a quick scroll through Instagram and Snapchat, I shove my phone in my purse and step into the café.

"Hey, Brianna." Joel, the bartender, calls. "What's up, babe?"

"Not much." I place my forearms on the cool smooth bar top. "How was the lunch rush?"

"Kinda slow, but it'll pick back up tonight. You know how Fridays are." He wipes down the bar as the overhead lights twinkle off the rows of hard liquor bottles lining the shelf behind him. "Sam's gotta new dish on the menu tonight. He said some food critic might be in so he wants to impress him."

"Mmm, do we get to taste test it?" Even though I just ate, I'm hungry again.

He laughs. "Even Sam may be swayed by that smile of yours."

"I can hope." I wink cause Sam's not exactly known for being laidback.

I say goodbye to Joel, then head toward the back to drop off my things before touching base with Sam to see what he's expecting tonight. Steam rolls through the kitchen as the sound of sizzling food on the grill fills the air with heavenly scents.

I grab a menu to memorize the specials as Macy sidles up next to me and gives me a playful nudge.

"Hey, hot stuff," I say to her before setting the menu back down. As usual, Macy's dark hair is expertly styled, and her fitted top shows off her voluptuous curves. "Ready for a Friday night?"

"Am I ever," she replies. "Rent's due on Monday, and if I don't kill it with tips, I'm gonna be short."

Since we're both poor college students, I totally get her worry. "You got this. Fridays are always good."

"I'm counting on it."

My shift passes quickly since Fridays are busy. Our eclectic French inspired menu draws in a regular crowd, but it's doubly crowded tonight since there's a concert at the convention center a few blocks away. The streets are packed with Ariana Grande fans, and a line to get into the café weaves around the corner. Everyone's hoping to grab a bite to eat before opening.

"Shit. My feet are killing me," Macy complains when we run into each other in the kitchen a few hours later.

I deposit an armload of dishes by the sink. "You and me both."

"How are tips for you tonight?" she asks.

"Pretty good. Those dudes in the corner just tipped me fifty. What about you?"

"I got snaked by that middle-aged couple. That dickwad pulls up in a Jaguar and only leaves me ten bucks. Ten freakin' dollars on a two-hundred dollar meal that I busted my ass on."

She nibbles her lip, and I know she's stressing about paying rent. I pull a twenty from my pocketed tips. "Here take this. I got over-tipped by those guys."

Her eyes widen. "What? Girl, no! That's your money. You worked for it."

I shove it in her hand and grab my plates from under the warmer. "And you worked hard on that last table but got stuck with a tightass. That's not your fault. Just keep it."

I head out before she can return the money. I know some on our team feel what's theirs and theirs and mine is mine, but I don't see if that way. We don't pick and choose our customers, and some customers tip better than others. As long as we're all working hard, I'm happy to share tips.

By the time my shift ends, it's almost eleven at night. Fatigue rolls through me in steady waves as the busboys wipe down all the tables. I give them and the bartender a cut of my tips before pocketing the rest.

The wad of cash in my pocket makes some of the grueling work worth it, but between the early morning class I woke up for, school all afternoon followed by a game, and then work, I'm beat.

"See ya tomorrow babe?" Macy asks when I grab my purse.

"Yeah. You still wanna meet up in the afternoon to study? That composition exam is gonna be killer."

Macy groans. "Tell me about it. And yeah, meet at the library around two?"

"Works for me. See ya!"

I sail out the door and around the corner. The sidewalks are still busy despite the late hour. Elated concert goers fill the streets as drunk college students bar hop.

I skirt around most of them and welcome the less busy streets the closer I get to my apartment. Above me, the full moon shines, visible even through the city lights.

My feet tap quietly on the sidewalk, and my shoulders begin to relax the farther I get from the commotion of downtown. Another block passes, and I'm alone on the street.

"Finally," I murmur, welcoming the peace.

But when I cross the next intersection, walking diagonally north, I feel it again.

That sense of something being . . . off.

The hairs on the back of my neck stand on end, so I stop in the middle of the street and twirl around. My hand flexes around my purse's strap as I search the sidewalks and alleys between buildings.

I don't see anything, but I still make sure to thoroughly check every dark corner. Living in a city for the past four years has taught me to be wary when I'm out walking alone, and considering all the weird feelings I've been getting lately—a tingle of unease slithers down my spine.

But after another careful search of the area, I still don't see anything suspicious or out of the ordinary. The dark street has a few parked cars. Some lights are on in the apartments above. And other than a stray cat dashing around a corner, there's no sign of life.

Standing straighter, I resume walking but quicken my pace.

"What the hell!" I whisper. That niggling suspicion that someone is watching me breathes down my neck like wildfire.

Picking up a jog, a part of me thinks that I'm overreacting, but I don't slow. Ahead, my block waits. The marigolds and petunias are visible in the streetlight.

Almost there. I breathe a sigh of relief.

Not slowing, I leap off the sidewalk to cross the road when something brushes up behind me. I'm not even sure what I'm feeling until a warm and heavy hand clamps over my mouth and nose while an arm snakes around my waist.

I immediately thrash, my eyes widening in terror. A million reactions ricochet in my brain as I'm lifted off the street before my attacker flies us into an alley.

NO!

My lungs heave as terror explodes in my chest. The alleyway flashes by at an alarming speed while my attacker runs surprisingly easily.

How can someone be carrying me this fast?

That thought leaves my mind at the same moment I scissor my legs and pummel my attacker's shins. But he doesn't stop despite me landing vicious blows.

I scream, or try to, but the thug's hand is covering my mouth so tightly that my air's cut off.

But I don't stop.

I thrash and kick more, struggling so hard against him that I'm surprised he doesn't fall over.

He's strong.

Incredibly strong.

He's still running and carrying me from alleyway to alleyway at superhuman speed.

What the hell is happening?

A small part of my brain knows that nobody can run this fast, but I shove that thought off and try to bite down as my vision darkens.

No! Stay conscious! You're dead if you pass out!

But my mouth and nose are completely covered. *Shit! Shit! Shit! I can't breathe!*

My attacker grunts when I land another kick on his kneecap. He still doesn't slow. If anything, he tightens his grip on my mouth, and I'm losing consciousness despite willing it otherwise.

This can't be happening. No. Please. No. This can't be real.

It's the last thought I have before I sag against him.

CHAPTER THREE
COLLIN

She's heavier than most women. Unlike the emaciated druggies and skinny prostitutes I'm used to carrying after the beast's kills, she's solid muscle and warm flesh. She's tall, too, but nowhere near my height. And her fragrance. That caramel-and-sunshine scent fills my lungs.

The beast stirs, pushing against my control. His bloodlust rises like a deadly wave.

"Fuck off," I growl and slam him down.

I dip into the last alleyway where the stolen car's parked. With silent movements, I flip the lid on the trunk and deposit her inside. I try to be gentle, and the irony isn't lost on me. I just clamped my hand over her mouth so tightly that she passed out.

But unconsciousness is necessary if I'm going to take her.

And even though she's knocked out cold, I know it won't last long. She'll likely be awake in minutes.

After grabbing the duct tape, I rip a piece to cover her mouth, grimacing at the slash of silver against her smooth skin. I don't let the growing guilt stop me, though. I make quick work of her arms and legs until she's fully restrained.

She's got a purse strapped across her chest, and with a start, I realize I don't even know her name.

I take it off her and search inside for her driver's license. The beast pushes against my control again, his impatience growing when I pull it from her wallet. Clenching my jaw, I shove him back, but his enhanced eyesight allows me to see the details on her ID.

Brianna Keller.

Her name's Brianna.

I scan the rest of her details. She's twenty-six—older than I suspected given she's an undergrad. The license states her height is 5'10" and she weighs one-hundred-sixty pounds. Brown hair and brown eyes.

After slipping the license back in her wallet, I toss the purse beside her. Now that she's completely restrained, I allow myself a moment to study her. Up close, she's even more beautiful than I realized.

Lush dark hair falls down her back like a waterfall. Her eyes are closed, and long lashes rest on her smooth tanned cheeks. She's breathing evenly again, but she's still unconscious. Her chest rises, drawing my attention to her round firm breasts before I take in her slim, muscular legs folded awkwardly against her toned stomach.

I step back, and the dim moonlight illuminates a picture from a horror film. I blanch and rake a hand through my hair.

I have a passed-out beautiful woman bound and duct-taped in a stolen vehicle's trunk.

Something stirs inside me. Something entirely human. With a start, I jerk back.

What the hell am I doing?

This isn't like the beast's victims. With them, the beast

raged inside me, completely in control when he snatched them off the street and devoured them only feet away at the end of barren alleyways. Those attacks were impulsive, primal, and fueled by my insane wolf.

But this woman . . .

I've stalked her for two weeks as a *human* even though the beast grew impatient. And now, I've bound her, stuffed her in a trunk, and am taking her away.

Far, far away where no one can take her from me.

Except for the beast.

I shake my head. *No. He won't. I won't let him.*

But still . . .

I've abducted her.

I've never done anything like this before.

You're a sick fuck, Collin. What would the pack think of you now? They would say your human mind's turning rogue too.

But my self-disgust fades when I gaze down at her. She's so beautiful, so exquisite. I *need* her.

Without another thought, I slam the trunk closed and slip silently into the driver's seat. The engine roars to life, and I pull onto the road. I drive for a good ten minutes before I hear her.

Between her kicks against the seats, muffled screams, and banging from side to side, I know she's fully conscious.

Another twinge of regret fills me. My grip on the steering wheel tightens as nerves flutter in my stomach. *You could stop, Collin. Pull over right here and let her out. You could walk away and pretend none of this happened.*

Hatred for myself rises inside me, yet the inexplicable pull she has on me doesn't lessen.

I really do need her, I try to reason with myself. *Selfish fuck,* I counter back.

I'm on the interstate now, heading out of the city as the

full moon shines above. The moon calls to my beast, making him stronger.

My human emotions disappear when his teeth elongate. A quick glance in the rearview mirror reveals my distorted features—half wolf, half human as he fantasizes about what he wants to do to her.

No! I roar at him. *She's mine! This one's mine! You can't eat her!*

But despite my efforts, hair sprouts on the backs of my hands as I drive toward the mountains in Utah. I grit my teeth and fight him. Thankfully, I don't fully shift, but my human side knows that we couldn't do this drive during the day given how hard I'm fighting him. My horrific half-beast appearance would be noticed by passerby. The authorities would be called. The SF would show up.

But in the middle of the night, with the moon calling to the beast and darkness covering the land, we're practically alone.

A maniacal sound leaves my lips—half cackle, half howl and comes entirely from the beast. The banging in the trunk stops. I know she heard me.

A sob reaches my ears. Then another.

Another twinge of regret fills me, but I don't stop, and a part of me is thankful for the beast. He never feels regret or shame, so I let him out more until he swallows up my misery like the rats he consumed last night.

A second howl leaves my lips. The beast urges me along, beckoning me to drive farther and go deeper into the mountains. I willingly succumb to his persuasions.

I know exactly where the beast and I are going. I visited it yesterday to make sure it was intact, and after stocking it with food and supplies that will last for several weeks, I returned to the city only to collect her.

And then I can keep the woman that I've taken for my own.

BY THE TIME I pull onto the old logging road several hours later, Brianna's grown completely quiet. The beast has retreated, bored of the long drive. He's still restless for blood, but when it becomes apparent to him I'm not letting bloodshed happen, he goes to sleep.

I cock my head, listening. Nothing greets me except the night wind through my cracked window. Brianna's incredibly silent, and if I couldn't smell her, I would wonder if she'd escaped.

But even with the backseat separating us, her sunshine-and-caramel scent permeates the air, and I know she's there.

It's strangely comforting.

I shove my foot down on the accelerator, the engine protesting as I gun it up the old logging trail. Thick trees scatter my view since a dark forest lines the dirt road. The sedan protests, the ruts and bumps in the road scraping the bottom of the car at times, but it keeps going.

A new scent fills the air, wafting into the cab like ozone before a thunderstorm. It's a scent I've become very familiar with.

Fear.

The sour smell oozes from Brianna like a dying fox ensnared in a hunter's trap. Even though she's quiet, she's awake, and she must know from the rough road and slower speed that we're approaching our destination.

That guilty feeling again steals my breath, but I ignore it.

When we finally reach the top of the desolate mountain, an old hunting cabin waits. It's small and sags into the earth like a worn out barn. I only know of it from a run I did years ago in my wolf form. I'd still run with the Wyoming pack then, when I still had brothers to run with.

Now, I only have the beast.

I shove the car into park and kill the engine. Silence descends. I get out, the packed earth smooth under my shoes. My nostrils flare as I take in the scent of pine, earth, and rodents scurrying in the trees.

The side view mirror reveals that my features are human again, but a glow lights my eyes.

The beast has awoken. He stirs within me, growing tired of the game I'm playing. He wants to eat her while savoring her flesh and crunching her bones.

"This one's mine!" I remind him with a snarl.

Anticipation builds in me as I walk to the back of the trunk. We're finally here, and she's with me. I long to touch her hair, feel her skin, and smell her scent. I have no idea why I long for these things, but they pull at me like the moon calls the tides.

With a squeeze of the latch, the lid springs open. "We're—"

I pivot out of the way just as she launches herself from the trunk, but with her arms and legs bound, all she does is land on the ground. *Hard.*

"Shit," I mutter and kneel down.

But she doesn't stop struggling, and a wild look fills her eyes. She thrashes and kicks more, screaming behind the duct tape as she does everything she can to knock me over.

"It's okay," I say quietly. "I won't hurt you."

I finger a lock of hair from her face, and she flinches back. Panic coats her expression like a terrified animal, but when our eyes lock, something changes in her. Her face pales.

With a start, I remember that she's human and has never seen a supernatural's eyes glow with the power of their wolf.

I straighten and rake a hand through my hair, turning so she won't see when I wrestle the beast.

He lunges against my control, making me double over. Images of him eating her fill my mind.

Sweat pops on my brow, and my breathing turns so rapid that my lungs barely fill with shallow inhales.

No, I say internally through gritted teeth.

I double over, yanking him back. *Submit, you fucker!*

It takes minutes to fully subdue him, and I'm still panting when I turn back to the waitress.

She's gone.

Thrashing in the trees and the flash of her bright white top twenty yards away catches my attention. *Holy shit, she's trying to get away.*

But she's hopping on restrained limbs. Nobody can hop down a mountain, then an additional fifty miles to safety. That twinge of guilt needles my heart again.

But a ripping sound comes next, and I gape like a fish when the tape around her ankles comes free. Before I can take another breath, she's running, truly *running* away.

"Are you fucking kidding me?" I exclaim, but the beast howls in delight.

He loves nothing more than a good hunt.

CHAPTER FOUR
BRIANNA

The forest is dark. Trees and branches block my path, and cool air washes across my cheeks as my heart beats so hard I can hear it in my ears.

Go! Go! Go!

Dense brush sweeps against my calves, cutting my skin when I barrel through it. I know I'm not running straight. I know I'm making a racket, but that fucking *psycho* back there kidnapped me and had glowing eyes.

Glowing eyes! WTF!

Harsh breaths make my chest heave, and I'm so close to losing it that I can barely breathe. Another branch scratches my face, but I ignore the sting when I rip through the foliage.

"Shit!" The forest slopes abruptly downward and before I know what's happening, I'm stumbling.

Somehow I manage to stay upright as I flee down the embankment. I gulp in another lungful of air and thank the stars that he hasn't caught me. I don't hear him either, which is weird, but maybe he's become too consumed with his alternate personality to have realized that I escaped.

The downward slope evens out, and I momentarily stop and search frantically for any signs of human habitation.

Dammit! There's nothing here except for dark trees and a moon barely penetrating the canopy above.

Which way? I'm still breathing heavily, and the adrenaline pounding through my veins makes it hard to think.

Come on, Bri. Think! Which way?

I need to find a road.

Yes. That makes sense. I debate how I'm going to find a road when—

His arms lock around me.

I scream. He came from behind me, like a ghost in the night. I shriek and thrash, but he pins me to him, his chest like a rock against my back.

"Shh," he whispers in my ear.

Shh? Yeah right.

I scream at the top of my lungs as my heart thuds a million miles an hour again. His hand is near my mouth. I bite down on it like I'm tearing into a drumstick, but he merely lifts me and begins running up the hill.

Fuck! Fuck! Fuck! Where did he come from?

I keep struggling and fighting, trying to break his hold, but he continues to *run* up the mountain slope with me in his arms.

How is this possible?

I barely have time to process all that's happening when the derelict cabin appears again. My mad dash through the trees did nothing.

Absolutely nothing.

"How did you get the duct tape ripped off so quickly?" He sounds surprised and awed, as if he didn't think anyone knew how to rip duct tape.

Instead of answering, I scream my head off. My ear-piercing wail sounds like it carries for miles, but Psycho doesn't seem to care. I punch his ribs when he opens the cabin's door, but that also does nothing.

"You're strong." That weird tone fills his voice again, as if he's proud. "And you can scream all you want. Nobody will hear you."

Hearing him sound so matter-of-fact and unconcerned about a rescue cuts my cries short. Besides, my throat is so raw now that it hurts.

Inside the cabin, it's dark and smells old. Only a few moonbeams penetrate the crooked windows. Vague shapes morph in the darkness, furniture probably, but I can't be sure.

I still don't know what my abductor looks like, but he's tall, I know that. My feet dangle from the floor as he walks in slow deliberate steps across the floorboards.

He abruptly stops. His hard arms are still around my waist and chest, and I've never felt anything more repulsive in my life.

"What do you want from me?" I ask through heaving breaths.

He takes another step. "I don't know," he finally replies, "but I couldn't leave you."

A growl vibrates his chest, rippling through me. I tense before another snarl tears from his mouth.

"No!" he snaps, which makes me jolt. "I told you, she's *mine!* Now, fuck off!"

I gulp. My breathing is so shallow that my vision swims black for a moment. He's doing it again. Talking to himself. He's a grade-A motherfucking psycho. Probably a serial killer or something equally terrifying, and he's going to kill me.

I know he's going to.

"Please," I beg quietly as he moves us to what I think is a chair. "Please don't do this."

He turns me so fast that my head spins before he sets me down. A plume of dust clouds up around me when my weight settles on a hard chair. I barely suppress a cough when I realize his grip has loosened.

Go!

I launch myself against him, lunging for the door, but his superhuman hands clamp onto my arms, keeping me in place before he rearranges himself to have one arm pressed flat against my chest while the other pins my legs.

And . . . I can't move.

How is he so strong?

"I'm sorry, but you can't leave." He squats down, and in the darkness, I still can't make out his features. All I see are those terrifying glowing eyes.

"What are you?" I recoil, barely getting the words out.

He doesn't answer, and I expect him to kill me, but instead he ties me to the chair. There's hardly any light in the cabin, but I hear him move. He moves impossibly fast, whizzing around the room as he secures me to the chair with a thick rope. Not once does the darkness impede him.

I struggle at first, fighting at every turn, but as before, it's as if I'm a small ant on the sidewalk that he's merely toying with. Despite me being strong, fit, and not afraid of lashing out, it makes no difference.

He's completely unaffected when I fight.

Goose bumps pepper my skin when he finishes, and I swear something in his face has changed. When a beam of moonlight hits the window just right, his jaw looks longer and more pronounced.

"I have to step out." He stumbles toward the door, muttering under his breath again, talking to himself similar to how he had been in the car.

The second the screen door bangs shut behind him, I'm thrashing. I test the rope, his knots, the stability of the chair, everything, but other than the chair teetering nothing budges.

I'm panting by the time I give up. All I have to show for it are rope burns making my skin raw and stinging every time I shift my weight.

"Dammit." I hang my head and the tears start up again. "What the fuck am I going to do?"

I can't let him kill me. I'm not ready to die, and I'm *not* willing to be his murder victim because I have no doubt that's what he intends for me. The entire ride here, he was growling, talking to himself, or howling. I could hear it all through the seats. Even though I haven't encountered many crazy people in my life, I'm certain he's certifiably deranged, which means I'm not sure if I can talk my way out of this.

But he also has glowing eyes. That's not normal even if he's crazy.

Another shiver hits me, making my flesh pebble more.

I shove that thought off because trying to rationalize this is . . .

Panic threatens to set in when an image of his burning irises fill my mind, so I quickly shake myself and force myself to concentrate on the roughness of the rope, the pain in my wrists, and the chill on my skin.

After a moment, I feel focused again.

Okay, so what do I know about psycho killers? What should I do?

Escape. That's what you need to do.

No shit, Sherlock.

OMG. I'm losing it. I'm talking to myself just like he does.

I take a deep breath and force myself to stop trembling. It takes a few minutes, but eventually, my heartbeat slows. *Okay, stay calm and keep it together, Bri. It's your only chance at escaping and making it out of this alive.*

I wrack my brain as the first hint of sunlight penetrates the trees. Dawn is still an hour away, but a very faint glow fills the forest.

Talk to him. That's what I need to do. Talk to him, and make him realize that I'm a real person with a family and friends. I'm not just a random body. That's what I'm supposed to do, right?

I curse myself for not watching more crime shows. What little I know is from my freshman year of college when my roommate, who was obsessed with *True Crimes and the Monsters Behind Them*, sat in front of the TV and watched episode after episode. I still remember my annoyance when she had it blaring from the TV at all hours of the night.

Now, I wish I'd joined her on the couch.

I squeeze my eyes shut, forcing the tears back as I take another deep inhale. I still don't hear Psycho, but that doesn't mean he's not right outside. Both times he's snuck up behind me, I didn't hear him coming. He was completely silent, like a predator.

That thought comes from out of nowhere, but I'm certain that's what he is. A hunter. A predator. Nothing about him is normal. Nothing about him seems *human*.

I shudder again.

I know I didn't imagine his glowing eyes. *But what the fuck does that mean?* People's eyes don't glow. They *don't*, yet I know I didn't hallucinate it.

A keening wail builds up in my chest before I clamp it down. *Remember what you have to do, Bri! Don't lose it, keep it together, and find a way out of this shithole.*

But despite determination settling into me like an anchor that won't budge, my thoughts still return to his glowing eyes, because if he's not human, then the next question is: what is he?

He's gone for hours, and I'm left with nothing but my internal questions that swirl around inside me like a tornado. *Will he come back? When? What will he do to me? What the hell is he?* Next comes the escape questions. *What's the best way to make it out of these woods? How far did we drive? We're in the mountains and it's not as dry as home, so he took me north, right?*

I'm practically dizzy from them.

The sun rises in earnest during his absence, highlighting the numerous dust motes in the air.

Those tiny dots are all I have to watch as my gaze darts between the door and walls. The cabin's rustic—no power or running water. There's hardly any furniture. Only my chair and a two-seater table and chairs in the kitchen. A cold fireplace sits off to the right, the only heat source, and the cabin's small, only one room.

At least I know there aren't any surprises lurking behind me, and I don't see a trapdoor to a cellar or someplace more ominous that he could move me to.

I stifle another sneeze. The cabin has an old musty smell, as if it's been around for decades and not been taken care of properly. Given the cracked window on the left wall and the floor that's so dusty footprints are left in it, I imagine it's abandoned. If not for the freshly bought supplies that sit on the rustic kitchen counter, I would have assumed Psycho only just found the place.

But those supplies mean that he knew we were coming here. He'd *planned* for it.

After what feels like forever with nothing but the silence and occasional bird call outside, I finally deflate, and somewhere between the bright sunlight filling the room and the trill of mourning doves penetrating the air, I doze off into a fitful rest.

Dreams plague me. Horrific dreams filled with screams and pain.

The next thing I know, a finger is touching my chin.

I jerk upright so fast that my neck pinches. I hiss in pain as my eyes flash open.

Even brighter light fills the cabin, and for one mind-numbing moment, I don't know where I am. But then I see a man in front of me, and it all comes crashing back making my stomach sink like a stone.

He's squatted down and is watching me with a reverent expression, but he looks so *normal*, which means he can't be my attacker. Right?

I don't say a word. I merely stare back at him.

Blond wavy hair brushes against his shoulders. He has bright-blue eyes, a strong jaw, smooth skin, and damp hair as if he's been out for a vigorous run. He's clean, young, and built. Like seriously built. His shoulders have to be at least three feet wide, and not an inch of fat lines his sculpted arms.

He's also carrying a backpack.

Hope floods me. *Maybe he's a hiker.*

I struggle against the ropes. "Can you help me?" The question tumbles out of me as desperation takes root. "He'll be back soon, any minute really. Will you untie me? Please! He's coming back. I know he is!"

But the only response my hiker gives me is a regretful look before he says, "I'm sorry. I shouldn't have taken you, but I . . ." He hangs his head. "I couldn't leave you."

Couldn't leave me? What the hell is he talking about? And then it hits me, like a million volts of lightning.

It's him.

He *is* the psycho who kidnapped me.

My shock is so huge that it takes my breath away. *He's seriously the one who abducted me?* But he looks so normal, and he's so freakin' good-looking. Disbelief comes next. *How can he be that deranged thing that took me last night?*

A hysterical laugh bursts from my lips just as I realize my mouth tastes like cotton. I'm so freakin' thirsty, but that thought is there and then gone as my laugh turns into a sob.

Psycho abruptly stands and begins pacing. Tension springs from his shoulders as his hands flex and unflex, and in that movement, I *see* it. I see his alternate personality emerge.

That crazy glow fills his eyes again, and something in him changes and morphs. His shoulders round over slightly, his jaw grinds, and for the barest second I swear something ripples in his face, as if something alive wants to birth from beneath it.

I heave myself back in the chair, nearly toppling it over but the wall stops my fall, then something I never anticipated happening occurs right before my eyes.

All I can do is scream.

CHAPTER FIVE
COLLIN

The beast's power tears through me, and he bursts from his restraints as explosively as an erupting volcano. He wants blood, and he wants flesh, and nothing will stop him. I fucked up. Dammit, I fucked up!

I denied him too long, and now Brianna will pay the price.

The horrific sound of crunching bone and slicing muscle fibers fill the small cabin. Brianna's scream comes next just as my body fully shifts.

The beast emerges, and I struggle to maintain control of my thoughts. He wants flesh. He wants to taste her, and a single thought enters my brain as rage at what he's about to do consumes me.

NO!

Brianna's eyes are so wide, and her face is so pale that she looks like a ghost. The beast lunges forward, stopping an inch from her face as a snarl tears from our throat.

But it's not my snarl. It's entirely his.

NO! I scream inside again. I grasp desperately for my

human side that's fading like the blood from her complexion. I know if I completely lose control of him now he'll kill her.

And I don't think I can live with myself if that happens.

I wrestle him back, making his head whip away just as he lunges for her throat.

She flings herself erratically to the side, but she's still bound by the ropes. Her chair topples over, and she lands hard on her side, cracking her head. She cries out in pain just as I shove the beast down.

I somehow force the shift. He howls his protest, but I manage to shift back to human before I take off for the door, snarling in anger that I let him tear at her like that.

I barrel down the cabin's steps and take off at a run through the woods. I'm completely naked. The clothes I'd been wearing are in tatters on the floor back in the cabin. Rocks, branches, and brush cut into my soles, but I welcome the pain.

The pain grounds me and makes me feel all of the self-loathing that's been rising inside me for months, ever since my wolf turned rogue and became something I no longer recognize.

There's truly no hope for me.

I fly down the mountain, blindly running as that thought cuts through my senses like a saber. I know I can't stop the beast. I know there's no way I will ever lead a normal life again, but that doesn't stop me from putting as many miles between me and Brianna Keller as I can.

You stupid fuck, Collin. You never should have taken her!

I welcome those thoughts, too, because as long as I'm thinking and still maintaining conversation as a human in my head, I can keep the beast from killing her, and suddenly, I know that's exactly what I need to do.

I took her, and now I'm responsible for her. I can't let her die.

You need to let her go.

But another vicious snarl tears from me at that thought. I should let her go. It's the only way she'll survive, but terror fills me at the thought of losing her, even though I know if I keep her, the beast will destroy her.

∼

Over an hour passes before I stop running. I'm so many miles away from her that I know for the moment I don't pose a threat.

I collapse to the ground, my muscles trembling from the exertion.

I need to go back. I need to give her something to eat and drink. Fuck, I also need to let her go to the bathroom. It's been so many hours since I took her. Although, given the terror in her eyes when the beast emerged, she probably wet herself.

A humorless chuckle escapes me, but there's nothing funny about this situation. The truth is, I fucked up. I shouldn't have abducted her. I should have ignored this bizarre longing I have and walked away.

But I didn't, and now she's been hurt because of me.

I take a deep breath before making myself stand. Thankfully, I don't feel the beast pressing against my control. It's as though he knows I would keep running away until he gave up. With any luck, he'll stay sleeping, which means I have a few hours reprieve.

I begin the long walk back to the cabin as the late-morning sun beats down on my back while my dick dangles between my legs.

Growing up a shifter means I'm used to walking naked in the woods, but I also know if any remote hikers happen to stumble across my path I'll make a memorable encounter.

And I'm trying to avoid detection from humans in this area.

So I keep my head up, sniffing continuously in case I catch a human scent. But all that fills my nostrils are pine, damp earth, and the musky smell of squirrels hiding in the trees.

It has to be noon by the time the old wooden planks of the cabin appear through the trees. The stolen car is still parked out front. One of the back tires looks flat, which means it probably got punctured on a sharp rock on this forgotten mountain road on the drive in.

I open the car's back door and pull out a pair of basketball shorts. I have a dozen pairs on hand just for moments like this, when a shift emerges against my control and leaves me naked and exposed.

After pulling them on, I'm still shirtless, but it's the best I can do. I pause and feel inside for the beast.

His hulking dark form shifts in my belly, but he's still sleeping. I need to take advantage of that while I can.

With quick movements, I climb the steps silently to the cabin and open the door. She's still lying on her side, but instead of instantly recoiling when she sees me, she stays still.

I cock my head but then realize her eyes are closed.

I take another step closer, and the coppery tang of blood filters to my nostrils. For one heart stopping moment, I can't breathe. The beast killed her. He tore out her throat after all.

My fear is confirmed when I see the pool of blood

beneath her head. She's still lying on her side, the chair still toppled over.

She hasn't moved since I left.

I dive toward her and slide to a stop at her side. The dusty wood planks leave burns on my shins from my desperate attempts to reach her, but I don't pay it any attention. My skin will heal within a few minutes anyway.

"Brianna!" I lift her head, inspecting her neck for the slash from the beast. He loves to go for the throat, a killing strike every time, before he tears the flesh away and wolfs it down.

Tears pool in my eyes, making my vision blur, but her moan renders me completely still.

She's alive.

I blink the tears away and carefully inspect her skin. She's chaffed from the ropes, but her neck is smooth and unharmed. I wrap my hand gently around her head and feel for injuries.

There.

My fingers alight on the cut and large bump on her scalp. It's sticky from dried blood, and she moans again before wincing.

"Fucking hell, Collin." I gently lift her and the chair until she's upright again and give silent thanks that the beast hasn't woken yet.

I don't know how long I have before he'll be fighting my control again so I make quick work of her restraints.

Within seconds, I have the knots undone and am lifting her gently from the chair. My jaw locks when I see her rope burns. She's fought nonstop. In some areas, the skin is worn completely away. Only dried blood is visible in those spots.

Disgust with myself cuts through me like a knife. I *hate*

that I hurt her. Hate it so fucking much that I want to rip my hair out.

But I shove the self-loathing down and move toward the kitchen. There's no running water, but I carried up barrels of fresh stream water two days ago in anticipation of keeping her with me for weeks. Most of those barrels are for cooking and bathing, but a few I filtered for drinking.

In the corner, I lay out one of the blankets I brought and set her down. I prop her against the wall. She winces but her eyes remain closed, so I reach for my supplies.

I don't know how bad her head injury is, but it's bad enough that it knocked her out.

Grabbing a pot of water and a clean cloth, I get to work on her numerous wounds. But it's only after I've completely cleaned the dried blood away and begin dabbing antiseptic on the open areas that she hisses and her eyes flash open.

The second her gaze alights on me, terror fills her eyes and she shoves herself against the wall so hard that the planks heave in protest.

"It's okay," I say. "I won't hurt you. I'm just trying to clean your wounds."

The distrust in her eyes remains as well as the fear, and then it hits me.

She saw me shift.

She saw the beast emerge, and she's a *human*.

I want to smack myself. She has no idea supernaturals exist, and I introduce her to us by shifting into a bloodthirsty rogue and lunging for her throat.

Nice one, Coll.

She whimpers, and before I can say anything to reassure her, she lashes out.

Her kick connects with my jaw, snapping my head

back, before she shoves against me and bolts to her feet. Upright, she sways. Her body looks like a slender tree about to topple over, but I push up and catch her right before she falls.

"It's okay," I say again, lowering her back to the corner. "You hit your head. You're probably dizzy from that, and it's been hours since you've had anything to drink."

Her mouth parts, and I see how dry her lips are.

Once again, I realize what a piss-poor job I've done. All I could think about was taking her, keeping her, and making her mine. I didn't think that she's a live human being who would no doubt fight me every chance she got.

Duh, dip-shit.

"Here, have something to drink." I pour a glass of the filtered stream water and hold it to her lips.

She watches me warily. There's a foggy glaze in her eyes, and worry fills me that she's more injured than I realize.

I coax the drink into her mouth, and once the cool water touches her tongue, she grabs the glass and greedily consumes all of it.

When she finishes, she lowers the glass. Her distrustful expression is back, but fear lurks behind it.

It feels as though someone punches me in the gut. I rake a hand through my hair and take the glass from her. *Fuck, I've blown this.*

But even though *nothing* about this is working out, I'm still glad she's here. I have no idea why, but sitting here with her, when she's not fighting me or trying to escape, a strange feeling of contentment slides through my veins.

You're seriously fucked up, Ward.

I fill the glass again. When I hand it to her, she takes it hesitantly and our fingers brush. The second we make contact, she flinches and yanks the glass away before drinking it.

I sigh heavily. Everything about this was a bad idea. And on top of that I have no idea what she's thinking, and it's driving me crazy.

"You must think I'm a real maniac," I finally say, anything to break the silence. This close to her, I can smell her underlying sunshine-and-caramel fragrance, but now it's lined with sweat and blood. I try not to dwell on that.

When she doesn't answer, I reach into the bag behind me, all the while keeping a close eye on her in case she tries to bolt again.

"Hungry?" I ask.

She stays quiet, so I pull out a packet of granola bars. "Chocolate chip or honey nut?"

She wraps her arms around herself. "What do you want from me?"

Her voice is low and trembles with uncertainty. My shoulders sag, and I grind my jaw, but the second my teeth grate her eyes widen, so I make myself stop.

"I don't know," I finally say. I hand her a chocolate chip bar, and after a moment, she takes it.

She's still wound as tight as a drum, but when she peels the wrapper back, I breathe a sigh of relief. At least she's going to eat.

But she doesn't take a bite, instead she asks, "What are you?"

That barely controlled fear tinges her words again, and I curse the beast for making an appearance like he did.

Knowing there's no point lying, and hell, she's already seen me shift so it's not like I can effectively hide anything from her anyway, I reply, "A werewolf."

Her eyes grow as wide as saucers. "A werewolf? Like in the movies?"

"Yeah, like in the movies, except my wolf . . ." But I can't finish my sentence. How do I explain to her that my wolf has turned rogue? That he's no longer like other wolves that live as one with their human? That being on my own for so long has turned him savage and murderous, and now, there's no going back? That it's been so long since I've been around another wolf that I've lost him to the darkness and I'll never be normal again?

No, it's probably best not to tell her all of that.

It doesn't matter, though. She doesn't seem to catch my hesitancy. From her confused look, it seems she's trying to come to grips with what I just revealed.

"So, that thing that you turned into . . ." She swallows audibly. "That was you as a werewolf?"

"Yes, although, when I turn into him I'm not really *me*, I'm *him*, if that makes sense." I sit down on the floor beside her but make sure to keep two feet of distance between us. For the first time since taking her, her gaze isn't darting around looking for an escape, and I don't want to scare her by sitting any closer.

"And is that why you took me?" She pushes a long strand of dark-brown hair behind her ear. "Because of your . . . err . . . wolf?"

"No, he didn't want to take you. I did. If it were up to him, he'd have eaten you by now."

Her jaw drops, and the granola bar clatters to the floor. I grimace when it lands in a pile of dust.

"You're going to eat me?" She tries to back up more, but there's nowhere for her to go. She's already cornered, quite literally.

"No," I say sharply. "I won't let him do that."

But her chest rises and falls quickly despite my reassurances. I try to ignore how her breasts heave up and down, but I can't help noticing for the merest second.

But any wayward thoughts I have disappear like snow in the underworld when that fearful look returns to her warm brown irises.

I hate that I'm the reason for it.

I rake a hand through my hair again and back up another foot. "Shit. I'm sorry. I shouldn't even be telling you this. It's going to be hard enough getting you back to your home with that flat tire, but since you've already seen so much the SF will be after you now."

"SF?" she squeaks.

"Supernatural Forces. They're like the military and law enforcement combined into one in the supernatural community. They're currently hunting me, but so far, I've evaded them, but once they discover that I took you, you'll be on their list too."

"Wait. What? Why? What did I do?"

"Nothing," I say wearily. "Other than being aware of our existence that is. Humans aren't supposed to know about us, unless they have family connections."

If I thought her look had been frightened before, she now looks damn near petrified.

Fuck a duck, Ward. Can you screw this up any more?

I sigh and try to say in a soothing tone, "It's okay, really. The SF will take you to their headquarters to have the sorcerers wipe your memory of this entire experience, and then you'll go back to your normal life. And this—" I wave at the cabin then me. "It will be like it never happened. You'll wake up with a bad headache and won't be able to explain why you can't remember the past few days, but you truly won't remember anything."

She sits up straighter. "Wait, you're serious. You're really going to let me go?"

I try not to be affected by the eagerness in her tone. Something inside of me withers, and I know whatever chance I had of making her feel this crazy irrational attachment to me that I feel toward her, was gone the moment I abducted her.

Of course you don't stand a chance, you stupid shit. How did you ever think anything good would come from this?

I hang my head before forcing a tight smile in her direction. "Yeah. I'm going to let you go."

CHAPTER SIX
BRIANNA

He says he's going to release me, and I try not to feel too eager because I'm not stupid. I know that at any moment he can change his mind.

Wolfman stands by the chipped kitchen counter, going through supplies.

My stomach churns with unease as I watch him, but I also know that I need to eat—feeling weak from low blood sugar isn't going to help me if I need to make a run for it—so I sit quietly in the corner of the cabin munching a new granola bar after he insisted on tossing the first.

It has to be early afternoon by now, and I still don't know what to think of the past twelve hours. I do know that 2 p.m. is coming, and when I don't show at the library, Macy will try to reach me.

I finish off the bar and take another drink of water, then close my eyes and think of my friends. I'm assuming none of them know I've been abducted, but by this evening, after missing practice, my library date with Macy, and my shift at work...

Someone will start asking questions.

I take comfort in that and open my eyes, settling more onto the hard floor while leaning my back against the musty smelling wall. I'm not full, but at least my stomach isn't growling anymore. And for the first time since being snatched off the street, my heart isn't beating painfully.

Still, flashbacks of the moment he abducted me keep clouding my thoughts. I don't want to remember that terrifying moment when he'd lifted me from the ground and clamped a hand over my mouth, so I concentrate on what else I've learned.

Werewolves. Sorcerers. Some organization called the Supernatural Forces.

They all exist. They're real.

I mean, seriously, WTF?

If I hadn't seen my abductor shift right in front of me into a wolf, and if I hadn't seen his glowing eyes on numerous occasions, I would know for certain that he's a complete psychopath who obviously doesn't live in reality, but now . . .

I'm not so sure.

He seems genuinely remorseful about my violent abduction, but I also know that I can't trust him. At any moment, those glowing eyes could emerge, and that vicious beast could return.

I shudder when I picture his golden wolf with snapping teeth lunging for my neck.

When he'd shifted, I'd thought for certain I'd gone crazy—the stress of my kidnapping manifesting into psychosis—but when I'd watched him morph just as suddenly back into a naked human before he barreled out the door as my vision grew dark . . .

I shake my head. It *wasn't* a hallucination. I'm certain of it, and his supernatural origins explain his inhuman strength and speed.

Still . . . WTF?

It doesn't help that I have a headache the size of Alaska. Thanks to the blow to my head, trying to contemplate what he is only makes the pounding worse. Fingering above my ear, I wince. A goose-egg, from where I'd fallen to the floor and hit my head, rises from my scalp like a mountain. But at least the rest of me is in better shape. Wolfman cleaned me up and applied ointment to my various cuts and rope burns. They don't hurt as much anymore, but I still don't let my guard down.

Because it appears I've been abducted by Dr. Jekyll *and* Mr. Hyde. One moment, Wolfman can be sweet and caring, but the next . . .

My breath catches.

The floorboards creak around me. Wolfman is currently trying to decide what to pack and what to leave. He stands in nothing but a pair of shorts. He doesn't even have shoes on.

I've noticed a few things about him in the hour since he untied me. He's young, probably around my age, yet despite his youth, despair is etched into his features every time he thinks I'm not looking, as though the weight of the world rests on his shoulders.

I keep quiet as I watch him. I study his movements, taking in his predatory build. He has broad shoulders and a tapered waist, and he's strong, like freakishly strong. A part of me isn't sure how much of his strength comes from his rippling muscles versus his werewolf origins. Yet, he still looks like a human. His skin is clear and tanned, his jawline strong and powerful. Nothing about him screams *different* or *other*, and everything about him definitely exudes sex appeal.

A flutter of something runs through me when I take in his taut muscles and defined abs.

My head snaps back. I did *not* just feel that.

But that feeling is still there. I've recognized that he's attractive, like crazy-hot attractive, as much as I was trying to ignore it.

I hang my head and sigh. Am I seriously attracted to him? *That is so fucked up, Keller.*

I fiddle with the granola bar wrapper, not realizing it's making a quiet noise until he whips around. I stop and the wrapper flutters back to the floor. My stomach drops.

But his blue irises remain clear.

"Everything okay?" he asks.

I suck in a shuddering breath. Dr. Jekyll is still with me. "Yeah, I'm fine."

His bunched-up shoulders settle back down. "I'm about done here, then I'll load up. I've got to change that flat tire, but then we can—"

"You don't need to accompany me. I can walk if you point me in the right direction and give me a few water bottles and granola bars."

I hold my breath as I wait for his reply. I've been debating if he would let me leave on my own. I have no idea how far it is to get home, and it's still hot enough this time of year that dehydration is a real concern, but I'm willing to take my chances even if I have a goose egg and a headache that rivals Alaska. I have a feeling that Mother Nature will be easier to contend with than Mr. Hyde.

A flash of regret crosses his features, but he smooths it before he breaks eye contact and reaches for the backpack. He fiddles with some supplies on the counter, putting them in the bag, then taking them out, before putting them back in. "I'm sorry, but it's too far for you to walk. We're easily fifty miles from any town. I'll drive you, and don't worry. I'll take you home, then I'll let you go. I promised I would, so I will."

"Where are we?"

"Southern Utah. Trust me. You can't walk from here."

He goes back to loading the pack. It's practically bursting with supplies.

"What's your name?" I ask, anything to keep him acting normal and talking. I figure if I engage Dr. Jekyll, he's less likely to morph into his malevolent side.

"Collin Ward."

Such a normal name. "I'm Brianna."

"I know."

"How do you know that?"

"I looked at your driver's license."

"You did?" I sit up straighter. "Does that mean you still have my purse?" *And my cell phone?*

"It's in the trunk."

My heart beats harder, and I tentatively push to a stand. "Do you think I could . . . uh . . . get it?"

"If you want."

I walk slowly past him, making sure to keep a wide berth between us. He watches me the entire time, his body tensing more with each second that passes, like a coil that's been pushed too far and is ready to spring. *He probably thinks I'm going to run for it.*

And maybe I should.

But once outside, I go to the trunk, knowing that calling for help on my cell phone is better than any sprint and knowing that he could change his mind at any moment about me acquiring it. The screen door bangs behind me, and out of my peripheral vision, I see him standing on the small porch watching me.

I fling the trunk open. My stomach lurches when I spot the duct tape. *He tied me up using that. He gagged me with that.* Shoving those terrifying thoughts to the side, my eyes alight on my purse.

With frantic movements, I grab it and rip it open to search for my phone. A quick look over my shoulder shows Collin still on the porch, except now his arms are crossed and a frown covers his face.

Shit. Mr. Hyde may be emerging.

I whip my cell phone out and almost squeal in delight when I see that my battery isn't dead. It's low, just above ten percent, but it's still working.

I start to tap in 911 but then my stomach lurches.

There's no signal.

There's no freakin' signal out here!

A shuffling sound on the dirt has me whipping around. I clutch my phone tightly to my chest. Collin's right in front of me. He's only a few inches away, and I'm fairly certain that he shuffled his feet on purpose. He's proven to be silent on every other occasion.

His gaze dips to my phone, and his eyes dim. In a quiet voice, he says, "I told you that we're too far away from anywhere. Your cell phone won't work here. That's why I don't want you trying to walk anywhere. I'm not sure you'll make it, and you wouldn't be able to call for help if you couldn't."

"But I'd be fine. Really, I would. How about I just take a few water bottles, and then I'll—"

"I said no!" His voice changes, growing deeper.

I open my mouth to reply when he suddenly doubles over. A snarl tears from his throat, and the veins in his neck bulge.

Oh shit.

I scramble backward, bumping into the open trunk in the process.

Hairs sprout on the backs of his hands, and even in the bright sunlight, his eyes glow when he looks up at me. His jaw has changed again, elongating in that terrifying way.

"Lock yourself in the car!" he says through clenched teeth.

I back around the car so fast that I almost trip. With a wrenching movement, I have the backdoor open and am throwing myself inside just as the sound of ripping clothing reaches my ears.

"Oh shit! Oh shit!" I chant over and over as I scramble to click the locks.

I've only just engaged the final lock when a snarling wolf lunges at the side of the car. I shriek and fall backward, slamming into the opposite side of the sedan.

The huge wolf lets out a terrifying growl and checks his body into the car again. The door heaves in protest, and I'm pretty sure the beast created a dent, but the glass doesn't shatter.

I squeeze my eyes shut and begin whispering a prayer. I've never been a religious person, but in this moment, I turn into one.

"Please, please, just let me live. Don't let him kill me. I'll be good. I'll help others. I'll devote my life to a good cause, if you just—"

But my prayers aren't being answered today, because the next thing I hear is the sound of shattering glass.

CHAPTER SEVEN
COLLIN

uck!
F   The beast is gaining ground. When she spoke about leaving, about getting away before he could eat her, I lost control of him.

I know I'm losing the battle when he lunges at the car again. The force of our body shatters the back passenger window and the next thing I know, he's wiggling through the broken glass, oblivious to the shards sticking to his fur.

He wants Brianna *now*.

She screams, her blood-curdling wail piercing our ears painfully. She's curled into a ball, her legs bent at the knees against her chest to protect her abdomen. One of her legs hurls out, attempting to kick us away.

But the beast is too fast for her. He feints to the right, her leg never making contact, and then he's on her. His entire weight sits on her chest, pinning her in place. She screams again, but this time her cry is a high shrill.

It's the sound a prey makes when they know they're going to die.

No! I fight harder, clawing and thrashing inside him. But it's no use.

His mouth opens, her throat calling to him. Her carotid artery flutters in her swan-like neck, and the sound of her heart, beating as rapidly as hummingbird wings, only calls to him more.

I'm sorry.

Agony grips me when he lunges at her. Whatever control I had over him is gone. His teeth lock onto her throat at the same time her hands clasp his neck, her fingers digging into his fur as her caramel-and-sunshine scent—tinged with the sour stench of fear—permeates our senses.

I wait for it—the taste of her blood filling our mouth and the sound of gurgling from her voice box as her body bleeds out.

But it doesn't come.

The beast pulls back. Bite marks are evident on her skin, and her fingers still dig into his scruff.

He inhales again, his face only inches away from hers. Wild eyes meet his as her entire body goes still.

She's going into shock. I can see it in the glaze of her eyes and the way her face goes slack.

Brianna! I silently call to her.

A whimper fills the sedan, but Brianna's lips never part. It takes a moment before I realize it came from the beast. He pulls back more, confusion flooding his senses, before the need to run, to flee, nearly overwhelms him.

But I can't leave her. Not this time.

I struggle to get him out of the car, wiggling his huge wolf body awkwardly through the broken window before the warmth of the sun shines on our back.

I force the shift, and surprisingly, the beast doesn't fight me.

A second later, I'm naked on the ground. The basketball shorts I'd worn earlier are torn halfway up the side, but they're still wearable. I frantically slip them on, yanking the drawstring into a knot so they don't fall off, before I fly to the car door.

A locked door greets me, and inside Brianna's trembling body makes my stomach plummet.

I rip the door off the hinges, not having the patience to search for the lock on the other side of the broken window.

"Brianna? Bri?" I say to her.

I tense, waiting for another kick, but she doesn't fight me when I climb over the seat toward her. Rapid breaths make her chest rise shallowly, and her complexion is terrifyingly white. Puncture wounds mar her neck, and small trickles of blood run down her skin.

I wince.

I did that to her when I let the beast gain control.

A part of me is afraid to get any closer. I could lose control again, and the beast could finish what he started. But I don't feel him trying to assert his dominance. If anything, he's retreated to a deep dark corner within my belly, agitation oozing from him, but something else rises off his deranged mind.

Confusion.

He's as entirely confused by this situation and his reaction as I am.

Being careful not to jar her, I inch more over her. Her long, toned body is clenching, her muscles spasming as she shivers.

"Shit," I mutter under my breath.

As gently as I can, I lift her from the seat and carry her back to the cabin. When the bright sunshine hits her face, her pupils constrict, but she doesn't close her eyes.

My jaw tightens. I bound up the steps two at a time until we're inside. Making quick work of the few blankets I have, I spread them out awkwardly while still holding her. Once the makeshift bed is complete, I lie her down.

Her gaze is still vacant, her face still pale. "Brianna?" I call.

She blinks, but it's as if she doesn't see me.

"Brianna?" I run a finger down her neck to the bite marks. My chest heaves again when I see what the beast did.

But as soon as I make contact with the shallow puncture wounds, Brianna lurches from my grasp.

"Stay away from me!" Her eyes are wild, but my relief at her return to the land-of-the-living is short lived when she grabs a thick jagged stick from the floor.

It had sat near the fireplace, beside a small pile of firewood, one of many things left behind in this forgotten cabin. But I don't have time to comprehend what she intends to do with it until she's swinging at me.

"Whoa!" I'm on my feet and jumping back but she's already lunging at me again.

I feint right, then left, amazed at her speed and agility. Most women wouldn't have been able to get a weapon anywhere near me, but she's managing to come within inches of my face every time she swings.

"Stop smiling, you egotistical psychopath!"

The venom in her tone has me smoothing my expression. I honestly hadn't realized I'd been smiling at all, but considering the relief I feel at the feisty side of Brianna returning, I'm not surprised at my response.

"Can you put it down?" I ask calmly.

But she just swings more. "Why? So you can attack me again?"

She's inching toward the door. With each swing she makes, she's also taking a step. I know she intends to make another escape, except this time, I don't think she'll stop.

Another arc of the firewood has it careening toward me. Instead of jumping back, I grab it mid-air. The force of my interception makes her teeth chatter, but that doesn't stop her from trying to wrestle it free.

But I don't let go. Instead, I close the distance between us until my other arm wraps around her waist and brings her flush against me. "Let go."

My quiet command doesn't have any effect on her. Instead, she thrashes and kicks, landing more well-placed blows against my shins.

I grunt but hold onto her and call up the dominant power inside me. "Brianna!" My voice is firm and rings with magic, heady with alpha power. "Let. It. Go."

Her body goes stock-still, and I curse that I called on my magic to command her. A part of me is surprised that it worked on a human, but since it works on all supernaturals, I know I shouldn't be that shocked.

Whatever the case, I take the wooden stick from her and throw it back with the rest of the firewood. It makes a hollow *thwack* when it lands on the floor.

I wrap my other arm around her, holding her captive. She struggles again, trying to push against me, and the feel of her warm body pressed so intimately against mine makes something else stir inside me. Something I haven't felt in a very long time.

I abruptly let her go.

That's a mistake.

She runs for the door, my short hold on her with my dominant power dispelling. With a sigh, I give chase and feel hesitantly for the beast.

But he's still curled up inside me, letting me know that he has no intention of making another appearance anytime soon. At least with this chase, I won't have to worry about him resurfacing.

CHAPTER EIGHT
BRIANNA

What the hell was that?

Branches scratch my face as I sprint wildly through the trees. Not only did Collin's psychotic wolf almost kill me, but he commanded me in a strange voice that brought goose bumps to my arms while electrifying my nerves. My entire body had gone still, my grip on the stick slipping. I'd wanted to hold onto the firewood, *needed* to if I wanted to keep fighting him, but it was as though my brain had other ideas. I'd let go, just as he commanded, and I'd been helpless to resist.

Fucking psycho! I don't even want to know what kind of weird werewolf mojo he just used on me.

I breathe deeply, and the rhythmic feel of my legs pumping beneath me helps quell some of my panic, but then images of being attacked by his vicious wolf surface again. I'd felt certain I was going to die when his fangs latched onto my throat.

That memory fortifies me with speed.

I leap over a log and know what I have to do. Despite

Collin claiming he's going to take me home, I'm not falling for it. Even though he's been acting like he cares about me and won't hurt me, I know I can't trust him. Because if he *did* care about me, he wouldn't let that terrifying wolf of his try to murder me.

Besides, for all I know, he and his wolf carry the same conscience, and Collin's just toying with me in some big fucked up cat-and-mouse game. He's probably laughing at me right now.

But what about how he talks to himself? Memories of him in the car, carrying on conversations, as if he's talking to his wolf, fill my mind.

Okay, so maybe they don't share the same conscience.

But still, he can't be trusted.

Heavy breaths fill my chest as I continue to tear down the mountain. I'm still running as fast as I can, not caring in the slightest that I have no supplies, no water, no cell phone—nothing. But at least, out here, I'm alive and away from him.

I haven't heard him behind me, but I know that doesn't mean he hasn't given chase.

But this time, I won't stop.

When I reach the embankment I stumbled down last night, my footsteps aren't panicked. They're now confident and sure. I'm getting the hell out of here, and I'm not going to let him catch me again.

I sail over a small stream, my feet sinking into the muddy embankment on the other side. My white waitressing top snags on a branch when I run past it. A tearing sound follows, but I don't slow.

My lungs are burning now, and my legs are thick with lactic acid. I've been sprinting for at least five minutes, and I know I can't keep up this pace. I'll need to slow to a jog if I want to escape him and keep putting distance between us.

Just a few more minutes, keep going until—

"Umph!" Something locks around my waist and stops me mid-stride. I'm lifted from the ground, and I know it's him before I recognize the feel of his hard arms or detect his cedar scent. Instinctively, I thrash. "Let me go! Fuck you, you psychotic asshole! Let me go!"

I pummel and kick him, and when he turns me in his arms, I scratch at his face.

He hisses in pain when my nails rake down his cheeks. The sight of blood doesn't stop me. If anything, it fuels my need for vengeance.

This asshole abducted me. He held me captive against my will. His psycho wolf has nearly killed me *twice*, and he won't let me leave now even though I desperately want to. And that's after he *promised* to take me home. He promised to let me go, but he's *not*.

"You lied!" I scream. "You lied to me! I want to leave, and you said I could go!"

His arms tighten, pinning my limbs to my sides. I don't give up despite his Herculean strength. Even though I'm gasping so hard I can barely breathe, I don't stop fighting.

"Brianna." The sound of my name on his lips sounds foreign. His voice is soft and tinged with regret. "Please stop. I don't want to hurt you, and I'm sorry that my wolf attacked you. I want to take you home. I do, and I will, but if I let you leave like this, you probably won't survive. Please, let me take you back to the cabin. We'll finish packing, and we'll go."

"You mean you'll finish packing while I'm tied to a chair?" I spit back.

"I won't tie you up again. I promise."

I finally go still. It's useless to fight him anyway, and my body is burning so much from adrenaline and lactic acid that my thrashes have turned painful.

I shake my head and blink rapidly as tears threaten to fill my eyes. "You're lying. You're not going to take me home. You're going to carry me to that cabin and then if you don't kill me, your wolf will."

His lips part, and his breath stops. Out here, in the bright sunshine, his eyes look stormy and troubled, as if a chasm of emotions lurk within their depths. I gasp when the scratches I inflicted on his face heal right before my eyes. The skin sews itself together like magic.

He swallows, his throat working, before he says, "I may be a lot of awful things, but I'm not a liar. I said I was going to take you home, and I will."

"But why not just let me go now? Let me leave. Right here. Right now. *Please*."

My plea comes out in an agonizing tone, and that pained and regretful look crosses his face again.

"I can't. For your own safety, I can't."

I stiffen as he turns and begins marching us back up the mountain just as I predicted. The rational side of me, the tiny side that is still holding onto reason, knows that what he's saying makes sense. Even though I'm in good shape, I'm on foot which means I'm days away from any town. And it's dry and hot here. While I have no doubt I can walk the needed distance and survive the cooler nights, I don't have any water, and I can't survive dehydration.

But the other side of me—the one that's running purely on instinct—doesn't want to be anywhere near him.

He can't be trusted. I *know* that, but at the moment, I'm helpless to stop him.

∽

IF ANYTHING positive comes from my second failed attempt at escape, it's that Collin seems to be making good on his promise. An hour later, I'm outside sitting on the cabin steps as Collin finishes putting the tools away that he used to change the flat tire.

The small spare is on the back of the sedan, and the blown one is propped against the cabin. The car is now missing its back door—thanks to Collin wrenching it off after his wolf attacked me. It looks totally ghetto.

"Ready?" he calls.

He turns toward me in the sunshine, his expression hopeful, then apprehensive. His hair is loose, and the blond wavy strands rest lightly on his shoulders.

For a moment, my breath stops, and that strange flutter runs through me again. The man is pure masculine perfection with his cut muscles, dazzling blue eyes, and magnetic presence. He reminds me of one of my favorite actors from those superhero movies.

But then a sneer lifts my lips. He's no fucking Thor.

I stand but don't move any closer to him. Instead, I narrow my eyes. "You're really going to take me home? No tricks?"

"No tricks. I promise."

Despite his promise and hot-as-hell appearance, I'm loathe to get in the car with him even if it's the only way he's willing to let me leave.

I eye the backpack in the backseat. He's latched it with the seatbelt so it won't fall out. "What if you just give me that backpack of supplies and cut me loose? I can walk back. There's enough food and water in there."

He rakes a hand through his hair, his bicep bulging in the process.

Dammit, Bri! Don't notice stuff like that!

"I have no doubt you're a very capable woman who could probably walk a thousand miles if she was determined to do so, but how do you know you won't get lost?

There's no cell phone reception for miles, so you can't use your phone's GPS. And even if you take the pack of food and water, it won't last more than a week, and that's *if* you're rationing. So then what? You'll be on your own with nothing but your own survival skills to keep you alive. And you may make it a few weeks by drinking dirty water from streams and eating berries—if you know which ones aren't poisonous—but you still have to contend with exposure. This heat is unforgiving during the day, and the nights can get cold. So tell me, after knowing all of that, how are you going to survive?"

I cross my arms and look away. I had hoped to follow the road to a city, but he's right. What if there are intersections? And there probably aren't any streams near the road. Where would I find water? Under my shoes, a few pebbles sift in the dirt. I roll them a few times before kicking them clear to the trees.

Dammit. He has a point.

Grumbling, I begin walking toward the car. He's still looking at me expectantly, as though waiting for my reply, but I'm not going to give him the satisfaction of agreeing and letting him know that he's right.

The only comfort I take is that he hasn't been talking to his alternate personality since we returned to the cabin, and his eyes haven't glowed since his wolf attacked me. I've come to learn those glowing eyes mean his wolf is close.

Too close.

He opens the front passenger door for me.

"Such a gentleman," I mutter under my breath.

His lips quirk up, and I have a sneaking suspicion he heard me. "We'll be out of gas soon, but with any luck, we'll make it to a gas station before that happens."

I pause before sinking into the seat. I wipe the sweat from my upper lip. It has to be at least ninety degrees even at this altitude. "You don't have any gas here to fill the tank?"

He shakes his head. "I didn't bring any."

"Cause you didn't think we'd ever be leaving?"

My scathing comeback makes his eyes dim. He shuffles his feet before saying quietly, "Something like that."

Before the realization fully sinks in that he intended to kill me all along, he leaves my door open before darting around the front of the car to the driver's side. He moves silently, his large form unnervingly graceful, before he slips into his seat and slams the door.

I let out the breath I've been holding. *He never intended to let me leave.*

Despite the heat, a shiver runs down my spine. I glance toward the trees. The tall pines sway at their tips while the clouds in the sky drift lazily above. I could make another run for it. I know I probably won't get any farther than last time, but I could try, and maybe just maybe, I would find a way to outsmart him.

But then reality sets in. Collin's right. Even if I did manage to escape, I would be leaving one possible death for a much more probable one. I have no idea where I am and without food, water, a map, and compass, how could I ever get home?

I finally settle into the sedan even though my instincts are telling me I may never make it back alive. *Just don't trust him, Bri, and don't let your guard down. Mr. Hyde can return at any moment.*

With that thought firmly in place, I slam my door and fasten my seatbelt while Collin fiddles with some wires under the steering wheel. A moment later, the growl from the starting engine penetrates the quiet mountain air.

I cock my head, eyeing the loose wires. "No key, huh? Did you lose it?"

He won't meet my eyes when he shifts into drive. "Something like that."

I shake my head. *Right.* He stole this car. It's not even his. No wonder he doesn't seem to care about the broken door.

He pulls away from the cabin, and we begin the long lumbering trip down the mountain. Several times, he drives up the embankment when the road thins. Each time, I grip my seat in alarm.

After the third one, his lips curve into a crooked smile. "Don't worry. I've driven on rougher roads than this."

"From your other kidnapping escapades?"

His crooked smile turns into a chuckle until he realizes I'm serious. "Um, no." He sobers. "I've never . . . uh . . . kidnapped anyone before. You're my first. I just meant from back home the roads can be like this. I grew up driving mountain passes."

He returns his attention to the narrow dirt path in front of us, and I only fully relax when the car is back on an even keel. But despite the harrowing road, that would be a nightmare to navigate if it turned muddy, he seems at ease.

"So where's back home?" I ask, trying to distract myself from the sharp turn coming up. I then reason that maybe keeping him talking is a good idea, even if it's self-serving. He seems pretty normal right now, more human than vicious animal, and maybe conversation will keep him that way.

"Wyoming."

"Anywhere in particular in Wyoming?" My eyes widen more when the turn approaches.

"Hidden Creek."

"Never heard of it."

He shrugs. "Most haven't. It's not exactly a tourist destination."

We hit a huge rut, making me bounce just before he steers up the embankment again. The car tips precariously. "Is your family still there?" I squeak.

"Yeah, they all live there."

We make it around the turn, and I try to untie the knot in my stomach. *Maybe being in the trunk was better.*

"Where did you grow up?" He glances at me and the sunshine makes his blue eyes sparkle.

"A small town in southern Arizona. My dad's still there, and most of my high school friends are too. It's one of those towns where everyone knows everyone. I couldn't wait to get out of there and explore the world, but now that I live in a city, I'm not sure that city life suits me." I realize I'm babbling and bite my lip, but now we're headed straight for a huge crack in the dry road. *How the hell are we going to get over that?*

But Collin doesn't slow. The bottom of the car scrapes, and I'm pretty sure the tailpipe falls off, but the car keeps going.

Still, I can't help my, "You couldn't have stolen an SUV?" complaint.

He grins. "The easiest model in your area to break into happened to be this one. Beggars can't be choosers."

My hold on the door handle loosens momentarily when I let out an anxious laugh. I then realize I just laughed with my abductor, as if we're old college buddies, and I swallow the sound.

I frown and immediately sober. *Don't let your guard down, Brianna.*

Collin, however, seems immune to my waxing and waning moods. He asks, "So if your dad's still in your hometown, where's your mom?"

"Um," I debate how much to tell him, then remember I'm supposed to keep him talking, while *not* letting my guard down. "She's dead. She died when I was a little girl."

"Oh. I'm sorry."

I shrug. "It's fine. I barely remember her." And what I do remember are not memories I like to dwell on. Images of a tall woman with long hair who drank chamomile tea and smelled of cheap drugstore soap fill my mind. My sharpest memories of her are when she's standing by the kitchen sink peering out the window. She would do that for hours even when I was standing right beside her, tugging on her pant leg because I was hungry or wanted her attention. She still wouldn't move. It was as though I didn't exist.

I shake my head, dispelling the memory.

"What about brothers or sisters? Do you have any of those?" he asks.

With a start, I wonder if he's trying to distract me. My knuckles are white on my door handle. "Nope, no siblings. It's just me."

"So you moved away to go to college cause you wanted to experience the world?"

"Yeah, but I started college late. I was twenty-two because I worked for a few years before college to save money and help my dad. That's why I'm a twenty-six-year-old senior."

"A senior, eh? Does that mean you're going to graduate soon?"

"Yep, I'm done this spring. I just need to—" I stop, realizing mid-sentence that he's just spoken about my future, as if I still have a future. Does that mean he's really going to let me live?

I try not to dwell on that or the insane way my heart surges at the thought of getting out of this alive.

"What about you?" I ask, completely losing track of our

conversation. "Where do you live and work?" *When you're not abducting women that is.*

He returns his focus to the road as a muscle tightens in his jaw. "Nowhere really. I don't have a job, and I haven't called anywhere home in a very long time."

"How long have you not had a home?"

"Two and a half years."

"And what happened two and a half years ago to make you not call anywhere home?"

His grip on the wheel tightens, and he doesn't look at me when he replies, "I left my pack and didn't look back."

Pack? I'm assuming that has something to do with him being a werewolf, but I have no idea how to respond to that. And from how tense he appears, I've just stepped into very sketchy territory, and I'm pretty sure a faint glow just lit his eyes.

Shit.

"So . . . have you seen any good movies lately?" I ask in an overly cheerful voice. "I haven't been to the theater in ages, but I try to watch a flick every week with my friends. It's one of our fave things to do as a study break." I begin babbling again, but it seems to help. His tension eases, and his lazy smile returns.

I don't even notice the huge rut that practically bounces me to the ceiling I'm freaking out so much, but Collin does. He laughs when I rub my head, then apologizes for the bump.

"It's fine, really," I say with a forced smile. "We've got to almost be down by now, right?"

"Yeah, not too far," he says and flashes me another dazzling smile. Dr. Jekyll is still firmly in place.

But that's not necessarily a good thing. When he smiles like that, a flutter stirs my stomach. And it's one of those flutters that I need to suppress. I groan inwardly. *Did I seriously just find him sexy again?*

I'm going to need serious psychological help after I get home, cause not only did I meet a werewolf who tried repeatedly to kill me, but I also continuously admired his muscles and fawned over his sex appeal.

So fucked up, Keller.

My breath stops again as images of Thor fill my mind, but I quickly shake it off and leap into a new benign subject. Food. Who doesn't like to talk about their favorite foods and the best meal they've ever had? And there's no way a conversation of food can remind me of chiseled biceps, tangled blond locks, or breathtaking smiles.

Thankfully, Collin has a long list of what he likes to eat.

I sit back a little easier and concentrate on what he's saying, all the while keeping my gaze straight ahead so my wayward thoughts don't once again land me in hot water.

CHAPTER NINE
COLLIN

Not long later, we're almost to the bottom of the mountain. Brianna's been asking me questions non-stop, and I have the sneaking suspicion she's doing it to keep me distracted. Or maybe she's trying to distract herself.

Whatever the case, her latest round of questions are about where I've traveled and my favorite place in the world. When I ask her the same, she replies, "British Columbia. I spent a few weeks up there last summer with a couple of friends."

I'm not surprised when she further digresses that her favorite activity was deep-sea fishing. Something tells me this woman has a love of adventure.

When we finally reach the gravel road at the bottom of the mountain, it's mid-afternoon. Brianna lets out a sigh of relief. "Finally. How far to the nearest town?"

"About fifty miles." I turn left, going south.

"So only an hour?"

My gut tightens at how eager she sounds, but I brush it

off. I abducted her so of course she can't wait to get away from me.

At least the beast hasn't stirred again, not since she asked about why I left Hidden Creek. When Brianna brought up my hometown, I'd tensed, waiting for him to overtake me, but then she switched subjects and images of my nemesis from back home disappeared, and the beast calmed.

Still, I know it's only a matter of time until he awakens again, his bloodlust surging to the surface and his insistence that Brianna be our next meal. But at the moment, for whatever reason, he's withdrawn.

Regardless of that, my grip on the steering wheel remains fixed. Just the thought of him hurting Brianna . . .

Veins pop on my forearms, so I say the first thing that comes to mind. "Do you like waitressing?"

She angles her body my way, and it's only from sheer force of will that I keep my gaze on her eyes. Her breasts are straining against her shirt again, and her shorts have ridden up her lean muscular legs giving me an ample view of her shapely thighs.

"How do you know I'm a waitress?" She fingers her polo shirt. It sports a small tear from her mad dash through the trees, but there's no emblem on it. It's just a plain white shirt. With a start, I realize there's no way I could have known she waitresses if not for my stalking.

I return my attention to the road. "I uh . . . I may have—"

BOOM!

The car swings violently to the left.

"Shit!" I wrench the steering wheel to straighten the car, but it still pulls hard to the side.

"What the hell!" Brianna exclaims as I slow the vehicle.

I pull over and put it into park. "The spare," I mutter

under my breath. I get out and round the back of the car, and sure enough, the spare has blown.

Brianna joins me as the hot sun beats down on us. She crosses her arms as we both eye the useless tire. "Another one went flat? Seriously?"

I rake a hand through my hair, then kneel by the tire. It's *completely* flat. "We must have hit something in the road."

She groans and pulls her cell phone out. "Do you have a phone charger? My battery's almost dead."

I shake my head. I haven't carried a cell phone in months.

"Still no signal." She lifts her phone up, moving it back and forth, as if a signal will magically appear if she holds her phone at just the right angle. But the mountains around here are too steep, and the valley we're in is too low. It will probably be miles before her phone works.

"Are you still up for walking?" I ask her.

She slips her phone back into her pocket and narrows her brown eyes. "Now you'll let me walk home?"

I laugh. I can't help it. "With me along of course, just to ensure you make it."

She snorts. "We wouldn't want any dangerous creatures in the woods hurting me, now would we?"

My mood lifts at her teasing tone, but just as quickly as amusement fills her eyes, it vanishes. She shakes her head and steps back. "Anyway, are you going to let me leave on my own now? Since you can't give me a ride . . ."

She lets her words hang, and it's like a punch in the gut. She wants to leave, and she doesn't actually want me around. I remind myself that her questions on our drive down from the cabin were just to keep me occupied and nothing more. She's not actually interested in me.

I stand back up but keep my gaze averted. It's fucking

ridiculous, but I have a feeling she'll see my anguish if I look her directly in the eye.

My next words are near impossible to get out, but I force them. "I can give you my map and the backpack so you have enough food and water. You should get cell reception at some point, so you probably won't have to walk the entire fifty miles to get help."

My insides are churning, and with stiff movements, I retrieve the pack, then stuff my worn map into it. The pack's heavy, but something tells me that won't bother her.

I hold it out as sweat pebbles on my skin. It's fucking hot here, and I really want to punch something, but I keep my arm extended.

Her eyebrows draw together, and I can tell she's wondering why I never mentioned the map before, but how do I explain that I couldn't let her leave because something inside me is broken? I wanted her near, if only for a while on our drive because I like the contentedness I feel around her. *Yeah, better keep that to yourself, Ward.*

With a tentative hand, she reaches for the pack. Our fingers brush, and the feel of her sends a thrill through me, but she quickly pulls away, taking the pack with her.

Strapping it to her back, she secures it with the buckle around her waist, her gaze never leaving mine. "You're really letting me leave?"

I give a curt nod.

"So what are you going to do?"

I place my hands on my hips and eye the wilderness around us. With a shrug, I reply, "Not sure."

She bites her lip, but I remind myself that I'm letting her go. She's not mine, and if I keep her, the beast will inevitably kill her.

For once in your life, do the right thing, Ward.

I turn away so she won't see the tornado of emotions

ripping through me. A sound comes from the gravel, next the trunk opens.

"I'm just getting my purse," she calls. A second later, I hear her footsteps. She's walking on the shoulder, growing farther and farther away with each step she takes.

I swallow the groan that threatens to tear me apart.

She left.

She really left.

I lock my jaw so tightly the muscle aches. The beast stirs. His growl comes next along with a rush of magic that explodes inside me.

Fuck!

I take off at a run, barreling through the trees as the beast's power grows. Brianna yelps in surprise, and with a start, I realize she must have turned back toward me. But I can't stop. I need to put as much distance between us as possible because the beast just sensed that she's leaving, and he doesn't want to let her go.

Not this time, buddy. This time, you're not going to win.

I ignore the pain coursing through my limbs and focus on the beast. He snarls and lurches against my control. I slam him down as far as I can, but my skin heats, and magic swells up inside me like a tidal wave. Hairs sprout on my arms. My jaw cracks.

No, you fucker!

Branches rip at my shirt. I pump my legs harder until I'm sprinting at top speed. Within minutes, I've put at least three miles of distance between Brianna and me. The pain of that realization opens a gaping hole in my heart. But now's not the time to dwell on the fact that I let her go and will never see her again, and that once again, I'm alone in the world, and it's only a matter of time before the SF catches me and ends my miserable life.

Keep running.

But the magic grows too strong.

I grit my teeth harder as the pain consumes me. Warring with the beast makes it feel as if I'm being eaten alive from the inside out. I stumble, then fall. Dry dirt, and course thorns from a cactus puncture my skin.

No. Get up! There's not enough distance between Brianna and me. I need to keep moving or she won't survive!

With a groan, I attempt to stand, but the beast has other ideas.

He howls in protest, then snarls and lurches, pushing against my control more. Magic surges through me, making me groan when I try to stifle it, but its burning strength is too consuming.

I fall back to the ground, and I writhe on all fours. Heat rolls through me, and the air next to my skin shimmers. I clench my hands into fists, my fingers digging into the sandy dirt. I fight him with everything I have, but his soft fur continues to sprout from my skin.

A guttural howl comes next, then the snapping of bones and muscle fibers.

Normally, shifting is instantaneous, painless, and causes an indescribable joy. But that was when my wolf and I were one—when I allowed the transition to happen.

Now, we're not of the same mind, and the shift is fucking agony.

No! I attempt again to stop him, but my sight changes, and burning needles stab through me as my human emotions dim.

He's coming. He's only a second away. No. No. No.

A howl penetrates the air.

Too late. It's too late.

It's the last human thought I have and then . . .

He's here.

CHAPTER TEN
BRIANNA

He let me leave.

I walk quickly along the side of the road. I'm still so shocked that I'm halfway convinced that I'm dreaming, as if the last few minutes will evaporate if I open my eyes.

But the gravel under my feet feels real. The dry hot air filling my lungs tastes dusty. And the gin-like scent of junipers fills my nostrils.

Those kind of details don't permeate dreams.

This is *happening. I didn't imagine Collin tearing off.*

After I'd started walking away, guilt had initially flooded me. The thought of leaving him here, without water or food, had made me pause and turn back to him, but all I'd seen was the flash of his clothing as he took off running through the trees.

I'd yelped more in surprise than anything. And now, while a pit has formed in my stomach, I'm not waiting to see if he returns. I have to remember that Collin can't be trusted. He and his wolf are one, and if his wolf wants me dead, it doesn't matter if Collin disagrees.

So I carry on, and my quiet footsteps fill the desolate surroundings. I keep glancing over my shoulder, though, waiting for him to appear through the trees or be walking silently in my tread, but each time . . .

He's not there.

All I see are the narrow gravel road behind me and the mountainous desert with its looming peaks and dry vegetation rising along the roadside.

I consult the map again, then pull out my cell phone. My battery's now below ten percent, and there's still no service. I power it down, knowing that I need to conserve the battery. I reason that I'll walk for a few more hours before turning it back on. With any luck, the closer I get to civilization the more likely it will be that I reach cell service.

I pick up my pace and wish I was wearing better shoes. *Maybe I should start jogging. It will go faster—*

A faint howl rises in the distance.

My breath stops, and I nearly trip. I right myself, but my heart is instantly beating a hundred miles an hour. I look left and right but don't see any animals.

Maybe it was a coyote.

I scoff.

Yeah, right. And maybe I'm the Queen of England.

I break into a run, the backpack jostling awkwardly against my spine. It's too big for me, and the straps aren't adjusted correctly. Despite that, I don't slow. I know I can't out distance him, especially if he's turned into that crazy wolf again, but I can sure as hell try.

Another howl sounds. Closer. To my right.

I glance through the trees again and don't see him, but he's coming. I know he is.

My mouth goes dry as the hot hair wicks all moisture from my tongue. *Shit! What the hell should I do?*

I breathe heavily but keep up my pace. I can't fight him, at least, not without a weapon. But maybe if I find another stick, or a large sharp rock—

The faint sound of a truck reaches my ears.

I stop and twirl around. Blood pounds through my ears, but I hear it again.

A semi. I'm certain of it. I'm not imagining it.

I run into the middle of the road just as a logging truck rounds the corner in the distance. It's headed in my direction.

"Help!" I wave both arms overhead and jump up and down. "Please stop and help me!"

I don't move from my position in the center of the narrow gravel road even though I know the crazy wolf is closing in. The approaching driver is either going to have to stop, run me over, or witness my death when Collin's wolf attacks me.

The semi gets closer, and I give another anxious glance toward the trees. A flash of something golden flickers by a rock before it disappears behind a large cactus.

It's him!

I bolt to the truck's passenger door, before the logger has fully stopped, and climb up the steep steps awkwardly. I wrench the door open and throw myself inside before I'm invited.

"Whoa!" the driver exclaims. "My goodness, young lady. What's going on here?"

I slam the door behind me and engage the lock. "Please! Can you give me a ride? A guy . . . he . . . he took me . . ." But I can't continue. My attention has returned to the trees, to the wolf that's lurking in them. I know he's out there. I can *feel* it just like I'd felt him watching me before he'd abducted me.

That's how he knew I was a waitress. I think about all of

those strange sensations I've experienced during the last two weeks.

Sweat moistens my hands. I now understand what those sensations were. For the past few weeks, when that prickly unease stole over me, it was my sixth sense telling me that danger was lurking, and each time, it was Collin. I'm certain of it.

Another second passes before I realize the truck driver is talking to me.

"... took you? Did someone hurt you? Do I need to call the police?"

I force my attention back to him and nod but then shake my head. "Yes. No. I don't know." I bring a hand to my forehead. My heart is still beating too fast, and I can't think rationally.

A part of me wants to tell the trucker that Collin abducted me outside of my home and intended to kill me, but then I remember that Collin's a werewolf. I saw him turn into one, and nobody on the police force will believe that. But do I need to tell them that detail? Should I just report it and say a man took me?

But he also let you go.

That small voice in the back of my mind reminds me that in the end Collin did the right thing. He didn't hurt me, and he let me leave. He also said I was the first person he ever abducted.

He'll go to prison if he's caught.

I grit my teeth, feeling so discombobulated that I don't know what to do, but then I reason that it really wasn't *Collin* that hurt me. It was his wolf. Collin's remorse is genuine. I feel as certain of that as I do that his wolf is out there right now watching me.

And Collin said something about the Supernatural Forces being after him. Maybe I should leave him to get caught by them. They deal with werewolves, right? And didn't he say something about the SF coming after me now too? What if alerting the police pisses the SF off? What if they do something bad to me for reporting Collin to the police?

Shit. I don't know what to do.

"Miss? Are you alright?" The driver's expression is guarded, as if he's unsure if a crazy woman just jumped into his cab.

I force a smile, but my lips quiver. "Can you please give me a ride and drop me off at the nearest town? There's no need to call the police. I'm fine."

The logger tips his Oakland A's baseball cap up and frowns. He has to be around fifty and looks as if he's spent most days working with equipment if his grease-stained fingertips are any indication. The scent of acrid sweat wafts off him, and stubble lines his cheeks. He's in need of a shower. I eye my torn shirt and dirty limbs. *That makes two of us.*

"Are you sure? I can call on the radio for help." He nods toward his equipment then eyes the side of my head.

I never did wash the blood from my neck and hair, and I wonder if my goose egg is showing. I finger it self-consciously, then unclick the pack from my back and slip it around me to rest on the floor. I quickly stash my purse in it so I don't lose it. "No. Really, it's fine, but I would appreciate a ride to the next town if you're willing."

He shrugs. "Fine by me. We're about an hour out." He shifts the truck back into gear, and it rumbles as we pick up speed.

Something flashes in my peripheral vision, and this time when I look out the window, he's not hiding.

Collin's wolf is twenty yards away, and if the logger's

attention drifted to my window he would be able to see him too.

The wolf's eyes glow brightly in the sunshine. He shuffles his feet, the movement anxious as the logger and I drive farther away.

The wolf bobs his head, and a faint whine reaches my ears.

For a brief moment, pain fills my chest, actual *pain*. It feels as if my heart is being torn, and for one crazy second, I consider opening the door and throwing myself back on the road.

But just as quickly, I right myself and wonder what the hell's the matter with me. Collin's wolf would kill me. Have I not learned that? Why would I go back to him?

Perhaps the logger was right to be leery of me after all, cause at the moment, I'm acting like a lunatic.

~

AN HOUR LATER, we cross the state line into Arizona, and not long after that, I spot a country bar off the road. It's the first business we've come across in the hour I've been riding with the logger, so I jump at the opportunity to leave.

"Do you mind dropping me off here?" My hand's already on the door handle.

"You sure you don't want to drive on a bit farther?" he asks. "I have to turn off this road in a mile, but I know there's a gas station a few miles down after that if you don't mind walking a bit. A few stores too."

"Nah, this is fine. I'm back in civilization, which is all I was hoping for."

He nods. "All right then." He slows the truck and when it comes to a stop, I jump out.

"You take care," he calls.

"Thanks, you too, and thanks for the ride."

He flashes the peace sign, then shifts back into gear. I slam the door and breathe in the hot air.

Evening's arrived, and the sun has begun its descent. That hasn't stopped the heat, but at least there's life around here. The two-lane highway has cars driving on it, and the front door bangs on the small bar when someone enters it. Rowdy laughter comes from within. Several pickup trucks and beat-up cars fill the parking lot. Beyond that, it's endless desert.

But there are people here.

Inside my pocket, my cell phone presses against my thigh. Its comforting weight makes me feel even more secure. Thankfully, its battery is mostly replenished since the logger let me use his charger, so I pull it out and turn it on.

As my phone glows to life, I hitch the backpack higher on my shoulder while the logging semi-truck rumbles off and leaves a plume of diesel smoke in its wake. I finger the backpack's strap. Now that I'm back in civilization, I no longer need the supplies in it.

That strange guilt steals over me again. It's so ridiculous, and I've had an hour to stew about it. Collin abducted me. He may not have hurt me in the end, but he still took me. It's absolutely crazy that I haven't called the police even though I have no idea what the Supernatural Forces might do to me—other than wipe my memory.

Still if I'm being honest with myself, fully honest, I haven't called the police not because of the SF but because I'm protecting Collin.

But why am I doing that?

I bite my lip just as my phone's home screen pops up. Seeing the familiar apps and the background photo of me and a bunch of my girlfriends following a match we won brings a smile to my face. I wait for that happy feeling to grow. I'm alive and officially free. I got away. I lived. I accomplished exactly what I set out to do the minute I roused in Collin's trunk, but . . .

That feeling of elation doesn't come.

I nibble on my lip again. I'm about to call my friends so I should be ecstatic. Instead that feeling in my stomach —that feeling I've had ever since I left Collin behind me and had the ridiculous urge to jump *out* of the semi— grows.

I take a deep breath and let my gaze wander toward Utah. In the distance, the mountainous peaks look more like small mounds. It reminds me of a pack of chewy Dots candy scattered on a kitchen counter. From here, the mountains look small and inconsequential, yet when I'd been held captive on one of their peaks, that environment had felt unsurvivable.

Shielding my eyes from the setting sun's glare, I scan the peaks. *Where's Collin now? Is he still a wolf? Or is he a human again? What will he do in the middle of nowhere with nothing but a car that he can't drive anywhere?*

I reason he could return to the cabin. There were still supplies there that he had left behind. But then what? What will he do when those supplies run out?

I shake my head. *Seriously, Keller? You're worrying about him?*

Something is definitely wrong with me.

My phone buzzes, and I jump. I completely forgot that I was even holding it.

It's fully powered up now, and dozens of text messages roll in. At least I have cell service here. *Hallelujah.*

I open the first text that pops up. It's from Kate asking where I am. I had practice at ten this morning but obviously didn't show. The next one is from Macy this afternoon. I scan it quickly.

Girl! Where are you? I thought we were studying today at 2.

She texted again twenty minutes after that.

Did I get my times mixed up? No biggie. See ya at work tonight!

Her next message came just half an hour ago after I didn't show up for my dinner shift at Café Trois Soeurs.

Okay, girl. I'm getting a little worried. You weren't at the library and now you're not at work. That's not like you. You better be shacking up with some hottie otherwise I'm gonna freak out at you next time I see you. Call me just so I know you're okay?

A missed call shows from Café Trois Soeurs five minutes after Macy's text along with a voicemail. The voicemail's from my boss, asking where I am. If I'd actually had my phone on when I'd been driving with the trucker, I could have answered it.

But my thoughts had been too consumed with Collin. I hadn't even thought to turn my phone on.

"Shit. I hope I don't get fired." I hastily call my job and get the manager. Sam sounds majorly peeved.

"I'm really sorry," I say. "Something came up suddenly." I nibble my lip, realizing I'm doing it again—protecting a man who abducted me. Now would be the perfect opportunity to tell somebody what *really* happened.

"Fine," Sam replies curtly. "I'll give you a pass this one time because you've always been so reliable, but don't miss work again. You're scheduled tomorrow at four. You better be here."

"Sure. Of course, and I'm sorry again."

I hang up and text Macy back. I lie again. I make up a story about my dad and him needing me. I say I had to travel home unexpectedly. I feel like the most horrible person on earth for doing that, but it's the only excuse that she'll actually believe.

She replies right away.

Oh shit, girl! I'm so sorry. Are you okay? Look, don't worry about anything. I'm off tomorrow so I'll tell Sam I'm covering your shift. Just take care of you, hun. xx

Tears prick my eyes. I'm so damned grateful. My heart feels happy that I have such amazing girlfriends, but at the same time . . .

It hurts. My heart still hurts and it has nothing to do with my life back on campus.

Fuck. What's wrong with me? I bring a hand to my forehead and can't stop my glance toward those northern mountains again. I need a serious psychological evaluation.

Maybe my brain got scrambled when I hit my head on the floor.

It's the only rational explanation I have for my behavior. I've gone from knowing that I can't trust Collin and wanting to get as far away from him as possible to wondering what he's doing at this moment and hoping he's okay.

"Coming inside?" someone says.

The question snaps me from my mulling. A guy who looks to be in his early thirties is standing at the bar's entrance, holding the door open for me. His gaze dips to my neck, and I can only imagine what I look like. Not to mention, who knows how long I've been standing here looking like a deranged woman who can't tell up from down or left from right.

"Um . . ." I pocket my phone and heft the pack up higher as I gaze at the bar. Maybe an alcoholic beverage is exactly what I need, but I don't have a ton of money, and what funds I can put on my credit card I should really use for a rental car or Lyft to get back home. Come to think of it, I don't have *any* cash on hand—

But then my hand flies to my other pocket, the one I stuffed my tips into last night. My eyes widen when I feel the slim wad. I have over two hundred bucks.

A smile lifts my lips. "On second thought, yeah. I can definitely use a drink."

The guy grins. "And some company?" He raises his eyebrows, and I groan internally.

Is this dude seriously hitting on me?

When I don't respond, he says, "Or not."

He's so quick to backtrack that I laugh. "No, it's fine. Maybe company would be good too." At least it would keep my mind off Collin and provide a distraction until I figure out how I'm going to get back home.

CHAPTER ELEVEN
BRIANNA

The bar has loud blasting music and is crowded with patrons who are already full of drink. With a start, I realize it's Saturday night.

The familiar feel of an eating establishment filled with customers and servers reminds me that I'm supposed to be working right now. *Thank you, Macy,* I say silently to her.

I'm going to do everything I can to make it to my shift tomorrow night so she doesn't have to cover for me. Now, I just have to figure out *how* to get all the way back home.

"There's a table by the wall. Want to sit there?" The guy who opened the door for me waves to it.

"Yeah, sure," I reply distractedly. I follow him to the table and pull out a tall rickety wooden chair. Its leg catches and squeaks. I drop the heavy pack on it and finger my hair self-consciously. "Um, I'll be right back."

The guy picks up one of the menus stacked near the napkins and condiments. He nods, and I briefly contemplate that I've been hanging out with one strange man after another since my shift last night. *WTF.*

A sign for the restroom hangs near a hallway in the

back, right next to a scarred pool table and a wall full of dart boards. A group of guys standing near the dart boards all stop talking when I pass. I can feel their eyes following me.

I sigh internally. Drawing attention from men is nothing new to me. I know my tall strong build and long hair have always been a natural magnet for attraction, but this time, I'm guessing it's from my disheveled appearance.

Once in the bathroom, the mirror reveals exactly what I expected. My skin is dirty, tiny bruises line my neck where Collin's wolf bit me, my wrists are chaffed from the restraints, some of my hair has dried blood in it near the goose egg, and my shirt is torn. All in all, I look as if I'm one step away from a body bag.

The faucet groans when I turn it on full blast. Leaning down, I splash water on my face and neck, then wash with the cheap hand soap that smells of chemicals. I wash away the blood in my hair as best I can. After that, I grab a handful of towels and wipe my arms and legs down until all of the dried blood and dirt are gone. I wince when I rub the tender skin on my wrists. Most likely, that skin will take a few more days to fully heal.

Once done, I thread my fingers through my hair until the tangles work free. I'm still in need of a shower, and I'm not wearing a lick of makeup, but at least I no longer look like I spent the weekend camping in the woods with a werewolf intent on murdering me.

A hysterical giggle bubbles out of me, and my heart lurches at the thought of Collin. I stare at myself in the mirror for a moment, my expression vacant. *Is he still a wolf? Did he turn back to his human form? Where is he now?*

Shaking my head, I throw the used paper towels in the waste basket and exit the bathroom.

The guys by the dart boards grow quiet again when I

pass. One of them leans to his friend and whispers something. Both snicker, then the tall one smiles and nods in my direction.

I ignore them and push through a few more groups. When I get too close to the speakers, I subtly cover my ears. It's freaking loud in here.

I finally make it back to the table. At least it's in a section of the bar that's buffered by a thick wall so the music isn't overbearing.

The guy who accompanied me is sitting with his legs spread on the tall chair while one of his arms drapes casually across the table. He's tall and broad, but a belly hangs over his shorts. I'm guessing a desk job or lack of exercise are to blame for the extra weight. His brown hair is a bit long by the ears, but his clothes are clean and he's still sober. That makes him an anomaly in this place. And all in all, he's not bad looking. I'm just not interested.

When I sit, his eyes widen. He looks me up and down, smiling, then hands me his menu. "You sure clean up well." He clears his throat and speaks loudly to be heard over the music. "The waitress stopped by. Special tonight is a mushroom swiss burger."

My stomach growls. The granola bars from this morning feel a long way off.

"I'm Declan by the way," he says when I don't reply.

"Oh, right. I'm Brianna." I give a little wave, then turn back to my menu.

The waitress appears a moment later and we both order.

"Are you sure you don't want a beer?" Declan asks after the waitress saunters off.

"No, I'm fine with water." I cross my arms on the table and scan the crowd again. "Pretty lively bunch for it only being early evening."

Declan shrugs, and his gaze runs over me for the third time. "It's a small town, and this place is known for being the hot spot on weekends. It can get pretty crazy at times." He leans back in his chair and slings an arm around the chair back. He's got full lips and an easy smile. Something about him reminds me of the countless jocks I went to high school with.

"Does that mean you grew up here?" I ask.

Our drinks appear in front of us when the waitress plops them down. I pick up my water and guzzle half of it. I hadn't realized how thirsty I was.

Declan drinks his beer almost as fast. Over the rim of his glass, his eyes keep straying to my breasts. "Yep. Born and bred. What about you? Where do you live? I haven't seen you around here before."

"You're right. I don't live here but instead in Quintin Valley, and I actually need to get back. Is there a car rental place around here?"

"Not here, but there's one at the regional airport."

I take another drink of the icy water. "How far is that?"

"About ten miles."

"That'll work. I better see if they have any cars available."

He cocks his head and leans forward in his seat. "So how did you get here if you don't have a car?"

"Hitchhiked."

He raises an eyebrow. "Ballsy."

If you only knew. I don't comment further and instead pull out my phone to check for car rental agencies. Declan doesn't seem to mind, though. As I'm scrolling, he launches into a monologue about himself. I hear all about him: where he works, what he does in his free time, how he spends his weekends.

As long as I comment occasionally or nod my head, he

doesn't seem to care that I'm multitasking. I don't mind the monologue since it allows me time to figure out how the hell I'm going to get back home, but he's getting a bit too familiar with his hands. Twice, he's run a finger down my arm when he's reached for his beer, and I've lost count of how many times he's told my breasts his stories instead of me.

Note to self: don't accept invites to sit with strange dudes next time you're abducted and get free.

Declan gives me a cocky grin. "I scored more points than anyone. Nobody was surprised. I was always good in sports, especially—"

"Here ya go." The waitress returns and places my plate of chicken fingers, fries, and coleslaw in front of me. Declan went with the burger special. "Ketchup? Another drink?" she asks.

"That would be great," I reply, thankful for her appearance. Declan was in the midst of telling me—or rather my boobs—about the touch football game he played with his buddies last night and I was getting a bit sick of it.

Declan nods yes to both as well and grabs the ketchup bottle from the waitress before she can fully extract it from her apron. When he finishes squirting a large dollop on his plate, he sets it by his side instead of handing it to me.

I reach awkwardly for it, but the waitress slides it my way. She then grabs my drained water and Declan's empty beer bottle. "I'll be back with another beer and a refill on your water. Got everything you need?"

"Yes, thank you," I reply.

Declan just keeps eating.

The waitress winks at me. "Sure thing, hun." She's probably in her fifties, and I wonder if she's been working at this bar her entire life as she saunters off.

I grab a chicken finger off my plate and focus on my

food. Declan's eating with gusto but still manages to launch into another monologue around a mouthful of food. I'm regretting my decision to join him more and more as the minutes tick on.

When the waitress returns and Declan reaches for his fourth beer, I can't help but notice that his words have begun to slur. I concentrate on eating as Declan drains his current beverage. After he sets it down, he grabs his next one and again casually runs a finger along my arm. It's the fourth time he's touched me.

What a douchebag.

I pull my arm back and concentrate on my meal. The only good thing about this dinner is that I found a car to rent, and it's available tonight.

It's a ten mile distance to the rental, though. I'll most likely have to walk some of it, if not all of it. There aren't any Ubers, Lyfts, or taxi services around here. I've checked. But maybe, with any luck, another nice trucker will pick me up.

Just as I finish my last fry, Declan starts talking about his job again. He uses words like "real important" and says constantly that he's "the man in charge."

I roll my eyes, but he's too drunk to notice. He probably also hasn't realize that in the thirty minutes we've spent together, he's only asked me two questions: where I live and how I got here. The rest has been all about him.

"I'm gonna go." I reach down to grab the backpack and then slip a twenty on the table. It's more than enough to cover my meal with a generous tip.

Declan's eyebrows rise, and he polishes off his fifth beer. Or is it his sixth? I've lost count. "Go where?" He raises his empty bottle and waggles it at the waitress across the bar.

Classy. That's one of my biggest pet peeves as a waitress

—demanding customers who treat you as a servant instead of as a human being.

I sling the backpack over my shoulder. "Car rental place. Remember?"

He leans back in his chair and gives me a sly grin. "You don't need that. I'll give you a ride."

I arch an eyebrow. "Do you really think you should be driving right now?"

He abruptly leans forward. "Course I should." A hiccup escapes him before he adds, "Where you wanna go?" He's staring at my breasts again.

I shake my head. "I'm good, thanks, don't worry about me. You just get yourself home safely." I turn to leave, but his hand clamps down on my forearm. I freeze.

"I said I'd give you a ride."

I pull my arm away. "And I said I'm good." It's too loud in the bar for anyone to notice Declan's aggressive behavior. Everyone carries on drinking and talking, but I level Declan with an icy stare to let him know I mean business before walking away.

Massive douchebag.

Once outside, I breathe a sigh of relief. I'm not looking forward to the long walk, but the temp has cooled, which means I won't be sweating the entire way. I eye the sun that's almost set. A deep-red glow fills the horizon.

After rubbing my hands on my forearms, I head toward the airport.

$\sim$

I MAKE quick work of the distance and am at least a few miles down the road before I hitch my thumb out. One car passes me but doesn't slow.

I grumble and keep walking. This obviously isn't a well-traveled road, but I figure sooner or later someone will stop.

Stars are twinkling above when I pull the pack around to dig inside it. Despite it being the end of summer, a chill has set into the air. High mountain deserts are like that. Hot during the day, cool at night. I'm used to it after living in this state my entire life.

My hands close around an old flannel when the sound of a second car in the distance reaches my ears. A cedar wood scent flutters up around me.

My nostrils flare when the scent hits me. "Collin?" I whisper. My heart patters, and with a dropped jaw, I realize my reaction isn't from fear.

But then I recognize the scent I've detected is from Collin's shirt, and that he's still miles away in those forgotten mountains, and he's definitely not in the approaching vehicle.

That heavy feeling in my stomach returns, but I stand back up, forgetting about the flannel. I hitch my thumb out as the bright headlights draw closer.

It's fully dark now, and I realize hitchhiking by myself in an unknown area isn't the smartest move. I briefly wonder if I should come clean with my friends and tell them where I am. I know Kate would drive up here in a heartbeat to pick me up.

But then I frown. If Kate comes here, she'll ask questions. She'll want to know how I got here, who I was with, why I missed work, and why I didn't tell anyone I was leaving.

I could feed her the same story I told Macy, the one about my dad, but that wouldn't make any sense since I'm in northern Arizona. I could tell her the truth about Collin abducting me, the reclusive cabin, and the trucker giving me a ride to this area, but if I did that she would insist I go to the police to report everything. And when I refuse to, she would want to know why.

Screw it.

I keep my thumb out.

To my relief, the car slows and pulls onto the shoulder. The passenger window hums when it rolls down, so I jog to the door and lean over to look inside.

My eyes pop. "Declan?"

He leans sideways from the driver's seat, the stench of booze on his breath. "How about that ride you need? Hop in." He unlocks the door and pushes it open for me.

"You're drunk."

"No I's not."

I back up and cross my arms. "Yes, you are, and I told you I'm not interested. You shouldn't be driving anyone anywhere right now, not even yourself. Can't you call a friend to get you home?"

He makes a disgruntled sound and throws the car into park. "I'm driving just fine. I's—"

But I don't stick around to hear the rest of his argument. I begin walking down the road again. Seriously, this guy is a loser with a capital L.

A car door slams behind me, then comes the sound of Declan running on gravel. "I said I's give you a ride!"

Goose bumps sprout on my skin. *Just get away from him, Bri.*

I strap the pack tighter to my back and pick up my pace. I curse the remote area, especially when I hear him getting closer.

"Hey! I's talking to you!"

"And I'm not interested in talking to you," I call over my shoulder.

His footsteps quicken and within a second, I hear him directly behind me. A sharp tug comes from my pack, stopping me.

I swing around.

"I said I's give you a ride. Why are you being such a stuck-up bitch?" His face is dark in the night. The glare from the headlights outlines his frame, so I can't see his expression.

My lips thin since he's called me a bitch, but fighting with him won't get me anywhere, so I take a deep breath and reply in a neutral tone, "Look, I appreciate you offering to give me a ride, but I'm not interested. Okay?"

He puts his hands on his hips. "So you's gonna walk all the way to get a car? Really?" He reaches for my pack, as if he's going to take it from me and carry it.

I sidestep, and his hand catches air. He falls forward slightly off balance. A prickly sensation grows on my neck, and the goose bumps on my arms rise higher. I need to get out of here and away from him.

"Go home, Declan." I keep my voice even, but inside I'm growing warier. The smartest thing for me to do right now is to get out of this situation without provoking him further.

But instead of letting me walk away, he grabs at me again, this time connecting with my arm. He encircles my bicep and pulls me toward him.

My blood turns cold.

"Get in the car."

I wrench my arm back, but his grip tightens. He yanks me forward, and I know any chance of this ending peacefully has evaporated like dew drops on a sweltering morning.

"Let me go," I say through gritted teeth.

He laughs and begins to pull me.

Fuck diplomacy.

I grab his shirt and slam my heel down on the arch of his foot. The move catches him by surprise, so he doesn't have time to deflect my twisting body and an upper cut to his chin. His head snaps back, and he howls in pain. I use the distraction to shove him off me.

He stumbles back in his drunken state, and I take off at a run in the opposite direction of where he's parked. There aren't any other cars around, and internally I scream in frustration at how incredibly shitty this entire weekend has been.

I run past his car intent on putting distance between us. He's drunk, and I'm sober and strong. I know I can easily outsmart him.

But I'm not running long before I hear the sound of his car revving. Headlights illuminate the road ahead of me, and I know he's turned around. I dare a glance over my shoulder, and my eyes widen when I see him barreling down on me. He's swerving back and forth, obviously having a hard time driving straight. And he's going way too fast.

"Holy shit!" I leap for the ditch just as he zooms past. The abrupt maneuver has me rolling, and the pack comes off. I come to a stop on my belly. Cold unease slithers through me. This is getting bad *fast*.

I'm going to have to run into the fields and surrounding trees. There, he can't run me over, and in the dark, he won't be able to find me.

FML. Seriously.

I push to a stand and grab the heavy pack. I'm already halfway up the ditch when his car skids to a stop twenty yards away. The white reverse lights come on. I'm just about to the top of the ditch when his door flings open, and he comes flying out. Well, stumbling out.

"You're a real bitch, you know that?"

"Declan just leave me be!"

I don't understand where his hostility has come from, or maybe his ego is so fragile that he can't handle any woman rejecting him, or maybe he's just a mean drunk who turns into a complete ass anytime he gets beers into him. Whatever the case, I'm so fucking over this.

"Get in the car!" He's running toward me now like an ataxic giraffe, his limbs clumsy and uncoordinated.

Something wet drips on my chin. Wiping it with the back of my hand, I realize it's blood. I'm bleeding again. *This is just great.*

I buckle the pack around my waist and briefly contemplate leaving the bulky weight behind me until I lose Declan in the dark.

But it would be just my luck that Declan would take it, and if he did I wouldn't have anything—no phone, no driver's license, no keys to my apartment, no food, no water. Nothing. All I'd have is the wad of cash in my pocket. That's it.

Just run, Bri.

I take off through the dry fields. Taller trees and brush fill the distant mounds. If I reach them, I can easily hide.

Heavy breathing comes from behind me, and I realize the douchebag's trying to follow me. I dare a look over my shoulder, and my pulse races when I see how close he is. He's breathing like a bull—spit and froth bursting from his lips.

"Get in the car!" he yells again.

Genuine fear grows in me. He's not losing interest.

"You better stop, bitch!"

I don't reply. Only ten feet separate us, so I pick up my pace.

It's not hard to outrun him even with the pack on. I

know I'm gaining ground when his labored breaths fall behind me. A triumphant feeling fills me. I'm a fast runner and outrunning a drunk isn't exactly challenging. Maybe I'll get away from him after all. He may even get lost out here or pass out in the field.

Serves you right you pompous—

I shriek when my foot lands near a huge lizard that comes from out of nowhere. I stumble then fall.

My cheek hits the dry ground, the heavy pack making me land awkwardly.

Fucking shit on a brick.

A gila monster stares back at me.

In the twilight, its black and orange scales stand out like a warning flag. The venomous nocturnal lizard normally leaves humans alone but considering I tripped over the damn thing I'm not surprised that it opens its mouth defensively. If that thing clamps down on me, it won't let go. It will chew into my flesh until its venom is deposited.

I scramble back. Course sand scrapes against my palms and knees, but it isn't until something sharp tugs on my scalp, yanking my head back that I realize I've failed to pay attention to where Declan is.

The most massive of massive douchebags. He's grabbed my hair.

"I's caught you!" He weaves his fingers through my long locks, his statement idiotically proud.

"Let me go you drunken ass!" I grab onto his wrist and twist. Even though I'm at a disadvantage being on the ground, I still give him a nasty snakebite when my right hand twists one way while the left twists the other.

He howls in pain and pulls me upright. I keep a hold of his wrist and try to work his hand free. Pain sears through my scalp, and I grit my teeth.

Once standing, he gazes down at me with glazed eyes, and his full lips open as he mouth-breathes heavily. "You's a feisty one. You know that? I's like that."

I swallow a cry of pain and jab him below the ribs. Following that, I nail him in the knee cap with a kick. He grunts and begins to fall but keeps his hand knotted in my hair.

Dammit. That didn't go as planned.

Declan lands on top of me. Panic sets in as his heavy weight settles, crushing my ribs.

I yelp when the burning in my scalp increases. He's pulling on my hair to steady himself. The only positive aspect of this fucked-up experience is that the gila monster has disappeared. In other words, I only have one toxic creature to contend with.

Declan relaxes more on top of me, and his large body is now completely covering mine. "That's more like it." He leers.

I push against him, intent on getting him off me, but he's so heavy it's hard to move, let alone force him away. It doesn't help that the backpack is making it even harder to move. I'm squished between him and it.

"You're a nice piece of ass, you's know that?" He's slurring again, and I can barely breathe. "It was the first thing I's thought when I saw you. Those curvy hips, nice legs, and full tits. I's wondered what it'd feel like to have you beneath me. I's—"

I spit in his face, which stops his monologue.

But before I can act further, a blinding slap explodes on my cheekbone, catching me completely by surprise. Stars shine in my vision.

"You's gonna pay for that!" He yanks my head more before reaching for his pants. The sound of his zipper opening comes next.

No! I begin thrashing wildly.

He pulls my hair again, making me yelp. "Don't fight this, or I's—"

A terrifying growl comes from my left. The deep menacing sound has my eyes widening just as a flash of tawny fur enters my peripheral vision.

Collin?

Declan cries out when the wolf barrels into him. One minute the drunk is on me, and the next second he's off.

I scramble back, the grainy sand cutting into my hands just as Collin pins Declan beneath him. Collin's wolf is huge, easily fifty pounds heavier than a large natural wolf, and the beast's eyes are glowing brightly.

Dread fills me when Collin's wolf opens his mouth. Saliva-tinged teeth glow in the moonlight.

Declan screams pitifully. He flails, doing everything he can to dislodge the werewolf. But despite his best efforts, he can't. The drunk's screams turn shrill when Collin's wolf leans down.

"Collin!" I scream when I realize what he's about to do.

But my terrified exclamation doesn't stop him. The wolf doesn't even pause.

He locks onto Declan's throat, and with one terrifying jerk, he tears Declan's neck wide open.

My hands fly to my mouth as blood gushes out of Declan. A gurgling sound comes next.

I watch in horror as the man I had dinner with—the man who was probably going to rape me—dies before my eyes. But Collin's wolf doesn't stop there. He growls again before leaning down to bite into Declan's shoulder. Declan can't cry out. He's dying too fast.

Collin's wolf shakes his head back and forth until another piece of flesh tears free.

My horror increases when the torn flesh slides down the wolf's throat after he tilts his head up. And that's when I see it, the deranged gleam in the wolf's eyes.

He's crazy. Absolutely crazy.

But instead of standing and sprinting away, I sit frozen. Nothing I'm doing will make my limbs move.

It's not until minutes later, when the wolf has had his fill of Declan—who now lies in a mangled bloody heap in front of me—that a strange glimmer fills the air around the wolf.

I blink, and a man appears.

Collin breathes heavily. His limbs are quivering, like a newborn fawn trying to stand for the first time.

"Shit. I . . ." Collin shakes his head, then turns his still-glowing eyes toward me. "Brianna? Bri? I'm sorry. I didn't mean for you to see that, but he was so enraged."

I stare at him dumbly. *Who was enraged? The wolf? Or Declan? What the hell is he talking about? What the hell is happening?*

A shiver strikes me, then another.

In the moonlight, dark-red blood glistens on Collin's face. Blood. He's covered in Declan's blood.

"You . . . You . . ." But the words won't come. I'm hyperventilating, and I'm losing it, but is he freakin' serious? He just killed a man right in front of me, and he's covered in blood.

Even though adrenaline is pounding through my veins, I still can't move. I tell myself to get up, to run, to *flee*, but my legs and arms feel as heavy as concrete.

I wait for Collin to shift into that hideous beast once more. I know he'll leap on top of me. He'll kill me and eat me, just like he did Declan.

I whimper. "Please don't hurt me."

Anguish distorts Collin's features. "Brianna, I'd never hurt you."

My lips part.

Collin's kneeling in front of me. He moved again in that silent way of his.

The moonlight illuminates his broad back and muscled thighs. He's naked. For the first time, I realize he's not wearing a lick of clothing. My gaze dips down to the appendage dangling between his legs. Holy hell. The man is huge on every level.

I squeeze my eyes shut. *Did I seriously just check out the guy's dick?*

"Bri?" He moves closer, not seeming to care that he just killed a man and is crouching beside me in his birthday suit. "Did he hurt you?"

Rage coats his words. His breath sucks in when he turns my head, inspecting my cheek where Declan slapped me. He surveys the rest of me, taking in the cut on my mouth that started bleeding after I flung myself into the ditch. The fury rolling off him increases.

"I got here as fast as I could. It took me a few hours to pick up your scent since it disappeared when you got in that logger's truck. I would have come sooner—"

"You followed me here? As a wolf?" The screeched statement leaving my lips sounds foreign. Is that really my voice? I then reason that it's not every day I'm attacked twice in the same weekend. I figure a meltdown is appropriate.

He takes a deep breath. "I can run faster as a wolf."

"But you . . . he . . . it . . ." I shake my head. "You just killed someone." I pull back more. "Are you going to kill me now too?" After all, he said he would let me leave, yet here he is, probably returned to lock me up again.

Collin's shoulders droop. "I would never. I meant it when I said I would never hurt you."

"But you almost did earlier today!"

"I know, but that was before."

"Before what?"

His eyes glow brighter. "Before I recognized that you're—"

CHAPTER TWELVE
COLLIN

I clamp my mouth shut.
 No, I can't tell her. Not here, and not like this. She already looks like she's going to pass out. My fucked up werewolf problems are not something she needs to deal with right now. *I'll tell her later.*

"That I'm your what?" she asks. She's still eyeing me warily, that distrust filling her gaze as strongly as it did back at the cabin.

I shake my head. "Nothing. Just please believe me. I won't hurt you, and my wolf won't either. Never again. Really. We won't."

I take a deep breath, but it's not enough to slow my heartbeat. It's pounding erratically. When I heard her scream, I'd run as fast as I could, but I was still too late. The asshole was already on top of her. He'd slapped her. He'd been yanking off his pants, intending to *rape* her.

The beast had gone apeshit when he'd seen that. I couldn't have controlled him if I wanted to, but I hadn't wanted to. I'd craved the fucker's blood as much as my psychotic wolf had.

But dwelling on that now won't help. The brimming anger inside of me will only add to her worries.

Brianna's face is pale. She's been through so much this weekend. And all because of me.

Her eyebrows draw together, and she tries to inch back, but the boulder stops her. Her suspicion is palpable. I'm sure my silence isn't helping.

I offer my hand. "Come on. We need to go."

She recoils. "Go where? You just killed a guy. Or have you already forgotten?" Her tone turns high-pitched.

Shit.

I take a step back, crouch down, and tilt my head to bear my neck. Assuming a smaller, less dominant position is meant to reassure her, but then I remember she's not a wolf. She doesn't communicate like we do. Still, I try.

I quiet my voice and say, "I know I killed him, which is why we need to go."

"But why are you even here? I thought you were letting me leave." That fear creeps into her eyes again. It's in her scent too. Her beautiful, intoxicating scent turns slightly sour. *Fuck.* I hate myself more than anything.

My mate is afraid of me.

It wasn't until she'd stepped into that logging truck that I'd realized she's my fated mate. The beast had howled forlornly, already understanding who she was. He'd begun understanding it when he caught her scent—right before he'd almost torn her throat out in the back of the stolen car.

It's why he'd stopped.

I rake a hand through my hair. *Fucking hell.* Who would have thought I would meet my mate like *this*?

This isn't how it's supposed to be. She's supposed to want me too. We're supposed to fall for each other so hard and fast that nothing else matters. We should want to be together every second of every day to rut and fuck and lick and bite and taste. The first few months of a new mating are animalistic in every sense of the word. If she were a wolf in my pack, and we were back home, the other wolves would chuckle and give us room. We'd be left alone until we came out of the honeymoon period that all new mates experience.

But nothing about *this* is normal.

My wolf is psychotic. I've gone rogue. She's human. And my pack is nowhere to be found.

It doesn't help that Brianna's staring at me like I'm the plague. As though I'll infect her if I get a millimeter closer.

It's not exactly what most females feel around their destined wolf.

What did you think would happen, Ward? You tried to kill her this morning after breakfast.

"Collin, we have to go to the police."

Her statement has me tensing. Her gaze dips again. She's eyeing my dick for the second time. Right. I'm still naked. I grab the backpack and find a pair of shorts. She averts her eyes when I pull them on. I then soak a rag using the water bottle and wipe the blood off me.

When I do that, she says in a rush, "I didn't want to go to the police, but now we have to. There's no way we can cover this up." She gestures toward the body.

"No police," I say firmly.

Once dressed and free of blood, I cram the bloody rag back in the pack, then survey the carnage. I make sure to keep a wide berth from Brianna even though the sour stench has left her scent. She's no longer afraid of me. At least, not at the moment.

My lip curls when I peer down at what's left of the guy the beast killed. The asshole who attacked her is bones and bloody flesh now. His face is gone. The beast took care of that. The dickwad will have to be identified by dental records—if there's any teeth left in that bloody mess—because by the time he's found, his fingerprints will probably be too decayed for identification.

I place my hands on my hips. "They'll think it was an animal attack. They won't know I killed him. We're leaving him here."

"An animal attack? Collin, you can't be serious! We can't leave him here!"

I swing back around, and my hands ball into fists. Just the thought of what he wanted to do to her makes my blood boil, and she's *wanting* to do what's best for *him?*

"And why can't we leave him here?" I counter. "He doesn't deserve any better."

Fire returns to her eyes. I'm coming to admire that fire so much. She pushes to a stand and takes a step toward me. "He deserves a proper burial even if he was a mean drunk."

I move closer until we're toe to toe. She doesn't retreat. "A mean drunk? Is that all you think he was? Do you know what he wanted to do to you?"

Her eyebrows draw together, and she gnashes her teeth.

"I think you know, Brianna. He was going to rape you. I could smell it on him. His excitement grew when he got you beneath him. He became aroused. Did you know that?"

She swallows but doesn't reply.

She knows. She just doesn't want to accept what almost happened—what could have happened.

"He would have raped you." My fists are so tight now it feels as though my forearm muscles are going to jump right through my skin. "So if you think I'm going to call the cops and turn myself in, all so dipshit here can go home to granny for a proper burial, you're wrong. He's staying here. The coyotes can finish what I started." My tone is cold, and I know I'm showing her a side of myself that I'm not proud of.

Can I be an asshole? Yes. Can I be a cold motherfucker? Yes. And it's not something I can blame entirely on my wolf. I was like this before the beast emerged, and now that my wolf's psychotic, the dark side of my personality has grown.

Brianna looks back at the dead guy. She shakes her head but not as assuredly. "He still didn't deserve to die like that."

I sigh heavily. "We can agree to disagree." I reach for the backpack and pull out an old long-sleeved flannel shirt. Wearing it paired with the basketball shorts isn't the greatest look, but I've got nothing else.

I scoff. *How far I've fallen.* I used to wear expensive clothes, designer cologne, and I showered daily. *Now look at me. I look like Hobo Joe.*

But, it will have to do.

I cinch the pack close and sling it over my shoulder. "His car's still on the highway. We'll get in that, and I'll take you home."

"What?"

I wince at her tone. "If we leave his car here, he'll be found in no time. If we take it, it will most likely be days, even weeks, before he's found. We'll be long gone by then."

"*We?* What do you mean by *we?*"

"I'm taking you home."

"I thought you were letting me go?" She plants her hands on her hips, and the wind picks up, ruffling her hair. *Damn, she's hot.* All fire and steel. Who would have thought my mate would be so fierce?

I raise an eyebrow. "I *am* letting you go."

"Then why would I get in a stolen car with you after you just killed its owner?"

I survey our surroundings, then raise my arms as if it's obvious. Nothing's around us but dry brush and cactuses. A coyote howls in the distance. Inside my wolf stirs. He's very much awake now, prowling around in my belly, letting me know that he'll take over if I can't protect our mate.

"You want to get home, don't you?"

"Well . . ." She frowns. "Yeah."

"And how do you propose to do that? Were you going to walk the entire way?" It suddenly occurs to me that she stopped in that bar a few miles back. Her scent was all over it. But she hadn't stayed there and waited for a ride.

"Why hasn't someone picked you up?"

"I . . . was going to rent a car."

"Where?"

"There's an airport that away." She points.

I raise my eyebrows. "You were seriously walking that entire distance to rent a car? Why wouldn't you call someone to pick you up?"

Her gaze drifts away, and her chin dips. She kicks the sand by her toes. "I don't know."

"Does that mean you haven't called anyone?" *Not even the police?* But I'm too nervous to ask her that. I know I'm taking a risk by showing up like this. She ran from me once, or rather three times now, so she'll probably run again. But there's no way in hell I'm leaving her. I can't now. She's destined to be with me.

She just doesn't know it yet.

"No, I didn't call anyone. Not really. I mean, I texted my friends to let them know I was okay, but that's it."

She didn't call the police? That's not something I expected. The wind quiets between us. Blood pounds through my ears. "Why didn't you turn me in or tell anyone about me?"

A long moment passes before she shrugs. I want to know so badly what she's thinking and to understand what she's feeling. Does she feel it? This innate need to be together? The attraction that crackles between us like electricity?

Or is she immune to it? She's human. She's not a werewolf, so maybe she doesn't feel it. Maybe she feels nothing at all.

My wolf snarls.

I know. I don't like the thought of that either.

With a start, I realize it's the first normal thing I've said to him in months.

"So what now?" she asks, completely avoiding my questions.

I take a deep breath. She obviously doesn't want to talk about what's motivating her silence. I have to respect that.

"I'll drive you home, and we're taking the car. Trust me. I've been doing this for longer than you. Leaving his car will only cause more problems for us."

Her eyes widen. I can only imagine how she's interpreting my blunt honesty.

Yes, mate. I'm a killer and a thief. That's what I've become. I dip my head, so she won't see the shame in my eyes.

"Let's go." I begin walking back to the road, the pack slung over my back. I try to pretend I'm not wound as tight as a rubber band while I wait to see what she'll do. I don't want to force her. I really don't, but I will if I have to.

When I hear her footsteps behind me, my tense shoulders relax. She only pauses once, when she steps near the body, but then she quickens and her scent flutters toward me.

I inhale. Her sunshine-and-caramel scent is tinged with sweat and a womanly musk. The fear is completely gone.

Fuck, she smells good, and she's not afraid of me right now.

The satisfaction of that makes me smile. It does something else to me too. My dick tightens, swelling more as her scent floods my senses. I subtly rearrange myself, hoping she doesn't notice.

Just cool it, Ward. One step at a time.

My jaw tightens, and I grind my teeth together, because I'm determined to do this right.

CHAPTER THIRTEEN
COLLIN

The car is still running, headlights on, door open, and sitting in the middle of the road. It's pure luck nobody has driven by and noticed. I don't intend to press that luck. We need to get moving.

"What if we get stopped by the cops?" Brianna pauses at the passenger door, her hand on the door handle. She doesn't open it.

"Then we get stopped."

"You aren't worried?"

"No. Should I be?"

"Do you even have a driver's license?"

"Of course I do." It might be a fake with a fake alias, but I have one. I laugh at her expression. "Don't look so shocked."

She gives me one of those looks, a look that says she knows I'm completely crazy, but she still gets in the car.

If my psychotic wolf could purr, he would be purring like a lion right now. His contentment heats my insides because our mate is *choosing* to come with us.

I slide into the driver's seat and slam the door. I don't

bother with a seatbelt, but Brianna is dutifully putting hers on as I shift into drive and hit the pedal. I eye the gas. Full tank. *Score.*

"How long do you think it'll take to get back to my apartment?" she asks.

"Three hours as long as traffic isn't bad around Phoenix."

She settles in, her lean muscular thighs angled toward me. *Damn.* I could drink in the sight of those legs every day.

I make myself shift my attention back to the road, but my cock responds again. I suck in a breath. This drive is going to be harder than I thought it would be.

At least five minutes of silence pass before Brianna says, "Why did you try to find me again?"

The headlights illuminate the dusty county road. I slow for the approaching intersection and put the blinker on. "What do you mean? You got in a truck with a strange guy. For all I knew you weren't going to get home safely. I found you to make sure you were okay."

She makes a little noise. "And you don't see the irony in that? You abducted me last night, you intended to kill me, you *almost* killed me this morning, and then you were worried for my safety?" She sounds genuinely confused.

I frown. "I know it doesn't make much sense."

"Exactly. It makes *no* sense."

I can feel her looking at me. Waiting. As if I'm supposed to say more. "What?"

"Aren't you going to explain yourself?"

I sigh. "What do you want me to explain?"

"For starters, why did you abduct me in the first place?"

I work my jaw. Given that she doesn't ask another question, and she's still looking at me, I know she's going to insist that I answer.

"There was something about you. Something that called to me. I couldn't leave without you."

She folds her fingers together, then unfolds them. Her nervous movements continue when she asks, "Have you been watching me?"

"What do you mean?"

"You know, *watching* me. Following me. Stalking me. Were you doing that before you took me?"

Damn. She's more perceptive than I thought, but telling your fated mate that you met by stalking doesn't bode well for a healthy relationship.

"Is that how you knew I was a waitress?"

I cock an eyebrow.

"Back in the car, when we were driving down the mountain, you asked if I liked waitressing. How could you have known that unless you knew where I worked?"

Dammit all to hell. Now I *have* to admit to stalking her. *Way to go, Collin. You're officially the creepiest mate to ever come out of the Wyoming pack.*

"Okay, yes. I was stalking you."

She plucks at her shorts' seams. "For how long?"

"A few weeks."

"I knew it," she whispers.

"You did? How?"

"I could feel it, during the past few weeks. It was like my sixth sense was warning me that someone was watching me, and all along it was you."

"Seriously?" That's incredibly perceptive for a human. In the previous months, most humans had been none the wiser that the beast had chosen them for his next meal, but Brianna had sensed us. A flush of admiration fills me.

She stops fiddling with her shorts. "So is that what you do? You stalk women?"

"Um . . " I clear my throat and turn us onto the interstate. The air flowing in through my cracked window has cooled, so I turn the A/C off and roll my window down more. A rush of wind enters the cab. It smells of dusty earth, sage, and creosote.

"Collin? Is that what you do? Do you stalk women?"

Okay, so she's not letting this go.

I sigh harshly and rake a hand through my hair. "On occasion."

"And did you kidnap them and let them go too?"

I hear the hopeful tone in her voice, and it nearly undoes me, but I can't lie to her. I can lie to a lot of people but not her. "No."

Her breath sucks in, and she turns to look out the window. Her body is rigid, her shoulders still.

The beast growls inside me, unhappy that I've upset her. His obsession with Brianna is growing. Maybe obsession is normal when one finds one's mate, but with him, I can't be sure. He's still a sick motherfucker. However, I do feel confident now that he won't hurt her. At least there's that.

"I wasn't always like this." I'm aware that my tone sounds desperate, but that's exactly how I feel, desperate for her to accept me. It's crazy. I've never felt that with a female before, and I've had my share of flings. "I didn't start doing this until this past year."

"How many?" She angles her body again, facing me. Tears brim her eyelids. "How many have you killed?"

Fuck me. Fuck me to the moon and back. I instinctively reach for her. I want to comfort her, hold her, dry away those tears, but just as quickly I pull my hand back. She's already recoiled. Anger and disgust line her expression.

My shoulders sag. She's never going to want me.

"More than I can remember," I reply quietly.

I tighten my grip on the steering wheel just as her

breath catches and a little yelp of surprise leaves her throat. She presses her lips together. "Those poor women."

She shifts away again and props an elbow on the windowsill. The wind blowing in through my cracked window lifts her hair, but she doesn't seem to notice.

My heart aches. It fucking *aches*. Who would have thought that I would meet my mate this way? That I'd kidnap her, hurt her, nearly kill her? It's so fucked up on so many levels that I don't know how I'll ever make this right.

∽

BRIANNA'S quiet for the next hour. I don't push her to talk. I want to, but I don't. I know she's mulling things over from the way her forehead scrunches up and from how she keeps biting her lower lip.

The beast is unhappy again. He's pacing in my belly, nearly unhinged. Thankfully, he doesn't test me, because I'm fairly certain that if I lost control of him right now Brianna would never speak to me again.

He seems to sense that, too, which is why I'm guessing he hasn't.

My knee moves up and down like a jackhammer. I've been fidgeting for the past thirty minutes. I set the car on cruise control miles ago, and the endless interstate passes slowly beneath us.

It's fucking agony to sit here with her, knowing she's upset with me and not being able to do anything about it.

I curse fate again. I curse the gods too. They have a pretty sick sense of humor if they thought this was a good way to punish me for all I've done. But it's punishment indeed. Finally, after months of being lost and alone, I've finally found my purpose and my home.

She's sitting right beside me.

Well fuck you too. I rale inside to whatever higher power thought this was amusing.

I sigh and fiddle with one of the knobs on the dash. I never thought I'd meet my fated mate. So few werewolves do even though mating in the werewolf world happens all of the time.

But fated mates? Not so much. I can't remember the last time it happened in my former pack. Most wolves choose their mates, only rarely does one encounter the other half to their soul. But that's who Brianna is. She's my mate, and she's my true mate in every sense of the word. I can feel it.

Ever since that moment, when my beast nearly killed her and her scent flooded his nose, the bond began to form.

But it wasn't until she walked away from us back by the mountain, that I truly understood what had happened.

The beast had recognized it first. He'd scented something was different about her, which was the only reason he hadn't killed her.

As for me? I'd been a bit slower on the uptake, but it makes sense now. My obsession with her. The reason I couldn't leave her behind in Quintin Valley when I should have.

My body had recognized that she was my mate before my mind had.

Another ten minutes of silence passes, and I can't take it anymore. "Are you hungry?" I ask. A sign flashes by the window. A Sonic is at the next exit.

"No."

"I am. Do you mind if we stop?" I've burned a shit-ton of calories today. My metabolism has been on overdrive, and I've been ravenous most of the day. Ever since Brianna got in the logging truck, I've been going at full-speed, and it feels like I'm starving—even if the beast ate Declan.

I pull off at the exit and let the car coast into the drive-thru. I lean over and pop the glove box. She tenses when my arm brushes against her leg, but she doesn't pull back.

"What are you looking for?"

"Cash." I rummage around in the compartment. "A lot of people keep a few spare bucks or change in their car."

Her lips part. "You don't have any money to pay for food?"

I grind my teeth. Two and a half years ago I had more money than I knew what to do with. But I'd left that money behind when I went rogue.

"Here." She reaches into her pocket and extracts a wad of bills. When my eyebrows rise, she adds, "These were my tips last night. If you're hungry, I can give you money."

Shame creeps up my neck, making my skin hot. My mate is offering me her hard-earned cash to pay for my meal, because I don't have any money. But that's not how it's supposed to work. *I'm* supposed to provide for *her*. Not the other way around.

I know it's an archaic way to think, but that's how it is in the werewolf world. Or rather, how it was. Things were beginning to change when I left my pack. Daria was seeing to that. For all I know, those chauvinistic tendencies died when the new alpha married his mate.

Of course I wouldn't know since I didn't stick around.

Regardless of whether or not that tradition has changed, I was raised to take care of my woman. My dad always provided for my mom. He took care of her, even if their marriage was strained at times. Bottom line, I intend to do the same for my woman.

"You know what? I'm not actually that hungry." I turn the steering wheel away from the drive-thru just as my stomach lets out a huge growl. *Traitor.* The scent of burgers in the air did it.

Brianna's hand lands on my arm, and my entire body goes still. I stop the car, my foot hitting the brake hard enough that she lurches forward in her seat.

She snatches her hand back, but I can still feel it—the feel of her palm on my skin, the heat of her body.

"You're obviously hungry. Let me buy you some food. Please."

The shame that I felt a moment ago quadruples. "I don't need you to buy me anything. I'll eat something from the backpack."

She snorts. "Oh for God's sake, just pull up to the window. Cause you know what? On second thought, I am hungry."

"You really expect me to fall for that?"

"No, because there's nothing to fall for. I *am* hungry."

I begrudgingly do as she wishes even though I'm ninety-nine percent sure that she's not hungry, and she's insisting on staying for my sake, but I'm not about to let her pay for my meal.

When we reach the speaker at the drive-thru menu, a bored sounding teenager asks us what we want.

Brianna's eyebrows rise. "Aren't you going to order?"

I shake my head stubbornly. "I'm good. Just get what you want."

She stares at me, those warm-brown irises lighting a fire inside me. Hunger for something else entirely has my breath stopping.

"Are you sure?" She leans over and stops only inches away. She's challenging me, and the alpha inside me wants to rise to the bait, but I force myself to relax. Still, I can't help it when my gaze drifts to her mouth.

Her lips part. Abruptly, she leans back, putting more

distance between us before calling loudly to the speaker, "I'll have a double bacon cheeseburger, a crispy chicken sandwich, two all-American dogs, a strawberry shake, and an order of onion rings."

When she finishes, she sits back and looks at me defiantly when I cock an eyebrow.

"What? I'm hungry."

My nostrils flare, but I pull forward after the total is read.

After we have the food, Brianna pulls out the burger, then one of the hot dogs. My mouth waters, and I try to concentrate on driving. I pull out of the parking lot and head back to the interstate.

Brianna makes a little sound of contentment when she bites into the hot dog.

I don't know if it's the sexy little noise she just made or the smell of the hot dog that stirs my appetite. But I do know that the way her lips wrap around her dinner is something I could stare at all night.

"Mmm, this is really good." She takes a second bite, then licks her lips.

I side-eye her and stomp on the gas pedal. The interstate lays in front of us again.

"Are you sure you don't want some?" She pulls out an onion ring and pops it in her mouth.

"Nope. I'm good. I was just thinking of pulling out one of those granola bars." I hook a thumb toward the pack in the backseat.

"Are you sure?" She extends her arm, putting the hot dog closer to my face.

I tighten my jaw and don't reply.

Sighing, she pulls it back and takes another bite before taking a drink from the shake. My stomach is growling so much now that it's bordering on painful.

"I can hear that, you know."

"Hear what?" I ask innocently.

She rolls her eyes and unpacks the cheeseburger. She takes one bite—if you can call the tiny dent in it a bite—then wraps it up again. "I'm full."

"You haven't even eaten it, and you haven't even finished half of that hot dog."

She shrugs. "Apparently, my eyes were bigger than my stomach. It's too bad. I hate to waste this."

I snort. "Nice try, but I'm not eating your food."

"Seriously?" She gives me another look, but instead of her look saying she thinks I'm crazy, it's telling me that she's getting annoyed. "Are you always this stubborn? I know you're hungry. Your stomach is growling loud enough to wake the dead."

"I'm fine."

Her shoulders droop. "Will you just eat this? Please?"

My stomach clenches at the plea in her tone. The beast stirs too. He wants to please her, and he doesn't like that I've made her upset, even if she did it all to manipulate me into eating.

"Fine." I grab the bag of food from her, and in less than a second, I have the chicken sandwich and burger unwrapped in my lap. I lift the burger, take a giant bite, and wolf half of it down.

I make quick work of the rest as Brianna sits quietly and sips the milkshake. When I finish, she hands me the rest of her shake which is still half-full.

Without saying anything, I take it from her. Our hands brush in the process. I go still, and I may be imagining it, but I think she does too.

But then another second passes, and whatever I thought was there, or maybe *hoped* was there, disappears.

She pulls her hand back and turns to look out the window again.

I polish off the rest of the food and despite the grease and exorbitant amount of calories, I feel strangely content. I know it's because she's near me again.

Brianna, however, doesn't seem to feel the same. She's got that unsettled frown again, she's nibbling on a fingernail, and she doesn't turn toward me. She seems lost in her own thoughts.

I don't push her to talk. Instead, I settle with tilting my head to watch her every few miles. I memorize the line of her jaw, the curve of her neck, and the swell of her breasts. Everything about her fascinates me. But it's only as we near her city that the aching sense of what lays ahead begins to settle in.

She thinks I'm going to drop her off at her apartment, and I promised her I would. But where does that leave me? I can't afford to rent something near her.

I have no money. No apartment. No job. The SF is looking for me, and I'm showing up in the city that had SF members prowling the streets not even a week ago. It's pure mania.

But I can't let her go. I know I have to find a way to stay with her and see her again.

All I can hope is that the SF doesn't catch me in the process.

CHAPTER FOURTEEN
BRIANNA

We've been driving in silence for two hours. It's been the longest two hours of my life. Never have I felt so physically aware of a man's presence before. When he's watching the road, I've found myself admiring the swell of his thigh muscles and the width of his fingers.

He's got huge hands. *Manly hands*, is what Macy would call them. And his face is utter perfection—deep-set blue eyes, perfectly symmetrical features, firm lips, and a pleasantly rounded nose. His hair is shoulder-length and tangled. Images of heartthrob actors on the big-screen again fill my thoughts. Collin is just as good-looking and sexy as any of them.

Oh poppycock. What have I gotten myself into?

An uneasy breath stifles my lungs. I keep telling myself that my body's awareness of him is because I can't trust him. It's merely my instincts making me hyperaware, because awareness of him will keep me alive.

It *has* to be that, because anything beyond that is pure

lunacy. I *cannot* be attracted to a murderer. And I *will not* be attracted to a man who abducted me.

I press my lips firmly together, then scan the horizon. Outside my window the city lights of Phoenix appear. My finger works its way into my mouth again. I've never been a nail-biter, but it seems I've turned into one during this drive.

I again contemplate what the hell's going on with me, and I'm really hoping it's because I hit my head. Because if my actions are truly survival instincts then why did I want to make sure Collin ate earlier? That doesn't make any sense. Wouldn't starving him be more logical if I simply wanted to survive?

It was crazy, the compulsion that came over me at that Sonic. Collin had been hungry and on-edge. That shouldn't have bothered me, but it had. So what did I do? I pulled out my tip money and bought enough food to feed a family. And then I basically force-fed it to him. All because I knew he was hungry.

What is the matter with you, Keller?

It's nearly ten o'clock when Collin parks at the curb outside of my apartment building. The marigolds and petunias are bright in the streetlight. The sight leaves me paralyzed for a moment. *Was it really only last night that I was in this same spot when he abducted me? How has it only been twenty-four hours?*

"We're here." Collin doesn't look overly happy after he parallel parks. He turns the car off, his expression grim.

I almost say *thanks for the ride* but then realize how ridiculous that sounds. "Yeah, we're here."

I open my door and get out. I'll have to grab my purse from the backpack since it has my apartment keys. Without them, I won't be able to get inside.

When I open the backdoor, I expect Collin to wait in

the driver's seat, but he gets out. A moment later, he's at my side. "I'll just make sure you get upstairs safely."

My entire body goes still. He's only inches away from me. He's still dressed in his mismatched clothes—long basketball shorts and a flannel with the sleeves rolled up. The shirt is entirely unbuttoned. I can't blame him because it's hot out and that flannel has got to be sweltering, but that open attire also reveals his well-defined six-pack.

I gulp. Why does he have to be so freakin' sexy? The universe is obviously playing some sick joke on me.

"Are you okay?" His voice drops.

I whip my head away from his abs and hurriedly dig my purse out of the pack. Once I have it, I extract my keys and clutch my purse closely to my side.

Behind us, a few college students stroll by on the sidewalk. The lone girl in the group gives Collin an appreciative second glance. I barely control myself from scowling at her.

My breathing grows ragged. *What is wrong with me? Who cares if she's checking him out?* I bring a hand to my forehead. *I'm sleep deprived, and I hit my head. That's what's going on.* That's *why I'm acting like a nut case.*

I still don't know why Collin's insisting on following me to my apartment, but once we're inside my building he dutifully walks behind me. His heavy footsteps echo on each step as we trudge up the stairs. He must be relaxed, since normally he's as silent as a cougar.

Two stories later, we reach my floor. "I'm just down the hall." I keep my gaze on his chin even though those damn abs are calling to me. My heart is beating painfully fast, which it normally doesn't following a quick jog up to my apartment. But I refuse to consider the other culprits for my tachycardia.

"Lead the way," he replies.

This is where you say goodbye, Bri.

But instead of telling him that he can leave now, I turn stiffly and count the steps to my apartment. Just as I reach my home, the door across from my apartment opens. Music spills into the hallway along with the sound of talking people within.

"Oh, hey, Bri!" my neighbor says. Mel's one of the few residents in the building who's not a student. Although, she did just finish her PhD last year, so she was a student not too long ago.

"Hi, Mel." I fumble with my keys. My fingers are trembling so much I can't get them in the lock.

Mel cocks her head when she notices my clumsiness—her frizzy red hair like a halo around her—but then she notices Collin. "Hi there." Her gaze slides up and down him.

Collin just looks at her. He doesn't even say hi.

Right. He's a psycho. Remember, Bri? Or have you forgotten that already? I finally give up with my keys and stop trying to get inside my apartment.

"You guys want to come in?" Mel swings her door open wider. "I met some really cool people this afternoon, so I invited them over. And some of my friends from Phoenix are here too. You guys should join us."

"No, that's okay. It's, um, been a long weekend." As much as I love Mel, I'm in desperate need of a shower, and fatigue is really setting in. Not to mention I'm acting weird. The last thing I need to do is alert other people to that.

"You sure? I was just popping out to grab a few more drinks, but I'll be back in twenty."

"Brianna's tired. She really needs to rest." Collin takes my apartment keys from me and opens my door. Before I know what's happening, he's pulling me inside and saying goodbye to Mel.

When he closes the door behind us, I stiffen. "What are you doing?"

He drops my keys in the turquoise ceramic bowl on the small table by my front door. "I'm making sure you get home safely, just as I promised."

"Right, but why are you still here, and why are you in my apartment?" I try to insert some venom into my tone. I don't know why I'm having a hard time remembering that he's a brutal murderer who needs to be locked up. As soon as his *stolen* car hit the curb, I should have jumped out and run.

Instead, I'd admired his six-pack.

He's quiet for a long moment. He's so quiet that the cheap wall clock ticking above my couch resonates in the room. I'm counting the seconds.

Three more seconds pass before he says, "Do you want me to go?"

His voice is so quiet I barely make out the words, and he's watching me, his expression unreadable. I cross my arms and grip my biceps, then open my mouth to respond. Of course I want him to go. He *needs* to go, but when I try to speak, my throat tightens and nothing comes out.

His entire body loosens, and the corner of his mouth tugs up. "Why don't you take a shower? I'll make us something to eat."

Before I can reply that he's not making us dinner, and I'm not showering with him here, I find myself turning around and heading to the bathroom.

What the hell are you doing, Bri?

But it's as if my limbs have taken on a mind of their own. I know he needs to go, yet—

The thought of him leaving and never seeing him again makes a physical ache fill my chest.

I'm clearly losing it.

The sound of running water comes from the kitchen just as I close the bathroom door. I'm vaguely aware that the man ate enough food to feed ten children only a few hours ago. He can't be hungry already, but he's right about me. I'm famished. A few bites of a hot dog several hours ago hasn't tided me over. My early dinner with Declan was five hours ago, and following that I'd hiked several miles through the desert.

I squeeze my eyes shut. *Holy shit. Declan.* I'd completely forgotten about him.

A swell of nausea makes bile rise up my throat. Collin's wolf killed a man only a few hours ago. We left his body in the desert. And since I'd willingly gotten into the dead man's car with Collin, I am now an accomplice to murder.

What have I done?

I strip my clothes, and the entire time I'm asking myself what I'm doing. I could go to jail. No, I could go to *prison* for life. Even though Collin abducted me, I'm not sure if that completely absolves me of everything that's happened. *Or does it?*

My head is pounding again when I step under the shower's spray. By the time I turn the water off, my lids are drooping from exhaustion and the craziness that has become my life. And on top of it all, I haven't been able to talk sense into myself.

This entire messed-up weekend is catching up with me.

Fuck it. I don't want to deal with this. I just want to go to sleep.

Standing in just a towel with wet hair dripping down my back, I thread a comb through my locks while staring in the mirror. The puncture wounds on my neck, that

Collin's crazy wolf inflicted on me have closed. Small bruises highlight what he's done, but by tomorrow those will probably be gone too. My wrists are still pink, and there's still a bump on my head even though it's decreased in size, but other than those few afflictions, physically you can't really tell that anything happened to me.

If I go to the police now, I'll still have physical evidence of what he did.

That small voice of reason speaks in the back of my mind. But then I remember why I didn't go to the police in the first place. How the hell do I explain wolf puncture wounds on my neck? A human couldn't do that.

A soft knock comes on the door followed by Collin saying, "I've got food on the table if you're hungry."

Hearing his voice slows my rapid heartbeat. It was beating so fast I thought it would leap right out of my chest but knowing that he's still here . . .

I feel like I can actually breathe again. "Okay. I'll be right there."

I wait until I hear him walk away before darting out the door to my bedroom. My apartment is tiny, only one bedroom, a bathroom, and a small kitchen and living area. But considering I don't see Collin, I know he's retreated to the kitchen. Otherwise, I'd have a clear view of him in the living room.

In my bedroom, I hastily throw on comfy shorts and a T-shirt before I walk to the kitchen. All ten steps has my heart pounding again, but the scent of food draws me in. I can't tell what he's made, but my stomach growls in appreciation.

"I made buttered noodles."

I shriek and jump around. The bastard snuck up on me again. When I shoot him an accusing glare, his eyes widen and he holds his hands up.

"Sorry. Do you hate buttered noodles?"

Before I can stop myself, I smack his arm. "Stop sneaking up on me. It nearly gives me a heart attack!"

He laughs and catches my hand before I can pull it back. "Sorry, I'll try to remember that." His firm warm grip closes around me. He makes no move to let go. The laughter dies in his eyes, and his gaze follows mine.

I'm staring at our joined hands. He's touching me. His hand feels solid, slightly rough, and incredibly warm.

It feels . . .

Right.

It feels like how it's supposed to.

What the actual fuck?

My heart pounds again, and I yank my hand away. I immediately feel empty, and my body lurches in Collin's direction.

No, you idiot. You're going the wrong way!

As fast as I can, I force myself to move the opposite way and stumble toward the kitchen table. Two plates of steaming buttered noodles sit across from one another. I'm in such a hurry to get to the table that I trip, but I manage to catch myself right before I fall onto the chair.

I don't wait for him to join me. I grab my fork and begin inhaling my food. It's hot and slippery. I barely chew as I swallow the noodles down. I'm vaguely aware that Collin has joined me. But he sits immobile in his chair, not touching the food.

He's watching me again, but I'm too afraid to look at him. I have no idea what's happening inside me, or why I'm in the situation I'm in, and it's scaring the hell out of me.

The second I finish, I bolt from my chair. "Good night."

It's not until I've slammed my bedroom door and am lying on my bed that I realize he's still in my apartment. I hear dishes clinking and know he's cleaning up. Following that, the shower starts. He's now taking a shower. In my apartment. Which means he's naked.

I roll to my side and am pretty sure I'm hyperventilating.

I wonder if Collin's truly the only crazy person in my apartment. I already know that he's certifiable, but considering how I'm acting . . .

I've apparently lost it too.

CHAPTER FIFTEEN
COLLIN

She feels it too. I know she feels the bond.

I'm so happy that I have to stop myself from singing in the shower. I suspected that she felt something when she didn't run the second I pulled up to the curb outside of her building, but it wasn't until I touched her in the kitchen that I knew.

My dick grows hard thinking about her. My mate. She's just across the hall from me, *and* she wants me. I smelled her arousal in the kitchen when I held her hand. That underlying musky scent had clung to her like salt after a dip in the sea. She hadn't been consciously aware of it, not really, but she'd been aware of *something*. That was why she'd run from me. She still isn't ready to accept it.

I finish in the shower after taking time to properly scrub myself. I don't know when Brianna will let herself succumb to our bond, but it's inevitable that she will. Once both parties feel it, it's only a matter of time, and I don't want to smell like a sweaty sewer rat when it happens.

As I'm toweling off, I imagine Brianna lying naked on her bed. I picture her with her legs spread and her pussy dripping. The mental image nearly undoes me. I groan, and my erection grows.

Fuck. This isn't good. I'm already like a randy wolf smelling a bitch in heat. All I want to do is rut with her. I imagine plunging my length into her sweet depths and making her scream. Another quiet moan tears from my throat.

Knowing she's not ready for anything like that yet, I grab my dick in one hand and begin pumping it. I imagine Brianna sucking me. She's naked, and her bare tits brush against my thighs, but it's the look in her eyes that really turns me on. Those warm chocolate irises gaze up at me with lust shining so brightly in them I swear she's a wolf too.

My release comes fast—embarrassingly fast. Hot liquid squirts all over my hand after only thirty seconds of the dirty fantasy.

Fucking hell, Ward. You better last longer than that when it actually happens.

I grab some toilet paper and clean up the mess. All the while, I picture doing things to Brianna that I can't wait for. I'm going to worship her body when she lets me. I'm going to make her feel so overcome with desire that she won't want to leave our bed for weeks. *Or maybe she won't want to leave the kitchen counter or the living room floor.* I'll take her in any location she's willing.

I barely suppress my frustrated sigh.

I can't even *try* anything like that yet, because I know she's not ready. Hell, I don't even know *when* she'll be ready, or *if* she ever will be even though she feels the bond too. She doesn't trust me, and I have nothing to offer her except a life on the run. I don't have any money. I don't know how I'll provide for us.

But I'll find a way.

I'm bound and determined to give her the life she deserves.

Which means you need to stop killing people, I tell my deranged wolf just as I flush the toilet paper. He's prowling around inside me. He's as awake as I am.

I know he's eager to make Brianna ours, but he's still a sick fucker. Bloodlust still rules his thoughts. Given the images I'm getting from him, he's frustrated and horny too. Although to burn off his frustration, he wants to maim, kill, and devour innocent humans.

But . . .

He also wants Brianna.

It's the only thing he and I have in common, which means that I now have to convince him that the only way she'll want us back is if he stops being a psycho.

If only there was a rogue werewolf rehabilitation program. I laugh humorlessly at my thoughts as I turn the bathroom light off and open the door. Of course, there's no such program, because *no* rogue has ever returned from the land of insanity.

That dejected realization has my shoulders slumping as I walk toward the kitchen. I have no idea if the beast will ever lose the impulse to murder people, but if I give up that hope then my life will be entirely meaningless.

At least he hasn't tested my control again, not since we found that asshole attacking Brianna in the desert, but I don't know if my control will last. I can only hope that I'll find some way to make him see reason, because if I don't, Brianna will be lost to both of us.

Shrugging those depressing thoughts aside, I pad to the small closet near her kitchen that holds her washer and dryer. I pull out a pair of freshly washed and dried shorts. The rest of my clothes are clean now, too, so I repack them in the backpack.

I'd thrown everything I'd owned into the wash before making Brianna dinner. I hadn't asked her if she minded, but I didn't think she would since clean clothes mean I won't smell like a pig.

If there's one thing I know, it's that I need to win her over. Because I *know* it's going to take me pulling out all of the stops to get Brianna to see me as a normal human, and what better way to start that than to act like one? Which means I need to shower regularly like most humans and wear clean clothes.

It's near midnight before I finally contemplate going to sleep. I've already checked all of the locks and windows and have peeked through the living room blinds every few minutes to scan the street below. I'm not used to staying in a city dwelling like this, and I don't like it. I feel exposed, as though the Supernatural Forces can see me right now even though all of the shades are drawn.

I part the blinds again to make sure nothing's changed because even though Brianna lives two stories up, that wouldn't stop a supernatural from entering her apartment, and it sure as hell won't stop an SF member.

But I don't see anything suspicious. The only people wandering the streets at this hour are drunk college kids and the occasional homeless person.

Satisfied, I drop the blind, then tip-toe toward her bedroom one last time to check on her.

I'm more than aware that watching her sleep borders on creepy, but I can't help myself. I want to look at her.

That and I need to make sure she's still safe. *Exactly. It's all about her safety. I should check her windows one last time.*

I tell myself that's the only reason I'm entering her room again, even though I know it's not.

Silently, I push the door open. The beast stirs in appreciation when Brianna's sunshine-and-caramel scent reaches us.

Our mate is lying on her back, tangled in her sheets. One leg is out, revealing a perfectly defined calf and toned thigh while an arm is bent beside her with one finger brushing her temple. The sheet is riding up, but it still covers the mound between her thighs but barely.

I let the beast out more so my eyesight sharpens. His glow allows me to see every detail of her. Her long dark hair splays over her pillow, and her full lips part as quiet puffs emit from her. She's a silent sleeper. She doesn't snore, and if it weren't for my enhanced senses, I would barely detect her breathing.

My dick twitches again. I can't help it. Her breasts push against her T-shirt, and her dark areolas are visible underneath the thin material.

Fuck me. My mate is beautiful.

She stirs, a slight noise coming from her. "Collin," she whispers.

I go completely still. *Dammit.* I've woken her despite being absolutely silent, but then she murmurs quietly again.

"Collin. Yes." Her eyes are still closed, and she moans quietly.

Holy hell. She's dreaming and talking in her sleep.

My heart rate increases when she arches slightly, another moan parting her lips. My nostrils flare. Fucking hell, my mate is having an erotic dream. I can smell her arousal.

She moans more, and her hips begin to swirl.

I stand completely still, absorbing all of it as tiny noises come from her.

"Yes. Yes."

Her barely whispered pants have blood throbbing in

my cock. She's on the verge of an orgasm. Her musky arousal is so sharp I can taste it. My gaze zeros in on her, and my dick is wound so tight now, it feels as if I'm going to explode.

"Ahh!" She arches off the bed, and the scent from her grows a thousand-fold. Her hips move more, and the sheet between her legs grows damp.

My breathing turns erratic. *Yes. Holy shit. Yes.* I just made my mate come—in her dream.

An ear-splitting grin stretches across my face. My erection is still bobbing in my shorts, but I don't care. Elation sweeps through me that Brianna's subconscious has recognized me for what I am even if her conscious self hasn't yet.

Still smiling like a baboon, I watch as she settles back onto her mattress, a soft content smile on her face as she succumbs to a deeper sleep.

Forcing myself to move, I do one last perimeter check of her bedroom before leaving as silently as I came, but that doesn't stop my satisfaction.

My mate just had a wet dream about me. *Me.*

I never knew I could feel so enthused about getting in a woman's pants even though I've never been in her pants.

Once in the living room, I lie on the couch and throw the spare quilt on top of me. The quilt tents, thanks to my Brianna-obsessed cock. I could jerk-off again to relieve my frustration, but after seeing what's waiting for me in the bedroom, I would rather hold out for the real thing.

Faint music fills the room. Mel's party is still going strong. I don't mind the noise, though. I don't even mind that my cock is still so hard it rivals steel, because for the first time in months, I'm going to bed happy.

Brianna's body rubs against mine. *She moans and gasps every time we touch. She feels like heaven.*

Fuck, this woman is amazing. I grip her ass and plunge into her from behind. Her neck arches, and her lips part when she moans.

"Yes," she whispers.

My cock hardens even more. I pick up my pace, rhythmically moving within her. Her back bucks, and every time I pull out too far, she begs for me to slide back in.

I chuckle. "Don't worry, baby. I'm not going anywhere."

A quiet scratch comes from behind me. I keep pumping into Brianna, not wanting to stop. Her channel is so wet and hot, it wraps around my length like warm silk.

But that damned scratch penetrates my senses again. I look over my shoulder, but there's a vast cloud of nothingness.

It's because I'm dreaming. None of this is real.

With regret, I survey the dream-Brianna. As much as I don't want this dream to end, something's wrong.

A whisper filters through my senses. The feeling of dread grows.

Someone's at the window.

Shit.

My eyes fly open. For a moment, my body is still heavy with sleep, but when I hear a second whisper, adrenaline pumps through me, snapping me wide awake.

I spring off the couch, the after-effects of sleep disappearing from my brain, just as two darkly clad individuals slip through the now fully-open window in Brianna's apartment. They're robed in black from head to toe, each carrying SF weapons, and they're crouched low.

They found me.

But no way in hell am I going down without a fight. I lunge toward them.

"What the hell?" one of them says just as he stands fully

upright. He's big, over six feet, and I'm guessing he's a werewolf even though I haven't caught his scent.

The second SF member gasps before yelling, "Down on your knees!" She raises her weapon, and the sound of her magically-infused particle gun buzzes just before she fires.

But she's not fast enough. I spring out of the way just as her shot goes off. The beast slams against my control, wanting out, but I manage to keep him down when I tuck and roll.

Brianna's couch explodes behind me, but I know none of her neighbors hear it. A cloaking spell shimmers in the air around us, depressing all sounds and smells in the area. That means the female SF member is a witch.

Both SF members point their guns at me and shoot. I dive at the last moment, barely managing to avoid the second shot as Brianna's chair blows to bits.

Dammit all to hell. They're shooting to kill, not to capture.

Brianna.

I don't know how far the witch's cloaking spell travels—if it's confined to just this room or Brianna's entire apartment, but I need to get to my mate.

"He's gonna make a run for it, Phoenix!" The woman shoots again, but I jump clear to the ceiling to avoid it.

The beast howls inside me, demanding that I let him loose, but if I do, he'll kill both SF members.

Three days ago, I wouldn't have hesitated. I would have shifted and torn both of their throats out, but now I have my mate to think about.

She wouldn't want them to die.

"Watch it, Priscilla!" The male SF member waves one hand, and a blue ball forms in the air.

So not a werewolf but a sorcerer.

I dodge left just as his hex flies. It smashes into the wall, leaving a crater, but the singeing ring it leaves around it has me side-stepping just as the ball reforms and flies toward me again.

A fucking tracking hex. *Shit. Shit. Shit.*

The blue ball forms over and over as I dodge out of the way. It explodes into everywhere I was standing just as I jump clear of it. And couple that with the SF witch and sorcerer continually shooting at me—it takes only seconds before Brianna's living room and kitchen are completely destroyed.

Sweat rolls past my ear as I dive toward the hallway again. The witch's blast comes within millimeters of me and singes the hair off my calf.

My attention drifts for a nanosecond to my mate. Since Brianna hasn't made a terrified appearance in the living room, I know that means the witch's cloaking spell is only protecting the immediate area. In other words, Brianna has no idea what's happening fifteen feet away from her, but time is running out.

The damn tracking hex is growing bigger, and it's getting faster. That's how they're designed. They learn their opponent's moves and sooner or later, they take you out.

Even I can't beat a tracking hex. Killing the sorcerer who created it, or making him call it off, are the only ways to stop it, which means I'm only left with one option.

CHAPTER SIXTEEN
COLLIN

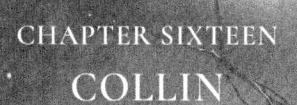

I leap across the room and catapult over the sorcerer. If I hadn't already spent months on the run, honing my skills and growing stronger every day because of the beast, I wouldn't have been able to pull off the move.

But I do, and before the duo even knows what's hit them, I'm behind the man with my arm locked around his throat.

"Call the hex off now, or I'll snap your neck." My words come out gravelly since I've let the beast out more. I know my eyes are glowing like headlights, and given the witch's terrified expression, I know she believes I'll do it.

The blue ball hovers in the air in front of me and the sorcerer. It feints right, then left, looking for a way to burn me while protecting its maker, but each time it moves, I move, too, and I use the sorcerer's body to shield me.

"Take him out, Priscilla!" the sorcerer manages through my chokehold. He's wheezing, and the woman's eyes grow even wider.

"Phoenix."

I know he's going to call off the spell when I hear her

pleading tone. Whoever these two are, they care about each other, and I'm going to use that weakness against them.

"Call it off now, or you die," I say into his ear. I tighten my hold more, until he makes a gurgling sound.

"Phoenix!" the woman yells. "Do it!"

He mutters a counter-spell under his breath, and the blue ball vanishes. Before he's finished uttering the last syllable, I head-butt him, effectively knocking him out. He hasn't even crumpled to the floor before I'm on the woman.

She tries to raise her gun, but I'm too fast. I slam my fist into her head, and she falls unconscious beside her partner. The shimmering cloaking spell in the air disappears, leaving in its wake a room resembling a war zone.

"Fuck!"

I jump over the fallen SF members and am in Brianna's room before I can blink.

"Brianna? My love?" I pull the sheets off her and haul her into my arms. I'm already striding out of the room, grabbing her clothes and whatever belongings I can snatch along the way.

"Collin?" she murmurs sleepily.

I throw what I've grabbed into the pack before calling upon the beast's strength and speed and flying from the room. In the hallway, I sail over the stairwell's handrails and we drop two stories to the foyer below.

Brianna lets out a squeal of surprise from the freefall, but I'm already up and running us out the main door.

Her eyes are wide open when I tuck her carefully into the stolen car's front passenger seat. "Collin! What the hell are you doing?"

My heart is thumping so painfully that I can't reply. I turn into a blur to get around the back of the car.

Brianna makes another sputtering sound of disbelief when I slip into the driver's seat. The car roars to life, and I stomp on the gas pedal. We peel out of the parking spot, the tires squealing as the moon shines down on us.

Brianna sits straight up. "Collin! Stop!"

Her command falls on deaf ears. My mate was just put in danger because of me. She's not safe in her apartment. The SF knows that I took her, and they came looking for her. I suspected this might happen, but to actually experience it . . .

"Fuck," I growl as we pick up speed.

The SF obviously didn't expect to find me in her apartment, too, since there were only two of them. It would explain their surprise after they realized I was there. And while I don't know much about the Supernatural Forces, I do know that when they purposefully confront a rogue, they always send a team of four to five squad members. Never two.

Which means those two weren't there for me, they were there for Brianna.

I slam my fist into the steering wheel.

Of course, you stupid fuck! They were already onto you last week, and then you took a college student right in the area where they were looking for you. You probably left your scent outside of her work, where she plays sports, and right outside of her fucking apartment. It doesn't take a genius to deduce you were stalking her.

I don't know how the SF found out so quickly that I'd taken her, unless they tapped her phone and were able to read her texts or listen into her phone calls. I don't know what's been said between her and her friends, but I'm guessing someone said something that alluded to Brianna being missing.

I slam my hand against the steering wheel again, which

elicits a yelp from my mate. I've been so stupid. But even though I know I've been reckless, I would still abduct her all over again.

Otherwise I wouldn't have her with me now.

"Collin what's going on?" Fear still lines her words. "You need to tell me. You're scaring the crap out of me."

Brianna's terrified plea has guilt eating me from the inside out. I rake a hand through my hair and try to stop the blood that's boiling under my skin. After taking a deep breath, I reply, "Your apartment isn't safe anymore. You can't stay there."

"What?" She licks her lips. "What do you mean it's not safe? What are you talking about?"

With a start, I wonder if she saw any of the destruction in her living room. Maybe I carried her too quickly for her to see those details.

"Two Supernatural Forces members just broke into your apartment, except they weren't there for me. They were there for you. I still don't know if they were checking to see if you were home, or if they already knew that I took you and you had returned." I shake my head. "Maybe they didn't expect to find you at all. Maybe there were simply coming to investigate your home and my being there surprised them. I don't know, but I do know that you're on their radar now."

She gulps just as I swing the car onto the interstate. I know I need to ditch this vehicle and find something new. We can't keep driving around in a dead man's car, and the SF is probably monitoring every vehicle around Brianna's building if they're looking for her, but I don't have time to find a new car right this instant.

We need to put distance between us and Quintin Valley —at least a few miles before I stop.

"Collin," Brianna says. "What do you mean they were there for *me*?"

I take another deep breath as my mind continues to spin. There's so much that I need to do.

I somehow manage to reply, "Do you remember what I told you? About how the Supernatural Forces have sorcerers that can manipulate a human's thought process?" She nods so I continue. "They were there to either check on your safety, learn more about you by investigating your apartment, or capture you and take you to their headquarters. If it's the last, that means they already know that I took you. And the only reason they would sneak into your apartment was because they knew you were back and their intention had been to wipe your memory."

Or maybe access her memory. For all I know, they would have first plundered Brianna's mind to gain information about me.

The thought of anyone violating her like that makes me grip the steering wheel so tightly it begins to bend.

But given Brianna's dazed expression, she's oblivious to the rage inside me. She sits quietly for a moment before shaking her head. "But how do you know that? Did they tell you that?"

"No, they didn't tell me anything. But didn't you see what your living room looked like? Did you not see the destruction?"

I hold my breath as I wait for her reply. If she truly hadn't seen any of it, then she may believe I'm making all of this up and that I simply abducted her again. *Fuck a duck. I'm up shit creek if that's the case.*

Her forehead scrunches up more, and her frown grows. "Actually, I think I did see some of it." Her eyes grow to saucers just as the horizon takes on a faint glow. "My couch was blown up!"

"Yeah, and that wasn't the only thing they blew up."

Her hands fly to her mouth. "But how could I have slept through that?"

"One of them was a witch. She used a cloaking spell around the living room. Everything that happened there was muted to everyone outside of it."

When Brianna just stares at me, I add, "A cloaking spell is what the SF uses when they don't want anyone aware of their whereabouts or actions. It effectively cloaks the area under the spell to resemble exactly what the witch wishes. The witch can change how outsiders see the area, or it can just mute all sounds within. The witch can essentially create the perfect illusion. So while I was fighting for my life in your living room, you and all of your neighbors were sleeping soundly in your beds, none the wiser."

"Wow." She sits back, her fingers trembling.

I can only hope she believes me.

CHAPTER SEVENTEEN
BRIANNA

I have no idea what to say. The last ten minutes of my life are all a blur, but I did see some of what Collin's talking about.

I close my eyes and concentrate, trying to remember exactly what happened after Collin whisked me from my bed.

Vague images come to mind. Holes in the wall. My exploded couch. A lump near the window.

My eyes flash open when I realize that lump is actually two bodies garbed in black and piled on top of each other.

Horror slides through my veins. "Did you kill them?"

Collin shakes his head. "No. I just knocked them unconscious."

I want to believe him. I really do, but what I've seen . . . "But how do I know that?"

A pained expression crosses his face. "You can't. You'll just have to trust that I'm not lying to you."

He looks so dejected, and his hands keep rhythmically gripping the steering wheel.

My stomach plummets. Before I know what I'm doing,

I'm reaching for him. My hand lands on his arm and squeezes. His muscle pops beneath my grip, his bicep like a boulder. "It's okay. We'll figure it out."

Some of the tension eases from his shoulders, and with a start, I realize I just did it again. He was upset, and seeing that upset *me*, so I did the first thing I could think of to comfort him—I touched him.

Stunned, I jolt away as if I've been burned.

What the hell's the matter with me?

Collin gives me a side-eye, then pulls off the next exit and slows.

I perk up again. "Where are we going?"

"We need a new vehicle. We can't keep driving this one."

My lips downturn when I realize what he means by "new" vehicle. *More like stolen one.* He's on the hunt to commit another crime and since I'm not opening my mouth to protest, I've truly become his accomplice. We're a regular Bonnie and Clyde.

Bri! Snap out of it! You need to stop this.

"Isn't there another way?" I ask when he pulls into the parking lot of a Burger King. The street we're on reveals a gas station another block down, along with a McDonald's and a Walmart. I twist my hands in my lap when his eyes alight on a powder-blue hatchback.

"That one will be easy to break into."

In the back of the Burger King, three cars are parked side by side. They probably belong to the employees inside who've just started their shift.

"Collin. You can't steal another car."

He completely ignores me.

The hatchback's gotta be circa 1990 or older, but it's rust free, and it actually looks as if the owner takes care of it. The guilt in my stomach grows.

"Collin, please. We can't do this."

His response is to turn off the engine. "Wait here."

He's out of the car before I can suck in another breath. My heart is beating quickly again, and I keep looking around, convinced that we'll be caught any minute.

But when my attention drifts back to Collin, I swear I'm seeing things. He's holding his pointer finger near the car's window, and the nail visibly *grows* in length until a thin claw emerges from his nail bed. My eyes bulge, especially when everything else about him stays the same. Using his wolf-like claw, he pries through the rubber lining the window.

I gasp when his claw connects with the door's lock *inside* the vehicle and pops it up. He's in the car leaning under the dash in less than fifteen seconds.

Dumbstruck, I fly out of the vehicle just as the new car's engine roars to life. Wires dip from the underside of the dash—thanks to his hotwire—and a determined expression fills the werewolf's face.

When Collin sees me standing outside of the door, he gives me a disapproving glare. "I told you to wait in the car."

"And I told you not to steal another vehicle."

"Then what do you suggest we do? Stay in the car we were in? Those plates are going to be on every trooper's radar soon. It's only a matter of time before they realize its owner is dead and that will mean we're considered dangerous. So what do you suggest? Because the police officer who pulls us over will have his gun drawn, and he'll shoot if I don't comply, and I can guarantee that I *won't* comply, which means I'll be out of options. I'll have to kill him."

My face pales. I can literally feel the blood draining from my cheeks just as Collin curses.

Shaking my head, I clench my hands into fists. "So if I

don't go along with stealing this car, and we get pulled over in the old one and you're forced to kill a cop, then it's *my* fault? Is that seriously what you're saying?" My blood heats at how he's trying to manipulate me.

"Shit. No." He rakes a hand through his hair. "I mean, yes. That's a fair assessment, and you're right. I was just trying to guilt-trip you into going along with my plan." He dips his head, then mutters, "Old habits are hard to change."

I blink. *Was that his version of an apology?*

He moves closer until he's standing in front of me, looming like a mountain, and even though I'm tall, I have to tilt my head back.

"I'm sorry. I don't mean to put this on you." He runs a finger across my cheek, his nail once again normal. The movement is so fleeting and gentle, so unlike the volatile power he's capable of. "I don't want to scare you, but you need to trust me. This is the only way I'm going to keep you safe from the SF, while also not harming other humans."

My lips part, more from surprise at the tingle that's still present on my cheek and my body's blatant reaction to him. As much as I should be concentrating on what he's saying and yelling at him for being such a dick, my body has other ideas.

What happened to fighting this attraction, Bri?

Even though I try to remind myself of that, it doesn't work. Shivers run down my spine. His cedar scent, which for the first time doesn't carry a hint of body odor, makes my head spin.

His eyes darken, turning into gray storm clouds.

When I don't say anything, he adds, "I'm sorry. Will you forgive me? It was a shitty thing to do—to try and make you feel you would be responsible for my actions—and I shouldn't have done it."

"Then why did you?"

"I don't want you to be in danger, and I'm trying to protect you in the best way I know how."

I want to argue with him, but any fight that was left in me drains out. His apology sounds sincere, and he looks genuinely aggrieved.

And he's right.

I'm in way over my head.

So I can either leave him right here, right now and accept whatever fate the Supernatural Forces has in store for me, or I can trust that he's making the right calls even though that means I'll be an accessory to another crime.

I bite my lip. "What happens when the human police catch up with me?"

The storm clouds in his eyes are about to unleash a torrent. "I won't let them touch you."

"You can't guarantee that. Before—when you abducted me—I could have used that as an excuse to explain why I was with you, but now . . ." My stomach twists into knots when I remember running into Mel last night. She'd seen me with Collin. I hadn't been trying to get away from him, and I'd let him enter my apartment. She may be forced to tell the cops that I'd been with him—that I *hadn't* been his prisoner.

And then it hits me. I'm truly no longer his prisoner. I could walk away right now, confess to everything I've been involved in and take what's coming to me from the law—human and supernatural.

Because if I leave Collin now, I may still be able to salvage some kind of reasonable future for myself even if it involves jail time and a nasty encounter with the SF.

My breath stops, and my heart clenches.

Just the thought of parting with Collin now has my heart ripping. It feels as if someone's plunged a dull blade in the muscle and twisted. I actually purse my lips together to keep from crying out.

Collin reaches for my hand, entwining his fingers through mine. "We'll figure this out together. Isn't that what you said? I won't let anyone hurt you."

He watches me intently as the blare of distant cars and trucks on the interstate filter through my senses. And it isn't until he has our bags packed in the new car that I realize I've already made my decision. I made up my mind hours ago on that gravel road back in Utah.

I just hadn't known it then.

"Brianna?" His brow furrows. "We need to go."

His hand brushes against my forearm, but he doesn't grab me. I can tell that he's waiting for me to make a decision. He's not forcing me to do anything.

And that's when I realize something else—I'm utterly helpless to resist this attraction to him. We're like magnets, and as fucked up and crazy as that is, I can't stop these feelings.

"Okay." I make a move to walk to the passenger's door of the new car, but he reaches out and stops me with a gentle touch.

"I need you to drive the old car into the city. I'll follow with this one. We need it well away from this area."

My lips part as comprehension dawns. "Because you don't want the authorities to put two-and-two together? They'll link this stolen hatchback to Declan's car and subsequently, his murder?"

He nods curtly. "Correct."

His shoulders bunch as he waits for my response, and he's right to be nervous. Not only have I chosen to go with him, but now I'm *helping* him break the law.

Can I really do this?

But the stormy sea in his eyes calls to me, pulling at me as the moon controls the tides. I can't leave him.

"Fine. I'll follow you, but that's it. Don't ask me to help you break the law again, because I won't."

He lets out a breath, and the tense lines around his mouth vanish. "Got it. I won't."

On stiff legs, I slip into Declan's sedan and follow Collin from the parking lot.

∼

WE DITCH Declan's car in a seedy Phoenix neighborhood and leave the keys in it. Collin says it will probably be stolen soon by some bored teenager, but that doesn't stop him from efficiently wiping our fingerprints from the interior and dousing the seats and carpet in some solution he retrieves from the backpack. He says he picked up the solution on the magical black market. Apparently, it breaks down any remaining clothing fibers and hair so no trace of our DNA will be found.

I watch all of it wide-eyed and come to realize that Collin truly is a seasoned criminal.

Yet, I still get into the newly stolen car as squealing tires and shouts from this derelict part of town float up around us.

And as Collin and I peel out of the deserted back alley with its putrid scents while Declan's car sits waiting for its next thief, I don't look back.

CHAPTER EIGHTEEN
COLLIN

We need money. Badly.

I drum my fingers against the steering wheel in time to the rhythmic lull of the interstate. We have the backpack that I packed from the cabin and some of Brianna's clothes that I grabbed on my dash out of her apartment. Other than that, we've got nothing.

Brianna shifts in her seat, angling her legs. The shorts she wore to bed last night ride up her thighs, and her tits are still visible through her thin T-shirt.

At least the view's nice.

She's been sitting quietly, but I can tell that something's changed in her. She's still tense and jumps every time another car passes us—and I know she keeps thinking it's a cop—but despite that anxiety, she hasn't said anything about being on the run again.

The beast stirs inside me. He wants out. He's not content with being locked away, especially since our mate is sitting with us. He's curious to get more acquainted with her, but obviously that can't happen in a moving vehicle.

I chuckle when I picture him pinning her to her seat and licking her face while we barrel down the interstate at seventy miles per hour.

"What are you laughing about?" she asks.

I shake my head. "Was I really laughing?"

She nods, and her dark hair falls over her shoulder. I wonder what it feels like. The long strands look soft as silk. They're thick too. I could knot my fist into it and arch her neck back before sucking on her neck and nipping her earlobe.

I shift in my seat when blood rushes to my cock. It's been getting worse, this draw to her, and now that she's grown a bit softer, less likely to cut my head off, my desire to claim her is growing.

I blink rapidly, hoping my eyes aren't glowing.

"So are you going to tell me?" she persists. From her innocent curiosity, she obviously has no idea how dirty my thoughts are getting.

Seriously, Ward, you've got the SF after you, you have no resources, and all you can think about is Brianna spreading her legs?

I clear my throat and drop an arm on my thigh to hide my erection. "Nothing, really. It's just something about my wolf."

"What?" She angles herself more my way.

"He's happy. That's all." She raises an eyebrow so I add, "I haven't felt him happy in a very long time."

"So if he's not happy normally, then what is he?"

I cock my head and try to think of the perfect word to describe him but then realize he's too complex for that. "He's angry, crazy, vengeful, and a whole slew of other adjectives, but he's nothing good. That's what happens when a wolf goes rogue."

Her brow furrows as the desert landscape zips by her

window. "What exactly does going rogue mean? I'm just a normal person, remember? None of this makes any sense to me."

A pit forms in my stomach, but then I remind myself that she already knows the beast is a murderer, and she's still here. She *chose* to come with me. Still, I can't help but wonder if that would change if she learns just how horrifically brutal my wolf has been.

I vow to keep the worst aspects of my dark past to myself. She knows he killed people—hell, she watched him massacre that prick who attacked her—but that's the extent of what she needs to know. Because if the beast and I want to keep her, the killing needs to stop, which means she doesn't need to ever see that side of us again.

You hear that? I say inside to the beast.

He whines, and I know that he understands.

In other words, today has become the first day of a new future. I won't let the beast kill anymore, and as long as he knows that murdering people means losing Brianna, I think he may try to stop his impulses.

But he's still crazy. His deranged mind hasn't changed. I can tell that from the random bloodlust images I get from him. When a car passed us not even ten miles back, a vision had filled my mind of wolfing down the driver's intestines. I'd pushed it aside, like I usually do.

Another vision comes to me. It's of Declan on top of Brianna, pinning her to the ground back in northern Arizona. Red coats my gaze, and I understand what he's showing me.

Well, as long as no one's threatening her, you can't kill, but if someone's hurting her...

The beast snarls.

I know. I feel the same. If someone hurts her, you can kill him. Will that keep you satisfied?

His response is to curl up back inside me, his restlessness abating.

Glad we finally agree about something.

"Collin?" Brianna says.

I jolt in my seat and realize she's still waiting for my answer. I give her a sheepish smile. *Don't mind me. I'm just conversing with my psychotic half.* "What did you ask?"

"You were going to tell me what a rogue is."

I clear my throat. "So rogues are male werewolves that have left their packs. When a werewolf is on his own for too long, he begins to change. Packs keep us civil, more human than animal, but without a pack, our wolf side can go insane. When that happens, we call a werewolf a rogue."

I make myself keep my gaze on her even though a deep sense of shame fills me, especially when her eyes dim.

"And you knew that your wolf would turn into that if you left your pack?"

I shrug. "I knew it could happen, but I didn't think it would. I thought I was too strong and that I could keep my wolf in check." My lip curls. "But I was wrong." *And I was an arrogant prick who's now paying the price.*

"So you can't control your wolf-side at all anymore?"

"I can but barely. During the last few weeks, it's been harder. He's grown stronger, and his impulses have been harder to control."

At least my human mind hasn't succumbed to the beast, but that could change if I'm not careful.

Some rogues eventually give into the darkness and let their beast completely take over. Even if they walk around in their human form, the beast is still ruling their mind.

But I refuse to let that happen even though it would be the easy way out. If the beast were in complete control, I wouldn't feel guilt or shame anymore. I could live like an animal.

But if I do that than I truly am no better than a murderer. Up until now, my beast has committed all of the killings, but if I forsake my human mind I would be no better than him.

I'm clinging to the fact that I can still *choose* the fate of my mind. I have to. If I no longer have that choice, I might as well give up and let the SF catch me.

Brianna shudders just as a cloud drifts in front of the sun. Some of the land dips into shadows. "And that's why your wolf tried to kill me back at the cabin? Because he loves to murder?"

"Yes."

"So why did he stop?"

I can tell from how she's looking at me that she genuinely has no clue. A female werewolf would have sensed it immediately and understood the mating bond, but since she's a human and didn't grow up in a pack, she has no idea how males of my kind get when their mate appears. Nor does she know how females of our kind get.

All wolves are hot-blooded.

I shrug and keep my answer vague since I still feel like she's not ready for the full truth. "He likes you."

Her head snaps back. "Likes me? He tried to kill me."

"But that was before."

"Before what?"

"Before he decided you were different."

She shifts completely in her seat so she's facing me squarely. "How am I different?"

In this position, her breasts jut out as the seatbelt cuts into the middle of them, accentuating the two perfect mounds. I lick my lips. Her tits are begging for my attention. *Fuck my mate is hot.*

Brianna squirms for a moment, and my nostrils flare. A slightly musky scent wafts from her.

A grin wants to stretch across my face.

She's also horny.

For me.

But relishing that scent right now will only make my shorts stand up like a tee-pee. I rip my gaze away from her and shrug. "He just decided you're different is all."

She takes a deep breath, and her scent dampens. With a quick movement, she squeezes her legs together, and I know she's fighting her innate attraction to me again. But fighting it is hopeless. For whatever reason, this human and I are fated to be together, and she can't fight it any more than I can.

"So why not just go back to your pack?"

Her abrupt question has my dirty thoughts falling to the back of my mind. "Why would I do that?"

"Doesn't your pack have werewolves in it?"

"Yeah, of course."

"So wouldn't going back home and being around them solve whatever problem your crazy wolf has?"

I grimace. She truly has no clue about rogues. "I wish it were that easy but no, that won't work."

"Why not?"

"Because no rogue in history has ever come back from insanity."

"So that means your wolf is beyond saving? That he'll always want to kill?"

My jaw locks. After a moment, I manage a curt nod.

Her lips part, making a surprised O. The musky scent coming off her completely disappears. Nothing like talk of a little murder to really kill the sexy vibe.

Another long moment passes before she asks, "So what have other rogue werewolves done when this has happened to them? Surely, there's a way to still live normally?"

With a regretful shake of my head, I tell her something that's been nagging at me. Ever since my interest changed toward her, I've been wishing for the impossible, but the truth is that even though I want a future now, I don't have one. "No, Brianna. None of them ever live normally again. Once your wolf has gone rogue, there's no coming back."

"But then, how will you not kill . . ." Her words trail off, as if she's too afraid to ask the question.

"I don't know. My wolf won't hurt you. I'm certain of that, but as for everyone else—" I feel him rise from his slumber and stretch. He's obviously sensed that our mate is talking about him. "I'm going to do everything I can to keep him from killing again, and I *will* be successful, but his impulses will never go away. He's always going to want blood."

She shudders. "So he's like an alcoholic? He's always gonna want booze, but as long as he goes to meetings and stays away from the bottle, he'll be okay?"

I laugh at her analogy. "Hopefully something like that."

"Then why are we running from the SF? Why don't you just tell them that your beast isn't going to kill any more so they stop following you?"

Her naivety is endearing, but I can't let her wish for things that will never be. "The SF will always hunt me. That's not going to change. Never in the history of werewolves has a rogue ever stopped murdering."

Her mouth parts but then determination lights her gaze. "But you could be the first. You could show them that you're not going to do it anymore. I mean, if your wolf isn't going to murder me then he's obviously capable of stopping. Right?"

"Yes, we can hope for that."

She nods, and some of the tension eases from her shoulders. It doesn't sit well with me, though. Cause while

I didn't lie, I also didn't tell her the full truth, because not only has no rogue ever stopped murdering, but no rogue has ever been able to run forever.

Sooner or later, the SF always catches up with them, and when that happens . . .

Death is waiting.

CHAPTER NINETEEN
COLLIN

By early evening, we're in southeastern California. I stay in the eastern part of the state. It's less populated here and will keep us well away from LA.

Heat wraps around the land like a glove. It's sweltering this time of year, but it's also less populated, and the less populated area may thwart the SF.

Rogues typically dwell in cities where it's easy to pluck off humans. As for rogues hanging out in deserted areas of states? Not so much.

The dry desert flies by my window. We've passed a few cheap motels, some open but most boarded-up and closed. There have been a few gas stations, too, and the random small town. But that's about it.

"Where are we going to stay tonight?"

Brianna asks the obvious question, and the unsettled feeling I've been dealing with for the past hour grows. "I'm working on it."

Once again, it becomes obvious that I can't provide for my mate. I have no money, no shelter, and hardly any food. I can't even fill the hatchback with a new tank of gas since

I have no cash, which means we'll need to ditch this vehicle and find a new car soon.

Brianna's not going to like that.

My jaw tightens and then it grinds when her stomach rumbles. I don't even need my enhanced senses to hear it.

"You're hungry."

"I'm okay," she says.

"Right." She's not fooling me.

The only option I've come up with for surviving the next twenty-four hours is to knock some dude out and steal his wallet. If I can even find a dude to knock out...

Regardless, pretty sure Brianna's not gonna like that either.

I'm almost desperate enough to use my old credit card. If I did, I could pull into the next open hotel along this stretch of highway and book us a room. Following that, I could take Brianna out for dinner, then I could spend the rest of the night pleasuring her until she screams my name at least three times.

Three? No. Four.

It's so very tempting. I know the credit card still works. My parents haven't cut me off from our family money but using that card also means alerting the SF to our whereabouts.

That obviously isn't an option.

Shit. What's your plan, Ward?

The beast is awake, too, which only adds to the tension building in my shoulders like a volcano. He's prowling around again, blood on his mind. He knows Brianna's hungry, and he doesn't like that. However, instead of knocking a guy out and stealing his money, the beast is throwing me images of hunting down wild hares and coyotes and bringing their carcasses back to Brianna.

I can just imagine her expression if the beast trots up to

her with the entrails of a rabbit hanging from his mouth before he drops her "dinner" at her feet.

Yeah, bud, thanks, but that ain't gonna work either.

He circles again, low growls coming from him.

At least he didn't suggest killing a human and bringing *that* carnage back to her. I suppose that's progress.

I cup the back of my neck as Brianna's stomach gives another rumble. She slaps a hand over it and smiles sheepishly.

"Take the last granola bar," I tell her.

Her lips part, a flush filling her cheeks. "No, I'm fine. Besides, you should take it. You've barely eaten anything today."

"I'm not hungry."

She raises her eyebrows. "You have to weigh at least fifty pounds more than me. You need more calories. You should take it."

I clench my jaw and give her a look that I hope conveys, *fat chance*. Keeping one hand on the wheel, I reach into the back and fish through the pack until I find the small bag of food. I plop the entire thing on her lap. "Eat."

"What about you?"

"I'll find something. Don't worry about me."

Her stomach grumbles louder, and she reaches for the bag's lip but then stops. "How much money do we have?"

And there's the question I've been avoiding. "Enough."

"Really? Cause yesterday you didn't have any when we stopped at that Sonic, and my purse is still back at my apartment along with my cash."

"I found some spare change in the trunk." I'm not lying. I *did* see a few nickels in the trunk.

"Seriously? How much?"

"Enough to buy myself some food when we stop next." *If I'm lucky, maybe a cheap piece of beef jerky.*

She frowns but finally acquiesces. However, it's not until her hand dips into the bag and pulls out an apple and power bar, before tearing into them, that I finally relax. Well, relax a little.

"I was supposed to work tonight," she says in between bites. "Macy said she would cover for me, but I'll need to call her if I don't make my next shift. She'll worry if I miss that one too."

"When's that?"

"Tuesday evening."

"So we have two days."

She bites into the apple, the loud *crunch* filling the sedan. "And I'm supposed to go to class tomorrow. It's my last year. I can't skip class forever if I want to graduate, but I can miss a few days."

I know where she's going with this, and I'm dreading it.

"So do you know how long I'll need to avoid my apartment? Do you know when we can go back?"

Despite wanting to avoid that question, my grip on the steering wheel loosens. She just said *we. Do you know when* we *can go back.* She hasn't given up on my sorry-ass yet.

"Is going back to school what you want?" I ask her.

She finishes the apple and throws the core out the window. Hot dry air blows in until she rolls it back up.

I expect her to say *yes* without hesitation, but instead her brow furrows. She looks so damned cute with her forehead all scrunched up that it's hard not to reach for her and touch her. And right now, I desperately need to touch her. I want to feel her smooth skin, inhale her sexy scent, and pull her into my arms. I don't have any answers for her at the moment, but fuck me if I don't want to try to be who she wants me to be.

"I thought I did." Her frown remains.

Hearing that unlocks my jaw. It's the bond. The bond is

making her second guess everything. What we have is real. We're fated, and right now, nothing else matters. She just doesn't fully understand that yet.

Problem is, I'm not sure how to make her understand it without scaring the shit out of her.

She finishes the last of the power bar and takes a drink from the water bottle. Now that she's no longer hungry I can concentrate on where we'll sleep tonight.

"So what did you do before you turned rogue?" She asks the question from out of nowhere. When I don't answer immediately, she adds, "I mean, if you don't mind sharing. I just thought that since we've only known each other for a few days, that we should try to get to know each other more, since we're . . . you know—" She clamps her mouth together, and some of the color drains from her face.

Shit. She's thinking about how crazy our current circumstances are. She's second-guessing herself again. It's as obvious as a blazing neon sign.

"I worked on my family's ranch back in Hidden Creek. I spent most of my life there, but I traveled a bit, too, when I had time off."

She takes a deep breath, and some of the anxiety lessens around her warm chocolate eyes. "What's ranching like?" Her hands are still clasped tightly together, her knuckles white, so I launch into everything I can think of.

I tell her about the horses, the smell of grass on an early summer morning, the lull of the cattle at night, calving in the spring, and the business side of it that isn't always pretty but keeps the pack well-fed and provided for.

By the time I finish telling her everything about how my life used to be, she's relaxed back against her headrest and the car's running on fumes.

"What was it like growing up in a community that close-knit?"

I slow the car, knowing it's twenty miles to the next town and that we need to make it. Better to drive conservatively. "It was better than I ever realized. I didn't fully appreciate how great my life was until I left."

"And you really can't go back?"

I shake my head. "It's not an option."

"What would happen if you did?"

"Besides every woman and child running for their lives when they spotted me followed by all the males shifting and circling me to protect their families? It would be great." I grin for good measure, but sadness pricks her eyes.

"You must be very lonely now, if returning to your old life or living in the human world aren't possible."

"Would you believe the loneliness never really bothered me? The beast—I mean my wolf—has become so strong that most of my time is spent struggling with him to keep him under control. I don't have much time to dwell on the past." *Until now.*

"So you can feel your wolf right now?"

"Yeah. I can always feel him."

"Is that weird? I mean, what's that like?"

"Before he turned rogue, it was normal, although he wasn't as strong then so it was easier to forget that my wolf resided inside me. It was more like he and I were one, even though technically we've always had two separate consciences. But when a wolf is healthy, he's like an extension of yourself. He's always there, ready to make the shift, but he's not in control, although your decisions are often in-tune so it doesn't matter if your human side makes the decisions."

"And now your wolf is in control and you don't share the same desires anymore?"

"That's right. What he wants and what I want are two different things." *Until you.* Brianna has no idea that her safety and happiness are the first common wish both the beast and I have shared. For the first time in months, I've felt an inkling of what he and I used to share on a daily basis.

"Tell me more about being a werewolf."

I'm hopeless to resist her demand and so is the beast, so I spend the next ten minutes explaining how you don't experience your first shift until puberty and how dominance is revealed at that time.

"Dominance? What do you mean by that?" She tilts her head, completely enraptured in every detail.

I can't hide my smile. "Every wolf has an innate inner strength. We call it dominance. The more dominant a wolf is, the more he can bend the will of those around him when he unleashes his magic."

"Really? How the heck does that work?"

"Do you want me to show you?"

Her eyes widen before she nods.

I call upon the beast's strength. He's even stronger now, which means my magic—that has always rivaled an alpha's—is even more powerful than it was a year ago. The heat builds in me, and I let a small river trickle out.

When it hits Brianna, she grows rigid in her seat. Goose bumps sprout on her arms, and her shoulders fold inward. It's only when fear grows in her eyes that I go still.

I quickly suck my magic back inside, drawing that tendril of alpha power back to where it resides.

The air clears, and Brianna sucks in a lungful of air. "So that's how you did it."

"Did what?"

"Made me drop that stick back at the cabin when I was swinging at you. You used your power against me."

Her accusatory tone has me replying, "It was only to get you to stop. I wouldn't have forced you to do anything else."

"But you could have, couldn't you?"

"Yeah, I could have."

"Does the beast, or whatever you call him, use that power on his victims?"

"He doesn't have to. He's strong enough without it."

She pulls her bottom lip into her mouth, and I can tell she's mulling everything over. I can only imagine what she's thinking. All of this has got to be so weird to a human. "So can dominance be learned?" she finally asks.

"No. You're born with it. It's why werewolf families get so edgy when the first shift is coming. Dominance manifests at puberty when the werewolf gene is activated. That first shift signifies how powerful a wolf's dominance is going to be."

"So you could have made people do things with your dominant magic when you were only . . . what . . . thirteen or something?"

I give her a crooked smile. "Twelve, actually. I shifted a bit earlier than some, but to answer your question, no, I didn't have the strength then that I have now. It grows as we age, but you can gauge how strong a pup will become at the first shift."

She sits back again, that curious sparkle lighting her eyes. I eye the gas tank for what feels like the fiftieth time. We're going to need to ditch this car soon, but with any luck, we'll stop for the night first so I won't have to steal another vehicle again until tomorrow. I figure my mate has been through enough crimes and misdemeanors for one day.

"What about women? Do they have dominance, and can they shift into wolves?"

"No."

She tips her head. "But I thought you said something about female werewolves before."

"I did. Women carry the werewolf gene, and they have slightly enhanced senses compared to humans, but they don't shift and never will."

"Well that doesn't seem fair."

"Tell that to whoever created us."

"Speaking of which, how *were* werewolves created?"

I shrug. "How did humans come to be? A higher power? Evolution? Aliens from space? It's an interesting question, but no one can answer it."

Her eyes widen. "Wow, this is heavy. I don't know if my brain can process all of this right now."

I laugh, which gets a smile out of her, and seeing her like she is now, seeming to genuinely enjoy my company, that feeling comes back again that I felt last night—happiness.

I'm just so fucking content when she's around, and I realize I truly do admire her. It reminds me of those glimpses I got of her personality when I was stalking her, when I didn't want to admire her, but I begrudgingly did.

The woman's got grit. She's been through hell and back this weekend, yet she's never broken down and when my wolf attacked her she quickly bounced back. That kind of resilience will serve her well. My life won't be easy on my mate and knowing she can handle it helps make this feel a little less daunting.

Brianna angles her head to look upward out her window. "I hear the night sky out here is amazing. Have you ever seen it?" When I shake my head no, she adds, "Do you think maybe we could crash somewhere around here for the night?"

Her blasé attitude about sleeping in the wilderness with

nothing but the clothes on our backs has my lips tugging up. Not only does she have grit, but she's down to earth too. Most of the women I've been with, human and werewolf, would have wrinkled their noses at sleeping on the ground.

"Do you really want to do that?"

She eyes the gas tank. "It's not like we have much choice, right? Looks like it's almost empty so sooner or later, we're gonna be walking. We might as well take advantage of the area while we can. We may even see shooting stars this time of year."

Something lifts in my chest, and a hunger for something that will probably never be grows in my belly. For a moment, I can't breathe. This woman is amazing, and the more time I spend with her, the more I want her.

I just hope I can keep her.

CHAPTER TWENTY
BRIANNA

We've pulled over, and I'm rummaging through the trunk for supplies. There's an old picnic blanket tucked under a bag of tools and jumper cables. I lift it triumphantly but then remember that this blanket actually belongs to someone else, and we stole it from them.

Ugh. But even that memory doesn't completely dispel my excitement at seeing the night sky. I know that I should be worried and confused about what's going on, that my focus should be on school, my job, and my friends, and that this crazy compulsion to stay with Collin is fucked-up on a million levels. I also know that sooner or later, the law will catch up with us.

But for whatever reason, at the moment, I don't care, and I don't want to psychoanalyze it anymore.

"Find something?" Collin's standing near the driver's door.

He's wearing another pair of basketball shorts but today he's also wearing a T-shirt, and while I wouldn't mind seeing his six-pack, I can't help but admire the way his defined pecs are visible through the thin material.

He inhales, a knowing look in his eyes.

A blush stains my cheeks, and I quickly scurry to my side of the car and call out, "Yeah, there was a blanket, so with this one and yours we should be okay if we sleep on the sand."

Once again, my heart is pattering like a hummingbird's wings. I still don't understand how I can have such an intense physical attraction to this man, but then I reason that he's been quite normal and actually caring during the past twenty-four hours. Mr. Hyde has fully disappeared, leaving only Dr. Jekyll in his stead.

Lord help me.

I bite my lip when I remember the sensation of freefalling this morning after Collin hopped over the railing with me in his arms, and we'd dropped two stories to my apartment building's entryway.

Instead of leaving me to my fate, Collin had fought off two SF members, he *hadn't* killed them, and then he'd carried me out of my apartment and fled from Quintin Valley to keep me safe.

Even though he'd initially abducted me, and I'd been utterly terrified of him, since then, he's been continually proving that he means well, and that he's trying to do what's right.

Surely that counts for something?

Collin's scrounging around in the pack when I finally muster the courage to look in his direction. He pulls out the last of the packed food—what I didn't eat—and wolfs it down. He's got to be ravenous considering we've been on the run most of the day, but he doesn't complain.

Something tells me he's grown used to hardship.

"See a good spot to camp?" he asks.

His deep voice sends a thrill down my spine. *Seriously, Bri, you're acting like a hussy. At least try to act a little cooler?*

I survey the dry land. There's a break in the cactuses and brush, and a small mound looms about a hundred feet away. "There looks good." I point at it. "Just behind that little hill. Nobody should be able to see us from the road if we camp there."

"That works." Collin comes around the front of the car. The wind picks up the long strands of his hair. He's got such a rugged appeal to him.

I whip my gaze away. *Not being a hussy. Remember?*

A chuckle comes from him, but before I can ask what's so funny he's striding toward the sand. I sling the picnic blanket over my shoulder and follow. Wind brushes long locks of hair across my face, obscuring my view of Collin's broad shoulders and tapered waist.

Damn wind. But even with my hair blocking my view, that feeling begins in my girly areas again, that pulsing ache. I nearly roll my eyes so hard they fall out of my head. *Bri! Hussy!*

I grip the blanket tighter and take a deep breath. When we reach the area, Collin kicks several rocks out of the way before throwing the pack on the ground. He then spreads his lone blanket. One of the edges catches on a cactus, but he pulls it free. The thick woolen material doesn't tear, but there are a few holes sprinkled throughout it.

When he sees me looking at them, he says, "Rats."

Rats chewed holes in his blanket? I think he's joking so I smile, but when his lips don't lift, I reply, "Seriously?"

He shrugs and sits cross-legged casually on the ground.

I spread out the second blanket beside him, letting the edges overlap to hopefully keep the sand off. The breeze picks up, and a chill brushes over my skin like a soft kiss. It's still warm, and the night shouldn't be that cold, but it will probably dip into the sixties. I rub my bare arms and drop to the ground beside him but am careful to keep at least a foot of distance between us.

Once settled, I ask, "Where did you encounter rats?"

He leans back on his hands. Veins pop on his forearms. "Sewers."

"Sewers as in *Teenage Mutant Ninja Turtles* sewers?"

He chuckles again, and I realize I like that sound way more than I should. "Not quite that bad. The rats I encountered were still normal sized."

"What were you doing in a sewer?"

"Sleeping there."

My eyes bulge. "You're kidding."

"I wish I was."

I settle back, too, realizing we have a long time to wait for a fully dark sky. "Why would you sleep in a sewer?"

"It was the safest place for me. The SF is good at finding rogues, but the SF didn't realize how desperate I was to stay free. The sewer was one of the places I'd managed to avoid detection."

I scrunch my nose up. "That must have been interesting."

He laughs. "I can't say I liked it."

Since he's laughing and joking about such an abhorrent way to live, I'm struck again by how tough this man is. He's completely alone in the world. He has no money or resources, yet he's managed to survive on nothing but his own wits. The little I know of his upbringing sounds charming and privileged. I can't imagine he suffered any then what he is now.

"How have you done it?"

He cocks his head. "What do you mean?"

I bend my knees to my chest and wrap my arms around them. The temperature is steadily dropping. "Well, you grew up in a small town, right? With your family and friends. You had money, food, and a house, yet now . . ." I shake my head. "You've been living for months on absolutely nothing. How does someone who went from having everything to not even one dollar do it?"

A groove appears between his eyes. "I suppose I was determined to prove that I could." He shakes his head. "But I was an arrogant prick. I thought I could show everyone that I didn't need them, but in the end, I was no different than every other male who's left his pack. My wolf turned into a beast, and here I am." He raises a hand and gives me a crooked smile. Since he genuinely doesn't seem upset talking about it, I decide to appease my curiosity.

"So how long do werewolves usually last on their own before they turn into a rogue?"

"It's hard to say. I don't have access to SF files, but rumors in the community have said your wolf can go rogue anywhere from a month to a year without a pack. But once rogue, most werewolves are caught by the SF within a few months. Some, however, have gone years before arrest. They're the most dangerous ones."

"A *month*? You can turn into a rogue in less than a month away from your pack?"

"Not usually. That particular wolf I'm thinking of wasn't very dominant. His wolf changed sooner than most."

"And when did your wolf change?"

"Around a year."

I rub my hands up and down my shins. "So you've been dealing with your crazy wolf for the last eighteen months?"

"Yep." He stretches his legs out and crosses his hands behind his head. Since he looks so comfortable, I do the same. I lie down on my side, my head cupped in my hand so I can look at him. *Damn*. He's a fine male specimen. My gaze rakes up and down his long frame. His biceps bulge from how they're bent. His abdomen is flat and toned, and his thighs are heavily muscled.

"Like what you see?"

His question makes my cheeks flush. I bite my lip and pick at a loose thread on the blanket.

"It's okay, you know. You can look if you want." The amusement in his tone has me rolling my eyes.

"Aren't you the modest one? You're assuming that I *was* checking you out."

"Are you denying it?"

I pick more at the thread. "Maybe. Maybe not."

"It's all right, you know. It's not your fault that you find me attractive."

My jaw drops and all embarrassment leaves me. "How do you know I find you attractive?"

"So you do?"

"No. I didn't say that. I . . ."

His eyes twinkle, and I mutter under my breath at his cockiness, but as hard as I'm trying to tell him that I don't think he's attractive in the slightest, I can't get the lie out.

"Damned cocky male." I harrumph and look away.

That just makes him laugh more.

Pushing up on my elbow, I arch an eyebrow at him. "I thought you said you *used* to be arrogant."

He shrugs. "Old habits die hard."

"So this is normal, huh? Having women check you out and fawn over you?"

"It may have happened once or twice."

Even though I know he's goading me, I can't stop my swell of irritation. I recognized that he was good-looking from the first moment we met, when I thought he was a random hiker who was going to save me, so why wouldn't every other straight female feel the same?

It's a normal reaction. Hot guy. Look twice. But the thought of other women eyeing him or being with him...

I bite down on my lip. Hard.

Ouch.

But dammit. He's right. I *am* attracted to him, but it's even worse than that. I have this ridiculous notion that I *like* him now that Mr. Hyde is permanently gone, and the thought of another woman feeling the same about him...

I mutter another sound of disgust. *Bri, what is wrong with you?*

Whatever the case, jealousy is not something I'm used to feeling.

I take a deep breath and look him square in the eye. "You probably have women throwing themselves at you all of the time." I manage to say it matter-of-factly, and some of my embarrassment eases since I don't sound like a jealous hussy.

But my nonchalant statement brings a frown to his face. "I don't care about other women. There's only one that interests me."

He says the last bit so seriously that my heart picks up that staccato beat again. A faint glow lights the rims of his irises. He doesn't break eye contact, which only makes my heart flutter faster. Jealousy still rides me hard, and I'm not sure I want to know which woman has caught his eye, but I can't help my question. "And this woman you're referring to is where?"

"She's lying right beside me."

"Oh." My lips part, and I drop back to the ground. My head is cushioned by the sand, but it still thumps. "You have a funny way of showing interest in a woman, if you insist on kidnapping her first."

"I didn't know how else to get her."

Heat flares in my core, and I do everything in my

power to tamp it down. Crazy. This is so crazy, and even though I was determined to stop thinking about how none of this makes sense, at this moment, I can't because everything about him, us, the past few days . . .

None of it makes *any* sense.

He doesn't say anything as I lie there, struggling to find reason in something that's unreasonable.

After a minute, he says, "It's normal, you know, what you're feeling right now, even if you don't think it is."

I whip my head toward him. He's turned on his side so he's looking down at me. And even though twelve inches still separates us, it feels as if he's almost on top of me. My attention dips to his hard biceps, strong chest, and flat abs. The man is dripping with sex appeal.

"Nothing about this is normal." I look back up and see the first star appear through the darkening sky.

"It might not be to you, but it is to me."

He says it so seriously that I whip my head toward him again. "So you do this a lot, is that it? Abduct women, pretend to be a psycho, and then turn all sweet and caring just to get in her pants? That's so fucked-up."

"No, that's not what I meant." He scoots closer and brushes a stray strand of hair from my eyes. "I mean that what I'm feeling for you is normal, because it's normal to werewolves."

"Huh?"

"Don't tell me you don't sense it? This need to be with each other? To be close? To touch?" His hand strays from my face to trace a feathery path down my arm.

My breath stops. A trail of goose bumps and a shiver of pleasure rises in his wake.

His tone turns husky. "You respond instantly to me. I like that. That's how it's supposed to be."

I shake my head, snapping myself out of his spell.

Because that's what this has to be. He must be a sorcerer *and* a werewolf, and he's woven a love-spell on me, because nothing else can explain this.

"What are you talking about?" I whisper. "None of this is supposed to be."

"Not to you because you're human, but if you were a wolf you would recognize it for what it is."

He's staring at me so intently, as if waiting for me to understand this foreign language he's speaking. But I don't understand it. I don't understand any of this. "And what's that?"

He swallows, his Adam's apple bobbing before he says quietly, "That you're my mate."

My eyebrows rise clear to my forehead. "Your what?"

Uncertainty fills his eyes. "My mate."

"What the hell does that mean?"

"That we're fated to be together. When together, our souls are complete. I just thought you should know, because I can tell that these feelings are tearing you up. That you don't understand—"

I push up from the ground. My breath is coming so fast now, that I feel lightheaded. Before I know what I'm doing, I'm pacing back and forth.

"Brianna," he says, an ache in his tone.

But I don't want to hear this. I *can't* hear this. There's no way in hell I'm mated to anyone. "This is crazy, Collin. I'm not mated to you. What the hell does that even mean?"

Any uncertainty in his expression vanishes. A hard look takes its place. "Yes, you are mated to me. You're my fated mate. You're meant to be with me and only me."

I stop pacing. My chest rises and falls so fast that I can't catch my breath. "And what if I don't want that?"

His face falls. "You don't want me?"

I begin walking again, the sand sinking beneath my

feet. "I . . . I don't know, but what I mean is that I don't believe in that. Soulmates and shit. That stuff's not for me. I'm not a romantic. I never have been. I believe that women end up with who they choose based on a history of good experiences, which means there are a lot of men out there that I could be happy with. And whoever I end up with will be because he and I met at the right time and we mutually like each other, not because fate decided it for us." A soft growl rises from him, but I don't let it deter me. "I'm not looking for a relationship right now, Collin, and I don't intend to be with someone just cause he's good looking."

His growl stops, and he smiles. "So you find me good looking?"

I groan. "Well, of course I do. I thought you already knew that. But you're not the only good looking guy in the world. I've met quite a few hot guys."

His smile disappears, and a scowl takes its place. "You're attracted to other men?"

I throw my hands up. "Of course I'm attracted to other men! Haven't you been attracted to other women?"

His scowl increases. "I don't care about other women."

"But you have been, in the past, right?"

"All women in the past are not women I care to think about or remember. Now, there is only you. There will only ever be you."

I stop in front of him, my chest heaving. *Seriously, why can't I breathe?* "But this isn't how I imagined my life going. I have no intention of settling down with anyone right now."

He stands too. He does it so quickly, that one second I'm looking down at him and the next he's looming over me. "I'll wait. I'm not going anywhere. When you're ready to be with me, I'll be here."

I take a deep breath because his words are doing something to my insides, and it's not something I want to feel. It's too . . . *much*. It's just too much. Whatever is going on inside me, I know that if I jump off this cliff with him, there'll be no return. I'll fall so fast and hard, that nothing and no one could ever come after him.

I press the heels of my hands into my eyes. "But what if I want someone else? What if I *choose* someone else? I still want a choice."

He's silent for a full five seconds, yet I can feel his tension mounting. It's building and burning off him with each second that passes, like a vortex swallowing me whole.

"Who is it that you want?" His words are clipped.

I let my hands fall and gasp when I see the light in his eyes and the flare of his nostrils. "I . . ."

"Do you have a boyfriend?"

"No."

"But you desire another man?"

"I . . ." My stomach flips over and over, and my core is swelling again. Lord help me, this man is virile. Everything about him is calling to me, and seeing him right now, so worked up at the thought of me with another guy—

My lady bits begin to throb.

His nostrils flare more. "You say you want another, yet your body wants me. I can smell it."

Smell it? Did he seriously just say that?

He takes a step closer to me, until we're standing toe-to-toe in the soft sand, then he places his hands on my hips and pulls me close. My breath sucks in when I press flush against him.

"I won't share you, Brianna. You are *mine*."

His possessive tone makes my core flame hotter.

"And you may not be willing to admit it yet, but I know you want me too." He leans down and nips my neck.

A small gasp escapes me.

His mouth moves upward, pressing soft kisses on my neck, until he's right at my ear and whispers, "I'll wait for you, until you're ready, but I won't share you." His breath tickles my skin, and my knees threaten to give out.

Holy balls, how is it possible that just the feel of his body against mine is enough to make me come?

As if sensing how much he's affecting me right now, he loops his arms around my back and supports my weight. "But if another man tries to take you from me, I won't allow it. I won't push you, and I'll give you the time that you need to adjust to being my mate, but I will not share you. Do you understand?"

My lids flutter. With how I'm feeling at the moment, I don't give two shits about any other man, but then I remember that I don't believe in this stuff.

I put my hands on his chest and shove him despite my body begging me to keep him close, but I refuse to be ruled by fate. "I told you. I'm not interested in a relationship. I have too many things I want to do first, and I *don't* believe in mates or soulmates or fated mates or whatever the hell you're calling this."

He crosses his arms, and the muscle ticks in his jaw.

I don't trust myself to steer clear of him, though, so I return to the blanket and lie on my side, my back to him.

Even though I'd wanted to admire the night sky, right now, I can't. It's taking everything in me not to throw myself at him and wrap my legs around his waist.

I groan internally with self-disgust.

It's painful, this sexual attraction to him. But I will *not* be that girl.

At least a full two minutes pass before Collin sighs harshly and returns to his blanket. He continually readjusts his position, clearly unsettled if his frequent movements are any indication, but I still don't turn to face him.

Instead, I wrap my arms around myself to ward off the growing chill. So what if he looks like Thor? So what that my lady parts are practically spasming right now at the thought of riding him? And so what that he's been nothing but devoted, sweet, and caring for the past twenty-four hours?

He still abducted me, and he still has issues.

That's not something I need to be a part of.

Then why are you here?

I shove that rational question aside and embrace my indignation. I never signed up to be anyone's fated mate. I'm just a normal human, and I intend to stay that way.

CHAPTER TWENTY-ONE
COLLIN

Fucking hell. Well that didn't go as planned.

My mate is sleeping beside me. Sometime in the past hour, she finally drifted off. Her even breaths make her back rise and fall slowly. I try not to watch her sleep, since she would probably be creeped out by that. So instead, I stare at the sky.

Millions of stars shine above us. It's truly breathtaking, but even that sight isn't enough to alleviate my frustration.

I rake my hand through my hair for what feels like the twentieth time. My mate's a human, so it's understandable that she's having a hard time with this. She doesn't want to accept that she's meant to be with me and that I'm meant to be with her.

I can live with that.

For the moment.

But my jaw clenches again when I remember her saying that she may want another. Her skin had flushed at the thought of being tied to me—only me—and while that makes irritation build inside me like a volcano, I'm willing to give her time to adjust to this.

But what I can't live with is the thought of another man touching her, kissing her, and tasting what's between her legs.

The beast snarls within me, and I mutter an agreement.

You're right. She is ours.

She will never be anyone else's, and now, I have to figure out how to make her see that.

I know that with enough time, she'll give into the bond, but time is not something I have.

I sigh again. I can only hope that she'll soon believe that we're fated. I hold onto the knowledge that she's here with me now and has never attempted to run or leave me despite saying that she doesn't want me. That's proof that she feels it.

She's just being stubborn.

Of course I would choose a woman that's tough as nails. I smirk and imagine being fated to a softer more pliant woman. Inside, the beast yawns in boredom.

You're right. Our mate is perfect as she is. I wouldn't have her any other way.

So I do my best to be content with lying beside her even though my shorts are tented like a tee-pee again. Brianna's scent keeps drifting toward me, and her ass is only inches away. Her backside is round and firm. I keep imagining sliding my palms over those lush globes.

I growl. It's going to be a *very* long night.

I prop both hands behind my head and try again to use the night sky as a distraction, but movement from Brianna has me pausing.

Her body shudders then stops. But in the next moment she shudders again. Alarmed, I lean up on my elbow with the intention of waking her but then I spot the goose bumps on her arms. Another quiver vibrates her body, and I realize what's happening.

She's shivering.

My mate's cold.

Fucking hell. Of course, she's cold. Cool air blows through the desert. It's fallen to around sixty-five degrees, and she's only wearing shorts and a thin T-shirt.

I lean over her with the intention of pulling her blanket around her.

But the second my body touches hers, she rolls into me.

I go completely still. She snuggles against my chest, naturally drawn to my warmth.

I breathe shallowly. My erection brushes her thigh because I'm facing her now, and if she wakes up with me nearly on top of her and with a hard-on rivaling the Washington Monument, I can only imagine the accusations that will fly.

Moving slowly, I ease away from her. I'll have to pull my blanket out from under me and drape that across her. Perhaps trying to wrap her snuggly in her own blanket isn't an option.

But the second I move away, Brianna follows. She whimpers quietly, and her hands find my stomach and then the hem of my shirt.

Before I know what's happening, her arms are slipping under my T-shirt and she's burrowing against me.

My breath sucks in. Her limbs feel like ice. I try to focus on that instead of how she feels molded against me. I take another shallow breath. *Shit.* This is going to be harder than I thought.

"Brianna," I whisper. I don't push her away because I know she's cold, but I have to wake her. If I don't and she wakes up with us like this, she'll think I was trying something. "Brianna," I say louder.

She lays her cheek against my chest, and her sweet breath puffs on my collarbone. She's now pressed completely against me from head to toe. Every inch of her gorgeous body is touching mine. Her firm breasts rub against my pecs, her long legs entwine with my thighs, and her hair tickles my chin.

Fuck.

My cock is throbbing now and on the verge of erupting.

Nostrils flaring, I try not to inhale her scent, but of course I do. That musky scent tinges it again, and before I can take another breath, she's rubbing herself on me.

"Collin," she whispers.

I know she's still sleeping. Night two with my mate is revealing that she's an active sleeper, and holy hell, if this is what she's like asleep I can only imagine what she's like awake.

But I know now's not the time to fantasize.

I place my hand on her arm and squeeze gently. "Brianna, wake up."

But sleep still claims her, and now her hands have wound up my chest and around my back. Her tits are squashed against me, and her core feels hot and damp on my thigh. So fucking damp. Her arousal wafts up to me, beckoning me to taste her.

I tell myself to breathe through my mouth, not to inhale the scent coming from her swollen mound, but trying to do that is like trying to ignore an oasis in a baking desert.

Giving in, I tentatively lean down and bury my nose in her neck. I inhale once, just enough to dampen my insatiable thirst for her.

I intend to pull back, to force air between us, but she moves her hips. That subtle swirl rubs against my erection, and then her lips find the base of my neck. She kisses me softly, then runs her tongue along my skin. Her throaty moan follows.

Fuuuuuuck.

I have to stop this, or I'm going to be plunging into her and roaring my release in seconds.

"Brianna!" I yell.

She startles and goes completely still. I know she's awake when her entire body grows rigid.

"Collin? What . . ." she whispers, sounding confused, then she scrambles back, her lush body now inches away. Her eyes snap wide open as mortification fills them.

I'm relieved that she's embarrassed instead of angry. Still, my cock is prominently hard. I stay on my side so it's not standing straight up like a pyramid. "You were cold. I was trying to wrap your blanket around you, but then . . ."

She rubs her eyes. "Cold. You're right. I'm cold, but I was . . . I mean, we were . . ."

"You were shivering, so I reached over to try and cover you. I didn't make a move on you while you were asleep, I swear. But when I leaned over you, I think you naturally sought my warmth cause you kinda rolled back with me, and—" I don't elaborate because color blooms in her cheeks. Even without my enhanced vision I can see it.

She whips her gaze away and rolls flat on her back. Uneven breaths make her chest rise and fall. She licks her lips and after a moment says hesitantly, "Did I . . . um . . . do anything?" She's still looking at the sky, refusing to make eye contact.

"You put your hands up my shirt and rubbed yourself on my thigh."

I watch her closely. Her cheeks turn scarlet. "Right. I, uh . . ." She presses her palms to her cheeks. "Sorry about that."

I inch closer to her. "I didn't mind." But she still won't look at me.

"Did I do anything else?" she finally asks.

"No. I woke you before you could." My voice dips. "But you can do more if you want."

She groans and covers her eyes. Embarrassment coats her words when she replies, "No. I didn't mean to. I was having a dream, and I—" Her hand falls to the side, but her eyes are still squeezed shut. "Crap, this is embarrassing."

I tilt her chin toward me, and her eyes open. "You never need to be embarrassed with me."

Her gaze searches mine, but she remains quiet. After a moment, some of the tense lines around her mouth lessen.

I run my thumb over her lower lip, unable to stop myself. Her mouth parts, and her tongue darts out.

My gut tightens, and my abs seize when her tongue grazes my finger. But the second that sexy little gesture ends, her eyes grow wide.

"I'm sorry. I don't know why I keep . . . I mean, I didn't mean to—"

Fuck it.

I pull her against me before she can utter another breath and slant my mouth over hers. I can tell the kiss catches her by surprise. For a moment, she stiffens, her entire body going as rigid as a board, but then she melts against me like soft butter.

I grab onto her ass and haul her closer. She moans, and the sound sends meteors of pleasure shooting through me. I plunge my tongue into her mouth. She tastes as good as she smells, and she's mine. *All mine.*

The beast rumbles his pleasure, urging me on. Images of my teeth elongating and biting into her neck fill my mind. He doesn't want to eat her, but he wants to claim her. He demands that I infuse her with our magic that will seal her forever as our mate.

She's not ready for that.

He growls, but I push him down.

Oblivious to the war raging inside me, Brianna wraps her arms around my neck, and I concentrate on the feel of her lips. They're soft and pliant, but then they turn demanding and aggressive.

My blood roars when she nips at my lower lip and sucks it into her mouth. "Damn," I whisper. "You're as hot as I thought you'd be."

Her only response is to moan more and whimper my name again. I could get used to hearing those sounds all night.

"I need you closer." I drag one of her legs over my thigh. My hips thrust instinctively, nestling my erection between her legs. My tip prods her entrance even though we're both fully dressed.

When it spears her clothed core, her hips buck, and she arches against me. "Collin!"

Fuck me, my mate is hot.

I tear my mouth from hers to press kisses down her neck. She tilts her head back, moaning again. More urgent noises come from the back of her throat, and I want to sing in glee. My mate wants me. She's hot for me. She has erotic dreams about me.

And she's all mine.

She doesn't protest when I push her shirt up. A lacy bra greets me, covering a delectable globe of firm flesh and an erect nipple. I cup her tit, then unhook her bra in the back. Her breasts spring free when I discard the material.

Her fingers are tangled in my hair now, urging my mouth toward her breast as her legs ride up and down my sides. She's turned into a she-beast, all moans and heat, exactly the way a woman is supposed to respond to her mate.

I flick my tongue over her nipple. She cries out, her entire body coming off the ground, and my cock throbs.

I'm so hard now it's painful, but I'm determined to pleasure my mate first.

I cup her other breast and make sure to give it equal attention. With every suck, her core grows damper and her whimpers grow deeper. I can smell the growing wetness between her thighs, and when I finally reach down to run my hand under her shorts, I growl in satisfaction when I feel how soaked she is.

"Yes. Please. Collin!"

She's finally given into the need to be one. The beast urges me to move back to her neck, to bite into her, to make her ours, but I move down instead.

I pull her shorts off. Pausing for a moment, I inhale the wetness coating her womanly lips.

She doesn't protest when I work her panties down. I fling them to the side, then pull back and admire the view. Brianna protests, trying to move me closer, but I have to look at her. She's so beautiful and swollen. No woman has ever come close to what my mate is.

"Collin!" she snarls.

A deep chuckle fills my chest when I finally oblige. I bury my head between her legs and run my tongue across her swollen nub, and a scream tears from her throat. I lap at her clit, sucking it and tasting it over and over.

The beast growls in pleasure when our mate screams in response and locks her legs around my head, forcing me to stay as I am and continue licking.

"Yes. Yes. Yes!"

Her demands grow wilder as I vary the pace and friction. I can't get enough of her. I could spend the rest of my life nestled between her legs, pleasuring her over and over.

But when her climax begins to build, I know she needs more. I lap harder at her hard nub, but I also push two fingers deep inside her. Her channel feels hot and wet. *So* wet.

I thrust my fingers into her again and again as her body bucks uncontrollably, and when I feel her walls begin to spasm, I tickle her G-spot, and an orgasm explodes through her body.

She screams loud enough to wake the dead, and her fingers turn into claws in my hair. I pump into her unrelenting. My fingers are so wet they're like a river as her climax peaks.

It's only minutes later, when her shattering release finally begins to subside, that she goes limp in my arms. Her hands fall, and her thighs release their death grip around my ears.

I pull my fingers out, reveling in the smooth wetness of her before bringing them to my mouth to suck them clean.

Fuck. She tastes good.

I give her one long last lick, making her shudder all over again before I push up on my forearms to climb on top of her.

A dazed look coats her eyes. Her hair is wild, and her cheeks are completely flushed. A low growl of satisfaction fills my chest.

I did that. I did that to her.

"You're smiling," she says. The earlier hesitation and embarrassment she showed is gone. I've so thoroughly loved my mate that I've fucked it right out of her, even though I haven't properly fucked her yet.

"How can I not be?" I make a move to roll to my side so I can pull her into my arms, but she tenses.

"No. What about you?"

Before I can tell her that she doesn't have to reciprocate, she's flipped me onto my back and is stroking me.

My heart jolts at the feel of her hand slipping around

my clothed erection, and when she lets go to dip her hand inside my shorts, I lose all thought. "Bri," I whisper hoarsely.

The night sky shines above me as she makes quick work of my shorts, and when her mouth closes around the tip of my length, I'm already on the verge of coming.

"Holy hellfire woman," I whisper.

"You taste good," she murmurs before taking me completely in her mouth. I can't breathe when she pumps me in and out, swallowing my entire length before lifting again.

Fuck me. This woman can take all nine inches of me, and she's showing no signs of slowing down.

I try to breathe, to think, and not to look like a thirteen-year-old-boy who's about to jizz all over his pants, but when she begins sucking me in earnest, my eyes roll back in my head. It doesn't help that her tits keep bobbing up and down on my thighs, or that she makes low moaning noises in her throat every time she swallows me.

She's got me on the verge of climaxing in seconds. I try to grip her hair, to slow her down, but she refuses to let up.

And when she slips one hand around my balls and pumps the other up and down the base of my shaft while her hot mouth and tongue make quick work of the upper half, any control I have vanishes.

"Brianna!" I roar. My hot liquid shoots into her mouth as an explosive orgasm rocks my body.

She keeps sucking and licking as my cock pumps into her. The pleasure is so intense that my vision goes dark. I roar again, my release that momentous.

It feels like hours before I finally come down from the high. She's cradled her head on my belly and is absentmindedly stroking my thigh. My dick's gone limp, but I know all she needs to do is glance at it, and I'll be rock-hard again.

"That was . . ." I swallow and try again, but my head is still incapable of forming coherent words. "I . . . uh . . . fuck . . ."

"Yeah," is all she replies.

I keep panting. Blood is pounding through my veins as the aftereffects of the best orgasm I've ever experienced lingers. I had no idea it would be this intense with her. I mean, I knew that the sexual chemistry between fated mates was said to be off-the-charts, but to experience it firsthand . . .

Words don't do it justice.

When I can finally move, I haul her close. I do it so quickly that only a small gasp leaves her lips before I have her gathered in my arms.

"You are mine," I whisper to her, then kiss her softly.

I expect her to grow limp, to wrap her arms around my neck and declare a similar statement, so when her body goes rigid, I pause mid-kiss.

"I'm not yours," she says and pulls back. "That was just fooling around."

My jaw locks. She hasn't completely moved away, but she also doesn't seem in any hurry to mold her body into mine and proclaim her feelings of undying love.

I sigh harshly. "Fooling around?" My voice is clipped even though I try not to be angry.

"Yeah. You know, it's what two people do when they're attracted to each other."

Fuck me. Did she really just say that? "So this is normal for you?"

She inhales and trails a finger across my chest. My muscles jump in response, and my cock twitches. It hasn't even been ten minutes, and I'm ready for round two, but instead of pinning her to the ground and plundering sense into her, I grab her hand to stop her movements.

"Answer me. Is this normal for you? Is this how you feel every time you *fool around* with a guy?" The words taste like acid on my tongue. Both the beast and I snarl at the thought of Brianna with another man, but I have to know if she truly *doesn't* feel as I do. I need to know if that honestly wasn't the most intense sexual experience of her life.

It feels like a rock drops in my stomach at just the thought of her denial.

She looks down, and her lips tighten. "And if I said it was normal?"

My stomach sinks more. I grasp her chin and force her face up. "I wouldn't believe you." But even I hear the desperation in my tone.

She scoots away from me and sits up. Before I can protest, she's hooking her bra in place and slipping her shorts on.

"Brianna . . ." I plead.

But she's already standing and pacing. She rakes a hand through her hair, then does it again. She's so wild and beautiful, that once again, my breath stops. How did I get so lucky to be mated to a woman like this?

But her next words completely ruin my high.

"This is crazy, Collin! You're on the run from the law, I have a life back in Quintin Valley, and what the hell are we doing anyway? There's no future between us."

My nostrils flare when I sit up. Her gaze strays to my abs. At some point in the past twenty minutes, I lost my shirt. The fact that I can't remember when it came off just goes to show how nothing is normal between us even though she's claiming it is.

"Of course there's a future between us," I growl, my irritation rising.

"No there isn't!"

"How can you say that? How can you deny what's right in front of you?" I stand, too, and take a step toward her. She doesn't shrink back. "You're made for me, Brianna, and I'm made for you. Nothing about what we just did is normal. I've never come like that with another woman before, and I sure as shit know no man has ever made you scream like that." My chest is heaving now, and the beast is snarling. He's no happier about this conversation than I am.

She glances away, but the stubborn tilt of her chin remains. "You don't know that."

I close my eyes and take a deep breath. I even count to ten before opening them. Fucking hell, this woman knows how to push my buttons. "I *do* know that because we're fated, and you're mine. No man on earth can pleasure you the way I can. My soul knows how to please you. I was born to pleasure you."

"Stop saying that!" she hisses.

"Why? Because you don't want to accept it?" I take another deep breath. "It's okay if you're not ready. I said I'd wait for you, and I meant it, but don't you dare start lying to me and saying that what we have is the same as what you've experienced with other men." I glare down at her. I can't stomach the thought of another man licking her like I just did, but I know she's lying. It's the only thing keeping me from completely losing my shit.

She glowers at me for another long moment, then groans and collapses to the ground. She sits on the edge of the blanket and picks at a loose thread. She still hasn't commented on the beautiful night sky, which solidifies that I've completely taken over all of her thoughts and senses.

"I don't understand any of this." She covers her face with her palms.

Some of my anger diffuses when I see how torn she is. I remind myself that she's not a werewolf, so all of this has to be very overwhelming for her.

I walk silently to her side and sit down. Before she can protest, I haul her into my lap.

Brianna squeals, but when I lock my arms around her waist and press my mouth to her neck, she goes quiet.

"I'll give you all the time you need," I say quietly, "But don't ever compare what we have to what you've experienced with other men again. It . . . hurts too much."

I know I'm opening my soul to potentially being tormented by her. This woman has the power to break me. But when the vulnerable words leave my mouth, her expression falls.

"I'm sorry," she whispers. "I don't want to hurt you. I really don't. I just . . ." She hangs her head. "I don't feel in control, and I don't like it. It feels as if—" She shakes her head, and her mouth presses into a thin line.

"That something bigger than you has taken over your life?"

Her gaze whips up. "Yeah. That's exactly it."

"And how do you think I feel? Do you think I was looking for a mate to complicate my life? I mean, look at me, I have nothing to offer you. I'm a criminal who's on the run, and now I've dragged you into the mess that is my existence. Do you think I wanted to do that?"

Her brow furrows before she gives a slow shake of her head.

I dip toward her, until our foreheads are touching. "I didn't fully understand who you were that first moment I saw you, but now that I know, I'll never be able to let you go. I'll never *want* to let you go."

A shiver runs through her, and my gut tightens, but after a moment she relaxes and sinks into me. "I know. I think I'm only just starting to understand that."

I pull her back down until she's lying on the blanket beside me. She settles in the crook of my arm, and our bodies fit so well together that I know fate intended for us to be one.

She admires the night sky for a few minutes, finally finding constellations and marveling at the beauty that domes over us, but then her fingers find my skin, and her tongue tastes my collarbone, and before either of us can help it we turn into another tangle of limbs and need.

It's only after I've made her come two more times, and she's rocked my world just as many, that we finally settle back to sleep.

I still haven't penetrated her. I know she wants it, even though she pretends she doesn't, but at some point, when I sink my shaft deep inside her, the beast is going to demand that we make her ours. And a claiming, even a normal one, isn't to be taken lightly.

I need to prepare myself for that moment so I can stop it. I won't be able to claim her the first time we fuck, not even the second. Hell, I might never be able to claim her even though I desperately want to.

Because how can I do that when the SF could catch me at any second?

That wouldn't be fair to her.

Still, I can fantasize about it. My lips curve up as Brianna goes limp beside me. Quiet puffs from her mouth let me know she's sleeping. I pull the blanket up higher so she won't grow chilled as I dream again about what keeping her could mean.

CHAPTER TWENTY-TWO
BRIANNA

I rouse from a deep sleep sometime later to slip away from Collin to relieve myself in the bushes. He's sound asleep on the ground, the occasional soft snore floating up from him. I have no idea what time it is, but it's still pitch-black out.

I scamper away and crouch down, sighing when the pressure releases in my lower abdomen. Above, a millions stars shine. It's pure magic. I had no idea there were so many stars, and the Milky Way galaxy stretches from horizon to horizon in a cloudy opaque ribbon. Even though my brain is still heavy with sleep, I marvel at it.

When I finish, I pull my panties back up and steal back to the blankets. Collin's still asleep, his chiseled body bare from the waist up. I shiver and rub my arms, but Collin seems immune to the cool air. He'd pulled his shorts back on after we finally settled to sleep, but he hadn't bothered with his shirt.

A flush creeps up my neck. *How many orgasms did this man give me in the span of one hour?*

Even though I'm cold and want nothing more than to

lie back beside him and soak up his warmth, I stay standing for a moment to admire him. *Damn.* He's built like a Greek God, all chiseled muscles, smooth skin, and symmetrical features. My lady bits swell *again* at just the sight of him.

Seriously, Bri? So much for not being a hussy.

Even though I had intended to avoid his sexual pull, there's no stopping now. The man knows how to please me, and now that I've gotten a taste of what he can do . . .

The ache grows in my core.

I want him.

Now.

Again.

I sigh and finally lie back down, even though I really want to climb on top of him, but I'm not going to wake him. So I settle for the feel of his hard length pressed against me. His arms immediately lock around my waist, even in his sleep. I love the feel of it.

I love it too much.

I snuggle into him, not thinking about tomorrow or what the future could bring because he's right. As much as I don't understand it, he's right.

He and I fit together.

We just do, and I can't explain it.

I sigh sleepily, a smile curving my lips up. Even though we haven't had sex, I feel sore, thoroughly loved, and oh-so-fucking-fantabulous. I could spend a thousand nights in this man's arms and never grow tired of him.

You need to tell him that.

That little voice of reason, that has always been in the back of my head telling me to do the sensible thing, has disappeared. Now, it's urging me to stay with him, and any previous doubt I had that Collin and I would work together has vanished in the span of two hours.

Maybe that makes me shallow, but I feel deep down, all the way into my bones, that it's not all physical attraction. There's more to him and more to us.

I can feel it.

As crazy as it sounds, it's as if he and I were made for each other. He had alluded to feeling the same.

Mate.

The word rolls over in my mind. He told me I'm his fated mate, and he's mine.

But I'm not a werewolf.

I pull my lip into my mouth, nibbling on it as sleep begins to cloud my thoughts. *Maybe that doesn't matter.*

I yawn and finally give into the fatigue.

∾

Light penetrates my closed eyelids. Next, a feathery touch trails up my thigh. Following that, warmth presses into my side. A smile lifts my lips.

I'm dreaming.

I'm with Collin again. His strong fingers knead my legs, and then his warm mouth presses kisses near my navel. He's touching me again, kissing me, and running his hands over my body.

I sigh and arch my back.

He murmurs a sound, part growl, part groan before his hands travel around my hips to cup my ass.

My core swells when he massages my flesh. Something about this man gets me hot every time he touches me.

His rumbling pleasure follows, and the contentment oozing from him makes my breath catch.

"Part your legs," he whispers.

He sounds so real. The light penetrating my eyelids grows, and my mind registers other sounds and sensations.

A cool wind washes over my naked skin. Soft sand molds into my back beneath the blanket.

I'm not dreaming.

Collin's really touching me.

My eyes fly open to see a dawn sky above. I gasp when Collin's tongue flicks the nub between my legs. I cry out.

"Good morning, mate."

The sensations washing through my body don't give me a chance to reply. I close my eyes again, giving into the heat rolling through my core and parting my legs fully.

He settles between them as I tangle my fingers through his hair, and before I can take another breath, he's lapping my clit and doing indescribable things that make me scream.

And when his hand joins his mouth, I welcome his fingers, but it's not enough. I want *more*.

"Collin," I pant. I want him to climb on top of me, to give me what I crave. I can feel his erection by my calf. It's hard and thick, and I need it inside me.

But he ignores my demands and instead ravages me with his tongue and fingers.

I'm helpless to resist his domination.

Before I can take another breath, an orgasm has me exploding. I cry out, bucking wildly as his tongue continues to lick and lap. The waves go on and on, growing higher and higher as his fingers slip in and out of my pussy, tickling my G-spot each time.

It's agony and heaven wrapped into one.

After the earth-shattering sensations finally subside, I go limp, and he growls in satisfaction before moving up to lie beside me. I'm so thoroughly spent, even after a full night's sleep, that I can't bring myself to move. I know I should open my eyes and reciprocate what he just did to me, but I can't.

The man has completely undone me.

When I finally open my eyes, he's smiling down at me like the Cheshire Cat. I laugh, unable to help it.

"You look very pleased with yourself."

He leans down and kisses me before nipping my lip. "I am. I love making you scream."

My cheeks heat as I become aware of my bare limbs and wanton state. I'm half naked and splayed out on the blanket as if it's perfectly normal to be displayed for the entire world to see in the middle of a desert. But when I make a move to cover myself, Collin stops me.

"Don't. I love looking at you. I knew you'd be beautiful, but you're pure perfection." He runs another finger down my stomach to my thigh. My shiver follows.

"What about you?" I ask. He's wearing shorts again, but that doesn't hide his massive erection. My skin tingles, and my lady bits swell at the sight. I want to feel him, all of him, and not in my hand.

His nostrils flare, and another low growl comes from deep in his throat. "You have no idea how tempted I am, but I have to work something out first."

Before I can ask him what he means, he's on his feet and cleaning up the blankets. I roll onto my side and join him, deciding that a sandy bed isn't a bad place to sleep at all.

"What are we going to do now?" I ask, peering up at him.

The morning wind flows through his hair, making a few long tresses flutter into his eyes. He has the rest pulled back into a low ponytail, and for a moment, I just stare. The man is so freakin' attractive, it's unreal.

He gives me a crooked smile, and I swear he knows what I'm thinking. "I've decided to break one of my rules. It's the only way to properly take care of you."

"Break your rules?"

"I'm going to withdraw money from my account back home. With that, we'll have plenty to live on for a few weeks."

"A few weeks?" My eyebrows shoot up even though I sound like a parrot repeating him.

His movements slow, his brow furrowing. He finishes with the blankets, and it's not until both are tucked under his arm that he meets my gaze again. "I can't take you back home, Brianna. The SF will find you. So the only option is for you to stay on the run with me."

I swallow the thickness in my throat. I knew this was coming. As much as I didn't want to face it, deep down I knew that this was what I chose when I stayed at his side. "I'll have to call work and my friends. They'll be worried about me."

His crooked smile grows as he pushes a lock of hair behind my ear.

His touch makes my breath catch, but I manage to say, "Why are you smiling? This is hardly funny."

"No, it's not, but you're choosing to stay with me. I hoped you would, and the fact that you *are*—how can I not be happy about that?"

I bring my hand up to cover his and remember again what I felt during the night, how I knew that he means something to me even though I can't explain it. I should tell him, reassure him that it's not just him feeling things, but when I open my mouth the words don't come.

Still, his smile remains. "Let's get a move on. That town is still twenty miles away. With any luck, we'll have enough gas to reach it. And then we'll find an ATM, fill the car up and get outta here as fast as we can."

"You're not worried they'll catch us?" I step over small sagebrush as we walk back to the car.

He tenses but smiles, although it seems forced. "If we're smart, we'll evade them, but we'll have to lay low for a few days so they don't pick up my trail right away."

I manage a shaky smile, but my stomach still twists into knots. Collin has proven to be more street-smart than I'll ever be, but uneasiness fills me regardless.

Because we can't run forever even if he does secure enough money to keep us going.

Sooner or later, the SF will catch us.

CHAPTER TWENTY-THREE
COLLIN

We don't make it to town before the engine dies. Luckily, we're not far. An old Citgo gas station is a quarter mile up the road.

I put the car into neutral. "I'll push us there. Can you steer?"

Brianna nods so I get out. Through the back windshield, I watch her lithe form slip across the center of the car to the driver's seat. The beast grumbles in appreciation.

He's been strangely content since yesterday morning. Other than the random images he's thrown me of eating people's innards while I drive, he hasn't been acting unruly.

Something tells me Brianna's continued presence can be thanked for that.

Five minutes later, I push the car next to one of the station's pumps. Brianna applies the breaks and puts it into park as I check our surroundings. The lone highway stretches for miles. Mountains rise in the distance, but here, the desert rules.

I inhale the dry hot air and open the driver's door for Brianna. When she stands, I pull her close. Her scent consumes me, and before I can stop myself, I lean down to smell her hair.

Her hands automatically grip my biceps, and her small intake of breath follows.

The beast growls lowly, liking how our mate responds to us.

"We'll fill the tank with gas first," I say quietly to her. "Then we'll go inside together. Keep your head down, and use your hair to hide your face from security cameras. We can use the restrooms and grab some food before I withdraw the cash. Once I do, the clock is ticking. We'll need to move fast."

Her grip tightens. "Are you sure we need to do this? Won't we get caught if you use your debit card?"

I trail my hand across her hip. "Yes, the risk goes up, but we can't continue as we are. We need money, and this is the only way."

She's studying me, her expression impossible to read before she says softly, "You mean, this is the only way to get money without stealing it from someone."

I nod.

A slow smile spreads across her face, then she rises on her tiptoes and kisses me. She does it so fast that it catches me unaware.

"Thank you," she says and disentangles herself from my arms. "Why don't I wash the windows while you're pumping the gas?"

A warm feeling slides through me that I've made her happy. Her tall strong form dips around the back of the car. She's wearing shorts that barely cover her ass, and a tank top that highlights her lean arms and pert breasts. Thanks to what I grabbed from her room last night, her wardrobe choices aren't exorbitant, but I'm not complaining.

The warm feeling stays with me when I grasp the pump. Another car rolls up behind us, its engine loud and grinding as the scent of gas fills the air. I eye the vehicle suspiciously, but the driver gets out without giving me a second glance. He goes to the pump, his credit card already out, but when he spots Brianna, he does a double take.

She's cleaning the windows, her back to him. His gaze rakes her up and down as his credit card hangs in the air near the pump, entirely forgotten.

Brianna's none the wiser that this jackass is mentally fucking her in his mind. I slam the pump into the car and take a step toward her, positioning myself between him and her.

When the dude spots me, he takes a step back. I can only imagine what my expression looks like, but from how quickly he's backtracking I'm pretty sure I look like a scary motherfucker.

It's only when the dude completely shifts his attention back to his car that the scowl leaves my face. Still, jealously courses through me.

Jeez, Coll...

I was never a jealous man before Brianna. Women were simply something to fuck and forget. And even though I've had a few girlfriends in the past, I'd never truly *felt* anything for them, which obviously didn't go over well with them.

But with Brianna...

I rake a hand through my hair. Something tells me that this is a feeling that's going to bite me in the ass over and over again. My mate is hot, and men notice her, and even though I don't like it, I'm going to have to live with it.

"Collin?" Her question snaps me out of my mulling. She's washed the windows and is leaning against the car, her eyebrows raised as she stares at me. "Ready to go inside?"

I mentally shake myself and finish with the gas. "Yeah. Let's go." I slide an arm possessively around her waist. The dickwad behind us is looking anywhere but at my mate, but I still give him a lengthy stare just to ensure it stays that way.

Cocking her head, Brianna nudges me toward the gas station's door. I remind myself that I need to be focused right now and pay attention to the task at hand, but I also know that until I claim my mate, I'm going to have a hard time controlling these jealous impulses. I laugh internally.

Who am I kidding? Even if I claim her, I'll have a hard time controlling it.

Once we reach the door, Brianna whispers, "Can I freshen up first? I'll be quick." She twists her hands, "And since the SF is going to find out our location, can I call my friends? I promised Macy I would be at work tomorrow, and my boss is expecting me too. I need to let them know that I'm going to be gone for a while."

I nod curtly. "Just keep the calls quick."

We both head toward the restrooms, heads down. The guy at the counter barely glances at us, but I still keep our pace quick.

A few minutes later, we emerge from the restrooms. Brianna's washed her face and hands. I can tell from the cheap soap smell wafting from her skin, but it doesn't deter her natural sunshine-and-caramel scent that I love so much.

"Grab some food while I withdraw the money," I tell her. I slip my credit card into her hand. Since we're not hiding anything right now, we might as well go all out. "And make the call on my credit card on the phone back there." I jerk my thumb toward the phone in the back.

"I will." She makes quick work of grabbing food. She's strategic about it too. Instead of grabbing junk food, she loads her arms with fresh bananas and apples, bags of trail mix, power bars, a loaf of bread, a jar of peanut butter, and bottles of water and juice. She's not a junk food eater, and that pleases me. My mate takes care of herself physically, which is probably why she has such a knockout body, but it's more than that. She's smart. The foods she chose will sustain us longer than any bag of chips.

After she's dropped the groceries at the counter, the cashier begins ringing up the mountain of food while we both head toward our destinations—her to the phone and me to the ATM.

I mentally begin timing myself when I approach the machine, and a pit forms in my stomach when I pull out my debit card. I haven't used it in over a year. A part of me wonders if it'll still work. For all I know, the Wyoming pack has seized my accounts, but when I slip my card into the machine and it asks for my PIN, I let out a sigh of relief.

I withdraw the max the machine allows—three thousand—before I go to Brianna. She's on the phone, her voice quiet, but my enhanced senses allow me to easily hear her.

"Yeah, I know, but I'm fine, really I am. I'll just be gone for another few weeks cause my dad needs me right now." She gives me an anxious look, and I tap my wrist. With a quick nod of her head, she says, "Macy, I gotta go, but I'll call again when I can." She smiles sadly. "Yeah, bitch, I love you too. Talk soon."

I don't know if she's had time to call her boss yet, but regardless, we're out of time. We head toward the counter. She's wringing her hands again, and her forehead is furrowed.

Shit. She's worrying.

The cashier is waiting for us so I hand him my credit card. The entire transaction doesn't take more than thirty seconds, yet it feels like eons. I continuously look around because between using my debit and credit card, I know the SF now has a location on me.

The second the clerk gives me the receipt, I grab the bags, then Brianna's hand and haul her out of the store. She doesn't say a word.

We both slip into the hatchback, and the engine roars to life. With a stomp of the pedal, we're off. I don't look back because the clock is ticking. We have to get as far away from this place as quickly as we can.

As of three minutes and twenty seconds ago, the SF is actively hunting me, *and* they know where we are.

∼

SHE'S BITING her lip again. The Californian landscape zips by her window, but she doesn't pay it any attention. I keep my foot down on the accelerator. The old hatchback rockets down I-40, protesting at times on the hills.

We've put thirty miles behind us, but that doesn't mean we're safe. My plan is to get us to Sacramento by the evening. It's a well populated city, meaning we'll have an easy time booking a hotel without drawing attention to ourselves.

"Are you okay?" I ask her. We've both been quiet for the past half hour, me as I continually check my mirrors and surroundings for SF sedans, and her apparently lost in thought.

She runs a hand through her hair, and the long locks trail down her shoulder. "Yeah. I'm fine, I just keep thinking about my friends, job, and school."

My stomach churns. She's having second thoughts. "Do

you . . . want to talk about it?" *Shit.* I've never been good at talking through emotional stuff, but that look on her face . . .

I have to try.

She flashes me a smile. "You sound worried."

"I am." The beast growls too. He's prowling in my belly again, on high alert in case the SF shows up and knowing that Brianna's uneasy only makes his hackles rise more.

"It's fine," she says, but when I raise my eyebrows, she shrugs. "It's just that . . . I'll probably fail all of my classes this semester if I'm gone for a few weeks. I doubt my professors will be understanding, and I've already paid for my classes so that means I'm out of the money—" She shakes her head. "You know what? Never mind. You probably don't want to hear this."

I place my hand over hers to stop her fidgeting. "Actually, I do."

She bites her lip again, and if it weren't for her innocent expression, I would swear she's doing it to torment me. She turns her hand until our palms touch and our fingers thread together.

I squeeze. "Tell me. I want to know." And the crazy thing is that I *do* want to know what's eating her up. I don't know if I can make it better, but I sure as hell want to try.

"Okay." She shrugs again. "It's just that money is always tight for me, so the thought of having to pay for all of those classes again makes me kind of sick."

I frown but wait for her to continue.

"You see, I worked before starting college because I didn't want a huge debt when I graduated. I work hard now, too, six nights a week, so between that and my savings I've managed to pay for my schooling in cash. And knowing all of that hard work is now down the drain this semester because I'm here and not there—" She clasps my hand harder. "Don't look at me like that. That's not what I mean. I *want* to be here, but it's stressing me out too."

I smooth whatever expression stole across my face and take a deep breath. It's hard, though. My gut is so tight it feels like I ate rocks, cause the thought of her changing her mind and leaving me—

I remind myself that this conversation isn't about me. It's about Brianna.

"Has money always been tight? It sounds like it stresses you out a lot."

She nods. "I don't come from a rich family, and my dad has had a hard time holding a job so I send him money, too, when I can. And as you probably know, school is expensive, so I work a lot to try and make ends meet."

"Sounds tough even on a good day."

She laughs, and the sound eases some of my tension. "It can be, but it's a lot of fun too. I love college and being able to see my friends every day. I'm going to miss it when it ends."

She pulls her bottom lip into her mouth again. I'm quickly coming to learn that means she's worrying.

"You'll be able to finish." I don't know how I can promise that, but I want to reassure her. Dammit. I have to find a way to give her the life she wants. "I promise. I'll find a way to get you back to your life this semester so you can finish school."

Of course I have no idea how I'm going to do that, and from Brianna's dubious expression I have a feeling she doesn't believe me.

"It's okay if you can't." She props her elbow on the door. "Maybe I'll just have to write this semester off as much as that makes me feel sick."

"Then I'll pay you back for it. That's the least I can do.

You'll still be a semester behind your graduation schedule, but you won't have to worry about paying again."

She laughs. "And how would you do that?"

My lips curve up at the sound of her laugh. "Unlike you, I come from money, a lot of it, so getting you tuition money wouldn't be hard if I wanted to."

All laughter fades from her expression. "I don't want you to do that. You don't have to pay for me."

"Maybe I want to pay for you."

"But wouldn't that require you visiting your bank? And couldn't that ultimately lead to the supernatural police or whatever catching you?" She shakes her head vigorously. "No. No way. I'll manage just fine on my own. I'm not going to be responsible for you getting caught."

The beast rumbles in contentment at our mate's fierce tone, but the side of me that wants to take care of her, the side that says *I* should be providing for her, doesn't like the sound of it at all.

"That's not really how I work," I tell her.

She angles her body my way, and damn, her legs look amazing. "What's that mean?"

"It means that I want to pay for you and take care of you. Maybe you should let me pay your tuition."

She crosses her arms. "Do I not strike you as someone who can take care of herself?"

"On the contrary, you seem quite capable, but you're my woman, and I have every intention of providing for you."

"Your woman?" A twinkle forms in her eye. "Is that how it works nowadays, Caveman?"

I chuckle. "You can call me a caveman all you want. It won't change how I feel, and it won't change how I'll treat you. I'm going to take care of you from now on, and if you don't like it, well . . ." I shrug. "You better get used to it cause it's how I'm made."

Instead of that making her smile, she picks at her shorts.

My stomach sinks. *Shit.* Maybe she doesn't want that. But I don't know how to stop feeling this way.

"Or I could try not to take care of you, if you don't like that—"

Her large eyes glisten, and the emotion in them makes me stop. "No, it's not that. It's just that nobody's ever taken care of me."

"No one?"

She shakes her head.

"What about when you were a kid?"

She shakes her head again. "Not even then. My mom died when I was young, and my dad kind of fell apart after that. He tried to look after me, but he could barely take care of himself, so I was kind of left to deal with stuff on my own."

I frown, and my grip tightens on the steering wheel. "How old were you?"

"Five."

My jaw locks. "That's pretty young to be on your own."

"I mean, I wasn't entirely on my own. He still bought me clothes and food and whatnot, but a lot of times he'd forget to feed me, so I had to make my own meals, and I was doing my own laundry by the time I was seven. And when I had something going on at school, like a sports game, I usually had to get myself there cause he wasn't reliable." She presses her lips together, and an old pained expression forms in her eyes. "Sometimes it felt like I was the grownup, and he was the kid."

When she catches my scowl, she quickly adds, "But he's a good dad, really he is. He loves me completely, and he tries, really he does . . . he's just not very good at taking care of others, at least, not after my mom died."

"Sounds like he was pretty wrapped up in himself if he couldn't take care of his only daughter after his wife passed away."

"He's not a bad guy. He's really not. He just loved her too much." She picks at her fingernail. "My mom had depression, and she killed herself because of it, but my dad loved her, like *really* loved her. He's never remarried. And twenty years later, I still catch him staring at her picture. There's only one left of her in the house. It was too painful for him to be reminded about her after she passed, but when he does stop to look at it, he'll stand there for so long, and I can tell he's lost in his memories of her."

I frown again, trying to imagine how he must have felt. Even though I've only known Brianna for a few days, I already know that if something happened to her I would never get over it. Never. Maybe I'm being too hard on her dad, but then I shake my head.

"He could have at least done your laundry, I mean, could you even reach the buttons on the wash machine when you were seven?"

My lighthearted tone makes her laugh. "Actually, I could. I was tall even then so I just barely managed to reach them."

"Did you mix your darks and whites?"

She laughs again. "Oh yeah. My whites were a disaster. They were actually all gray, but I've learned since then. I now keep them separate."

I study her for a moment as we sail down the interstate. "You're really something, you know that?"

"Because I can do laundry?"

"Among other things but especially cause you can do laundry." I pinch her side.

She laughs again, and I take in her wide smile and tantalizing cleavage. I clear my throat and return my attention to the road, but I can tell she knew where my thoughts had shifted.

She squirms in her seat and rubs her legs together. "So where are we going?" she finally asks.

"Sacramento. We'll get a hotel room for the night."

"You mean we'll sleep in a bed?"

I give her a wicked grin. "Well, I don't know how much sleeping we'll do."

Her cheeks flush. "Does that mean we're going to . . ."

"If you'll let me."

She squirms again and the aroused scent coming off her increases. "So you don't need to work anything else out or whatever you meant this morning?"

The beast growls. He's not happy about the choice I've made. I've been thinking about it all day during the drive, and I've come to a decision. I can't claim her. It's not an option since my life is so messed up, but I *can* properly fuck her.

I'll just need to keep control of the beast so he doesn't take over and force me to claim her.

"Yeah, I have, and I can't wait to make you mine."

CHAPTER TWENTY-FOUR
BRIANNA

We arrive in Sacramento that evening, and I'm so happy to be done driving that I practically jump out. I stretch my limbs as Collin saunters to the hotel's reception area to check us in. He's wearing a cap and sunglasses and has cash and his fake ID ready. He said it's to conceal our location. Even the SF can't know our whereabouts if we use cash, fake identification, and hide our appearances behind hats and shades.

I wait by the car as a warm breeze flows across my cheeks. I'm wearing a baseball cap and sunglasses too. It was the first thing Collin insisted we buy when we stopped an hour ago to grab some supplies.

I tap my foot as I wait. We're at one of the big chain hotels that's sure to provide fluffy pillows, extended cable, and a mini bar. I'm ridiculously excited at the thought of spending the night here, especially after what Collin promised.

If you'll let me . . .

Yes please with a cherry on top. I want him. I don't know why I want him so badly, but I do.

I stretch my arms overhead as my restlessness grows. I'm so glad that the rope burns on my wrists have finally healed. The lump on my head is also gone, and only very faint bruises mar my neck from where Collin's wolf bit me. By tomorrow, I imagine I'll be one-hundred-percent.

Collin returns and gives me a key card. His fingers linger when he touches my hand. "Room 805. We should have a good view that high up."

I pocket the key card and open the backseat to pull out the backpack and the other items we picked up. Besides the hats, Collin also insisted that we buy me sturdy shoes and a few more garments. I'd protested initially, knowing his money would be burned through in no time, but he'd insisted.

And I have a feeling that insistence goes along the lines of taking care of me. Funny how I've never been a woman who needed that, but now that I have it—I grin. I'd be lying to myself if I said it didn't make me feel a little giddy.

"What's that smile for?"

I look over the roof of the car to Collin. His arms are flexed from the bags he's holding, and his bicep is the size of a grapefruit. *Damn. He's so freakin' hot.* "Nothing. Just happy I guess." And as weird as that is, I realize it's true.

He smiles and slams the door. "Are you hungry?"

"Yeah, starving actually."

"How about we order some food and then . . ."

He lets his words hang, and fuck me if it doesn't do indescribable things to my lady parts.

∽

AN HOUR LATER, we're sprawled across the king-sized bed with ten items from room service propped on various trays around us and the beginnings of a comedy movie on TV.

Collin insisted on ordering everything that sounded tempting on the menu, and I'm starting to see the difference in how we were raised. Whereas my eyes immediately went to the price tag, his only went to the descriptions. He doesn't care what everything costs, and says I shouldn't either, but I can't help but wonder how long we'll be able to stay on the run if we blow through all of his cash in a few days.

My worry must be showing because he says gently, "Brianna, There's nothing wrong with splurging on our first real night together, besides I can always withdraw more money if we need it."

"But the chance of you getting caught goes up—"

He presses a finger to my lips. "Let me worry about that."

I remind myself that he's been on the run for a long time and obviously knows what he's doing. Opening my mouth, I nip his fingertip.

His eyes darken and a rumble fills his chest. "Don't tempt me. I'm starving and want to eat, but as soon as this bed is cleared you can guarantee I'm going to fuck you senseless."

My lips part as heat floods my core. He takes a huge bite of his gourmet burger before polishing the rest of it off. I somehow manage to take another bite of the tender ribeye steak. The meat practically melts in my mouth. I then take a spoonful of the garlic mashed potatoes followed by a spear of grilled asparagus.

I swallow my bite before curiosity gets the better of me. "What did you mean earlier when you said you had to work something out first before we'd, you know . . ."

"Fuck?"

Damn if it doesn't get me hot when he talks like that. "Yeah. Fuck."

He takes another bite of food before saying, "I had to figure a few things out with my beast because he desperately wants to claim you, as do I, and that usually happens during sex."

"Claim me? And a claiming is what exactly?"

He grabs a kebab of grilled chicken and dips it into the Thai peanut sauce. He finishes it in two bites. "A claiming is what a werewolf does when he asserts ownership over a woman. If I claim you, my magic will flow into you, sealing us as one, and all other wolves will know that you're mine."

I sputter then cough, and somehow manage not to choke on my next piece of steak. *"What?* Ownership?" I sit up straighter. "If claiming me means that you *own* me, then you can tell your beast that's never happening." I pick up a piece of the chicken that fell off his kebab and throw it at him.

He grabs my wrist, stopping me when I try to pull my arm back. "I explained that badly. It doesn't mean I own you."

My chest still rises and falls at the thought of him and his beast wanting to claim ownership of me. I may be laid back most of the time, but to have any dude *own* me? Yeah, I don't think so.

I manage to pry my wrist from his grip, but I can tell he lets me go reluctantly. "Care to explain what you did mean then?" I ask and cross my arms.

He sighs. "Shit."

I just raise my eyebrows.

"Claiming is a werewolf thing. It doesn't mean I own you, not in the sense you're taking it at least. You're not a slave, and I can't boss you around, but when you're claimed it does mean to other wolves that you're off limits. All other males will be able to smell my mark on you, and if they were to touch you or try to make a move on you, they would be directly challenging me. Because of that, most wolves steer clear of claimed women." He shrugs and picks at the fries on his plate. "It's kind of peace of mind, for a werewolf, to claim his woman. It means you're mine forever, and no one else can have you."

He grows quiet after that.

I fidget and push the food away. "So being fated isn't enough? You want to claim me too?"

His eyes are glowing when he looks up. "In the worst way, but I'm not going to."

His wolf is shining through his eyes. I can see the predator in him as if he were in the room with us.

"Are all wolves this territorial?" I ask.

"Most are but especially dominant males. The more dominant a male is, the more he's driven to claim his woman."

"Is it like a status thing or something?"

He shakes his head. "More like an intrinsic response. You have to understand that wolves are naturally driven to mark what's ours, so when we claim a female, we're simply putting our stamp on her so other wolves know she's off limits."

"So it's like peeing on a tree, except I'm the tree."

He chuckles. "I guess you could look at it like that."

I massage my temples. "This is pretty weird."

"It wouldn't be if you were a werewolf. You would already know that I want to claim you based off how I've been acting."

"But I'm not a werewolf," I say with a frown.

"I know."

"So what did you figure out that means you're now okay with having sex?"

He pulls me closer to him, and I settle against his chest. "Quite simply, I realized that claiming you isn't an option, and I had to make sure my beast understands that too. Knowing him, he'll probably still push me to do it, but I'll have to resist."

"Do you think you can?"

"For you, I can do anything."

I run my finger along his chest. "And why have you decided that claiming me isn't a good idea?"

His eyes grow hooded when my finger strays down to his abs. "Because when a claiming happens the male's magic flows into the female, and not only does it permeate the female's scent so all other males know she's claimed, but it also links her to the male. They form a mental link, which means they can feel each other's emotions."

My eyes bug out, and I push against him so I can sit up straight. "Wait, what? If you claimed me, I could *feel* you?"

He nods. "Which means that if I ever get caught by the SF and taken away, you would still have me with you, but I'm not willing to do that to you."

"Why not?"

"Because then you would have to experience everything I was going through. Prison, a trial, and probably execution even though the supernatural community claims it doesn't have capital punishment. I don't know if I can do that to you."

My brow furrows. Just the thought of him being taken from me is hard enough, but to think he'd be subjected to execution . . .

I throw my arms around him. "You can't be taken away. We have to make sure you're not caught."

His arms automatically lock around me, holding me tightly. "I'm going to do everything in my power to ensure that never happens."

A deep shuddering breath fills my chest when I inhale. "Good."

He strokes my hair, threading his fingers through it before he inhales my scent. He lies me back on the bed and stretches my arms above me to rest on the pillow. He then runs a finger down my arm, which makes me shiver. "I would die for you, Brianna. You know that, right?"

Heat pricks my eyes, and I blink back the moisture that threatens to fill them. "I know. I can feel it."

He nuzzles into my neck and kisses above my collarbone. Another shiver follows. "Let me love you tonight. I won't claim you, but I want to feel you, *all* of you."

I arch my neck to give him better access. "Do you have a condom? I'm on birth control, so I won't get pregnant, but what about diseases?"

"I can't give you a STD. Werewolves don't carry them, and if you're on birth control, we won't need any further protection."

My lips part when he runs his tongue along my skin.

"Please, babe, let me fuck you. I'm dying to feel you."

My breath catches as my heart patters. All I can manage is one word. "Yes."

CHAPTER TWENTY-FIVE
COLLIN

The food trays are scattered on the bed so I make quick work of removing them, then shut the TV off. Silence descends except for the quiet hum from the fan and my mate's soft pants. The setting sun dips the bed into shadows, and the woman lying on it is the most gorgeous creature I've ever seen.

Brianna is still stretched out on the mattress. Her long arms drape over her head, and her lean legs bend at the knees. She's so beautiful that I want to stare, but the look on her face—the look that says she's dying for me to fuck her—makes my cock throb.

I'm back on the bed in seconds, climbing over her. She parts her legs, letting me nestle between them.

She's already wet. Dampness coats her thin shorts, and the heady scent filling my nostrils tells me she's thoroughly aroused. Still, I want her hotter.

"I want to make you scream," I whisper to her.

She moans when I nip at her neck, then run my tongue along her ear. The beast is prowling inside me again, urging me to elongate my teeth and bite her, but I vehemently push him down and concentrate on pleasing our mate.

One thing I'm sure of, a claiming won't be happening tonight.

Brianna threads her fingers through my hair when I kiss her. Her lips are so soft and pliant, but she quickly turns demanding. She meets my every nip and bite with one of her own.

We taste one another and explore. I run my hands up and down her limbs, soaking up the feel of her smooth skin and firm flesh, and when I peel her clothes off she readily complies until she's lying naked in front of me.

"Fuck you're amazing." I stare down at her strong body. She's toned and hard, yet has flaring hips and round breasts. I look my fill, and with each second that passes, I can smell her arousal growing.

"You're wearing too many clothes," she teases.

I chuckle and strip my shirt off, and when I drop my shorts, her eyes widen. My cock is hard and ready. It's pulsing with need for her, and she eagerly reaches for it.

Before I can pull back and demand that I please her first, her lips are closing around my length, and she's sucking me into her mouth.

I hiss in a breath and try to slow her down, but she's sucking me like her favorite lollipop.

"Bri," I say hoarsely. I force myself to sit back on my haunches before I blow my load in her mouth. The movement makes my dick pop out.

She looks up at me, her eyes dark with desire, her lips glistening. I groan and push her back on the bed.

She readily complies and reaches for me, legs spread and back arching. My cock is so hard now that it's painful, but I'm determined to make this last.

I yank her up the bed, and her boobs bounce. Her dark

areolas are pebbled with desire, and her nipples are taut buds, like sweet raspberries beckoning me to taste them.

I suck one of her peaks into my mouth while kneading the flesh. She cries out and threads her fingers through my hair again, holding me at her breast as I lick and suck before moving to the other.

I sample each tit until her nipples are thick and protruding, and when I dip a hand between her legs to feel her, her eyes roll back in her head.

I groan. *Wet. She's so incredibly wet.*

I pull back, getting a whimper from her, but I want to see her. I spread her legs wider, and she bucks, trying to get closer to my cock.

"Not yet." I let a hint of alpha power wash into my words.

She freezes as goose bumps rise on her flesh. A devilish smile spreads across her face, and the arousal coming off her increases a hundred-fold.

Ah, so my mate likes it when I dominate her. Good. That suits the wolf in me well.

"So beautiful." I run my hand along her mound again, and she sucks in a breath. Her core is moist and glistening, her womanly lips swollen and ready.

She grinds against my fingers. Her movements turn urgent, and the desire flowing between us works her into a frenzy.

"Collin. Now," she demands.

I tap her pussy. "Not yet." I use my alpha power again, and her hips stop.

"Please," she whimpers.

"No."

She groans but does as my power commands.

I chuckle and release my control over her, before I shift

upward and trail kisses down her neck. I then flip her over on her stomach. She's writhing now and pushes herself onto all fours.

I move behind her, and she rocks back on her knees forcing her ass against my crotch. My tip rubs against her entrance, and I nearly come undone.

She pushes more, and my cock slips inside her, just enough to cover the head.

Her deep moan fills the room, but I grab her ass before she can sheathe me fully and pull out.

She snarls and looks over her shoulder. If she were a lioness, her claws would be out.

I chuckle. "My hot little eager, mate. You're almost ready but not yet." Another rush of alpha magic flows from me, and she gasps when it hits her.

She's panting now. I lean down and run my tongue up her core, but she can't fight my power. Quivering muscles and harsh breaths come from her, but I keep my hold on her so she can't move. I know she needs release, but I'm not done tormenting her.

She pants harder as her tits hang, brushing against the sheets. The sight makes me groan as I slip a finger inside her, teasing her, before I pull it out and lick her clit again.

She moans loudly, her head and back arching. "Collin. Please. Now. *Please*."

Shit, this is agony.

With her pussy in my face, I'm clouded in her scent. I'm ready to come just smelling her.

I take a deep breath and get back on my knees. I grasp her ass and, jaw tight, I push into her. She moans in pleasure as I enter her slowly, inch by inch. Her body expands. She's so tight and hot. Shudders wrack her body as her channel stretches and clenches around me.

She cries out, and her fingers turn into claws, digging into the pillows. "More!"

"Damn, woman, you don't know what you're doing to me." Sweat drips down my temple. Not being able to slow myself anymore, I plunge my length completely inside her.

She screams again and arches her back. I feel every inch of her hot, slick channel. Even though she's a tall strong woman, her core is tight and grips my shaft like a glove.

"Fuck me. Fuck me hard." Her demands turn primal, but I'm more than happy to oblige.

I pull out until only my tip is inside her, then plunge into her again. I tilt my hips, rubbing her with my entire length.

"Yes," she moans.

I do it again, pulling out just enough to make her whimper before filling her again.

She groans and writhes, and I slowly pick up the tempo, going faster and faster, deeper and harder until Brianna completely loses control. She bucks and claws at the pillows, and I've never seen anything so hot in my life.

I'm on the verge of blowing my load, and I know she's seconds away from coming, so I pull out and flip her onto her back again.

My cock is glistening from her wetness, and she reaches between us and grabs my dick. Desire clouds her eyes, and a wildness coats her expression. Her long fingers encircle my length before she begins pumping me up and down and pulling me back to her core.

"I need you. Inside me. Now."

I groan. My erection is throbbing, but I'm not ready yet for this to end.

I growl and grab her wrists. She cries out at my rough touch, but the desire coating her gaze tells me that she likes it. Good. I'm not in a gentle mood.

I pin both of her arms above her head with one hand and reach down with my other. I touch her lightly at first, soft swirls that have her limbs tensing and her back arching. She cries out again, moaning when I run a finger up her slit.

"So wet," I murmur. I bring my finger to my mouth, first to smell her scent then to taste her again.

She tries to force me down. I know she wants me to enter her again, but I only place my tip at her entrance, still playing with her.

She snarls and raises her hips, trying to force me inside her.

"One more taste, then I'm going to fuck you senseless." I release her hands and she immediately reaches for me. I *tsk*. "Nah-ah. Hands up." Alpha power washes through my words.

She seethes, which makes me grin. My mate has turned into a she-beast, all pants and needs.

Once her arms are positioned above her head, I kneel between her legs and spread them open.

She willingly complies and shudders when I position my head between her thighs. I lick her core, and she arches again, crying out. She's so swollen, and her clit is a hard nub. I taste her again and again.

Within seconds, she's on the verge of coming again, and I know if I don't finish fucking her she'll come on my face, and I'll probably jizz all over the bed.

So I move upward until I'm kneeling, then take my dick in my hand. I prod her entrance with my tip. She moans again.

"Please, Collin! Please!" Her heels work their way up my thighs until she's digging into my ass, pushing me closer to her core.

"Only cause you asked nicely." I grab the headboard

with one hand and cup her ass in the other. She tilts her hips, and I plunge into her.

She screams, so I pull out and pound into her again. I don't mess around this time. I bang her in earnest, and I'm fucking her so hard that sweat erupts across my body. Within seconds, her orgasm builds.

She tilts her hips more, her moans growing louder, her screams sharper. I can feel her climbing the peak as her waves begin to build.

And I'm right there with her.

"Yeah, baby. Come for me."

My command is her undoing, and her orgasm explodes around me.

Her scream sends me over the edge, and I slam into her one last time, roaring when my seed shoots out. The headboard shakes against the wall as my mate's pussy tightens around my length again and again.

Her scream is relentless as our orgasms go on and on. I buck again and it feels as if my body is completely out of control. It feels as though it goes on forever until stars explode in my vision.

We stay locked as one, our bodies spasming, our skin slick with sweat, until I collapse on top of her. She pants in my ear, and her body turns to jelly.

Minutes, hours, days pass. I can't be sure. All I know is that we were just transported to another dimension.

"Oh. My. God," she finally breathes.

I'm panting too hard to respond. It still feels as if I can't get enough oxygen. My mate has completely wrecked me.

"That was amazing," she whispers.

I press my forehead to hers before kissing her softly.

When we both finally come back to reality, I push up on my forearms so I'm not squishing her completely, but I still struggle to speak. All I can do is stare into her eyes, completely at loss for words.

Sex has never—*never*—been that intense for me with anyone.

Brianna blows a strand of hair out of her eyes, then smiles lazily. She meets my gaze, and I know that my eyes are glowing because my wolf is so close. He still wants me to lean down, bite her, and claim her, but I know I can't. Still, I don't try to hide him.

Her chest heaves as she places a soft kiss on my lips. I kiss her back, my tongue flicking out to run along her lip.

"That was—" She moans and closes her eyes, obviously still savoring it.

I try to slow my breathing, but fuck, it's hard. "The most incredible experience you've ever had?"

She nods.

"Same, baby. Same."

Her lips part, and I lean down to kiss her again before I gather her in my arms. She snuggles into me, and our limbs entwine.

Outside, the sun has fully set and a deep red glow coats the horizon. I run my hand up and down Brianna's back and hold her closely.

I've never been an emotional guy after sex, but fuck me if my insides aren't twisting and turning right now.

I love her.

I love her more than I ever thought it was possible to love someone, and I think she loves me too.

"You are *mine*," I growl.

"Yes. Always."

Hearing her immediate conviction settles something inside my wolf. I can feel something crack in him, the deranged cocoon that encases his mind fissures.

The beast growls in contentment when Brianna settles in my arms to sleep. Our mate is safe. She's with us, and she's ours.

And if there's one thing I'm certain of—that I feel all the way into my bones—is that this woman is made for me.

Now, I just have to figure out how I can keep her, because I know I'm never letting her go.

∼

I WAKE her again an hour later. The second time is slower and more reverent. We explore each other's bodies instead of working into a fuckfest frenzy. Love shines in my eyes. I can't hide it. So I hold her to me, cherishing her and loving her until she screams my name again.

And after that, we do it a third time, except faster and more urgent, our bodies demanding that we bite and claw until my alpha power rises up and puts my mate in her place.

She giggles when I do that. I think my mate has secretly harbored a crush for some nasty domineering sex, and my wolf-side is more than happy to comply.

So it's not until the wee hours of the morning that we finally fall asleep, but come sunrise, we're at it again.

I can't get enough of her.

We make love two more times before we fall asleep and wake around nine in the morning for the day. And when we wake for good, we do it again.

"It's like I can't get enough of you," she whispers when she spreads her legs.

"It's because we're a new mating," I tell her. "It's like this when all mates find one another."

"But when will it be enough?" she asks when I slide inside her, and we begin to move.

I groan in pleasure but manage to say, "In a few months? There's a reason newly mated couples are left alone by the pack."

She shudders when I fill her completely. "I can see why."

CHAPTER TWENTY-SIX
COLLIN

Despite wanting to keep Brianna in bed for weeks, we don't stay long in Sacramento. After four days of endless fucking and loving and more fucking, we finally leave. I've pushed the limits by staying this many days, and we need to keep moving.

Sunlight fills the room, revealing a tangle of bedsheets that reek of sex. I inhale, and my dick hardens again, but I know we don't have time for another round, so I concentrate on collecting our things.

"Where will we go from here?" she asks as we pack our bags.

"Where do you want to go?"

She cocks her head. "We can go anywhere?"

"Within reason. We just need to keep moving."

A smile parts her lips. "I've never been to Seattle, and I've always wanted to go."

"Sounds like we'll be seeing the Space Needle then."

She laughs, and the sound makes the beast and I puff up in pleasure. Even though we haven't claimed her, the bond is growing stronger, and the beast is pleased. And on top of that, it's been twenty-four hours since I've received a sick fantasy from him. Considering the norm for months has been hourly images of him murdering and devouring—twenty-four hours of nothing is a miracle.

Of course, our obsession with Brianna can be thanked for that. She's all the beast thinks about now too.

"Do I still have to wear this?" She holds up the hat.

I zipper the pack closed. "Just until we're on the road. You don't need to wear it while we're driving."

She nods and slips it on. Her long dark hair tumbles down her back, and she looks so damned cute that I have to force myself to gather the last few things instead of pulling her into my arms, but when she turns and I eye her curvy ass filling out her shorts, I can't help myself.

I growl. "Just once more before we go."

She squeals when I grab her around the waist and drop her on the bed, but already she's reaching for me and spreading her legs.

I shake my head. "What have you done to me woman?"

Her eyes darken, lust filling them again and instead of replying she grabs my shirt and pulls me in for a kiss.

∽

We somehow manage to get downstairs before checkout time, and we make quick work of leaving the Sacramento. By evening, we're in Seattle. Watching Brianna's joy at seeing a new city and feeling her giddiness when the Space Needle appears clenches my heart.

I take a deep breath. I've fallen so fast and hard for this woman. It's crazy that it's only been a week since I abducted her.

"Where will we stay?" she asks.

"Are you up for camping?" I turn toward the Cascade

Range just east of the city and watch her anxiously. I want to give her the world, but I also can't afford to keep us in hotels every night. "We can explore the city tomorrow if we're careful, but I—" I grimace. My pride doesn't let me continue. It's embarrassing that I don't have enough money to keep us in five-star accommodations every night, but the reality is that I don't.

Her hand covers mine. "Camping's fine. I've always liked to camp."

The feel of her soothes something inside me. I turn my hand over, and our fingers thread together. The beast settles more, too, curling up inside me since our mate is still happy.

We stop along the way and buy a cheap tent and sleeping bags at an outdoor store, and an hour later, I pull into a rustic campground.

She doesn't blink an eye that I pick a tent-only campground. There isn't running water or electrical hookups, which means there aren't any RVs.

"How does this look?" I ask.

"Perfect." She eyes one of the hiking trails by the campsite check-in wistfully.

I follow her gaze. "Do you want to go hiking?"

She grins. "Could we? I would love to go for a run, and since we're in the wild now, we probably won't need to wear these, right?" She waves at her cap and shades.

"No, we don't." I run a finger along her arm, wanting to touch her for the sake of touching her. She shivers. "Do you want to set up the tent or run first?"

"Run."

We run for forty-five minutes and cover at least eight miles. The terrain varies, and since Brianna's not as fast as me I slow my pace to accommodate her, but that doesn't stop my frequent side-eye and grins when the trail's wide enough for us to run side by side.

She's panting when we get back to the campsite and cocks her head. "What's so funny? You've been smiling the entire time."

I raise my eyebrows. "I have?"

She nods and bends her knee to stretch her quad. "Yeah. Do I have something in my teeth?"

My smile doesn't lessen. "No, nothing's in your teeth and nothing's funny. Am I really smiling like an idiot?"

She laughs. "Kind of, although I wouldn't call you an idiot."

I shake my head and sling an arm around her shoulders, drawing her close. We're both sweaty, but it doesn't deter me. "I'm just impressed is all."

Her eyelids flutter when I lean down to press a kiss on her neck. "Impressed with what?"

"You. I don't know many human women that can run that fast for that long, especially on terrain that steep."

She tilts her head up and makes eye contact. "But you know werewolf women who can?"

I nod.

We head toward the car to grab the tent. Her eyebrows draw together as we approach the vehicle. "Have you ever dated a human woman before?"

"A few."

She stiffens and opens the hatchback's door. "How many is a few?"

Shit. I don't want to answer this.

She crosses her arms and faces me. "How many women have you dated?"

I rake a hand through my hair. "None that have ever meant anything."

She grinds her teeth together and mutters under her breath about her reaction being ridiculous and that she's dated other guys, too, but I can still smell the jealousy rolling off her. She's swimming in it.

I slam the car door and haul her against my chest. "You're the only woman I want now, Brianna."

She struggles and pushes me, but I don't let her go. "How many have there been?"

Shitting shit shit. I *really* don't want to answer that.

She makes a disgusted sound and tries again to free herself, but I refuse to let her go. "I've only had a few girlfriends before you, but yeah, I've been with a lot of women, and I'm sorry about that. If I'd met you sooner, that never would have happened."

She bites her lip. "How many girlfriends have you had?"

"Three."

"And how many others have you slept with?"

My jaw works, and I don't respond.

"Do you even know how many?"

I eventually shake my head. "No."

"*That* many?" She makes another disgusted sound before saying, "What about your girlfriends. How long were you with them?"

"I was with Cali the longest—"

She covers her ears. "I don't want to know their names!"

Man am I fucking this up. Wincing, I pry her hands away from her ears. "Babe, seriously, don't worry about them. Please. It's only you now. It will only *ever* be you now."

I gather her closer to me and nuzzle her neck. Her heart is still pounding, and I can taste her annoyance, so I press myself more against her before kissing her neck again. "Baby, you're the only one I want. Just you. Only you. I never wanted any of them like I want you." I keep up my reassurances until she sags against me.

She shakes her head. "I'm sorry. I've never been the jealous type. I don't know what's the matter with me."

I kiss her deeply, flicking my tongue against hers. The jealousy and irritation leave her scent as arousal takes its place. I growl in response. "It's okay. I don't mind that you're jealous. It means that our mating bond is strong."

"The mate thing makes me feel this way?"

I nod.

"But I'm human."

"It doesn't matter. We're fated even though you're human."

"Right." She pulls back and grabs the water bottle. When finished drinking, she hands the rest to me.

Our fingers brush when I take it. "Should we stake the tent? Before we crawl inside it together?"

She takes another deep breath, and my stomach tightens. I think she's forgiven me for being with so many women, but I'll reassure her all night long if she needs it to feel secure with me.

But instead of that jealous glint filling her eyes again, she smiles coyly. "Yeah, let's stake it and crawl inside together.

∽

BRIANNA SEEMS to have fully gotten over her jealous stint by the next morning. I'm pretty sure the fact that I made love to her three times during the night helped.

Mid-morning, we leave the campsite to venture into the city. It's easy to blend into the masses, but we're still careful about concealing our identities. I keep Brianna close too.

Seattle isn't that far from Boise—where the Supernatural Forces headquarters reside—which means we're more likely to run into SF members here.

"Have you ever been to the top?" she asks when we step into the Space Needle elevator.

"Can't say that I have." I smile down at her, loving how carefree she is today as the doors ding close.

Since we're not alone in the elevator, we don't talk further. It hasn't escaped my attention that neither of us have spoken of the SF since leaving Quintin Valley, nor have we mentioned Declan. I've kept an ear out for anything on the news about him, but so far, there's been no mention of a mangled body being discovered in an Arizona desert.

The elevator glides to the top, and when we step out Brianna tugs me to the window. It's a weekday so not overly busy, and it's easy to find an open spot to enjoy the view.

"Oh my god, Collin. Look!"

The panoramic image of the city is breathtaking. Puget Sound glistens like an ocean of sparkling rain drops, Mount Rainier rises like a dome, the Cascades loom to the east, and spread out beneath us is the sprawl of the city.

Brianna grins and takes it all in, and even though I find the view impressive my attention lingers on her. She's wearing shorts again, which reveals her long shapely legs. I could stare at them all day, even though I would rather have them wrapped around my waist.

And if that's not enough to captivate my attention, she keeps making little breathy noises whenever she sees something new, and she's been chattering in excitement nonstop since we reached the observation deck. The pure happiness radiating from her makes the beast and I growl contentedly.

"Collin! I think I just saw a whale!" She squeals again, which makes me grin.

We meander around the deck, taking our time to enjoy it all. When we reach the opposite side, she steps closer before slipping her arm around my waist. She tilts her chin up and smiles. "What do you think?"

"I think it's almost as beautiful as you." I kiss her forehead and she squeezes me more.

"Thank you for taking me here." She lays her head against my chest, and my heart swells at her quiet declaration.

"I'll take you anywhere you want." I wrap my arm around her waist, loving the feel of her pressed against me.

We stand like that for a few minutes before she says, "Do you think there's anything to drink up here?" She licks her lips. "I didn't think to pack a water bottle."

I lean down to kiss her again, except this time I press my mouth to her neck. Goose bumps rise on her skin, and she shivers. "I'll go check," I reply and nip her earlobe, which causes another intake of her breath.

Regretfully, I let her go and head toward the café. I have to step around groups and other couples on the way. Out of habit, I scan the crowd and keep an eye out for the SF. I don't usually run into SF members at random like this, but it has happened on a few occasions, so I never let my guard down. Luckily, during the other occasions, I detected them before they detected me.

After buying a couple of water bottles from the café, I head back toward where I left Brianna. I circle around the observation deck, the scents of humans, cleaning agents, cooking from the café, and exhaust from the city streets below filling the air.

But it's on my next inhale that I stop dead in my tracks. My grip tightens around the water bottles as my nostrils flare. I inhale again, more deeply, and know without any doubt that there's another werewolf up here.

My jaw clenches, and I pick up my pace. Most likely, the wolf isn't from the SF. If he is, I would have detected scents from other supernaturals since SF members never work alone unless they're doing a covert mission.

But my jaw still clenches when I round the corner because if I can smell him that means he can smell me, too, and as much as my mate is enjoying her time up her, I'm going to have to cut it short.

"Brianna, we—" I ground to a stop when I see her talking to a guy. He's around six-two with a scruffy beard, and he's wearing aviator sunglasses. His shoulders are broad, his stomach flat, and the scent coming off him confirms one thing.

I've found the wolf.

He's trying to engage my mate in conversation, but she's twisting her hands and biting her lip. Her blatant anxiety has my hackles rising and the beast snarling. I see red as I cross the distance between us.

When I come into view, a relieved smile parts her lips, and she steps toward me. I cross the remaining distance between us in three quick strides and wrap an arm protectively around her, my gaze never leaving the other werewolf.

Anxiety eclipses Brianna's natural caramel-and-sunshine scent, which makes my hands curl around the water bottles. The wolf is still watching her. With his sunglasses on, I can't assess his eyes, but everything about his stance and avid interest in my mate tells me that he finds her as appealing as I do.

My grip on the water bottles increases, and Brianna

pries them from my hands. "Brianna. Time to go," I tell her in clipped tones.

The wolf smirks. We both stare at one another, so I let a swell of alpha magic flow from me. I'm careful to control it, so it doesn't touch any of the humans in the surrounding area. When it hits him, he stiffens, and the amused smile on his face disappears.

Before I can turn, his own magic barrels into me. Brianna gasps when it hits her. She folds inward, and my jaw grinds when I feel his strength. I don't bow to it, but it does tell me one thing.

He's not a lesser wolf.

The beast's magic rises at the blatant challenge, so I concentrate on Brianna. I can't lose control of the beast here, not with so many witnesses.

And to make matters worse, since the other wolf doesn't retreat when I assert my dominance, and since his own magic rivals mine, I know he's one of two things: an alpha or another rogue.

And since he's not an alpha I recognize, I know that means I've just encountered option two.

Fuck.

He's not the first rogue I've run into during the past two years, but he is the first I've encountered with Brianna at my side. And right now, I know the only thing that's stopped us from shifting and fighting is this very public location.

I grind my teeth. He's probably on the hunt if he's at a tourist venue. Tourists are easy to pluck off. They're in strange cities, nobody knows them, and if they go missing, it's usually days or weeks before family and friends know.

But the fact that I'm a rogue and I'm here with a human will inevitably pique his curiosity. Since when do rogues travel with a woman?

I wheel Brianna around and haul her toward the elevator. Only one thought fills my mind—I need to keep her safe.

The other rogue's magic pulses toward me. I can feel him begin to follow us.

Fuck. Fuck. Fuck.

"Collin?" Brianna says worriedly as we step into the elevator.

But our retreat doesn't stop his interest. Before the doors can close, he slaps his hand between them, and they begin to open again.

Brianna gasps, and my claws are out before the rogue can act further. I slash his hand, breaking the skin wide open before I punch him in the chest. He flies backward, obviously not anticipating my aggressive attack, and the surrounding humans yelp at the display.

But I don't let the witnesses stop our retreat. The doors begin to slide close again as the rogue comes to his feet. That cocky smile is back on his face just as the doors seal, and that smile tells me one thing.

He's coming for us.

CHAPTER TWENTY-SEVEN
COLLIN

"Collin what the hell was that?"

It's the third time she's asked me the question, but I still haven't responded. Only one thought fills my mind—I need to get her out of here. Now.

I'm dragging her down the street, my long strides eating up the pavement. My skin is rippling, heat barreling through me. I'm seconds away from losing control, and my mate's still not safe.

"Collin?" she says again when we round the city block and the stolen car comes into view.

"Not now," I finally manage and wrench the door open before stuffing her inside.

She sputters again, but I'm already at my door, slipping into my seat, and hotwiring the vehicle before she can question me further.

The tires squeal when I pull out from the parking spot. I glance in my mirrors and catch sight of the rogue on the corner of the block. He smirks as he watches us retreat. Just as I suspected, he followed us.

"Fuck!" I bellow, which makes Brianna jump. It takes

another moment of erratic driving and weaving in and out of traffic before I realize I've completely terrified her.

I force myself to take a deep breath and eye her anxiously. "Are you okay?" I ask.

She nods and clasps her shaking hands together. "Yeah, I'm fine. I just—" She licks her dry lips. "He's another werewolf, isn't he?"

I nod once.

She drags a hand through her hair, and I clench the steering wheel tightly. All of my instincts are screaming at me to get her as far away from here as possible. My nostrils flare when I remember the push of his magic. He's strong—as strong as me—which means he's probably been a rogue even longer than I've been, which almost guarantees his wolf *and* human mind are completely psychotic.

In other words, we can't stay anywhere near here.

"We're leaving Washington."

She opens one of the water bottles and takes a drink. "Okay," she says, sounding worried but clearly not understanding how grave this situation is.

"We have to leave, Brianna. That guy was a rogue, and he's shown interest in you. And the fact that I just whisked you away will only intrigue him further. He probably thinks I've found a rare prize that I'm savoring, or he'll wonder why I haven't already killed and eaten you. Either way, he'll be doubly interested now."

"So he knows you're a rogue too?"

"Most likely. He had to have felt it in my power. Rogues are notoriously strong. It's the only reason we survive as long as we do."

She shudders, but it's important that she understands what just happened.

"So we need to keep driving and leave him far behind."

She nods firmly, and some of the tension leaves my

shoulders. "Okay, then you're right. We need to leave Washington."

I sit back in my seat and tell myself that distance will keep her safe. Most rogues lose interest in a victim if the hunt becomes too time intensive, but some . . .

My nostrils flare, and unease roils my gut.

Some rogues revel in the challenge and won't stop until they've found their prey.

∼

We stay on the move for three solid days, only stopping to camp at night. I can tell my mate doesn't enjoy the monotonous sixteen-hour travel days, but I need to put distance between her and the rogue. Not to mention the entire western region is crawling with other wolves since the three American packs reside in Montana, Wyoming, and Idaho. That and the SF headquarters are there. Sometimes hiding in plain sight has worked to my advantage, but with a rogue now interested in her—I'm not taking any chances.

It isn't until we cross the Mississippi river that I lessen my manic driving. Brianna seems to sense the change in me. Her mood brightens, and teasing once again laces her words.

We return to sightseeing and venturing to places she's never traveled to, but it's only when we begin our second week together that I truly breathe easier.

It's been seven days since the incident in Seattle. I haven't seen or detected the rogue since. We're now two thousand miles away, and I've only scented the SF once. That run-in had been in passing when we'd driven through Missouri. The SF hadn't been hunting me in that encounter—instead they were after a coven of witches practicing black magic—so we'd stolen away as quietly as we'd come, slipping right under their noses without them even knowing it.

The grassy Kentucky landscape surrounds us just outside Louisville. We've stopped for the night and have laid out a picnic dinner by a small creek outside the city. Brianna's stretched out on the blanket and munches an apple while she studies a pamphlet she picked up at the last gas station.

"Have you ever watched a horse race?" she asks. She's studying the colorful pages, flipping through the local attractions. Since we're in Kentucky, race tracks are prolific.

"Actually, no I haven't."

"Do you want to?"

"Yeah, we can do that tomorrow."

We haven't staked the tent yet. We've been mostly camping at campgrounds, but since nobody's been around this area all evening, I'm pretty sure we can sleep here even though it's not legal. The car is hidden by a patch of dense trees, and our tent is green so it won't be easily spotted by cars driving by on the narrow highway just around the bend. All in all, it's a pleasant spot to spend the night.

"Looks like the track's open in the morning." She finishes her apple and props her head in her hand. It's warm here, so she's wearing shorts and a tank. I drink in the sight of her.

It's crazy that I've already fucked her three times today, and I'm already looking for an excuse to get in her pants again.

She eyes me mischievously and rolls more to her side, which squishes her tits together and reveals her tantalizing cleavage. "See something you like?"

My cock hardens, and I chuckle. "Better watch what

you say woman, or I'll have you flat on your back before you can blink."

She flutters her eyelashes. "Is that a threat or a promise?"

I shake my head, my chest rumbling with laughter. My mate is proving to be quite an entertaining little vixen. "Come here, you," I say and dip a finger into her shirt to pull down her top more. The thin material isn't showing nearly enough of her delectable breasts.

She leans closer to me, her eyes already closing in anticipation of my kiss.

I'm less than an inch away from devouring her mouth when the hairs on the back of my neck stand on end.

Before her lids can fully close, I'm standing with my hands fisted at my sides. I inhale deeply, and my stomach turns to ice when a familiar scent taints the breeze.

No!

I haul Brianna up and off the blanket just as the rogue strolls into the clearing. A menacing gleam coats his eyes, and a grin splits across his face.

"Well, well, well. What do we have here?" He laughs, the sound both deranged and filled with glee.

I don't respond since I've already flown from the picnic area with Brianna in my arms. I have her locked in the car before she can scream.

"Start the car, Brianna, and get out of here!"

But her eyes stay wide, and she frantically shakes her head.

"Go!" I yell. I've taught her how to hotwire the hatchback, but it's not until my second bellow that she scoots under the dash and gets to work.

I've already wasted too much time. The rogue is only ten feet away, and he cackles when the car stutters but refuses to start.

"She must be something, that luscious human you've found." He cranes his head to try and see around me, but I've blocked Brianna from view since I'm standing at the car's edge. "Does she taste as good as she smells? Oh wait, you wouldn't know since you're keeping her for a pet, although I imagine you've tasted what's between her legs. Perhaps I'll start there before I rip into her flesh."

Rage explodes inside me. The beast lunges against his restraints, but I force him down. I have to keep the rogue talking. I can't fight him until Brianna escapes.

"How did you find us?"

He chuckles. "It wasn't easy. I had to, how shall I put it?" He taps his chin. "*Coerce* a seer to help me. Good thing I plucked a strand of your human's hair for the seer to use." His eyes flash, and that crazy gleam returns.

The car stutters again, then starts. My heart surges with hope, but in the next instant the engine dies.

Fuck!

The rogue takes another step my way. I bristle, readying myself for what will inevitably come. I know that the seer he consulted is dead, just as I know Brianna will be, too, if I don't kill the old rogue first.

The beast snarls and rages again. He desperately wants to be let loose. Fiery power rolls through me, and my magic swells like a tsunami. I'm seconds away from my control snapping.

"You don't touch her," I say through gritted teeth.

The old rogue grins wickedly. "We'll see about that."

He springs into the air and shifts instantaneously, but I'm just as fast. I unleash the beast, giving into his need for bloodlust.

We clash in mid-air, and Brianna screams. A part of me knows that she hasn't gotten away, but it's too late to stall him any longer.

Magic erupts in the clearing as the old rogue goes for my throat. He may be old and powerful, but I'm an alpha by birthright, and the beast has only made me stronger. I deflect his jaws by ducking my head and twisting. My unmerciful need to protect my mate infuses speed into my already blurred attack.

I will die before he touches her.

Snarls tear around us. Instinct takes over. My beast lunges, bites, rips, and tears at the rogue. He comes at us just as fast, his jaws snapping and slashing while high-pitched growls reverberate from his chest.

Blood pores from his wounds. Skin flaps by my leg. Only seconds have passed yet we're both relentless in our need to destroy one another.

A flash to my left shows movement just before the car revs and gravel spins. *My mate is getting away.*

A millisecond of relief flows through me, but that instantaneous distraction allows the old rogue an opportunity to latch onto the beast's shoulder. His bite is ferocious, and pain sears through my nerve endings.

The beast whines when our flesh is torn away before ducking and clamping onto the rogue's front paw.

The rogue howls in fury and spins. Our movements turn into a blur again as blood flies like splattered paint around us. The scent of magic and rage swell in the clearing, and the bubbling creek sloshes around the beast's paws.

I'm losing my grip on the beast. He's nearly taken complete control. I cling to the sliver of my human side that remains, knowing that the taste of blood could send the beast back into his psychotic mindset.

He could start killing again after this fight.

That means we would lose Brianna.

I can't let that happen.

But that sliver of my human side works against the beast. I'm clashing with the beast's instincts to maim and kill, and the old rogue must sense that. His attacks strengthen.

The old rogue kicks up dust from the gravel, trying to blind us. The beast whips his head at the last possible second, but the distraction allows the old rogue to tear another piece of flesh from our side.

Blood gushes onto our underbelly. *Shit!*

The old rogue's deranged compulsions make him deadly since fear of retribution doesn't cloud his judgment.

Not like ours.

But I can't allow the beast to digress to who he was. The risk of losing Brianna is too great.

The beast lunges again, fighting valiantly despite me hindering him. He pushes the old rogue back onto the grass, but the slippery bank snags the beast's paw. For the briefest moment, we sink down, and the old rogue is upon us.

A squeal of tires comes from the gravel road, then a slamming car door. A human scream follows when the old rogue lunges for the beast's throat.

Brianna appears behind him.

No!

Fury coats her gaze, and in her hand she carries a tire iron. She's swinging it before I can push her out of the way. It connects with the rogue's haunches. Against all odds, she managed to hit him in our tangled fight.

The rogue spins and lunges for Brianna.

She leaps back just as his jaws snap only inches from her abdomen.

A tornado of power and rage erupts inside the beast. My magic swells, and a surge of dominance blasts from our body. We deflect it away from Brianna, so it only hits the old rogue.

The rogue freezes for a hair's breadth of time. It's enough for his blurred movements to pause for less than a second.

But it's enough time for my mate to see him. Brianna's expression is still fierce, and she swings again just as I grab onto the old rogue's hind leg right where it connects at the joint.

Brianna lands another blow. It cracks the old rogue's jaw and sends blood flying like raindrops.

A millisecond of pride and admiration sweeps through me before red coats the beast's mindset. *Die. Die. Die.* It's the only thought that plunders the beast's senses.

The old rogue went for our mate.

For that he will die.

The beast rips the hind leg from the old rogue's body. One bloody tear and a surge of immense power is all it takes to tear the limb away.

A howl of pain comes from the rogue as the beast latches onto his throat. With one giant tear, the beast rips out the rogue's windpipe. A shudder wracks the rogue's body before blood pools on the ground around him.

Brianna is panting heavily when the rogue shifts back to human form before staring skyward, his eyes vacant and glassy.

The tire iron falls by her side, but pulsing anger still emanates off her in waves. The beast limps toward her, our body bleeding and battered.

When he reaches her side, he licks her hand and she falls to the ground and wraps her arms around us.

"Collin," she whispers. Her heart is thudding in our ears. A surge of love consumes not only me but the beast too. He tilts his head back and howls.

She fingers the beast's leg and then his side. Worry coats her gaze. But already our wounds are healing. Our flesh sews back together as our skin and muscle regenerates. It may take another day to be fully healed considering the extent of our wounds, but we'll be whole by tomorrow.

The beast licks her cheek and pushes his cold nose against her skin, trying to reassure her.

A relieved laugh escapes her, but I pull the beast back within me, and he goes readily. He knows that right now, our mate needs us in human form.

When I shift back, she launches herself into my arms and buries her head in my neck.

"Oh my God, Collin. I thought—" She gulps in a lungful of air as tears erupt from her eyes. They stream down her cheeks in warm rivers. "I thought you might die!"

I hold her to me. Blood covers my skin, and I'm naked against her clothed form, but I don't let it stop me from tenderly fingering a lock of hair from her face.

"I was never going to lose. I would have been the victor even if you hadn't interfered—"

"But when he came at you, and I saw your blood—"

I put my fingers to her lips. My heart is still thrumming wildly. Seeing Brianna put herself in danger for me, for *us*, had made terror explode in my chest until I saw just how capable she is.

My mate is fierce—as fierce as me.

That feeling of pride steals my breath again when I finger her chin and tilt her head up. I kiss the tears away before tightening my hold around her.

"I will never let anyone hurt you," I say against her ear.

She shivers before replying, "And I you."

A proud smile lifts my lips. "My mate, the warrior."

She snort laughs before threading her fingers through my hair. "I'm not a warrior, but when I saw him trying to kill you in the rearview mirror, I couldn't leave. I don't know, I just—" She shakes her head, a frown covering her face. "Something overtook me."

I glance behind me toward the highway to make sure we haven't been spotted before returning my attention to her. "I would say don't ever do that again, but I have a feeling I'd be wasting my breath."

She nods, the frown disappearing. "I know you want to take care of me and be the big, strong male, but I'll be damned if I sit on the sidelines and watch someone try to kill you."

I shudder because I know she would interfere again, and the only way I could ever stop her would be to command her with my alpha power, but I also know she would resent me for it.

"How about we don't make a habit of fighting old rogues?"

She eyes the dead werewolf again, and her breath stops. "Holy shit. We really killed him." Her lips part. "That's two now. *Two* men that have died because of me."

"No!" I force her attention back to me. "That's two *predators* that were going to rape or kill you that died at *my* hands, not yours. Don't you dare feel guilty about that."

She takes a deep breath, and I can sense something change in her—an acceptance, an understanding that this is how it works in my world. The supernatural community views death and battles differently than the humans. Mated werewolf males are known to go to any lengths to protect their mates. The supernatural community understands that. It's been our way for centuries, and modern human laws and rights haven't changed that.

"This killing is one hundred percent justified, my love. The SF would thank us. Killing him stopped him from murdering innocents. He would have murdered *you* if I hadn't killed him. Trust me, the SF would have taken him down without a second thought."

Another second passes before she nods. "You're right about him. He would have killed me, and after me, who knows how many people he would have murdered."

I pull her back to the car to grab new clothes before I jog to the creek to wash the blood from me. Once I'm dressed and relatively clean, I pick up the rogue's body and head for the woods.

"What are we going to do with him?"

I hide a smile. She said *we*, not *you*. My mate and I are truly a team.

"Bury him. He's like me. The Supernatural Forces is after him, too, as they are with all rogues, but I'm not going to make their jobs easier by leaving him here for them to find. If they find him soon, they'll be able to scent both you and me on him, but if we bury him, it's possible he'll never be found."

She follows me into the woods, and I make quick work of the body. When finished, I'm covered in dirt and know we're going to need to check into a hotel so I can properly wash. But I've been smarter about spending money lately and the cash we have should still last us a few more weeks.

By the time we return to the car, twilight has arrived and the moon shines through the clouds.

I pull Brianna to me. Even though I'm dirty and my stomach is rumbling like an earthquake, she readily wraps her arms around my neck.

"Have I ever told you that I love you?" I whisper to her.

Her breath catches. She and I damn well know neither of us have spoken those words yet, but when she tilts her chin up to press a kiss to my lips, I see the same love mirrored in her gaze.

"And I love you," she replies.

We bounce from city to city and state to state. Each night is somewhere new. Sometimes we stay in hotels, other times we sleep in the wild, but no matter where we are our appetites for one another only grows.

Despite our sexual chemistry, I worry that Brianna will grow tired of the constant moving, but she never complains.

Still, our arrangements don't sit well with me. I would take her out of the country if I could, but my contact who can secure fake documents is clear across the country, and I'm not willing to risk a border crossing without a passport since that could put her in jeopardy.

So we stay on the move and keep a low profile. It helps that the beast is no longer killing. After the old rogue, there's been nothing. And as each day passes without the beast throwing psychotic images at me . . . well, I start to cling to the hope that maybe he's changing.

I also take heart in knowing that the longer we go without leaving bodies in our wake, the more the SF will struggle to find us. I don't fully understand how they track rogue werewolves, but I know murder sprees are one of them, and since the beast isn't committing homicides anymore, well . . .

That's one less thing for them to work with.

I actually start to think that maybe we can do this. Maybe we can spend our life on the run, hiding, and evading them.

But there's only one problem.

Money.

It's a constant concern since neither of us have an income coming in. To do that, we would need to stay put somewhere and pick up employment, and I don't know how we can safely do that without the SF detecting us.

So we live frugally while I try to think of a plan, but by week four, the three thousand I withdrew back in the desert is gone and neither of us have jobs, which means I'll need to do another ATM withdrawal.

I imagine my family knows about the first withdrawal, and the SF is now monitoring my bank accounts, so when I go to make a second attempt and the money is seized, I'm not surprised.

"Good thing I have a backup plan," I whisper to myself.

I slip my brother's ATM card into the machine and withdraw several thousand. It weighs heavily on my mind, though. I don't want to steal from Pete, and while I think he would understand, I don't know that for sure. But right now, it's the only option I have to keep us funded until we figure out what to do.

After pocketing the cash, I hitch the collar of my jacket up and head back outside.

Brianna is waiting in the car. We're in upstate New York, and the nights are growing cold. We'll have to head south again to warmer climates, which is where I plan to take us tomorrow.

Brianna's biting her nails when I slip into the hatchback. I haven't stolen a new car—more to please my mate than anything—but I have stolen license plates. Every week I change the plates on the hatchback to help avoid detection.

Brianna's not happy about the continued petty theft, but considering that's the worst of my crime sprees now, she grumbles but turns a blind eye.

"Did it go okay?" she asks and angles toward me. She's wearing a sweater and jeans since the weather is so cool up here, and the frosty temperature matches her cool expression.

I know she's trying to hide her anxiety, but I can smell the fear that surrounds her, so I don't tell her about my accounts being seized because I don't want to worry her more.

"Yeah, went fine." I give her a smile, but it does little to ease the worry on her face. "Babe," I say gently. "We'll be okay."

I run a finger across her cheek, and she closes her eyes, seeking my touch.

It's crazy that over a month has passed since I initially abducted her. Each day our love only grows. I keep waiting for the moment of our frenzied mating to end, to feel like I've had enough and don't need to fuck her every minute of every day. But each time she gives me one of those sexy looks that I love so much, I only want her more.

That desperate feeling I have to love her, keep her, and possess her has made me fiercely determined to find a solution to our problem. I know I have to find a way to secure us fake aliases so we can settle down somewhere and gain employment. Until we do, our only source of funds is from my family.

"How much did you get?" she asks.

"Another three thousand. We'll be good for a few more weeks."

I hotwire the car and shift into drive before pulling back onto the road. A light drizzle falls on the windshield so I flip on the wipers as I automatically check for a tail even though it's too soon for the SF to be here.

Brianna leans back in her seat and bites her lip.

I reach over and clasp her hand. She readily turns her palm over before gripping me tightly.

"We'll make it work," I say. "We can go south to where

it's warmer, then head west again. I'll contact my source in California when we get there. With enough money, he can provide the documents we need to start a whole new life."

"How much will those cost?"

I grind my teeth. I know if I tell her ten thousand each, she's going to flip, so I say, "It's not cheap, but we'll get the money."

She takes a deep breath, then nods. "Okay, so that's what we'll do. We'll get aliases and start new."

"See?" I try to cheer her up. "We'll be fine."

She nods but a frown still mars her features. "Yeah, we'll be fine." A moment later, she adds, "We have to be cause I can't live without you."

The desperation in her tone soothes and encourages me.

I have to protect her, and I know I will. The beast, who's grown calmer every day in Brianna's continued presence howls inside me. I can feel his agreeance, and even though I haven't let him out since the old rogue attacked, he also knows that Brianna's safety is our top priority right now.

We need to secure our future first, then he can enjoy weekend runs again.

I eye her as we speed down the dark highway. She's leaned back against her headrest, her eyes closed. Love swells in my chest.

Brianna's united my beast and me. She's *saved* us. How she's done that, I don't know, but I do know that for the first time since leaving my pack over two years ago, I actually feel like a normal werewolf again.

CHAPTER TWENTY-EIGHT
BRIANNA

The end of October looms when Collin and I pull into a dusty travel station in central Utah. We have to withdraw money again, and the anxiety swirling in my stomach feels like a buzzing hornet's nest.

"It'll be okay." Collin gives me a smile. He's been reassuring me all evening, but I still detect the tightening of his jaw. As much as he always tries to be strong for me, I know he's worried too.

"Just be quick. I'll leave the car running."

"You don't want to come in and call Macy, Jill, or Kate?"

I bite my lip. I miss my friends, and Collin knows that, but after the last call I had with Kate...

"No. I don't want to argue anymore. Since they know now that I'm not at my dad's, they always have questions, and honestly, I don't want to lie to them."

He nods solemnly. He knows it's the one subject that makes me question if I should have left my old life. When I decided to stay with Collin, I turned my back on the friends I love.

He leans across the seat and kisses me softly. "You'll make up when you see them again. I'm sure of it."

If I see them again.

He kisses me once more, this one long and lingering. As always, the feel of his lips calms my mind while making my pulse quicken. It's crazy that after almost two months together, it still feels as if we just met. All of the excitement, attraction, and anticipation are still there. It doesn't matter that we live on the run, because when I'm with him, it doesn't feel like I gave everything up.

As much as it surprises me, I've officially turned into one of *those* girls, but even knowing that, I don't care. I belong with him, and he belongs with me, and even though I get why my friends are completely baffled by the choices I've made—I would still do it all over again.

Collin slams his door and saunters toward the travel station. I watch his ass, appreciating the view. He fills out his jeans like an underwear model.

After he disappears inside, the minutes tick by. I bite my lip and check the dash's clock again. He's usually out by now.

I lean back in my seat, hugging my jacket around me. My knee jiggles as I eye the time again. Another minute passes, and I'm about to get out and go inside when he comes through the door.

A stormy look covers his face, and his stride eats up the pavement.

Shit. Something happened.

A second later, he's in the car and we're peeling out of the parking lot.

"What's wrong?" I tug my seatbelt so I can see him better.

The muscle in his jaw ticks. "I couldn't get the money."

I let out a shuddering breath and lean back. "Okay.

That's okay. We knew this would eventually happen. We'll just have to find another way to get money for the documents, and—"

His hand slams against the steering wheel, making me jump. "Dammit, Bri! I don't want to have to find another way. I want to provide for you, and look at the mess that is my life! None of this is okay! It's not supposed to be like this!"

My heart slams against my ribs. Instinctively, I reach for him. I want to touch and soothe him. Our bond is so strong now, and I know my touch will help calm him.

His wolf is aggravated too. I can see it in the glow of his eyes. Even though Collin hasn't claimed me yet—something he refuses to do because of our tenuous life circumstances—I've never felt closer to another person.

My hand settles on his forearm. The rock-hard muscle beneath my palm tightens. His arm feels like steel, smooth skin, and hot blood. I squeeze. "Collin, we'll figure it out."

He sighs and rakes a hand through his hair. "Fuck me. Seriously. *Fuck me* and the shitty choices I've made."

I continue touching him, knowing the feel of me will do better than any words could. And sure enough, as the miles slip past us, the anger emanating off him decreases.

"I'm sorry," he finally says. "I didn't mean to lose my shit."

I lean across the seat and place a kiss on his cheek. "At least you didn't kill anyone. I count that as progress."

He chuckles, and the familiar twinkle enters his eyes. "What has it been? Six weeks since the rogue? I'm damn near a boy scout with how good I've been."

I laugh and squeeze him again. "Exactly, so please, don't worry. We'll figure something out. We can always look for cash work if you're not able to withdraw money again. There's always a way."

He frowns but doesn't reply. I know he hates the idea of me having a job and having to provide, but I'm used to working. I *like* working. It gives me purpose, and even though my mate is stubborn so am I. No way in hell am I going to sit back and not do something when I'm perfectly capable.

～

WE DRIVE until we get to the west side of Nevada. Since the SF was able to locate us at our last stop—thanks to the failed ATM withdrawal attempt—we keep moving until the car is nearly out of gas.

Dry land and sage brush surround us. Overhead, the night sky looms.

"Sleep outside tonight?" Collin asks.

"Yeah. I figured as much."

We get out and slam our doors. The loud sound echoes around us. There's nothing out here but dry land and endless stars. It should be a peaceful night.

"I'll get the bedding." He heads to the trunk.

After weeks of doing this, we've developed a routine. While Collin's grabbing the sleeping bags, I grab a water bottle and snacks. We didn't stop for dinner since we never stop moving after using an ATM.

My stomach grumbles as I reach for our toothbrushes and hats. Even though we've moved south, the temps fall at night. It will easily reach the forties, even lower if we hit a cold snap. And while Collin is always happy to keep me warm at night, I find the extra warmth of a cap helps.

We don't bother setting up the tent since the night should be dry. After eating our snacks and laying out the bedding, we slip under the covers. The cool night air makes my nipples stand on end, which brings a delectable glow to Collin's eyes.

He slips his dick inside me. As always, I'm ready for him, but because of the cold he takes me fast and hard. Within minutes, I'm coming. Afterward, he holds me close. Each night after we make love, his arms lock around me. I can feel his need to hold me and feel that we're one.

We lie on our backs and stare up at the stars.

"I don't think I'll ever get sick of this," I tell him. "As long as I'm with you, I can be happy anywhere."

His swallow is audible, and his arm tightens around my shoulders. "I just wish I could take you to Wyoming, to show you my home."

He doesn't talk about his home much. I know it pains him. The longer we've been on the run and the more his wolf has calmed, the more Collin realizes what he gave up when he chose to leave his pack.

"Maybe someday we can go there," I tell him.

He gives me a small smile, but it doesn't reach his eyes. "I suppose there's nothing wrong with wishing."

We lie together in silence as the night drifts on. Collin's soft snore soon fills my ear, and I snuggle closer to him. I've almost completely drifted off when something in the air changes around me. Heaviness descends like a blanket, as if the air has grown thicker and denser.

I frown, my eyelids fluttering open just as the hairs on the back of my neck stand on end.

I lift my head to look around and gasp. A dome of sparkling lights covers the entire area around me and Collin.

"What the hell?" I'm already shaking Collin awake when a blast of light shines directly in my face, blinding me. I slap a hand over my eyes, but it does little to stop the burning light. *What is that?* It's as bright as the sun.

"Freeze! Don't move!"

The blood drains from my face just as Collin rouses. "Collin!" I shake him more, panic creeping into my tone.

"We said don't move!" another person yells.

I whip around, trying to decipher where the voices are coming from, but the light has me as blind as a mole.

A growl tears from Collin, and before I know what's happening, he springs up and shifts mid-air. A huge golden wolf descends on top of me, pinning me to the ground. I yelp, more from surprise than fear, but now I'm flat on my back with Collin above me.

The burning light vanishes, but it's sudden disappearance doesn't give my eyes time to adjust. I still can't see.

But I can hear.

Terrifying snarls rip from Collin's wolf. His underbelly covers me, the soft fur brushing against my face when he crouches low, ready to spring. Every muscle in his body is tense. He feels like rock against me.

With a start, I realize what he's doing.

He's protecting me.

But then mayhem breaks loose, and any understanding I had of what was happening evaporates.

Screams.

Snarls.

I will myself to see again, but spots still dance in front of my vision.

Something pushes into me. Soft fur and hard muscle nudges me. *Collin.* He's trying to tell me something.

I rub my eyes and finally see six darkly clad people descend on Collin. They're coming at him from all angles. He pushes me one last time before springing up. Gunfire explodes where he had been directly above me.

Holy hell. They're trying to kill him!

And then it hits me, what his nudges had been. He'd been trying to make me get up and out of the way.

"Don't let him out of the circle!" one of the men yells.

Collin's tearing around, moving so fast that he becomes a blur, but he's still trapped inside the perimeter the group has made around us. Every time he leaps up, jumping fifteen feet into the air, one of the men follows.

They've all got to be supernaturals. Blue-lit balls fly from one of the man's hands. Sparkles of red light emit from a woman's fingers. And another is at least six-foot-six. Every time Collin does one of his impossibly high jumps, the tall man catapults after him and ensnares Collin's paw, forcing him down.

Yet despite the uneven fight, Collin is holding his own. And something tells me he's holding back. I've seen how incredibly fast his wolf is. I know he can move faster.

Yet he's not.

Course sand rubs against my splayed hands as I sit immobile on the ground. For a split second, Collin's glowing wolf eyes meet mine. Desperation lines them.

He wants me to leave. He wants me to get up and run. That's why he's holding back. He's creating a distraction right now.

Stifled breaths fill my chest.

I can't do that. He *knows* that I can't do that. I won't!

"Chloe! Now!" one of the supernatural's yells. A woman raises her gun.

"Collin!" I scream.

He whips around at the last moment and the shot misses him by millimeters. His wolf lashes out, fangs flashing in the moonlight. Blood-curdling snarls come next.

Chloe screams and buckles. Blood gushes from a tear in her leg as she falls to the ground. The gunfire increases, but somehow Collin manages to jump and dodge, missing all of it.

The entire circle moves inch by inch away from me. It's as if the team has forgotten I'm there. All of their attention is focused on Collins' wolf, and he's steadily forcing the circle back.

The sparkling dome above the team and Collin moves with them. When it washes over me, I shiver, but the heavy feeling in the air disappears when it passes, and then . . .

All sounds of fighting stop.

I gape. *What the hell?* Several yards away, the magical dome encases the group, but I can't hear anything happening inside it. I can still see them, but that's it. The action within the dome is like watching a silent movie.

I'm truly alone now.

No one is watching me.

I frantically look around, searching for something I can do that will help Collin.

One of the team members reaches behind him. A deadly looking arrow appears. The tip glistens, and I know something magical coats it. He locks it into a bow, and before I know what I'm doing, I'm pushing to a stand and sprinting toward him.

He pulls the arrow back. All of his attention is focused on Collin's wolf.

I leap through the magical dome just as he lets the arrow loose. Chaotic sounds fill my ears, but I'm already flying through the air.

Something hits my shoulder.

Pain tears through my arm. An agonizing burn follows.

I land on the ground. *Hard.*

A moment of complete silence follows before a shimmer appears above me, and Collin's face swims into my vision.

"Brianna!" Terror lines his words, but I can't respond.

He cradles me to him, his large arms encasing me as fear lines his face.

Then fire takes over my body. I'm dying.

I'm burning alive from the inside out.

Then everything goes black.

CHAPTER TWENTY-NINE
BRIANNA

"**G**ive me the serum!" a man yells.

"It's too late. We can't save her."

"Yes we can!"

"No, I don't think so. The magic is already in her bloodstream. Do you see the lines streaking up her arms? We can't stop it now."

"Shit, then we failed." The first man groans. "I failed. My arrow is the one that hit her."

"It may not be too late," a woman says. "That healer Daria Gresham could save her."

"Then get her," the first man says. "Use portal keys if you have to. We have to do everything we can to save this woman."

Darkness claims me again. I'm in an inferno. Fire consumes my body.

I don't know how much time passes before the voices around me come in and out of focus again, like a radio station I can't find the channel for.

"Brianna."

I tense when that achingly familiar voice washes over me.

"Brianna! Please! Look at me!"

Agony lines Collin's words. Rattling sounds come next. I jostle from wherever I lie, and the movement makes me wince. So I'm lying down. I'm aware of that much, but I'm not stationary. Rough movements make the pain unbearable.

"Brianna!" Collin's snarl tears several yards away followed by more rattling.

"You can't break those chains, Rogue, so quit trying."

"Fuck you! She's dying! You need to let me go to her—"

"So you can kill her? I don't think so. Shut up you murderous rogue!"

My stomach lurches when whatever we're traveling in abruptly drops.

"We're almost there," a female says. *"Wes was able to reach Daria. She's on her way and will meet us at headquarters. And Douglas is ready. He'll help Brianna cross the portal once we arrive."*

The bumps and dips continue. I'm in a vehicle or plane. I can't be certain which, but I know Collin is near. His rage is palpable, but his fear is even stronger.

The rattling sound comes again, as if a thick chain is being dragged. *"Brianna? Babe? Stay with me. Please."* Collin's tone turns raw and desperate. *"Don't die."*

I try to open my eyes, to see him one last time, but my lids are too heavy. Despite his plea, I know I'm on the brink of death.

I can feel it.

Agony fills my limbs. The burning is so strong that it's a miracle I'm not crying out. Then I realize my lungs have seized. I'm barely breathing. I can't even talk, let alone cry or scream. The magic swimming through my system is stealing my life right out from under me.

This is the end.

"They have the stretcher ready. The second we touch down, we move."

"Col—" But my whisper is so quiet, I doubt he heard me.

I try again to call for him, but my lips won't part. I want to reach for him, touch him, hold him, give him one last kiss goodbye.

But my body won't move.

This is the end.

∽

Small hands are touching me, feeling along my arms and around my shoulder. I must have died. The touch is so soft, like angel kisses.

"I don't have much time," a woman says. "She's on the verge of entering the afterlife."

The small hands lift, leaving me to drift away. The blackness is descending again, like a veil closing in front of my eyes, when burning light abruptly enters my body.

I arch and open my mouth to scream—more from shock than pain—as the burning increases. Rivers of heat flow through my bloodstream, trickling into every pore and cell in their path. Soothing coolness follows, dousing the flames and leaving me blissfully numb where the fire had consumed me.

So I'm not dead, but whatever's happening to me it's not of this world.

It goes on and on, over and over. The fiery light courses through my body again and again. I see the light even with my eyes closed. It's as if the sun is shining within me. I've never felt anything like it.

As the minutes tick by, my mind slowly clears. Awareness creeps into me with every second that passes.

I'm inside somewhere, and I'm lying on something hard and flat, maybe a table or bench. The room's cold, and a draft flutters air near my feet.

And I feel better. The burning from the poisonous magic is ebbing away as the strange light heals my body. I know I was at the brink of death, but this light is pulling me back.

"Collin?" I whisper.

"Shh," a man says. "Don't move, Brianna. Daria's almost done."

Another moment passes, and just as quickly as the fiery light came, it disappears.

Soft hands touch me again, cool yet firm. "Brianna?"

I flutter my eyelids open to see a small woman hovering above me—Daria I presume. She has startling turquoise-colored eyes, and long blond hair trails down her back. She smiles, and she's so beautiful that all I can do is stare.

"That was close," Daria says. "You were pretty determined to die on me." She clasps my hand and helps me sit up.

"Here, let me. You shouldn't be lifting in your condition." A large older man with salt and pepper hair intervenes. He takes my hand from Daria, his warm fingers closing over mine.

He easily props me up before swinging my feet over the side of the bed. It's then that I see Daria's round prominent belly. She has to be at least eight, if not nine, months pregnant.

"How do you feel?" Daria asks. Her voice is soft and melodic. My heartbeat slows just hearing it.

"Fine. I think." I feel my scalp, wondering if I got a head injury since I don't remember how I got here or where I am.

"I eradicated the magical poison in your blood," Daria says. "You should be good as new now."

I frown as understanding dawns. "Did you just heal me?"

"Yes. You were near death after that injection of *kuraia* from Mitchell's arrow. It was good thinking to call me. I'm not sure you would have recovered otherwise."

I shake my head and finally take in my surroundings. I'm in a small room, and I have no idea where, but foggy images of Collin as a wolf and us being surrounded by black-clad men and women has my heartbeat picking up all over again.

The Supernatural Forces. They attacked us while we slept in Nevada.

"Where's Collin?" I whip my head around, but all that surrounds me is Daria, the older man, and the bed I'm lying on in this sparsely furnished room. Dawn sunlight peaks through the large single window, so I know it's almost morning. "Is he here?"

The older man's lips thin. "He's being dealt with. You don't need to worry about him anymore. You're safe now."

I jump out of the bed, getting a surprised look from Daria. I race to the older man. "Where is he? Is he okay? Is he hurt?"

The older man and Daria share a confused look. Daria inches toward the door and says, "I'll just be on my way, Wes, so you can deal with everything else. I'll let Logan know that you've found Collin." She frowns, and her eyes dim. "I'll also let his parents know, but I'll wait for you to break the news to them about what happens from here."

Wes gives a curt nod, and Daria slips from the room. I never get a chance to properly thank her, but my heart is beating so hard I can barely breathe. My fingers tremble when I reach for Wes. "Please. Tell me where he is. Tell me that he's okay!"

Wes takes a step closer to me, his confused expression still in place. "Brianna, is it?"

I nod distractedly.

"Am I understanding correctly that you're worried about Collin Ward's whereabouts? We are talking about the same person, correct? The person who abducted you and would have inevitably murdered you if we hadn't stopped him?"

"Murdered me?" I shake my head rapidly. "No, he would never do that. I mean, at first his wolf tried, but that was weeks ago, but now, no! He's not like that anymore."

Wes's eyebrows rise. "His wolf—" He scratches his chin. "You know about his wolf?"

"Yes, his rogue werewolf."

Shock lines his face. "He told you about that?"

"Yeah, Collin told me, and he told me about the SF too." I glance around the room again. "That's where I am now, right? Somewhere that the Supernatural Forces controls?"

The grim expression on Wes's face grows. "So not only did Collin abduct you, but he also told you about werewolves and the Supernatural Forces?"

I suck in a breath, wondering if I just got Collin in more trouble. "He only did it to protect me, to warn me about what would happen if we were caught. He was only thinking of my safety."

Wes lets out a bitter laugh. "Your safety? I'm sorry to inform you of this, Brianna, but it seems you've been completely manipulated and used by him. Considering he's gone rogue, that behavior doesn't surprise me, but I'm sure all of this is very confusing for you."

"No, I'm not confused."

But he ignores my denial and reaches for my arm.

"Since you're fully healed now, you may return home soon, but first, we would like to ask you a few questions."

I stiffen, just as we step into a hallway. "What kind of questions?"

Wes cocks his head. "Just a few questions from our team."

My fingers tremble, and I dig in my heels. Collin told me this would happen. They'd first question me, then wipe my memory. I need to stay away from the sorcerers at all costs.

"I'll answer your questions if you tell me where Collin is and how he's doing."

"That's not how it works. You don't get to negotiate—"

I rip my arm free from his grip and take off at a run down the hall. I can see I'll get nowhere with Wes, and I know this is my only chance to find Collin. I know he's going to be punished for what he did, most likely put to death, but even though I have no idea where I am or where he is, I have to try to find him.

CHAPTER THIRTY
COLLIN

My heart is ripping with each breath I take. I know Brianna's probably dead. Even if they called Daria in to heal her, it doesn't mean she got here in time.

I prowl around inside my cage, murder on my mind. They took Brianna away the second we landed, and nobody will tell me anything.

I smash my fist into the cage's bars, making them rattle, but even that doesn't squelch my frustration.

I'm still chained within the cage, and they've moved me into an underground holding facility. My beast howls within me, not from rage, but from pain. We failed to keep Brianna safe.

My mate is probably dead because of me. Because of *us*.

I tip my head back and howl, too, and before I can stop him, my wolf makes me shift. The guard posted by the door takes a step back when I lunge at the cage. All of the pent-up frustration and regret over what I let myself become when I left my pack bleeds out of me.

Our mate is dead.
My execution is coming.
It doesn't matter what we do anymore.

CHAPTER THIRTY-ONE
BRIANNA

I run to the end of the hall and reach a double door. Wes shouts for me to stop, but I still push through it. Or try to.

The door doesn't budge.

Shit! Shit! Shit!

Rapidly approaching footsteps come from behind me. I frantically look for another way to escape. It appears I'm in some kind of hospital, but there's no staff around.

"Brianna!" Wes calls.

He's almost reached me, so I take off down the next hall. I can't believe he hasn't caught me yet, but just as I'm about to try another door at the end of this corridor, a large hand clamps over my bicep.

"Brianna, you need to stop."

Wes's voice is firm yet gentle. He's not even winded, which makes me realize he was humoring me. He could have caught me at any point, and I'd simply made a fool of myself.

I can only imagine what I look like when I turn to face

him. Desperation clutches my gut in an impenetrable hold, and I want to wail in frustration.

His eyes soften, but his voice remains firm. "If you don't cooperate, I'll have to restrain you, and I don't want to do that."

I grab onto Wes's shirt. "Where is he? Please, can't you just tell me?"

He frowns, that perplexed expression appearing before he removes my claw-like hands from his chest. "Brianna, Collin doesn't care about you. He's a murderer and demented. Whatever he did to you, it was for his own gain. I'm sorry if he made you feel that you mean something to him, but I can assure you that you don't. It was only a matter of time before he killed you. You're lucky we found you when we did."

"But he wouldn't kill me!"

"He would. That's what all rogues do." He pulls me back down the hall even though I resist. When it becomes apparent that he's as freakishly strong as Collin, I know there's no point trying to break free.

His grip loosens when he understands that I'm not fighting him anymore, but he doesn't let go. "We only have a few questions, and then we'll give you some time to clean up and get something to eat before you go home."

I press my lips together even though inside I'm raging. Maybe if I cooperate he'll be more likely to listen to me. If I just answer his questions, maybe he'll let me ask a few of my own.

It's the only thing that keeps me from screaming in frustration.

Wes takes me to an elevator, and we descend to another hallway. This one is long and devoid of rooms. Whatever infirmary we were in upstairs is long gone. Everything about this new area has military written all over it.

"This way." Wes's shoes click on the concrete as he guides me to the end of the hall. He stops at a door and places his palm on top of a scanner.

"Welcome, Wes McCloy," a robotic voice says. The door clicks open.

Inside, a table with ten chairs awaits. Seated at the table are two men and a woman. But even though they all look human, I'm assuming everyone in this place is some form of supernatural.

The woman stands and offers her hand. She's tall, like me, and also has dark hair. "Brianna, it's good to see that you're safe. I'm Priscilla, this is my brother, Phoenix, and at the end there is Ray. We're part of the rescue squad that saved you in Nevada."

I shake her hand, more from habit than anything, but I look her squarely in the eye when I reply, "I didn't need rescuing."

Her eyebrows rise.

Wes pulls out a chair for me. "Brianna is under the impression that Collin cares for her."

Priscilla's expression turns sympathetic. "Right."

She sits back down, and I reluctantly follow suit. Wes takes the chair at my side as Phoenix and Ray look on. I can tell that Phoenix and Priscilla are related. Both have dark hair, brown eyes, similar facial features, and the identical shade of honey-tanned skin. Ray, on the other hand, is huge. Even though he's sitting, I'm guessing he's around six-four. He's of African-American descent and watches my every move. Something tells me he doesn't miss much.

I fiddle with my shirt, wishing I was dressed in something other than my thin cotton pants and old university T-shirt. Having all of this happen while I'm wearing my pajamas only makes it worse.

Making myself sit still, I ask, "What questions do you

have for me?" I figure the sooner we get this done with, the sooner I can ask about Collin.

Priscilla props her elbows on the table and leans forward. "How long have you been held captive by Collin Ward?"

"I already told you. He wasn't holding me captive."

She shares a side-eye look with her squad members before addressing me again. "Our surveillance indicates that he began stalking you in August, but the exact date that he took you is still something we don't know. Do you care to fill us in?"

"How do you know he took me?"

She takes a breath, and I know I'm being difficult, but nothing about any of this is okay. I mean, they haven't read me my rights or asked if I wanted to make a phone call.

"And aren't I allowed legal counsel or something? I mean, how can you guys hold me here like this against my will?"

"We'll be letting you leave soon, and you won't hear from us again," Wes says. "I understand our way of doing things is unusual to you, but I can assure you, no harm will come to you, and you'll be able to return to your life as you knew it just after you help us clarify a few things."

What he really means is return to my life after the sorcerers wipe my memory.

Of course, he didn't add that part. But I suddenly understand how they can be so candid. They know I'm human, yet they're not hiding anything about their organization or magical powers, and that's all because I won't remember any of it.

"Brianna?" Priscilla arches an eyebrow. "What day did Collin take you?"

"I don't know the exact day, but it was at the beginning of September."

"And did he abduct you before or after he was in your apartment?"

"Before."

Priscilla and Phoenix share a confused look. "Then what was he doing in your apartment on the night of 7 September if he wasn't abducting you?"

"So you're the SF members that broke into my apartment that night and attacked Collin?" Since they just look at me, and obviously have no intention of answering my question, I add, "He was sleeping on my couch. That was the night after he took me, then returned me."

Ray leans forward in his chair. "So you invited him inside your house after he abducted you?"

"Yes."

Ray shakes his head. "And you believe that Collin cares for you after he *abducted* you?"

My stomach drops. They don't believe that Collin's anything but bad. They obviously think I'm some messed-up chick with a bad case of Stockholm syndrome. But maybe they'll understand if I use words they're familiar with.

"I'm his mate, and he's mine, so yes, I do believe he cares for me. Actually, I know he loves me."

Wes's sharp intake of breath follows. "Did you say *mate*?"

"Yes. We're fated mates."

"*Fated* mates?" Ray repeats, looking skeptical. "Isn't that rare, Wes?"

Wes nods, and I wonder if Wes is a werewolf. He certainly has the build for it, as does Ray.

"And you believe that?" Priscilla cocks her head. "That you're fated to be with Collin?"

I clasp my fingers together and look down. I fidget for a moment, trying to process exactly what Collin and I are.

Something connects us, and if that's called fated mates, then I guess that's what we are.

I look back up and meet her gaze. "Yes."

She sits back and folds her hands together. "That still doesn't change anything. He's still a rogue werewolf and a murderer."

"But he hasn't killed anyone in weeks, and he didn't kill me."

Ray scoffs. "Yet."

"No, you don't understand." I tell them how Collin's wolf had recognized me as his mate and not killed me all those weeks ago in Utah. I even tell them how I felt for certain that I was going to die when Collin's wolf pinned me in the backseat of the car back on that mountain. "But he stopped. He didn't kill me because he recognized me for what I am."

All four of them watch me with confused expressions. A full thirty second passes before one of them responds.

"Are you really telling me that a rogue werewolf in the heat of bloodlust stopped himself from murdering you?" Wes's dubiousness is apparent in every syllable of his question.

"Yes, that's exactly what I'm telling you. And Collin also let me go. I didn't understand then what he and I have, and I wanted to leave, so he let me."

Phoenix raises his hand, stopping me. "Wait, wait, wait. If he let you go, then why were you with him in Nevada?"

I sigh. "I told you. Because I *chose* to be with him." Knowing that their skepticism won't abate until I tell them all of the details, I rehash the last two months of my life.

The only parts I leave out are Declan's and the rogue's murders. Even though Collin stopped them from raping and killing me, I have a feeling the SF won't be as understanding. But I make sure to emphasize that neither Collin nor his wolf have gone on any killings sprees since he took me.

When I finish, they all lean back, their expressions impossible to read.

"Wes?" Priscilla finally says. "What do you make of all of this?"

Wes scratches his chin. "It's certainly something I haven't heard before."

"But she's human," Ray states. "How can a werewolf be fated to a human?"

Since Ray is looking to Wes for answers on werewolf clarification, I can only assume that Ray isn't a werewolf. As for what he, Priscilla, and Phoenix are, I can only guess.

"Fated mates in and of themselves are rare," Wes replies. "But I believe it can happen with a human. My grandmother told me that when she was a child, she heard of a wolf who was fated to a human. It's even rarer than fated mates between two wolves, but it can happen."

"So does that mean we're believing this story of hers?" Phoenix sneers.

"It does explain why he was in her apartment all of those weeks ago, why she's still alive, why she was on the run with him, and why they were sleeping together in Nevada." Priscilla shrugs. "I'm not saying I believe it either, but it does explain it all."

I rub my eyes, fatigue making them feel gritty. The stress of the last few weeks, while Collin and I tried to figure out how to start a new life together, is finally catching up with me. But I still feel sick at the thought of what's happening to him.

"Can I see him? Please?" I ask.

Wes frowns, and I know his answer before he opens his mouth. "I'm afraid not. Even if Collin is your fated mate, it doesn't change what he did or what he is. Rogues need to be held accountable for their actions, and unfortunately, we've never encountered a rogue who's been able to stop his bloodlust despite what you claim or believe."

"But he has stopped! I swear it! He stopped himself from killing both of you, didn't he?" I send Pricilla and Phoenix an accusing glare. "You were the ones who broke into my apartment in September. So tell me, if he's such a cold-blooded murderer who can't control himself, why are you both still alive?"

The siblings share another apprehensive look.

"You know it's true," I continue. "He chose not to kill you. That's why you're still here, which means your argument that he can't be saved is bologna. He wants to change. He said he's not going to kill anymore, and I believe him."

I'm near hysterics, and I know it, but desperation has taken a hold of me. I know I'm going to lose Collin if I don't make them see that he's worth saving.

"I think that's enough for now." Wes pushes his chair back. "Why don't we get you a fresh change of clothes and something to eat."

Ray, Priscilla, and Phoenix nod curtly and stand. They exit the room from another door at the opposite end, while Wes takes me back the way we came.

I follow him mutely, my heart heavy as I contemplate how saving Collin is even possible. Granted, I don't know much about werewolves or supernaturals, but I do know that Collin means to be good. Even if he didn't want that before meeting me, he does want that now.

Wes stops a few minutes later in front of another door. With a start, I realize we're now in a hallway with windows. I was so lost in thought I hadn't even paid attention to where we were going.

"There are a change of clothes and a hot meal inside.

You'll have to wait here until a squad member returns. It might be good to get some sleep."

"Where are we exactly?" I ask as he opens the door. I'm looking out the window at the rolling hills and a forest.

"Just outside Boise, Idaho."

The fact that he doesn't try to conceal their location makes my stomach drop. "You're still going to wipe my memory, aren't you?"

His eyes widen.

That's right. I know about the sorcerers too.

His composure smooths, and he says, "It's for the best, truly it is. Regardless of what you believe, Collin will be held accountable for the crimes he committed. A life with you isn't an option after what he's done."

"So I really get no say in what happens to me or him?"

He gestures for me to enter the room. I do so on wooden legs. Aromas from the hot meal waft up to greet me. Several slices of bacon, a hearty bowl of oatmeal topped with fruit, and a steaming cup of coffee wait on a tray at the end of a bed. A pile of freshly washed clothes sits at its side. It's a small room, similar to the one in the infirmary.

Wes crosses his arms and studies me. "I see that Collin told you quite a bit about us, especially if you know about our sorcerers, but tell me, Brianna, do you think you could go the rest of your life without telling anyone what happened to you during the past two months? Don't you think that your friends and family would know that you experienced something extraordinary?" Instead of waiting for a response, he continues. "We do what's needed to protect our kind. Even the most well-intentioned humans can't be trusted." He smiles sadly when angry tears pool in my eyes. "As much as I believe that you truly do think you're fated to be with Collin, it doesn't stop how our organization functions. We have to do what's best for the greater good, and sometimes that means making hard choices that affect one or two."

He doesn't elaborate, and I doubt anything I say will sway him anyway.

They've made up their minds.

To them, Collin is a murderer who can't be saved, and I'm a human who was stupid enough to fall in love with him.

It doesn't matter that Collin's changed.

To them, he'll always be a murderous rogue, and I'll always be a naïve human.

Nothing can save us now.

CHAPTER THIRTY-TWO
BRIANNA

Despite Wes's suggestion that I get some sleep, I can't. It's six in the morning when he leaves me alone in the room—the *locked* room. I'm a fucking prisoner here.

I storm about the place, knocking into things. Some of the coffee sloshes over the mug's rim when I hit the tray. Despite its mouth-watering aroma, I can't drink it. I feel sick about what's being done and what's to come.

If only I could see Collin and know that he's okay.

But I doubt I'll ever see him again.

Over an hour passes with me pacing and raging. All I can do is hope that Collin's not being hurt and wish for a future that will never come.

I understand now why he's never claimed me. If he had, I could feel what he's going through right now, especially if they're hurting him. The thought makes my stomach heave.

It's only when bright sunlight fills the room that I realize another day has truly begun. I finally head to the bathroom. As much as I dread what's coming, I don't care to have another "meeting" in which I'm wearing only my pajamas.

The bathroom has a full tub and shower. Fresh towels wait near the toilet, and a new bar of soap and a hair brush sit by the sink. I shake my head. Something tells me that I'm not the first human the Supernatural Forces have held here.

I clench my teeth and rip the shower curtain back. I'm so irritated that I don't wait for the water to warm before stepping under it.

My squeal fills the room when the cold water hits my head, but the spray soon warms so I set to work on scrubbing myself. It's only then I think to look where the arrow pierced my skin. The puncture wound by my shoulder is entirely healed. I don't even have a scar—it's as if the arrow never hit me.

And when I wash between my legs, I realize that Daria truly healed me on *every* level. I'd been sore last night. Collin and I had made love multiple times yesterday morning and then again before bed. He'd dominated my body, but it had been in a good way. A loving way. A way I wanted to remember. And now that's washed away, too, just like the water slipping down the drain. I don't even have that small affliction to remember him by.

My anger finally evaporates, and I crumble in the tub as the water continues to cascade around me. Tears want to form in my eyes, but I hold them back. *No. I'm not going to cry.*

Crying is something you do when you give up, when you feel all hope is lost. But it's not.

I will find a way to save him.

I don't know how long I sit like that. Anger and loss strums through me like the relentless spray hitting my back, but I refuse to believe there's nothing I can do. I *will* find a way to save Collin.

I finally get up and turn the water off.

And when I'm standing in front of the mirror, toweling off my hair, a fierce determination blooms inside me. Because if I can't find a way to make them see that Collin won't hurt anyone again, my mate will be gone forever.

Which means I have a job to do—a job that I cannot fail at.

∼

A knock on the door comes an hour later. I'm sitting on the bed, dressed in a pair of new jeans that fit surprisingly well and a cotton T-shirt that falls to a comfortable length at my hip-bone. They even got my bra size right—36B. The SF is surprisingly attentive to details.

I don't bother calling out because I know they're coming in anyway, and sure enough, after that short quick knock, the door opens and a woman steps inside.

"Brianna Keller? We're ready for you." She has pointy ears, sharp teeth, and glimmering skin. I may not be familiar with supernaturals, but I'm not an idiot. The woman is obviously a fairy.

If I wasn't so consumed with Collin, I might have stared in curiosity, but in this moment, I don't give a fuck how many supernatural species there are or what they look like. Only my mate matters.

"Where are you taking me?"

Instead of replying, she turns and calls over her shoulder, "Follow me."

I roll my eyes and get up. She leads me down a series of halls, all concrete, but I'm awarded glimpses of the outdoors through the numerous windows. A few steps later, she stops at a door and opens it.

A team of SF members are waiting inside the room for me. Three men and one woman stand around an examination table. They all wear friendly expressions, but considering my surroundings look like a surgical room—with a long table for a human to lie on—I immediately ground to a halt.

"Oh hell no." I shake my head. "You are not taking away my memories!"

The woman in the group rushes forward as the fairy disappears back into the hall. The door closes behind her, its lock clicking in place.

"You must be Brianna Keller?" the woman says. "I'm Kelly. Now, please don't worry. We're just going to lay you down for a minute. Nothing will hurt and then you'll be on your way. Really, I promise. There's nothing to be afraid of."

Kelly reaches for my hand, but I yank it back. "Touch me, and you're dead."

Her eyebrows rise at my threat, but from her unconcerned expression, I can tell she's undaunted.

"Brianna," one of the men calls. "Please lie down. We won't ask again."

I cross my arms. "No."

A resigned expression crosses his features before he replies, "Fine. Have it your way."

He swirls his hands together while muttering foreign-sounding words under his breath. The other men beside him all look bored.

My breath grows shallow since I have no idea what the hell's going on, but then my feet lift from the ground while my limbs seize like sticks. I yelp in surprise.

I try to fight whatever spell he's woven over me, but it

does no good. He turns me horizontal in the air, my body now stiff as a board as I float to the table. Even my voice is paralyzed. I can still breathe, but I can't talk.

What an ass!

Anger rises in me at his demonstration of power, but it's not until I'm lying firmly on the table, completely helpless against all of them that panic sets in.

No!

But it doesn't matter that in my mind I'm pleading with them to stop. This is it. They're going to wipe my memory, and then I'll never see or remember Collin again.

I grind my teeth. I want to scream, to wail, but these assholes have completely overpowered me. Still, I fight. I will myself to move, to lift my arm, to do *something*.

My hand flinches.

"Hmm," the sorcerer manipulating me says. "She's a strong one."

Another one with a shorter build and wavy hair cocks an eyebrow. "Can you handle it, Douglas, or should I join you?"

Douglas frowns but then shakes his head. "I got it."

When Douglas has me completely incapacitated on the table, the third male shifts to stand at my head. I'm panting as exertion sets in. I'm fighting Douglas with everything I have, but no matter how hard I try, other than a few twitches, my limbs won't move. I grit my teeth and try harder.

"Actually, Olaf, I might need your assistance," Douglas says.

The shorter sorcerer swirls his hands and whispers those foreign-sounding words, just as my forearm breaks through Douglas's spell, but in the next instant, it's as if a cement block suddenly drops on top of me.

My arm falls, and my breath catches.

Olaf cocks his head. "You're right. She is strong."

Thanks for talking about me like I'm not here, numb-nuts. I grit my teeth again since I can't scream at him.

"Shall we begin?" The third sorcerer widens his stance. He spreads his fingers and places his palms alongside my ears, but Kelly cuts in.

"Hold on, Geoff. We need to identify her."

Geoff rolls his eyes but drops his hands. "Right. Go ahead."

She gives him a pointed look and says sternly, "Protocols are in place for a reason."

He dips his head. "You're right. Sorry."

I breathe faster as sweat pours from my temples. The immense pressure is still on my chest, but sometimes it feels for a fraction of a second that I may be able to move.

Still, I'm helpless to resist when Kelly flips my arm over like a ragdoll's. "You'll have to forgive us for all of this, Brianna," she says as she holds up a tablet and aims it at my wrist. "We take no pleasure in this, but it's necessary for our survival. Please know that we'll be as quick as possible so you can go home."

I eye her as she does something on the tablet. An eruption of lasers swathes my skin before a glowing symbol appears on my inner wrist. My eyes widen, but just as quickly as the mark materializes, it vanishes.

Kelly's lips part. "What the heck . . ." She positions the tablet over my wrist a second time, and the lasers appear again.

Some of the fight goes out of me as I watch all four SF members lean over the table to peer at my wrist.

They all share incredulous looks when the same glowing symbol appears and then vanishes.

"Douglas and Olaf," Kelly says in a clipped tone. "Release her."

I gasp when the magic abruptly disappears from my body. The second I'm free, I fly off the bed to the corner of the room, ready to fight them if I have to, but Kelly just holds her hands up in surrender.

"Brianna, I'm sorry. We shouldn't have done that, but we didn't know."

I keep my stance wide, not letting my guard down. "Didn't know what?"

"That you're a female werewolf."

CHAPTER THIRTY-THREE
COLLIN

I've been in here for at least twelve hours. And in all that time, nobody will tell me how Brianna's doing, but I think I overheard one of the guards say Brianna was going to the sorcerers this morning.

When I'd heard that snippet, I'd yelled for the guard, pleading with him to tell me what he knew, but he'd ignored me and slammed the door.

Still...

My mate's alive.

Such an enormous weight lifts from my shoulders. For the first time since the SF caught me, it feels as if I can breathe.

But they're taking her to the sorcerers. She won't remember me.

A new dread forms in my belly, but I shake it off.

No, don't think that way.

I do my best to distract myself. It would be easy to go mad in this place even if one's wolf was sane. Above my cage, a light buzzes. It's the only light source here. The fancy electronics, and high-tech lighting used in the personnel section don't extend to the prison cells.

Here, the walls are thick, the lighting dark, and the air humid. I know I'm underground, as for how far underground, I don't know.

The guards changed an hour ago, and the new one brought me a hot meal. It was a meal made to accommodate a werewolf's high metabolism. I inhaled the three steaks, four potatoes, and pile of vegetables. I need to keep my strength up, which means I need to eat when food's provided.

Because Brianna is alive, which means I need to be on my best behavior in case there's a sliver of a chance they'll let me see her again.

My wolf prowls within me, snarling at every turn. He wants to find Brianna as much as I do, but neither of us know how to make that happen.

"How many others are down here?" I ask the guard.

He stands near the door and wears the uniform all SF squad members don. He's young, probably early twenties, but his military-precise movements and flat affect let me know he's no spring chicken. I won't be able to manipulate him.

When he doesn't respond, I add, "I know there are others down here. I can hear them."

His attention stays focused on the wall, unwavering.

I sigh in frustration and pace the few steps my confinement allows. My cage is placed within this dank cell. A cage within a cage—how fitting—but I've figured out I'm in their prison block. Despite the thick steel door, sound still penetrates it. During the night, I heard maniacal laughter, howling, and desperate calls from other inmates. And given that they all sound bat-shit crazy, I figure this is the mental-hospital side of their prison. The SF obviously thinks I'm a deranged rogue, so they probably think I fit in perfectly here, and a few months ago, I would have.

But now? No.

I grip the bars of my cage, which makes my chains rattle. "I'm not a rogue anymore," I tell the guard.

He rolls his eyes but remains quiet.

I shake the bars, trying to get his attention, but then realize that makes me look aggressive so I stop. "I'm not, I swear. My mate changed me. She healed me. I was a rogue, I was deranged, I *was* a wolf who couldn't be trusted, but that was before I met her. Brianna pulled me back from the brink. She saved me."

I wait, hoping for some kind of reaction from him, but . . .

Other than his initial eye roll—nothing.

"Dammit!" I yell. "Are you listening to anything I'm saying? I'm not crazy anymore! I won't ever kill or hurt anyone again, human or supernatural. You've got to believe me. I've changed!"

He finally turns to face me. His eyes are cold and devoid of sympathy. They're the eyes of a guard who doesn't believe a word his prisoners' say. "Save it, Rogue. You're not fooling anyone."

I let go of the bars and rake a hand through my hair. "But I'm not trying to fool you. I'm being honest."

He smirks. "No one's going to fall for that."

"Even if it's the truth?"

"How can it be the truth when no rogue in the history of werewolves has ever stopped killing or come back from insanity?"

My arms go slack, falling to my sides. A deep sense of hopelessness settles within me. He's right. Nobody's come back from crazy-town when they've gone rogue, which means the SF won't believe me or anything I say, and if the SF won't—then the courts won't either.

My execution is coming.

CHAPTER THIRTY-FOUR
BRIANNA

"We won't be wiping your memory," Kelly says as I stand there in disbelief. "It's against regulations to manipulate another supernatural's mind."

My arms fall to my sides. "Wait. What did you say?"

She takes a step closer to me, looking apologetic. "Because you're a female werewolf, we won't be wiping your memory." She cocks her head. "Did you not know of your origins?"

I shake my head, and it feels as if the room is closing in. *A female werewolf?* I sway against the wall. I'm certain she's wrong. I'm not a werewolf. I'm *human*.

It must look as though I'm about to faint because she reaches out to steady me. "I'm sorry if this is news to you, but if you didn't know and Wes said nothing about you being a supernatural, then you're most likely not in our database, and that's a problem since we track all supernatural citizens. You'll need to come with me so we can sort this out."

After taking a deep breath, I follow her. The sorcerers

all stay by the table, talking amongst themselves, no doubt about me since they keep casting suspicious glances my way.

At least that's the only thing they're casting now.

I follow Kelly from the room as numb shock creeps through me. She says I'm a werewolf, but I'm certain I'm not. I know she's made a mistake, but if it means they're not going to wipe my memory, then I'm sure as hell going along with it.

∽

Kelly leads me to what I can only surmise is some kind of command center. We're still on the main floor, but the room we enter is huge. Dozens of SF members in uniforms are stationed throughout the circular area. All of them sit in front of computers with holographic screens.

In the center of the hustle, a large holographic display flashes in brilliant colors and shows various locations around the world: Barcelona flashes in red, Shanghai is green, Cape Town sparkles in gold . . . the list goes on.

The world display travels from floor to ceiling and is constantly changing, glimmering from city to city as beacons light up and identify individuals. I cock my head, and after a moment realize those individuals are SF squad members that the Supernatural Forces is tracking.

Wes is standing on the other side of the central holograph, visible through the impressive globe, as he talks to one of the technicians.

"Wes?" Kelly calls. "Can we speak with you?"

When Wes sees me at Kelly's side, his eyes narrow. He says something to the technician before striding toward us. When he reaches us, he plants his hands on his hips, and his eyes train on my escort. "Kelly, what's this? Brianna should be on her way home by now, and she shouldn't be in here. This is no place for a human."

Kelly wrings her hands. "I know, but something came up. Something you need to be aware of. It's about her background, and I didn't want to leave her."

"Is this something that needs to be discussed in private?" he asks.

Kelly nods. "It involves her personal identifying information."

"Then we'll go to my office." Wes turns on his heel, and Kelly scampers to follow, dragging me with her.

I still don't know what kind of supernatural species Kelly is, but she's six inches shorter than me and doesn't have pointy ears or glowing eyes. I'm assuming she's a witch.

Wes keeps looking over his shoulder as we leave the command center behind us. I'm guessing he wants to reassure himself that we're following since I attempted to flee in the infirmary.

But if there's one thing I've learned it's that I can't beat the SF, so if allowing them to think I'm a female werewolf works to my advantage, then I'm all for cooperating.

We step onto an elevator and ascend to the fourth level. Since the numbers in the elevator don't escalate beyond four, I know we step out at the top floor.

Large windows line this hallway. The beautiful Idaho hills surrounding the SF are filled with trees. The autumn landscape is even prettier this high up. Forest stretches for miles around us, and in the distance, I spot the city of Boise.

"This way." Wes leads us down the hall to a door and places his palm on a scanner beside it.

I jump when a robotic female voice says, "Welcome, Wes McCloy." The door clicks open.

Wes ushers us inside his office. The large room contains a huge desk and more computers and holographic screens than the command center. An entire wall is dedicated to the tracking system I saw downstairs.

I frantically search the map, looking for something about Collin. For all I know, he's been moved and isn't even here.

Wes catches me eyeing it and pushes a button on his desk. All of the images vanish.

Dammit.

Wes waves to the chairs surrounding a small boardroom table near the corner. We all sit.

"All right," Wes says to Kelly. "Now that we're guaranteed privacy, do you care to explain what the hell is going on?"

Kelly pulls at her shirt collar. "I'm sorry. I probably should have approached you first, but it took all of us by surprise." She grabs her tablet, which she'd secured to a clip on her waist. "Brianna, can you hold your wrist out?"

I readily comply and hope that the same symbol appears. If it doesn't, I have no doubt I'll be granted a one-way ticket to memory-scramble-land courtesy of SF airlines.

Kelly positions the tablet above my wrist, and those weird lasers erupt again. She swathes it over me, and the same glowing symbol appears before it vanishes.

Phew.

Wes's lips part. "Do that again."

She does it a second time, and again, the same symbol appears.

"She's a female werewolf," Kelly says and secures the tablet to her waist again. "Only, she doesn't know it."

Wes stands, his eyebrows knitting together. He paces a few steps before turning back to us. He looks down at me and cocks his head. "Were you aware that you're a female werewolf?"

"No." *Cause I'm not.*

He pulls out his own tablet and types something. "We have your parents listed as Neil and Bridget Keller of Creola Vista, Arizona, and although your mother is deceased, your father is still alive. Is that correct?"

"That's right."

"Have your parents ever given you any indication that they carry supernatural blood?"

I try to picture my dad howling at the moon and manage to smother my smile. I then think of my mother. Even though most of my memories of her are fuzzy, I never saw anything unusual in her either.

Although if I tell him the truth, they may realize I'm *not* a female werewolf, in which case I'll be back in my initial predicament, so I settle with, "I don't know."

Wes's eyes narrow, and I make sure to keep my back straight and my expression smooth, although I have a sneaking suspicion I'm not fooling him.

Wes types something else on his device and appears to be reading whatever he found. He looks back at me. "Your father's lineage can be traced back to Germany. His ancestors first arrived in the US in 1890. According to our database, there isn't a drop of supernatural blood in anyone on his side. As for your mother . . ." His fingers fly across the tablet again, he then frowns. "That's strange."

"What is?" Kelly asks and leans forward.

"Her mother's history can't be found." Wes secures his tablet to his waist again and crosses his arms. "Your mother died of suicide, correct?"

I flinch but nod.

"And your parents were married for eighteen months

before you were born, but she died shortly after. Is that also correct?"

"She died when I was five."

"So she was without her pack for over six years." He taps his chin, and my heart begins to pound.

I suddenly remember what Collin told me about female werewolves. While men who leave their packs turn into psychotic murderous rogues, the females who abandon their packs often suffer from mental health issues—mainly depression.

Holy shit.

My heart beats harder, but I shake myself. There's no way my mother was a werewolf. My father never mentioned anything like that, and even though he has his faults, he wouldn't keep something like *that* from me. I'm sure of it.

Wes looks me over. "You certainly have the build of a female werewolf. Tell me, have you always been athletic?"

I think about the multiple sports I've been involved in since I was a child. Sports come easily to me. They always have. "Um, yes."

"We'll need to test your blood to confirm your lineage." Wes begins issuing orders to Kelly. Apparently, it's a big deal that I'm not in their database. It seems that *all* supernaturals are tracked by the SF.

If I'm even a werewolf at all.

My mind spins as they hash out a plan to confirm my ancestry. Before I know what's happening, I'm ushered out of the door and am on my way to their lab.

I can't believe this is happening. *I'm a female werewolf? An actual werewolf?*

As much as shock fills me, I'm starting to see that it could be true. I'm tall, strong, and athletic—something Collin said all female werewolves are and which Wes just confirmed. A memory flashes through my mind of the first run Collin and I enjoyed together in the Cascades. He'd made a comment about not knowing any human woman who could run like I do.

But female werewolves could.

The familiar pain tightens my chest when I think of Collin.

"Wes?" I ask when we step out of the elevator on the second floor. "Can you please tell me how Collin's doing?"

I expect him to ignore me, since no one's bothered to give me any updates, but he surprises me by replying. "He's fine. He's being held in the prison block."

Nerves prickle my skin. *So he's here, he's alive, and he's okay?* "Is there any chance I could see him?"

"No." Wes gives Kelly another instruction before leaving us.

Dammit. So much for supernatural blood giving me that privilege.

I follow Kelly down the hall, my breaths shallow. What would Collin say if he knew that I was a werewolf?

I close my eyes, remembering my mother. The tall beautiful woman that haunted my dreams for years after she died flashes through my mind. *Were you really a werewolf, Mom? But why didn't you tell us?*

My stomach twists as a flash of betrayal seers through me. It was bad enough that she killed herself and left me without a mother, but to also lie to me and Dad about it? To keep something like that from me when it could affect *my* future?

Having to deal with her suicide was horrible enough, but if she truly was a werewolf and never told Dad . . .

How could she not wonder if *I* would also suffer from depression? After all, if I'm a female werewolf without a pack, I could end up in the same position as her. Or what if

I had a son and passed the gene onto him. Imagine his shock and mine when he hit puberty and turned into a wolf.

A sour taste fills my mouth. If that's the case, then what she did is a hundred times worse.

OMG, Collin, I need you. I wish so hard that he were with me. I have a feeling that learning my true history would be easier if I had him to lean on.

But even though the SF may now believe that Collin and I are fated—since apparently the odds are higher in two werewolves—I still know there's no guarantee that I can save him.

～

Hours later, I again wish that Collin were here. I've been poked and prodded, scanned and tested, and treated like a lab rat for several hours.

Well, I guess it's not that bad. Everyone has been really nice. It's all smiles and apologies now when they do a test that requires drawing blood. It's as if I'm one of them.

But my stomach is grumbling by mid-afternoon. Everyone is so caught up in the discovery of an undocumented supernatural that nobody's remembered that I haven't eaten in hours, and I can't bring myself to complain. I can tell an event like this doesn't happen often.

"There we go. All done," a fairy technician says after she withdraws her needle. She hands me a cotton swab to stop the bleeding.

I hold pressure over my arm as she attaches a label to my specimen. "Any answers yet?"

The fairy snaps her gloves off and grins, revealing rows of pointy teeth. "Not yet, but we'll have answers tomorrow morning. All of these tests need to process overnight."

I sigh and check my arm. The bleeding's stopped, so I throw the cotton ball in the garbage. The canister is fifteen feet away but, of course, I nail the shot. Come to think of it, I rarely miss shots like that. I've always chalked it up to being naturally athletic, when in reality, it was probably due to my werewolf genes.

"We're finally all done, Brianna," Kelly says cheerfully. "I'll take you back to your room now."

My room. *Ugh.* In my room I'm alone with no answers, and answers are what I desperately need right how.

"Is there any chance we could go for a walk outside first?" I ask and hop off the stool.

She checks her watch. "I suppose. I'm not due back for another hour."

The one benefit of my supernatural lineage discovery is that everybody is more accepting of me now. It seems I've just joined the supernatural club. Membership requirement is pretty easy—supernatural blood only, and yes, they're open to half-breeds.

I bite my lip and contemplate just how far I can use this new leverage. Cause while going outside will be nice, what I really want is to spend more time with Kelly. With any luck, I'll be able to get more answers out of her about how Collin's doing and what his future holds.

We exit the lab and head toward a set of double doors. Kelly does the security checks while I watch on. This place is essentially a fortress. There's no way I'll be able to sneak to wherever Collin is locked away.

Once outside, Kelly starts babbling about my undiscovered history and seems more excited about it than me. It takes a few attempts before I'm able to steer her to what I really want to know.

"That probably explains why Collin and I are fated," I

say casually. "If I'm a female werewolf, the chances of us being fated are higher, right?"

Kelly's eyes narrow.

"He told me about female werewolves," I continue. "Actually, he told me a lot about the supernatural community."

Kelly cocks her head. "You two talked about stuff?"

"All of the time."

She stops and faces me. The cool autumn wind blows through the trees behind us and lifts a few strands of her dark-blond hair. "Rogues aren't usually known for casual conversation."

"I know, and trust me, when Collin first abducted me, conversation wasn't something we engaged in, but within the first few days, it became apparent to both of us that we had a connection. At first, neither of us knew what it was, but eventually Collin recognized it. We're fated mates. That's why we were drawn to one another and why his wolf never killed me."

She crosses her arms, and her eyes narrow again. "Did he really have you for two months?"

"He didn't have me. He let me go on day two, but I didn't want to leave him."

Her eyes widen.

"It's because we're fated," I add quickly. I know I've finally caught her complete attention, and I'm frantic to keep it. "His wolf recognized it first. He almost killed me, but when he caught my scent in his wolf form, his wolf started understanding it. Collin took another day to process it, and by day three . . ." I shrug. "I felt it too."

She shakes her head, her frown deepening. "But he was still a rogue when he recognized it, right? His wolf was crazy?"

"Yeah, but even though his wolf was psychotic, the fact

that we're fated broke through his bloodlust, and the longer I was with him, the tamer his beast became."

"Beast?"

"It's what Collin called his wolf-side, although, he doesn't anymore. Now, he said he feels like a normal werewolf again."

Kelly bites her lip and shakes her head. "What you're telling me is unheard of."

"I know, but it's true."

She takes a deep breath, confusion still filling her eyes. "I heard a few things about you two. Most aren't sure what to think. No rogue has ever come back from insanity."

"But how many rogue werewolves met their fated mate? Is there any history of *that* happening?"

Kelly begins walking again, so I fall into step beside her, but her frown remains. She eventually shakes her head. "Come to think of it, no, I've never heard of a rogue meeting his fated mate."

A thrill runs through me. "See? Even the SF wasn't aware that a fated mate can affect a rogue, and you guys didn't know about my lineage, so isn't that proof that your organization doesn't know everything? Maybe you're all wrong about Collin."

She shakes her head. "Oh no. Trust me. Rogues are nasty business, and Collin was definitely a rogue, but you make a fair point. We haven't seen a fated mate's effect on a rogue before. I'll give you that."

We circle back around the field to the door we initially exited. I know she's going to escort me back to my room, so I grab her hand before she can open the door. "Please, can I see him?"

Her eyes bug out. "You want to see Collin?" She quickly shakes her head. "No. That's not possible. His ward doesn't allow visitors, for their own safety."

I know my face falls because her expression turns sympathetic.

"Then can you at least give him a message? Please? Not seeing him is killing me."

She frowns and scans us in at the door. That creepy robotic voice comes on again, welcoming us back to the building. "I suppose I could pass on a message to him, just as long as it's not some weird coded shit that tells him how to break out." My eyebrows rise, and she laughs. "Kidding. There's no way he could break out of here."

We begin walking back to my room, our feet tapping quietly on the concrete floor.

"My message is pretty simple. Tell him that I love him, and that I'm not going anywhere. I'm going to stay right here for as long as I can."

She pauses outside my door. "You won't be able to stay here for much longer. It's highly unusual that you've been here as long as you have and seen so much. You've seen some rooms that only SF members are allowed in."

I twist my hands. "Then I'll stay in Boise so I'm nearby if I'm needed."

She cocks her head, her expression perplexed. After a moment, she says, "You really do love him, don't you?"

My breath shudders out of me. "More than words can describe." I grab her hand when my door clicks open. I know it's my last chance. "Please, just pass along my message, okay?"

She eyes me for a long moment, then finally says, "I'll try." She steps aside and waves for me to enter my room. A tray of food waits on the bed, but even though my stomach was growling not even ten minutes ago, I could care less about the food. "Someone will be back to retrieve you in the morning. We should have answers then about who you really are. In the meantime, I recommend you eat and get some sleep."

The door shuts behind her, and I'm once again locked in my room. I can only hope that she passes along my message to Collin and that if I'm not allowed to stay here that I can find a job pronto in Boise, because if there's one thing I know—there's no way I'm leaving him.

CHAPTER THIRTY-FIVE
COLLIN

A loud knock comes on the steel door to the cell encasing my cage. The guard stationed at it flips some scanner on his wrist device just as a female calls out, "Supper time."

The guard unlocks a panel in the door and leans down. He grabs the tray, then says, "What are you doing down here? Shouldn't you be scrambling memories?"

My entire body stiffens from where I'm sitting on the floor in my cage. I bolt upright. My hands close around the bars as a female responds, "I should have been, but plans changed. Is he in there?"

The guard casts a glare my way. "Still here. He won't be going anywhere."

A pair of eyes appear through the narrow slit the tray came through. I can feel her watching me. A full minute passes before she returns her attention to the guard. "He's kind of quiet for a rogue."

The guard shrugs. "He's on his best behavior. Trust me, it's not that unusual, especially in rogues that have evaded us for so long. They're smart fuckers. Don't let him fool you."

She clears her throat and says in a hurry, "Well, I have a message for him. I promised I would try to pass it along."

The guard, still holding my tray, sets it down. "Kelly what the hell are you talking about? We don't pass messages to inmates."

She rolls her eyes. "Yeah, I know, Dane. Don't bust my balls about it, but it seemed harmless enough." She slips a piece of paper through the slit, and my hands are gripping the bars so tightly now that my knuckles turn white.

"Is it from Brianna?" My question comes out hoarse and desperate sounding. Damn. So much for playing it cool, but when it comes to Bri, my usual suave demeanor vanishes.

The woman watches me again, Kelly, or whatever her name is. Her laser-like focus is studying me, taking all of me in. I don't know what she expects. Maybe I'm supposed to lunge against my constraints or eat my own limb or whatever fully crazy rogues do.

I try to picture how the beast would have reacted if I'd been in this position two months ago. It's definitely possible that he would have forced a shift and lunged toward her. The smell of human flesh, when he hadn't consumed it in days, could drive him a bit mad.

But my wolf is no longer a beast.

Now, his emotions align with mine. All either of us think about is Brianna and if she's okay. If anything, it's such a consuming distraction that I rarely think about my own future or what's to come.

I dip my head so I can meet Kelly's stare. "Is that message from Brianna? Have you seen her? Is she okay? Please, just tell me what you know."

My enhanced senses catch her intake of breath. She

rights herself before mumbling, "She may be right about him."

"What was that?" the guard asks her.

"Nothing. Never mind. But if you're okay with reading him that message, his girlfriend would appreciate it."

The guard sneers. "You mean his hostage?"

Kelly sighs. "I know it's weird, okay? But she insists that she's his girlfriend, and that they're fated mates."

The guard shakes his head. "Poor stupid woman. She's been manipulated and doesn't even know it."

I slam my hand against the bars. "Don't call her that! She's a hell of a lot smarter than you!"

My outburst makes both of them go quiet. They share a confused look before Kelly says, "Anyway, I better get outta here. Don't want Wes catching me."

They say their goodbyes before the guard brings my tray over. He uses the proper safety equipment so he stays out of touching range. I have to pry the tray through the small opening at the bottom.

But I could care less about the food. "Please tell me what the note says."

He unfolds it and reads it quietly. My gut is twisting as each second passes, and I'm about to snarl in frustration when the guard frowns before reading it again.

I don't think he's going to tell me what it says, but then his brow furrows and he replies, "It says she loves you and she's not going anywhere. She's going to stay here for as long as she can so she can be with you." He shakes his head, his frown deepening.

I let out a breath and press my forehead on the bars. *Bri.* She's still here, and she still remembers me. I have no idea how that's possible, but I hold onto the hope that maybe, just maybe, I'll see her again.

CHAPTER THIRTY-SIX
BRIANNA

I'm in the lab again, and even though I knew this was coming, I still gape when I hear the results.

"You're definitely a female werewolf," says the fairy technician from yesterday. "Your ancestors reside in the Montana pack and have since the North American wolf packs were created. Your mother's maiden name was Drummond, and her line is from the Originals, which makes you a pure half-breed." The fairy smiles. "And yes, I'm aware that's an oxymoron."

"My mother's maiden name was Drummond and not Olson?" I sway on my feet. It feels as if the earth just moved beneath me. "So I *am* a female werewolf? There's truly no doubt?"

Wes crosses his arms from where he stands beside me. "There's no doubt. Your mother—Bridget *Drummond*—disappeared twenty-eight years ago. There was an extensive search for her after her car was found over an embankment in Montana, but her body was never recovered. It was believed she was swept away in the river, her body either eaten by predators or caught underwater so far downstream that she couldn't be located. But now we know none of that is true—because your mother never died in that accident—it appears that she faked her own death."

I plop down onto the stool behind me. "But why?"

Wes's lips purse. "From what we can gather, it was because she wanted to be with your father. Given her lineage and what was expected of purebred females at that time, she was slated to marry a wolf of equal standing in the Idaho pack. Arranged marriages were fairly common then, but it seems your mother was having none of that. Instead, she chose to leave her pack and refuse that marriage. It also seems that she already had plans with your father because they were married not even a month after her disappearance."

He retrieves a piece of paper from the folder he's holding and hands it to me. My fingers curl around the crisp copy of my parents' marriage certificate.

It holds my mother's name, or rather, her alias. Instead of the block print letters reading Bridget Drummond, they read Bridget Olson. She chose a common last name, probably to make it easier to blend into the masses.

"But how did they meet if she normally only hung out with werewolves? My dad said they met at a concert. Is that even true?" My fingers are trembling, so I hand the sheet back to Wes and shove my palms under my thighs.

He slides the copy back into his folder. "Yes. That sounds right. From what we can gather, your parents met at a rock concert in Park City almost twenty-nine years ago. It's the only location our database found in which both were present in the same location at the same time. The timing adds up too. Your mother's pseudo-death was eight months after the concert, which means your parents were most likely secretly dating prior to her disappearance."

"But how could my dad not know the truth about her?"

He shakes his head. "We may never know the answer to that."

I think about what my father has told me of my mom. According to him, she was orphaned and had a hard life. She didn't have any brothers or sisters and struggled to find her place in the world. He believes that struggle ultimately led to her suicide, when in reality, it was because she left her pack.

Wes is right. My father probably doesn't know my mother's true past.

I work my jaw when a memory slams to the front of my mind. It's of a summer day when I was eleven or twelve and thought I was home alone, but my dad had returned early from work after another firing. He'd found me in the study, going through a box of his old belongings. That box held numerous Bon Jovi CDs, and my dad had been furious when he'd found me playing with them. He'd yanked the box away and told me they were very special to him and not to touch them again. He'd hidden the box after that. I never did find it again.

Tears prick my eyes. Maybe those CDs reminded him of the concert he met my mom at. It was probably another memento he held onto. Mementos he never shared with me.

Once again, I'm reminded of the fierce love my dad fostered for my mother. If only that devoted protectiveness had extended to his daughter.

"Do you think your father knew about your mother's heritage?" Wes asks, snapping my attention back to him. Both he and the lab technicians are staring at me.

I blink rapidly. "No. I don't think he did. He always told

me that my mom was an only child whose parents had died when she was young. He said she'd been brought up in the foster care system." I shake my head. I suddenly feel very tired. "My dad's a terrible liar. I'm pretty sure if he knew about my mother's heritage, I would have seen cracks in his façade."

Wes nods curtly. "We'll look into it, although I wouldn't be surprised if she fooled your father. Your mother was able to fool her entire pack, the SF, *and* the human law enforcement that had been brought in to look for her body after she disappeared. Our organization has been so rattled by this deception that we are now combing through all missing person cases in the past two hundred years, just to ensure nothing like this happened at any other time."

I sigh bitterly. And to think, my entire life I'd attributed my mother's mental health issues to a rough upbringing when in reality it was her werewolf heritage that could be blamed.

"She was a wily old bitch, that's for sure," I mutter under my breath.

My tone sounds as bitter and hurt as I feel. Betrayal cuts my heart into a thousand pieces as I try to process everything. If it wasn't bad enough having Collin taken from me, I now have to deal with the deception that my mother forced upon me.

What the fuck, Mom. Seriously.

"Brianna?" Wes says. "Would you like to meet your mother's family? Your grandparents are still alive, as are her two sisters and brother, along with a dozen cousins, not to mention all of their kids."

My eyes widen. "You told all of them about me?"

He shakes his head. "No, not yet, we wanted you to know first, but if they're anything like most pack families, they'll be thrilled to meet you."

My hands are sweating so badly that I keep rubbing them on my jeans. Two days have passed since I discovered my true origins, and Wes has arranged a meeting for me and my mother's family. I'm so nervous I could barf, and it doesn't help that I still have no idea how Collin is.

Being parted from him has taken on a life of its own. When I haven't been with Wes, all I've been able to think about is Collin. He's invaded my thoughts and my dreams.

I don't feel complete anymore.

It's as if a part of my soul was cut from my body, and a cold empty void now resides in its place.

I sigh in frustration and use my current situation as a distraction. I'm locked in an SF conference room. My packed bag lies at my feet. After meeting my grandparents, I'll be escorted out. Since my lineage testing is complete, and they're not wiping my memory, I have no further reason to be in the SF's super-secret base.

And all I have to show for the past two months of my life—in which I fell madly in love, found out I was part werewolf, and left my friends and schooling behind me—are the clothes at my feet. The upside? I get to keep the little canvas duffel bag that I packed everything into this morning, a nice little souvenir of this tumultuous experience.

Frustration howls inside me, and I suppress the urge to kick something. All I want is Collin, and all I get is a damned bag.

I pace in front of the windows. The beautiful Idaho hills loom outside, yet I hardly notice them. I keep trying to figure out what I can do. Nothing I've tried so far has worked. I don't even know if Kelly passed along my message to Collin because I haven't seen her since. The only person I see now is Wes, and when I asked Wes about Kelly, he gave me an odd look, so I clamped my mouth shut.

I shake my head again, and anxiety coils in my stomach. I miss Collin so much, and I hope and pray that he's okay as I take a deep breath and try to concentrate on what's to come.

"Brianna?" Wes calls.

I jump when he enters the conference room. I didn't even hear that creepy robotic voice when he scanned himself in. Grief has completely consumed me.

"Carol and Bill are just outside," he says. "Are you ready to meet them?"

I somehow manage to nod. He gives me a reassuring smile, then opens the door wider. I swallow the lump in my throat when an older man and woman walk in.

The woman gasps, her hands flying to her mouth. She's tall with long dark hair streaked with gray. Strong shoulders fill out her button-up blouse. She's wearing jeans and sturdy boots. At first glance, I would have assumed she was a rancher's middle-aged wife. I never would have guessed that she was seventy-five and the grandmother of eleven grandchildren.

The man also looks fit and younger than his years. Salt and pepper hair covers his head, and the scent of Old Spice aftershave wafts toward me.

"Hi." I bite my lip, not sure what else to do.

But my grandmother doesn't hesitate. She rushes forward and pulls me into a hug. "You look just like her," she whispers and clings to me. "I can't believe how much you look like her."

Despite vowing that I wouldn't let this meeting get me emotional, a lump forms in my throat again. After an awkward second of me just standing there, I tentatively hug her back, and when her embrace only tightens, I slowly melt into her.

Even though she's athletic, there's some softness to her, and a cloud of scented detergent wafts up from her clothing. She smells good, clean, and a part of me feels like . . . I've come home.

My grandfather joins in and before I can stop myself, I begin crying. The emotions come from out of nowhere. I'm not sure if it's my fear and frustration about Collin, or if it's twenty years of bottled-up anger, loss, and the sense of abandonment from my mother's suicide that comes pouring out. Whatever the case, I completely lose it.

I cry and cry, and they continue to hold me. They rock me gently, crooning to me, rubbing my head, and sliding their hands up and down my back. I get lost in their embrace and don't have the wherewithal to snap myself out of it.

My grandma's crying, too, and out of the corner of my eye I see Wes leave the room and close the door behind him. I'm a complete mess, and I'm guessing he doesn't want to get wrapped up in this.

We're left alone and another few minutes pass before I manage to sniffle and wipe the tears from my eyes. I pull back, shuffling my feet. Warmth fills my cheeks as embarrassment floods me. I dab at my eyes with my shirt before my grandfather hands me a tissue.

"I'm so sorry," I say and wipe at the tears again. "I don't know what came over me."

My grandmother just smiles through her tears, and I'm so relieved to see it's not only me. Wetness coats her cheeks, and her eyebrows pinch together. "Oh, sweetie. I can only imagine what you've been through. When Bill and I found out about Bridget—" She brings her hand to her chest. "We couldn't believe it. We thought she died long before you were born."

"But we're so glad we have you," my grandpa says. He squeezes my shoulder, then pulls out one of the boardroom table chairs for me.

I collapse onto it, grateful for their kindness.

They sit beside me, and I squeeze my grandma's hand. It's crazy how quickly I've become comfortable with them. "Do you miss her?" I ask.

She nods. "Every day."

I avert my gaze, not sure how to ask what's been eating me up ever since I found out.

My grandma nudges me. "What is it, sweetheart?"

I let out a breath, hoping she won't hate me for being so damned angry at my mom that I would throttle her if she appeared again, but I can't help it. I have to know. "But how could she do that to me? She left me on my own, with a human father, knowing that I'm half-werewolf. She had to know that I could have also suffered from depression, that I could have gone down the same road as her. How could she do that? She couldn't have loved me at all."

The age-old ache of betrayal comes blazing back to me as hot and fiery as a wildfire.

My grandma takes a breath. "It's true. You could have ended up with depression, too, but you have to understand that when a female werewolf leaves her pack, the depression comes on gradually. A lot of the times, they don't see it coming. Bridget probably thought she would be immune to it, that it wouldn't happen to her, and when it did—" She shrugs. "She was probably so far gone with depression that she couldn't help herself, let alone you. It doesn't mean that she didn't love you. Our daughter may have made some reckless choices in her life, but she wasn't a bad person. She was kind. I *know* that she loved you. She just didn't know how to care for you given the state she was in. She probably didn't even realize that state so thinking ahead to what your future could be like . . . it probably never occurred to her."

I look at her hopefully. "Do you really think so?"

My grandpa squeezes my shoulder. "We believe so, and even if she did consider it, you have to remember that you're half human. Maybe she knew that your human side would protect you, because that's undoubtedly what kept you healthy. It's why you've been able to survive without your pack."

My pack. I bring my hands to my cheeks. *I have a pack.* I groan internally. How I wish I could share this with Collin. He would be so elated to know that I'm like him.

I consider their words and remember what Collin told me about his wolf changing. I'd seen firsthand what kind of beast his wolf had become without a pack. He'd been in denial that it would happen to him, just like my mother had probably been in denial that it would happen to her.

Fresh tears fill my eyes when I picture how hard he's fought to find his way back. He's told me repeatedly that I saved him, that being with me, finding his fated mate saved his wolf. He believes that anything less than that wouldn't have pulled him back from the brink.

If only my mom had found the same in my dad, but he obviously hadn't been her fated mate, just her chosen one.

My grandpa hands me another tissue, which I gratefully accept.

"Have you noticed anything about yourself that alludes to your werewolf heritage?" my grandma asks gently. She then smiles with pride. "You certainly have the build of our kind, but what about other traits."

I blow my nose quietly, then reply, "Wes said female werewolves are stronger, faster, and have enhanced senses.

I think I have the strong and fast, but I don't know about the enhanced senses."

My grandma pats my hand. "No matter. You're still one of us."

My heart fills at how quickly they've accepted me before my grandparents share a hopeful look.

"There's something else we're wondering," my grandpa says. "Wes told us that you won't be able to stay here anymore, that you've been asked to leave after this meeting, and well . . . your grandma and I were wondering if you wanted to come back to Montana with us? We'd love for you to meet your rightful pack and your extended family. You have aunts and an uncle and a whole slew of nieces and nephews. They all want to meet you if you're willing."

Tears fill my vision again. "You would do that? For me?"

They both nod vigorously.

"We want you in our lives so much, Brianna, but it's your choice. We won't force anything on you." My grandmother's words are gentle, but I hear the ache in them, the desperation, and it's exactly how I feel. I've only just found them, and I can't bear to let them go.

All I can do is nod as another fresh round of bawling begins.

My grandma throws her arms around me as my grandpa chuckles in relief. He pats my hand and says, "Welcome to our family, Brianna."

∽

A FEW HOURS LATER, I arrive in Crescent Crossing, Montana—the pack-run town of the Montana pack. Who would have known that an entire town could be owned and run by a werewolf pack?

Not me, that's who.

As I gaze out at the mountainous landscape, I realize that my life in Arizona is truly behind me. After all I've gone through and experienced, there's no way I can return to school and pick up where I left off.

My grandparents live in a huge home on their ranch just outside of Crescent Crossing. Mountains rise in the backyard like pyramids, and cattle low in the distance. All of the bedrooms in their sprawling house used to be occupied by their four kids, but now they're guestrooms, a sewing room, and one is dedicated to storage.

I have no idea which room was my mom's when she was young. Maybe someday I'll grow curious and ask, but right now, I'm still mad at her.

They help me settle. I choose one of the guestrooms with frilly curtains and a patchwork quilt bedspread and dump my SF bag on the floor.

"I'm going to get dinner started," my grandma says. "Why don't you rest for a bit. We'll eat in two hours."

I nod. It's all I can manage. So much has changed.

After she's retreated down the hall, I pull out my new cell phone that they bought for me on the drive here. My stomach is a jumble of nerves, but I can't put off the call any longer.

I tap in the familiar number, and my dad answers on the second ring.

"Hi, Dad. It's me."

I can practically hear the smile part his lips. "Well, hi, Bri. How are you? How's school?"

My jaw drops. It's been nearly two months since I've called him, and all this time, he thought I was still in Arizona—at school, hanging out with my friends, working my job, just living a normal life.

The truth couldn't be further from that.

My heart thumps, and I lick my lips. "I'm fine, but I'm not in Arizona. In fact, I have some questions for you."

"Oh?" He sounds genuinely curious.

"Yeah, because I'm actually in Crescent Crossing, Montana right now with Bill and Carol Drummond. They're mom's parents. Did you know that?"

"Her parents?" A pause follows. "Bri, what are you talking about? Her parents are dead. She was an orphan."

Some of the anxiety in my stomach lessens when I hear his genuine confusion. "Actually, no Dad. She wasn't."

We have a long talk, and I tell him everything I've learned about my mother—minus the werewolf part. It's the most open and honest conversation we've ever had, and I can tell he's as shocked by all of these revelations as I am.

And when I ask him to tell me more about her, for the first time in my life, he does. He tells me about their great love story, the little quirks that made her who she was, the day I was born, how happy they were to have me, and then . . . her inevitable downfall.

By the time we get off the phone, my heart feels shattered, but I'm certain that he's as shocked by my mother's deception as I am. But more than that, I'm certain that he has no idea she was a werewolf.

I didn't tell him about her true origins or mine. Maybe someday I will, but that day is not today. Because the truth is, I'm still coming to understand it all.

But some of the ice that encases my heart—the ice that has been with me since my mother died—thaws.

"Bri! Supper's ready!" my grandma calls from the bottom of the stairwell. Heavenly scents of roast beef, mashed potatoes, and freshly baked bread waft into my room, and I realize that I'm starving.

When I join them at the table, I tell them about my dad,

then ask if they're okay with him visiting so he can meet them.

My grandparents share a look before clasping each other's hands across the table. With smiles in their eyes, they nod.

"Oh, yes, sweetheart. We would love that."

~

I CALL my friends the next day as I wait to hear what's to become of Collin. Most of my friends don't understand when I tell them I'm not coming back, but a few of them are more accepting. Macy listens and tries to understand. She says she'll help me clean out my apartment when I finally come back, although that will be weird. Wes assured me that the witches fixed all of the damage after Phoenix and Priscilla made their surprise visit back in September, but still, it's weird.

I'm so thankful for Macy's friendship, though. She and I talk a few times a day. It's a much needed distraction, especially when two more days pass before we hear from Wes.

He calls my grandma to tell her that the date has been set for Collin's trial. It's the first news I hear about him, and I cling to everything she tells me.

"He's been officially charged with murder, sweetheart." My grandma holds my hand as we sit side by side on the living room couch. "His trial starts next week, and Wes gave us the name of his assigned magistrate."

"We have to go see him!" I immediately exclaim. "He has to understand that Collin's not a rogue anymore."

She pats my hand. "Honey, I don't know how to tell you this, but that's probably a lost cause."

"What? No. How can that be a lost cause?"

The timer dings on the oven, alerting her to the dish

she's cooking. She gets up and walks into the kitchen. I follow her, practically stepping on her heels I'm so anxious.

When the hot dish is sitting on the stovetop, she finally says, "Because most rogue trials are over before they've begun. Everybody knows what happens to a wolf when he leaves his pack, and everyone knows that lone wolves eventually turn into murderers." She steps closer to me and lays her hot mitts on the counter. "Because he did commit those murders, right, sweetheart?"

Tears well in my eyes. "His beast did. *He* didn't. That's a big difference."

She takes a deep breath and says softly, "But once a wolf has gone rogue there's no coming back."

"No! That's not true!"

I won't listen to her even though I know she's trying to break things to me gently, because I can't accept that there's nothing I can do.

I immediately get to work and seek out the magistrate that will be defending Collin. I manage to secure a meeting with him when he's at a stopover in Montana at the end of the week.

He listens attentively as I explain that Collin's no longer a rogue, but when he steeples his hands at the end of my monologue, I can tell that he doesn't think anything can be done either. Still, his words pierce my heart like an arrow.

"No one's going to believe you, Brianna." He's a middle-aged sorcerer and sports a little goatee. "Even if I put you on the stand, and even if you said everything you just told me, no one will listen."

"But we at least have to try to make them believe me, right?" I sit forward in my seat while my grandparents stay quiet at my sides. "I'll swear under oath—if the supernatural courts have that kind of thing—and state that my testimony is true."

The magistrate gives me a placating smile. "But you're forgetting one thing—you're Collin's mate. Of course you would say something like that."

"But I'm his *alive* mate! How many rogues have ever been with someone as long as Collin was with me and not killed them?"

He sits back and shrugs.

Frustration bubbles inside me when I see how unpassionately he feels about Collin's case.

"Please," I plead. "You have to save him. He can't die."

He raises his eyebrows and gives my grandparents a pointed look—as if asking them to take their kooky granddaughter from the room.

It's enough to make me scream, but even with my grandparents urging him to reconsider, the magistrate holds firm. He doesn't believe my testimony will do a damn thing.

~

Somehow, the next week passes by, and Collin's trial is set to start.

Apparently, the supernatural court system is much more judicious and efficient than the American legal system. There is no waiting for weeks until charges are pressed or months until a trial begins. From what I've been able to gather during the whirlwind of the past week is that rogue trials are usually short and sweet, and an execution is almost always the outcome, even though the community claims not to have capital punishment.

I take a deep breath as I stand in a lush Montana valley. All around me tall grasses sway as a grove a trees hides the glowing portal door to the fae lands. It waits in front of me, and all I have to do is step through it for a one-way trip to fairy-ville and my mate's trial.

"Are you ready for your first portal crossing?" my grandmother asks. She stands beside me in the field. We're less than a mile from Crescent Crossing.

I let out an uneasy breath but don't step forward. I stare at the swirling magical door with its opaque interior and glowing green trim and think of what waits on the other side—the fae lands, the supernatural courts, and Collin.

My grandparents wait patiently behind me. I can't believe I've only known them for two weeks. We didn't have our first *real* talk about Collin until after meeting his magistrate. During the previous days, I hadn't been ready. The ache growing inside me for my lost mate made rehashing what we had too painful.

But when I finally opened up to them and told them how Collin and I had met and how I *chose* to stay with him —they believed me. And when I told them that I was his fated mate—they believed that too. And when I told them that I wanted to be at his trial, and I was staying at his side no matter what transpired—they asked if I would like them beside me in the courtroom.

Never in my life have I had that kind of support. And whether their support is because blood runs thicker than water and I'm their long-lost daughter's offspring, I don't know.

But fuck it. They're here for me, and I love them, and I'll never forget what they've done for me.

"You'll be fine," my grandfather says. "Just remember, it goes quickly."

"Okay. I think I'm ready." I give them another unsure look. "So I'm really going to land in the fae lands after I step through this?" I know I'm stalling again, but the "door" with its glowing green border and milky interior has me completely freaked out. I've never done a portal transfer before, and I've never been to another realm, but it appears I'm about to do both. Now.

"Just remember why you're doing this." My grandmother squeezes my arm.

Her strong grip grounds me and reminds me that Collin's on the other side.

My mate is waiting for me.

"Yeah, you're right." Without another thought, I step forward and hurtle through space.

∽

THE PORTAL SPITS me out onto a golden cobblestone lane, and I somehow manage to land on my feet and not fall over.

The portal crossing wasn't as horrible as it could have been. Other than my bones popping and death feeling imminent, it was truly fine.

And what awaits me on the other side has my jaw dropping and my pulse racing.

Two tall humanoid-like creatures with golden complexions stand with pointed spears. When I make a move to step forward, their spears come together to form an X, and a rush of magic washes over me.

My eyes bulge. *WTF.*

A second later, my grandmother, then my grandfather appear. They dust themselves off and look me over.

"Looks like you made it out in one piece," my grandma says before linking her arm through mine. "Ah, the sentries. We'll just do this quick formality and then be on our way."

The two sentries stare down at us with blank eyes

before one of them says, "State your reason for visiting the capital."

"We're here for her mate's trial," my grandfather replies.

The sentry's eyes swirl to a silver color before returning to black. They pull their spears back. "You may proceed."

My grandparents act nonchalant as we step forward. When they see my bewildered look, my grandma whispers, "They're the gatekeepers. They keep nefarious individuals out."

Right. Of course.

I shake myself, and then gape at what's beyond the sentries. All around us, the capital gleams with its golden walkways, thatched-roof houses, and charming boutique stores.

Fairies mingle in small crowds, their colorful hair like bouquets of flowers. They go about their daily business, none of them paying me a passing glance, which must mean they're used to supernaturals popping into their city at random times.

"Where exactly are we?" I ask.

"The fae lands capital," my grandma replies. "Well, what do you think?"

I'm still staring at everything. "It's beautiful." And it is.

At the top of the looming hill in front of us a castle soars upward with jutting spires and stone walls. Fragrant scents and sizzling sounds come from what appears to be a café on the corner near the portal. Fairies with glowing skin and pointy ears walk along the main thoroughfare, carrying knapsacks or tugging children in their wakes.

And the sky. It's pale-green with wispy clouds, some white, others pastel colors.

Everything looks magical.

But I don't have time to fully take in the wonders of the fae lands capital. The courthouse is only a block away from the portal, and I catch a peek of its ivory columns and stone steps.

"We should get going. They close the doors at noon." My grandfather takes my hand, and he and my grandmother whisk me away.

I'm thankful for their firm grips and sure footsteps because the closer we get to the courthouse the weaker my knees become. I've never felt so overwhelmed in my life and knowing that I'm going to see Collin within minutes has me feeling faint.

My grandma pats my hand. "Stay strong, Brianna. You're a Drummond, and Drummonds can handle anything."

CHAPTER THIRTY-SEVEN
COLLIN

My chains rattle as I pace the few steps I'm allowed in my cage. They transferred me this morning to the fae lands. I'm in the prisoner chambers behind the courtroom. It's dark and quiet here, but through the thick walls I hear the magical workings of the courthouse.

My mother used to tell me stories of this place. She said the walls were spelled and hexes awaited criminals at every threshold. Those stories used to keep me up at night and made me fearful of breaking the law, which of course was my mother's intention.

But as I grew older, cockier, and more entitled, those fears subsided.

And now look at me.

I'm just another sad bastard who broke every rule in the goddamn realm and will no doubt have the book thrown at him.

It doesn't help that I've been confined to my cage's tight quarters—other than my minimal supervised exercise per day—ever since I was caught. The bars feel like they're closing in on me at times, and my wolf growls in anger.

And worst of all, I haven't seen Brianna in weeks. It's the one thing that can break me.

Other than the one message she managed to smuggle to me at the SF, I haven't heard anything more. I'm going mad with worry and the not knowing.

Because even though she said she was fine and still had her memory intact, it doesn't mean it stayed that way. For all I know, the SF was behind schedule in their mind-manipulation procedures and I've since been erased from my mate's thoughts and heart.

I hang my head and finally force myself to sit down. The cage's bars provide little comfort against my back, but I lean against them anyway.

I try to distract myself, so I pick at the hem of my pants. I'm wearing fancy prison garbs today. They had me shower, shave, and put on an SF-issued neon pink jumpsuit. The bright color suits the fae lands, although its main purpose is to make me clearly visible should I end up somewhere I'm forbidden. Still, the color's somewhat amusing. I have nothing against guys wearing pink. I was just never one of them.

I close my eyes and picture Brianna. Her image is seared in my memory like a brand. Her long lush hair, full lips, and wide luminous eyes have haunted my dreams every night since they took her from me.

If it weren't for that tiny message she managed to smuggle in, I would have never known what became of her.

I can only hope that she'll move on.

My wolf snarls when we picture Brianna with another man, but it's inevitable that she'll find someone else one day. I know the lucky bastard will never fill her heart like I do, but I do hope that he can provide for her and make her happy. As much as it kills me, I want what's best for her. She deserves a life of happiness and peace even if that means she's with someone else, because it's a life I'll never be able to provide for her.

I slam my head back against the bars when I picture someone else planting his seed inside her and her bearing his child.

Stupid Fuck! I berate myself.

None of this would have happened if I hadn't been caught, so cursing myself has become my new favorite pastime. I've wracked my brain every waking moment to try and figure out where I fucked up. I obviously did *something* wrong since the SF found us, but no matter how hard I try to place the crucial moment where I made the wrong move—I can't.

The only thing I've come up with is that the SF got lucky.

They knew where we were in Nevada when I tried to withdraw money for the third time, and as shitty as it is, they chose the right getaway highway to pursue me and found us sleeping under the stars.

So score one for the Supernatural Forces, and score zero for the motherfucking rogue.

I rake a hand through my hair just as I hear voices penetrate the thick wood door to my chambers. The courtroom is beginning to fill, and from the sounds of it, there are quite a few attendants.

I shoot to standing when the door opens, then peer downward. A gargoyle awaits. He stands no more than four feet tall and has a face hideous enough to induce labor.

He grins. It doesn't add to his charm. "Collin Ward?" I

continue staring at him, not bothering to reply so he adds, "I've been assigned to your trial."

Lucky me. If a gargoyle has already been brought in for my sentencing, then the verdict's already in. They're going to kill me. Considering a gargoyle's sole purpose at a trial is to carry out the sentence—leeching years off a supernatural's life—I can pretty much assume he's going to do that to me. I can only hope that he doesn't take all of the years I have left.

I snort inwardly. The courts are such a joke. They claim not to administer capital punishment, but everyone knows that rogue sentencing typically ends with one hundred and fifty years of life given to the gargoyles, which essentially means you're dead within months of the trial ending, or if you're lucky, you get a few years.

Whatever my fate, I know I'll spend the rest of my days in a cage dressed in clothes that rival cotton candy while I enjoy the meager time the gargoyle doesn't leech from me. Most likely, I'll be dead by New Years.

When I don't reply to him, the gargoyle shrugs and hobbles out of the room just as a witch appears behind him. Unlike the gargoyle, she doesn't feel the need to say hello.

She's wearing a business suit, and her dark hair is tied back in a bun. Her hands rise, and she begins to weave them through the air. She whispers a spell under her breath, and my cage rises like an illusion.

She transports me through the door and out to the courtroom.

The second I'm in the room, I smell it—caramel and sunshine.

My heart slams against my ribs, and I pin myself to the bars as I search the attendees for her.

She sits near the back—where all attendees are placed—and she's flanked by an older man and woman.

"Brianna," I whisper.

I know she can't hear me, but she spots me. Shock ripples through my frame, then my heart sings.

Brianna's here, which means she remembers me.

But as soon as that elation comes, so does a heady dose of reality. *She's here? But how is that possible? Humans can't portal transfer, so how the hell did she get into the fae lands?*

But I don't have time to consider it because the witch deposits me by the far wall. Even though I'm in a spelled cage, they still don't take any chances. I'm kept well away from all attending magistrates and court officials.

Rogues have a nasty reputation.

And then, the hubbub begins.

The judges and magistrates parade out in their long robes with their chins high. The clock strikes noon from the twelve chimes that ring through the square outside.

My magistrate sits behind his desk, shuffling papers. I've met with him a few times. Those meetings were enough for me to realize he doesn't believe he can save my life. If anything, our meetings were simply a formality.

The three judges sit behind their huge wooden panel at the front of the courtroom. The queen justice sits center and highest of them all. Given her pale skin and stark cheekbones, I'm guessing she's a vampire. She eyes me shrewdly from behind her black-rimmed spectacles.

Shit. She hates me already.

The next thirty minutes are filled with the officials introducing the case and outlining what my trial will entail. I don't hear any of it. My attention shifts back to Brianna and stays focused on her.

My mate.

Brianna watches me just as intently. As the opening

arguments continue, she mouths, *I love you* and a weight bearing down on my shoulders—a weight I didn't even know I carried—is lifted.

My mate still loves me. She believes in me. She knows I've changed. And she *remembers* me. How that's possible, I don't know, but in the end, that's all that matters. I'll die a happy man if I know her love for me remains.

But it's only when I see her gaze stray from mine that I finally hear what the opposing magistrate is saying. Worse. I see it.

At some point in the past few minutes, the counsel started showing pictures of the victims the beast killed. They don't waste any time in these trials. The magical slideshow flashes in the air above the courtroom in vivid detail—the grisly evidence on full display.

Brianna's face pales when a woman, one of the beast's first kills, appears. The woman is lifeless and lying in a pool of blood. Her throat is slashed and half of her face is missing.

I wince. In his early days, when the beast first emerged, I hadn't learned how to clean up after him. Some of his victims were left for the authorities—and SF—to find. I cringe. Make that *all* of his victims that I hadn't burned.

During the next hour, I'm forced to relive some of the beast's most brutal killing sprees. I continually seek out Brianna, but her attention doesn't waver from the display.

I'm not surprised. It's a captivating horror show, but agony rips through me. I hate myself more than anything in this moment. My mate is having to relive my awful crimes because of what *I* allowed my beast to become.

I growl in frustration and shake my head, but that movement causes me to finally see the other attendees in the court. My old pack's alpha is here with his wife, Daria. She meets my gaze and holds it. I try to communicate with my eyes how grateful I am to her. She saved my mate. I owe Daria so much, more than she will ever know, and I know I will never be able to repay her.

She watches me silently. Her brow furrows together, and I can tell that my clear gaze and steadfast behavior is perplexing her. After all, what kind of psychotic rogue is calm and thankful?

My parents sit beside Daria and Logan. My heart shatters when I witness the pain on my mother's face while my father's steely expression stays steadfast, however, his eye twitches. As much as he's trying to hide his pain, he's not. My brothers sit beside them, heads down. *Fuck.* I stole money from Pete not even a month ago. What they must think of me.

A few other members from my former pack are also present, and when I see the woman at the end, my lips part.

Cali's here. My old flame—the girl I dated a few years ago, for longer than any other woman, has come all the way to the fae lands to see my trial.

I scoff. *She's probably hoping that I burn.*

I take a deep breath and focus on Brianna again. Her face is still pale, and her bottom lip quivers.

My wolf howls forlornly. I can feel his confusion and regret. A part of me wonders how much he remembers of his beast-like days. Sometimes I think it's all a bad dream to him, but he senses Brianna's turmoil now, and it's tearing him up.

He howls again before curling up and trying to hide deep inside me. He's trying to escape a past that they won't let us forget.

I hang my head mournfully. His shame and regret are exactly how I feel.

CHAPTER THIRTY-EIGHT
BRIANNA

When court finally adjourns for the day, Collin is whisked away by the witches before I have a chance to look at him again. My stomach is roiling. Everything I've seen today and witnessed—it makes me sick.

"Are you okay?" my grandmother asks.

I nod quickly, but horror still swims through my veins. "Yeah. It's just a lot to take in. I mean I knew that his beast had killed men and women, he'd told me that, but other than—" I bite my lip. I almost said *other than Declan and the rogue who wanted to kill me*, I'd never witnessed that side of him.

She pats my hand, and her expression conveys she feels similar to me. It was hard to look at the pictures. But as horrific as those crimes were, I remind myself that Collin's psychotic wolf committed them, *not* Collin.

I cling to that. I need to. Fated or not, I couldn't stand by his side if he'd willingly killed people, but I can forgive his actions if they were committed solely by his wolf. I take a deep breath and remember that.

As much as I ache for the beast's victims, I still love Collin.

And I know the beast's changed and those days are behind him. His wolf isn't a beast anymore, and Collin regrets his actions that resulted in his wolf turning rogue. He wishes it never happened, and if he could go back in time and undo it all, I know he would.

But that doesn't absolve him of his crimes. I can only hope that the courts are more lenient if they see that he's remorseful, and I wish with all of my heart that they spare him the death penalty.

I try to imagine what the rest of my life will be like if he's allowed to live. Most likely, we'll spend it apart—him imprisoned and me on the outside. I'll only see him when I'm allowed to visit, and that will have to be enough.

I take a deep breath. It's not exactly the future I envisioned for us, but I accept it.

"Should we head back home?" My grandpa helps me stand, as if knowing I'm struggling to do anything right now. "Time moves differently here, so it will still be morning at home. Or, we can stay here and do a bit of sightseeing. Either way, we can turn in early tonight, so we're fresh for tomorrow."

I grip his hand tightly. "Yeah, that sounds good."

They give me placating smiles, and I can't help but wonder if they secretly think that I'm crazy for staying so committed to Collin.

The other attendees are also leaving the court. Collin's magistrate is still seated at his table looking through his court papers. I debate asking him again if I can testify on Collin's behalf, but I doubt he's changed his mind. He truly thinks my mate's case is a lost cause.

Anger burns in my gut. *I have to do something. Collin's going to die if I don't.*

I spot the woman who healed me from the poisoned arrow—Daria. She stands beside a massive mountain of a man. He has dark hair, broad shoulders, and keeps a protective arm slid possessively around her waist. I can tell he's a werewolf not only by his physical appearance but also by the way he treats his wife. It's as if she's the most precious creature on earth.

It's exactly how Collin treats me.

Daria gives me a sad smile when she catches me watching her. I step away from my grandparents to approach her. Since she's the only one I know here, and she seems to know most of the people in this court, I wonder if she can help me.

"Hi, Brianna. How are you holding up?" She places a hand on her pregnant belly, her demeanor sympathetic.

"I'm okay, really I am, but I'm a bit concerned after what I heard today. It doesn't look good and I know that Collin's attorney—I mean magistrate—doesn't believe Collin can be saved, and considering the light the opposing side is painting Collin in—" I can't continue because a lump forms in my throat.

"I know." Daria nods sympathetically. "Unfortunately, most rogues are judged before their trial even begins. Centuries of their compulsive behaviors can be blamed for that. There's really not much your magistrate can do to save him."

"But Collin's not like that anymore."

She cocks her head, and I can tell that she's listening.

I step closer to her, and my words tumble out. "I know that he was a rogue werewolf, but he's changed. Please, you have to believe me. He told me that the longer he was with me, the more normal he felt. And I *know* that to be true. When I first met him, he abducted me, and I saw how crazy his wolf was. I experienced it firsthand, but as the weeks went by he changed. Our love—" I pause and take a deep breath as emotions rise up inside me. "He says our love saved him."

Daria stands silently, still watching me. Her brow remains furrowed, but she doesn't automatically blow me off. "I have to say," she finally says, "that's rather interesting. I've never heard of a rogue being saved before."

"He thinks it's because I'm his fated mate."

Her eyebrows shoot up. "You're fated? Not chosen mates?"

"Yes, we're fated." I eye the werewolf at her side who's still engrossed in conversation with someone else before I turn back to his wife. "I can't help but think that if I testified that maybe I could help. Collin's changed. He really has. He's not a rogue anymore. Maybe I can help them see that even if his magistrate thinks no one will believe me."

Daria cocks her head, her expression turning pensive. "You truly believe Collin's changed?"

I nod emphatically. "With all of my soul."

She's silent for a moment, studying me with those arresting turquoise eyes of hers before she says, "Let me speak with the queen justice. She and I are on friendly terms, and she may listen to me."

My lips part. "You would do that?"

"I'll try, because unlike a lot of the people in the community, I do believe everyone deserves a second chance, especially if what you're claiming is true."

I thank her profusely before hurrying after my grandparents.

My grandmother clasps my hand, and we step through the doors to the foyer. A shimmer of magic waves around me, and I know I've just stepped through some kind of magical barrier. Out of the corner of my eye, I catch a flash of tawny hair and stumble. *Collin?*

I quickly right myself as my heart trips. But just as quickly as hope fills me, it disappears. It's not Collin but a man who looks suspiciously like him. It has to be Collin's father. He looks just like my mate only thirty years his senior.

At his side is a woman, also a werewolf given her strong build, and next to her are two men who I can only assume are Collin's brothers.

My breath catches. As if sensing my distraction, my grandparents stop.

"Oh, it's the Wards," my grandma says. I can feel her watching me. "Would you like to say hello to them?"

"I . . ." I'd hoped to meet Collin's family one day but this isn't how I envisioned it. Still . . . I'm his mate, and I'm not leaving him, and since any chance of Collin introducing me to his family disappeared upon his arrest, I know it will be up to me to make the first move. "Yes. I do actually."

"Bill and I know them," my grandma says. "We'll introduce you."

Nerves eat at my stomach as we approach, but I hold my head high and fight my trepidation.

"Jared and Andrea?" My grandmother touches Andrea's arm.

Andrea turns, her eyes widening. "Carol! I didn't know you were here." She pulls my grandmother into a hug, and I wonder if all werewolves know each other. After she pulls back, she dabs at her eyes and says, "Isn't it awful what they're saying? There's no way my boy could have done those things. Lies, all of it! He would never—"

"Andrea," my grandma says gently. "There's someone you need to meet. This is my granddaughter, Brianna."

Andrea wipes under her eyes again before extending her hand. "Nice to meet you. Are you a friend of—" She gasps before she grabs her husband's arm. "Jared! This is Brianna!"

Collin's father levels icy blue eyes on me. He looks so much like his son that all I can do is stare. Unlike his wife, he doesn't extend his hand. He merely cocks his head. "Aren't you the woman they found with Collin?"

I nod. "I'm his fated mate." *There. I said it. Now they know.*

Both of them raise their eyebrows.

"His fated mate?" his mother finally says.

I nod quickly. "I would have been another victim if his wolf hadn't recognized me for who I am. It's why he didn't kill me."

Andrea pales, and Jared clears his throat before saying, "Brianna, you have to understand that we don't believe anything they're claiming Collin did. Our son may have acted a bit overbearing at times, but he's not a bad person. He never would have killed those people."

I shift my weight to my other foot. *They don't believe Collin's a rogue?* "Um, actually, his beast did commit those murders. Collin told me he did, but those horrible things he did were when his beast was insane—when Collin was still a rogue—but he's not anymore."

A small noise comes from his mother. "Are you actually implying that my son's wolf killed those people?" Hysteria laces her tone.

"I'm not implying," I say cautiously. "I'm telling you. Collin's beast *was* a murderer. I experienced his wolf's psychotic behavior firsthand." I bring a hand to my neck, remembering the feel of his beast's jaws closing over my throat. I'd thought I was going to die.

Andrea's breath sucks in just as Jared takes her hand. "Andrea, let's be on our way. Carol and Bill, you'll have to excuse us."

A horrible sinking feeling forms in my gut when they hastily depart. *Fuck. I totally blew that.* It's only as his parents are walking away that I catch glimpses of Collin's brothers following them. Both have dark-blond hair and chiseled expressions. While they don't look identical to my mate, the resemblance is obvious.

One of them gives me a sympathetic look, and in it, I see that he knows what Collin turned into. He's accepted that his brother went rogue even if his parents are refusing to.

"Shit," I whisper when the courthouse doors close behind them. I want to hang my head, but I refuse to give into the dejected feeling. Instead, I whirl around to face my grandparents. "Why are they in denial?"

My grandma shakes her head sadly. "I'm sorry, Bri. That didn't go as well as I'd hoped."

"But how can they say that Collin's wolf didn't do those things? Of course he did. That's why he's here."

My grandpa pats my shoulder. "Jared and Andrea—" His lips press into a thin line. "Let's just say that in their eyes, their sons can never do anything wrong. And it doesn't help that Collin was always so strong and dominant. There had been talk in his pack that he could rise to alpha, but that didn't go as they'd hoped."

My frown deepens. "Instead he fell from grace and ended up a rogue." I shake my head. "Not exactly what they'd dreamed of for their firstborn."

My grandma nods. "They've had a hard time accepting Collin went rogue, and it doesn't help that they've always bailed him out from the bad choices he made as a youngster. I'm afraid he's now learning the hard way what happens when you go too far." She waves toward the courthouse and his trial.

Anger rises in me. I know it's not his parents' fault that

he left his pack, but dammit, if he hadn't been such an entitled spoiled kid maybe he would have learned that he's *not* invincible and then he never would have turned rogue.

But then you wouldn't have met him.

That little voice reminds me that all of Collin's poor choices led him down the road to the intersection in which we met, and I can never regret that—even though all of those innocent people died.

I must be more like my mother than I thought.

I have a feeling if my deceased mother had been in my shoes, she wouldn't have regretted what Collin did either.

Shaking my head, since I know these disturbing thoughts will get me nowhere, I make a move for the courthouse exit when a woman calls, "Brianna?"

My grandparents pause when a young woman approaches me. "We'll just head to the restroom, Brianna, before we go," my grandma says. "We'll meet you at the doors."

I nod and wave them off before cocking my head at the approaching woman. "Yes?" I say to her.

She stops in front of me at eye-level. Most likely, she's also a werewolf given her height. "You're Brianna Keller, right?"

I notice that she doesn't say Drummond. Since entering the werewolf world, she's the first to call me by my birth name versus my werewolf family name. "That's right. Do I know you?"

She smiles, revealing perfectly aligned teeth. The soft expression transforms her face, and despite her height, there's a delicate beauty to her. "No, but we have a mutual acquaintance." I cock my head, so she continues. "Collin Ward? I believe we've both been duped by him."

My eyes narrow. "I guess I don't know what you mean."

She encircles my forearm and pulls me toward the

corner before saying in a quieter voice. "I heard that you're Collin's fated mate, but it's important that you know who Collin really is."

I pull back and cross my arms.

"I used to," she drops her eyes demurely, "be with Collin too."

Jealousy flares in me. It's such a juvenile response, but I can't help it. "Oh?"

"He and I were together several years ago, and he told me the same thing, that I was his fated mate."

"But you're not. I am."

She gives me a placating smile. "The reason I'm telling you this is that Collin said that to most girls he was interested in. He would say it so they'd keep running after him, *and* it was a guaranteed way to get in their pants." She sneers bitterly. "Until he grew tired of us that is. Then he wanted nothing to do with us."

I try to slow my breathing, but my chest rises and falls too fast. "Well, I don't know what to tell you, but that's not why he told me that. I *am* his fated mate. It's not something he said to keep me *running after* him or to get in my pants. And by the way, what did you say your name was?"

"Cali Fogelson."

Cali. I'd heard that name before. My lips part when I remember where. It had been in the hotel room in Sacramento, when Collin began telling me about his exes before I stopped him. He'd said he had a girlfriend named Cali, someone he'd actually been with for a while.

But I shake my head. "I'm sorry, but you're mistaken. Collin and I truly are fated mates despite the history he has with you."

"Brianna?" my grandmother calls. She and my grandpa are standing by the door, watching me with worried expressions.

I can only imagine what kind of energy I'm giving off right now. Even though I know what Collin and I have is true, I'm still rattled by what Cali is implying. "I gotta go."

I don't wait for her to reply, but when my grandparents and I barrel through the courthouse doors even the charm of the fae lands doesn't improve my mood.

∼

My grandparents offer to show me around the capital, but I'm not interested in sightseeing so decline. We travel back to Crescent Crossing. At least the second time through the portal goes smoother. It's still not comfortable, but I know what to expect.

But even when we set foot back in Montana and leave the glowing green portal door behind us, my mind stays in the fae lands. So much happened today between seeing Collin, acknowledging the brutal murders his beast committed, meeting his parents, then hearing Cali's deceitful claim . . .

It's too much.

"You look tired," my grandmother says. We all get into the truck to drive the ten miles back to their ranch home. "Why don't you take a nap. It'll be another long day tomorrow."

"How long do these trials usually last?"

My grandfather eyes me in the rearview mirror. "Usually a few days, but never more than a week."

A few days. That's it. How different the supernatural community is from the human world.

I still can't believe that despite seeing all of those horrible photos today that my grandparents still haven't said one word about Collin.

The rest of the drive I'm quiet, and when we finally

arrive home and get inside I mean to head toward the stairs, but instead I take a seat at the kitchen table.

"Grandma?" I play with the plaid tablecloth that reminds me of a Scottish kilt. "Do you still think that Collin's my fated mate?"

I hate my questioning tone, but dammit, Cali planted a seed that even my mind's Roundup can't exterminate. Maybe that was her intention, to make me question if what Collin and I have is real. For all I know, she's a bitter ex-girlfriend. I mean, she certainly looked like one, but what if there's some truth to what she's saying? Maybe he *did* tell girls they were fated, just so he could mess with them and get in their pants.

Grandma sits down opposite me. The tea kettle whistles, but she makes no move to get up. Grandpa's still outside. He'd headed to the barn to tend to the horses right after we got back.

"You look like you're having second thoughts," she says.

I smile sadly. If there's one thing I've learned about my grandmother it's that she's not one to answer questions for you. Instead, she's unnervingly good at answering questions with a question until you've answered your original question yourself. It's been helpful as I've come to terms with my mother's deception and has only made me think my mom was completely nuts to walk away from a family like this.

I sigh. "I'm not having second thoughts, it's just something Cali said at the courthouse that got to me."

"Was Cali that woman you were speaking to before we left?"

I nod and she finally gets up to stop the whistling pot that now sounds like a runaway freight train. She returns and sets a mug of tea in front of me. The familiar scent of chamomile wafts up. It's my grandma's favorite tea.

I encircle the hot mug with my palms. "Yeah. She's one of Collin's ex-girlfriends from his old pack."

My grandmother sips her tea, eyeing me over the rim of her cup. She doesn't say anything.

I pick up my mug and blow on the hot liquid. "She claims that Collin also told her she was his fated mate. According to Cali, that's what Collin tells women to keep them around until he gets tired of them."

Grandma takes another sip before setting her cup down. "And do you believe her?"

"No. I don't think so. I think she's a jealous ex-girlfriend who's trying to get under my skin." *Too bad it's working.*

"Then what has you bothered?"

I sigh and take a gulp of the too-hot liquid, which makes me wince. "I don't know. I guess a small part of me wonders if it's true. It's not true. Right?" I stare at her with pleading eyes.

She covers my hand with hers. "Did you believe you were Collin's fated mate until you met Cali?"

"Yes, with every fiber of my soul."

"And what made you believe that?"

I sit back and smile sadly. "It was the way he tried to protect me even when his psychotic wolf wanted me dead. The way he came after me when I wanted nothing to do with him because he couldn't let me go. It was the way my body reacted to him from the very beginning, as if I was made just for him. And the way—" My breath catches. *Dammit. I don't want to cry.* "The way it felt when we first made love, as if I'd come home and finally found where I belong even though I'd never known I was lost."

When I finally meet her eyes again, her irises are misted over. "Has he ever been anything but good to you?"

I wipe at my tears. "When he first abducted me, his

beast tried to kill me, but that was before his beast recognized me as his fated mate. And the entire time, Collin tried to protect me, and once his beast realized who I was, his beast protected me too."

"So a rogue werewolf protected you instead of hurt you?"

I nod.

She sits back. "In all of my years living with our pack, I've never heard of such a thing. No rogue's come back from his murderous need for bloodlust no matter who the victim is."

I can't contain my tears any longer. A fat drop rolls down my cheek. "But that's what his rogue did with me, and every day we were together, it was like he healed a little more. By the time the SF caught up with us, Collin said he felt like a normal werewolf again."

She squeezes my hand. "So a young woman who didn't even know she was a werewolf pulled her rogue mate back from the depths of insanity. If that isn't a fated mate, then I don't know what is."

I take a deep breath and the rapid beat of my heart slows. "Yeah, exactly. I don't know why I second guessed it."

She sips her tea again, and I finish mine. And while the hot brew warms my insides I realize how lucky I am to have found Collin and my grandparents. If I hadn't met my mate, I would have never known the Drummonds.

I close my eyes. *Thank you, Collin. I'll never doubt you again.*

CHAPTER THIRTY-NINE
COLLIN

Day two of my trial begins and ends similar to the first day. I'm paraded out like a monkey a flamingo barfed on and shackled well away from the general public. Even though I've never thrown a rage, never shifted uncontrollably, and never lunged at my bars trying to break through them, they all still think I'm a rogue.

On day three, Brianna still sits on the bench in the back. I've come to look for her the second the witch flies me out. My mate's chin is high today, her expression resolute. Fuck, I miss her. I miss her fire, resilience, determination, and grit. She's as breathtaking on the inside as she is on the outside.

Our gazes connect repeatedly as the day drones on. I try to convey how I feel for her even though I'm not allowed to say one word. She's become my only comfort in my damned existence, so I sit, wait, and watch. It's all I can do now.

"As you can see, Collin Ward is a danger to society and

cannot be trusted. He murdered twenty-three victims, and those are only the ones we know of—"

I stop listening when the gasps and scornful looks begin in the crowd. Even my mother pales. I haven't talked to anyone in my family. I haven't talked to anyone at all. They keep me locked away and contained. It's how they treat all rogues.

And as more evidence of the abhorrent rogue my wolf had become is displayed for everyone to see, the evidence mounts until it's as if Mount Everest sprouted in this courtroom and looms directly over me.

As my crimes come to light, shame clouds me in a persistent fog. I've felt months of self-loathing and self-hatred prior to the start of all of this, but seeing my crimes advertised for other supernaturals to judge and witness . . .

I've never felt so much sorrow, guilt, and despair, and worst of all, nothing I can do will make it right.

I know that, but I still wish fervently that I could go back in time and change it all. I wish that I'd kept my ego in check, that I'd been wiser and smarter in my decision making. I wish I'd met Brianna on a random summer night while I was traveling with my pack brothers. That I'd seen her waitressing while I was out for a drink, asked her out, and swept her off her feet.

We could have married, had children, and grown old together. We could have done everything that fated couples are supposed to do.

But fate is a bitch, and that's not how my life turned out. Instead, my mate mourns for me as she sits in the back, flanked by the older couple who accompany her every day. Her shoulders stay straight, and I can see the stubborn tilt in her chin. I know she won't leave me. I know she'll stay by my side no matter what the verdict is, which means I need to make a choice.

Do I want this life for her? Do I want her to stay chained to a criminal who she'll never be able to touch, see, or be with again? Or do I set her free?

Only thing, setting her free means destroying all we have.

But I know what I need to do. My final sentencing is coming, and for once in my life, I'm going to be unselfish in my decision-making.

It's not about me anymore. It's about my mate and what's best for her.

I can only hope that one day she'll forgive me.

CHAPTER FORTY
BRIANNA

Collin's trial is winding down, which makes nausea roll in my gut. Each day has been more damning than the last. I know they're going to execute him given what's been said, and I can't let that happen.

My only hope is meeting with the queen justice. I've tried several times to see the judge, but she's always been unavailable. However, yesterday Daria told me that if I arrived at seven this morning, the queen justice would be free before the start of Collin's trial today.

It's my only chance.

I arrive at the courtroom early and smooth my A-line skirt and button-up blouse before walking to the judges' chambers. I'm hoping that if I look professional, I'll be taken seriously, but even my fancy clothes don't hide my trembling hands.

My grandparents aren't here yet. I told them that I needed to do something before the trial began so I left without them, but when I round the corner and two sentries stand guard at the judges' quarters, I wonder if I'm out of my depth. Maybe I should have brought them along after all.

The sentries watch me as I approach. Each one holds a wickedly sharp spear and stands ramrod straight.

When I reach them, their dark eyes stare down at me from their imposing heights. Both are heavily muscled, and their skin carries that strange golden hue.

I take a deep breath. *Okay, Bri. Don't blow it.*

They extend their spears toward the center of the hall creating an X, and a loud *clang* follows. A strong push of magic barrels into me. It's as if I've hit an invisible wall.

"State your reason for approaching the judges' chambers," the sentry on the left says.

My mouth goes dry. "I'm here to see the queen justice regarding Collin Ward's trial."

Something changes in the sentry's eyes. His dark irises whirl and turn to shimmery silver before becoming inky darkness once again. Another rush of magic flows over me but quickly passes.

With a swift move, the sentries pull their spears back to their sides and look forward once again.

"Proceed."

I hurry through the guarded threshold and head straight for the corner room. Daria prepped me beforehand so I would know where to go, and when I reach it, I knock twice on the solid wooden door.

"Enter," a woman calls from within.

The door opens before I can touch the handle, and when I cross the threshold, another vibration of magic flutters through me.

Fucking-A. This place is swimming in magic.

But I manage to maintain my composure when I approach her desk. She still hasn't looked up. Instead, the queen justice writes furiously on some legal-looking script in front of her. Daria had told me the queen justice is a vampire, and I can't help my curious appraisal of her.

Her complexion is snow-white and blemish-free. As before, she wears thick black-rimmed glasses. Her blond hair is piled into a stylish twist on the top of her head, not one stray strand is out of place.

"Are you done?" she asks without shifting her attention.

My jaw snaps close, and I swallow uncomfortably since she knew I'd been appraising her. I sink onto the chair in front of her desk while my cheeks flush.

"I didn't say you could sit."

I hastily stand. *Shit. Can I fuck this up any more?* "I'm sorry." I clear my throat. "I was just hoping for a few minutes of your time."

She finally sets her quill down and gives me her attention. Her eyes are ice-blue. She props her elbows on the table, then folds her fingers together. "Please sit."

I collapse onto the chair.

"Daria Gresham tells me that you're wanting to be a witness during Collin Ward's trial today."

"That's right. I tried to convince his magistrate to allow it, but he thinks it's a waste of time."

She purses her lips. "Well, I have to say that I agree with him, so tell me, dear girl, why should I allow it?"

"Because Collin's not a rogue anymore."

She quirks an eyebrow, but other than that, her frosty demeanor doesn't falter. "Says who?"

"Me."

Her thin lips rise in an amused smile before she sits back in her chair. "Ah, yes. The proposed fated mate comes to the rescue. Why am I not surprised."

"Please." I lean forward, desperation ringing in my tone. "Please, you have to believe me. I was living with him for almost two months prior to his arrest. I was with him twenty-four hours a day and in that time, he never killed anyone." I don't mention Declan or the old rogue because I firmly believe those incidents were different. Collin was defending me, not murdering for sport. "Please. I need to tell my story. Everyone needs to hear that he's changed."

She watches me for a full minute. Her gaze is unblinking, her expression blank. I have no idea if she's considering what I just said or has merely spaced out.

She sits upright so quickly that I startle, and before I can blink her quill is back in her hand and she's writing furiously again. "Fine. You may take the witness stand today. Now, is that all?"

I nod but wonder if she sees me since her attention is still on her writing.

"Very well then. You may go." She makes a swishing movement with her hand—still not looking up—and I don't waste any time exiting her room and crossing the sentry barrier.

I breathe a little easier when I reach the foyer. My grandparents are waiting and smile when they see me.

But while I'm ecstatic at getting the chance to defend my mate, I'm also terrified, because if I fail, his death will forever haunt me.

∽

An hour later, I step into the courtroom, and the prickly magic at the threshold needles me like thorns on a cactus. As has been the case every day this week, the courtroom is mostly full but by no means packed. I keep waiting for crowds to form, for news stations to show up, and for the fae lands and supernatural world to be as engrossed in Collin's trial as I am.

But it never happens.

My grandparents have told me that rogue trials rarely garner attention. It's the same old, boring story each time—wolf leaves his pack, wolf turns rogue, rogue murders others, rogue is caught, rogue dies.

There's nothing interesting about a revolving door that spins round and round in the same pattern of its existence.

But those that I've come to recognize are present again today—Daria and her husband, Collin's family, and a few members of his former pack.

I nod at his family. His parents and brothers acknowledge me in return. Even though our initial introduction was rather awkward, I've made a point to speak to them every day, and they've begrudgingly come to accept me. After all, they love Collin as much as I do, so dammit, we're on the same side.

My grandparents and I sit in the back again, and once the trial starts, my mate is paraded out. His chin dips, and his broad shoulders fold inward. Each day he looks more defeated.

I will him to look at me, but today he keeps his focus on the magistrates. As before, the magistrates drone on.

It's the same as it's been all week. More evidence. More pictures. More gore. After four days of this, I've almost grown immune, but that's only because I *know* my mate has changed.

"Brianna Drummond," the queen justice calls late morning. "You may approach the court and take the witness stand."

I stand hastily, and Collin's gaze whips toward me. I walk steadily to the front and look around for the bailiff to swear me in, but nobody steps forward.

"Brianna, the stand." The queen justice raises her eyebrows while the judges at her sides wait expectantly.

"Right. Sorry." I step into the seat, and my breath sucks

in when a powerful flare of magic coats my skin. *Holy balls, what was that?*

"State your name for the court," the judge on the left says. He's a short man with a paunch belly. According to my grandpa, he's a sorcerer.

"Brianna Bridget Keller, although in the community I'm known as Brianna Bridget Drummond." I say both of my last names cause I don't know which one the court wants. The magic glows green around my skin. *Um, okay . . .*

"State your race."

My race? "Um, human?" The magic glows red. Confused, I look to the judge for clarification while Collin's attention bores into me. I eye my mate for a moment. His eyebrows have drawn tightly together.

The queen justice shakes her head. "Do you care to try that question again?"

Oh, shit. Oops. "Sorry. This is new to me. I'm half-werewolf." The magic turns green.

Collin's breath sucks in, and a look of shock crosses his features. I flash him a wan smile, wishing he didn't have to learn my true origins this way, but he just stares at me, his expression unreadable.

My smile falters.

"—Ms. Drummond?"

I snap my attention away from my mate to see the judge eyeing me shrewdly. "Did you hear me?"

"I'm sorry. No."

The queen justice sits back. "I was saying that I advise you to keep your answers truthful, Ms. Drummond. We will know if you're lying."

So that's what the flaring magic means. I barely have time to react before she says, "And why do you want to testify today?"

"To prove that my mate has changed." The magic again flares green.

"Very well. Magistrate?" the queen justice states. "Do you have any questions for Ms. Drummond?"

The magistrate prosecuting the trial scowls at me before standing. I eye Collin again, hoping for his support, but his expression remains blank.

"Ms. Drummond," the magistrate begins. "Are you denying that Collin Ward's a murderer?"

"No. His wolf side was definitely a murderer, but he's not anymore."

When the magic shows that I'm being truthful, the magistrate's scowl deepens. "And how can you prove that?"

"Because he and I were together twenty-four hours a day after we left my apartment in Quintin Valley. I can attest that Collin hasn't killed or hurt anyone since then." I'm careful to state that *Collin* hasn't killed anyone, only his beast has and when the magic again states I'm being truthful, I let out a relieved sigh.

The magistrate frowns and changes tactics.

He comes at me from every angle, wanting to know how Collin treated me and came to meet me. When I tell them how Collin abducted me and almost killed me before his beast recognized me as his fated mate, the prosecutor puts his hands on his hips.

"He almost killed you, but you want us to believe he won't murder again?"

"He won't. That was the day his wolf started healing."

"Am I understanding correctly that you're claiming that Mr. Ward is no longer a rogue werewolf because you're his fated mate, and you've healed him?"

"That's exactly what I'm saying."

"That's quite an accomplishment to make considering *no* rogue has ever come back from insanity."

My lips part, and I eye Collin again, but his head has dipped. My heart rips. *Why won't he look at me?* Somehow I manage to say, "I know, but it's the truth."

When the magic glows green, a collective intake of breath is heard in the courtroom. The three judges all eye one another.

Leaning forward, the queen justice asks, "Can we confirm that Collin Ward has not committed any murders following the date of 8 September?"

I hold my breath, unsure if they've uncovered Declan's and the rogue's murders, but when the SF informant stands and states, "That is correct. To the best of the Supernatural Forces' knowledge, he has not committed any murders since that date."

Inwardly, I breathe a sigh of relief. As much as I feel guilty about Declan's death, there's no way in hell I'm letting that prick be the cause of my mate's execution.

"And what about you, Ms. Drummond, can you also confirm that you have never witnessed Collin *or his rogue wolf* killing anyone in the time you were with him?"

Shit. The queen justice wasn't fooled. My mouth goes dry. "Um, what?"

"Can you also confirm that you have never witnessed Collin or his rogue wolf killing anyone in the time you were with him?"

I glance around at my chair, my heart sinking when I realize I can't lie. The magic will alert them to my betrayal. I seek Collin's support, desperately needing it right now more than anything, but his gaze is down, his expression resolute.

"Well, Ms. Drummond? We don't have all day, and you've already held up this proceeding by requesting to be a witness at this trial, so state right now—can you also confirm that you never witnessed Collin or his rogue wolf killing anyone in the time that you were with him?" She taps her finger impatiently.

I clasp my hands together and look down before saying quietly, "No, I can't confirm that."

The light shines green, and a collective gasp sweeps through the courtroom.

The queen justice's lips thin. Her icy skin, as smooth as marble, betrays her slight frown. "So you *have* witnessed your fated mate murder since you joined him?"

I somehow manage to swallow the lump in my throat as tears prick my eyes. Nausea makes me want to heave. I've thoroughly fucked this up. I wanted so desperately to keep Collin alive that I unwittingly just revealed that his wolf has killed since we met.

"Yes, but it's not what you think." I glance up at her with tears in my eyes. "His beast killed two men in the time since we met, but both of them were trying to hurt me. One was going to rape me, and the other was going to murder me. He did it to defend me. He only wanted to keep me safe."

The opposing magistrate sits smugly, while Collin's magistrate shakes his head. There was probably more to his reasoning for not putting me on the stand than I'd realized.

Idiot! Fuck, I'm such a fool!

I lock my gaze onto Collin. He's sitting quietly in his cage, his head still down, his shoulders drooped.

He's totally and completely given up.

My heart shatters, and I plead to the judges. "Please, just listen to me. There was a man who was following me one night in northern Arizona. He attacked me and was on top of me when Collin's wolf came upon us. Collin's wolf killed him because he was going to rape me. And the second man he killed was another rogue. That rogue directly challenged Collin and stated he was going to kill me right before he attacked Collin. Again, my mate was defending me. In both circumstances, he was *defending* me. Those are the only people he's killed in the time I've known him."

Green light shines around me, but the judges' expressions don't change. My heart sinks.

"Very well," the queen justice says pragmatically. "Any further questions?" she asks the opposing magistrate.

The opposing magistrate shakes his head smugly.

"And you?" she asks Collin's magistrate.

Collin's magistrate twirls his goatee, then stands. He comes around his table. For a moment, he paces slowly back and forth in front of me, continuing to rub his chin hair.

"Ms. Drummond, you're stating that your fated mate is no longer a rogue werewolf because you helped bring him back from insanity. Is that correct?"

"Yes." The light shines green.

"And you're further stating that the only two men that Collin Ward's rogue wolf killed in the two months you were with him were both men that attacked you and meant you harm."

"Yes." Again green.

"And you are also testifying that you were with Collin Ward, in his direct presence, during the entire time up until his arrest?"

"Except for four hours when we were apart, the day after he abducted me—yes." Again, green.

The magistrate stops his pacing and faces me. "Ah, so not only did your *fated mate* defend you against grave harm and possible death, but he also *let you go* during a period of time, while he was a rogue werewolf."

"Yes." Green.

He resumes his pacing. "Now, as the court knows, never in the history of known rogue abductions, has a rogue ever let a victim go. And as the court also knows, the supernatural community does not punish mated werewolf males for defending their mate, even if that defense leads to the aggravator's death. If that were the case, we would have hundreds of mated werewolves clogging up our prison system." He stops and faces the judges. "From the true testimony that Ms. Brianna Drummond has provided us with, it seems evident to me that in the two incidents she's highlighted, Collin Ward was practicing his given right to defend his mate as sanctioned by the high courts in clause 19.2 of the 1837 mating law. And as you have seen from her true testimony, Collin Ward at no other times in the previous two months committed murders against innocent humans or supernaturals, which as we all know, has never before been seen in a rogue werewolf. So tell me, will you please, how can we condemn a man to gargoyle leeching if he is in fact no longer a rogue werewolf?"

"Because that's never before been seen!" the opposing magistrate states.

The queen justice raises her hand. "You make a fair point, Magistrate, but you've had your time to speak." She turns her gaze back to Collin's magistrate and asks, "Any further questioning?"

"No. I believe I'm done."

"Very well. Ms. Drummond, you may step down."

I shakily stand and look to Collin for support, or some form of response from him, but as he's been all day—nothing.

WTF.

When I sit back beside my grandparents, a stone settles in my stomach. My chest rises and falls rapidly. I love

Collin with all of my heart, and I'll do whatever is needed to keep him alive.

But right now, I'm wondering if my mate even wants to be saved.

∼

When the day comes to an end, Collin is whisked back into the locked chambers behind the judges.

As before, he refuses to acknowledge me. My body physically hurts at his blatant snub. I thought he would feel hopeful that I'd put myself out on a limb to testify for him, but maybe he doesn't care.

"How are you holding up?" A soft hand touches my shoulder, and I jump.

Daria's eyes go wide. She's standing behind my bench and must have approached when the attendees all stood.

"I'm sorry. I didn't mean to startle you. I just wanted to see how you're doing. You did well up there."

"I'm fine," I lie. "And thank you so much for your help. Without it, I don't know if the queen justice would have allowed me to testify."

Daria smiles, and her face radiates a womanly glow. Her large pregnant abdomen juts out in front of her like a beach ball, but she's alone at the moment, her husband nowhere to be seen.

"You're very welcome. I just hope it's enough to sway them."

I nod, but my chest feels heavy. "Yeah, me too."

∼

The next day is the final day of the trial, and I'm all nerves. I wait expectantly with my grandparents in our usual seat, and my breath catches when the back door to the courtroom opens. The witch appears with Collin's cage in her wake.

She glides his cage to its designated area. He still wears that ridiculous pink jumpsuit, as he has been all week, and his eyes stay downcast. I will him to look at me, but he seems intent on staring at the floor again.

I can feel Daria behind me. A haze of compassion and empathy surrounds the healer.

"The honorable queen justice," a fairy announces. He bows when another door opens and the judges parade out with their haughty demeanors and flowing robes.

The queen justice takes her place at the highest seat. According to my grandma, she's been on the supernatural courts for centuries and has a reputation for being fair but resolute.

I can only hope that she grants Collin some leniency given my testimony.

Daria squeezes my shoulder one last time just as her mate appears. The dark-haired werewolf slides onto the bench beside his wife, his large form silent. He moves just like Collin.

"Magistrates, please rise," the queen justice declares.

I grip my grandparents' hands tightly. *Here it is. Final sentencing.* I'll finally know Collin's fate.

After the magistrates are standing before her, the queen justice eyes them shrewdly. "I had a request from the prosecuting magistrate this morning, which I've decided to grant. We shall be calling more witnesses before final judgment is passed."

I turn wide eyes toward my grandmother, but she looks as confused as me. "I thought we would know first thing this morning what the judges decided."

She nods and gives me a tight smile. "So did I."

The magistrate prosecuting Collin glides around his table, his demeanor almost giddy. "I would like to call Cali Fogelson to the stand."

My lips part when Collin's ex-girlfriend stands from the front bench. She approaches the witness stand as I did. I whip my gaze toward Collin, but he's still staring at the floor, his jaw locked and his expression tight, so I turn around and say in a rush to Daria, "What's happening?"

But all she does is frown and shake her head.

"State your name for the court," the judge on the left says to Cali.

She sits straighter. "Cali Fogelson." The magic around her shimmers green.

"State your race."

"Werewolf." Again, green.

"Thank you for the formalities," the prosecuting magistrate says, taking over. "Now, for the court, please state who Collin Ward is to you."

"My ex-boyfriend." Another flare of green magic.

The magistrate cocks his head. "Was he truly just a boyfriend?"

Cali's jaw tightens. "Yes, although I thought we were more. He told me we were fated mates."

My heart stops. So here it is—what Cali was claiming. But Cali had to be a jealous ex-girlfriend when she told me that. She was trying to shake my faith in Collin.

But the magic shines green.

I drop my head to my chest and squeeze my eyes shut, but I still hear the collective gasp in the courtroom.

"So like Brianna Drummond, Collin Ward also told you that you were his fated mate?" the magistrate asks her.

"Yes."

"And are you? His fated mate?"

"No."

"Yet he was insistent that you were?"

"Yes."

"And did you believe him?"

Cali's chin quivers. "Yes."

My heart is in pieces by the time the magistrate finishes with Cali, but the torture doesn't end there. He calls another woman to the stand, and then another. They all testify that Collin told them he was their fated mate.

After the fourth woman, the queen justice intervenes before the magistrate can call his fifth witness. "May I ask where this line of questioning is going?"

"Of course, Queen Justice," the magistrate replies. "I'm merely convincing the court that Collin Ward is not in fact Brianna Drummond's fated mate. As we all know, fated mates are rare. Most packs only see one or two every century. Yet Brianna Drummond claims that it was *because* she and Collin Ward were fated mates that Collin Ward is no longer a rogue, but as you can see Collin Ward has told most females that they were his fated mate. So how can we trust that this time it's true? And if Brianna Drummond is not Collin Ward's fated mate, then how could she have saved him as she claims? Unfortunately, the reality is, is that Ms. Drummond was another one of Collin Ward's victims. Even if she wasn't a murder victim, he still abducted her and manipulated her, which we all know is very common *rogue* behavior."

"Very well," the queen justice says. "Are you done? I do believe you've made your point."

The magistrate bows. "I have three more witnesses who also attest to Collin Ward telling them they were his fated mate, but if it pleases the court, we can move on."

"Yes, that would please the court," the queen justice replies.

With tears in my eyes, I glance at Collin again. I'm

desperately hoping that he'll deny all that's been said, that he'll tell me that even if he did trick those other women that I truly *am* his fated mate.

But he still refuses to look at me.

His expression is blank and his demeanor rigid as he leans back in his cage.

After Collin's women are walked out, I feel so sick I fear I'll barf right there in the courtroom.

The queen justice calls a short break, and as each minute ticks by, I struggle to breathe. While everyone else stands and stretches, I stay as I am, watching my mate with my heart in my throat.

But Collin continues to ignore me. And any emotion I'd seen prior in him has vanished.

I can't help but fear that I've been made the biggest fool of them all, but then I shake my head. *No. What we have is real. I* am *his fated mate!*

Everyone returns and the judges emerge from their deliberation room. After settling her robes around her, the queen justice eyes Collin then the magistrates.

"Thank you magistrates for your time and expertise in the matters of the community versus Collin Ward," she says just as the clock chimes two in the square. "Collin Jared Ward, please rise for your sentencing."

My hands turn to ice. Collin stands, his expression blank.

My heart aches, and my stomach drops. Everything about him calls to me, and I will him once again to look at me—to reassure me, to tell me that everything I just heard isn't true, that I'm his only fated mate, and that I wasn't just another notch on his belt.

But his same indifferent expression remains.

Oh my God, I can't breathe! Why? Why won't he look at me? I'm trembling as I stand there, my body at the point of collapsing, and my grandparents grip me tightly around the waist, keeping me upright.

The queen justice eyes him shrewdly. "Collin Jared Ward, you are judged as guilty and hereby convicted of murder on twenty-three counts." The queen justice's icy voice cuts down my spine like a knife. "The usual sentencing for such a crime is gargoyle leeching of one-hundred-fifty years, however, since you have not murdered an *innocent* human or supernatural in the past two months—a remarkable achievement never before seen in a rogue, even though it was not definitively proven that you've been reformed—you will be spared leeching and are hereby committed to life in prison without the chance of parole." She picks up her gavel and slams it once on her bench. An eruption of magical sparks flare around her seat. "Court is adjourned. Your sentencing begins today."

My knees give out, but my grandparents catch me before I fall. Everyone else is gasping and whispering to each other, their surprise as great as mine.

He won't die. He won't die. Tears fill my eyes and trail down my cheeks as I sob in gratefulness, but even though my relief is so intense that I can't speak, the women's testimony comes back to haunt me.

I need to know that Collin and I are truly fated mates.

I need to speak with him.

"Collin!" I jolt to a stand and call to him, but instead of reacting to my call, Collin slams his head against his bars. A large cut splits his forehead, and blood gushes out.

I gasp in shock just as a flash of blue clothing streaks across my vision. Daria's running toward the front of the room, her pregnant form approaching Collin before anyone can stop her.

"Daria!" her husband yells, but his large body is blocked by a group of attendees.

The healer reaches my mate and slips her hands between the bars of Collin's cage. The witch who's in charge of Collin's cage rushes forward, but Daria is quick. She lies her palm across my mate's forehead, and Collin's cut is healed before anyone can stop her.

She pulls her hand out just as the witch reaches her. Everyone is so consumed with the spectacle Daria is making that they don't see me sprint along the wall and approach his cage.

"Collin." I leap the remaining distance to him and grasp the cage's bars. Magic thrums through my palms, heating my hands, but I don't let go. Collin's only two feet away from me, the closest we've been in weeks. "My love. Look at me."

My tone is pleading and desperate. It mirrors what I'm feeling within, but when he turns to meet my gaze, his eyes are empty.

My lips part. "Collin?"

He sighs and an irritated expression washes over his features. "Brianna, go home."

His words are like a punch to my gut. I bend forward, my stomach concaving, as if I took an actual blow. "What? How can you say that? Please, talk to me, touch me. Tell me that what we have is true. Please! Just tell me, and I'll stay by your side. I'll believe you. Just tell me that none of them mattered. Tell me that I *am* your fated mate!"

A commotion comes from behind me. I know I've been spotted. We only have seconds until the bailiffs reach me.

"Collin!" I plead.

Collin clenches his teeth and glares at me. "Stay by my side? Why would I want that? I had hoped by abducting you and showing the SF that I was capable of not killing that I'd be set free, but that didn't work. Now I'm stuck behind bars for life."

A wave of dizziness hits me. *What the hell is he talking about?*

Before I can ask, Collin levels me with an icy stare. "I don't love you, Brianna. I never did." He laughs bitterly. "You're not my fated mate, just like none of those women were, but my plan didn't work. Even though I'll be left alive, I'll spend the rest of my days rotting in a cell. Thanks for that."

His words cut me so deep it feels as though I'm sliced in two. I stand, reeling, feeling as if the earth has tilted off its axis when he growls, "Go home, Brianna. You don't belong here, and you don't belong with me."

"Collin . . ." My heart pounds as I wait for a flicker of something, *anything*, to flash in his eyes. "Why are you saying these things?"

He snarls and lunges toward me, just as hands enclose around my biceps and pull me away. "Don't you get it!" He seethes. "You were an easy fuck and a human shield. Why do you think I took you? I knew they were going to catch me. They'd been closing in, and I needed a way to stay alive." He laughs as a dark light fills his eyes. "You played your role perfectly, convinced that I loved you. You even testified on my behalf!" He laughs again. "You stayed devoted until the end." He spits at my feet, and I recoil just as I'm yanked away. "Stupid woman. Your roll is done, now get the fuck out of my sight."

My vision clouds as Collin's painful words cut me to pieces. I'm bleeding, hemorrhaging from within. My heart is splitting open inside me, and I'm dying as I bleed out.

Collin's lying. He has to be, but then I catch Cali watching me from across the room. Her sympathetic and forlorn expression says it all. *I told you so. I tried to warn you, but you didn't listen.*

And that look is the nail in my coffin.

Collin's hauled away. He doesn't look at me again. His jaw is set, his expression like stone.

But my tears don't come. I watch as the man who I thought was my mate is taken behind the courts. He'll be locked away, gone from me forever.

And the pain that is flaying me alive from the inside out is too much. I squeeze my eyes shut. I will myself to create a shield, a barrier, something, *anything*, to stop this unbearable pain.

And when I open my eyes, I've died and been reborn, only the new person I've become doesn't feel pain.

She doesn't feel anything at all.

CHAPTER FORTY-ONE
COLLIN

One month later

I hate myself, and every day I despise what I did to my mate.

The look on Brianna's face when I told her I never loved her will stay with me until I die.

I hurt her beyond repair. I said cruel, vile words to the woman that I love and worship.

But I had to.

It was the only way to give her a fulfilling life—the only way she would forget about me and move on.

But the pain . . .

The goddamn *pain* that sears through me every time I remember what I did to her . . .

This is my punishment.

This is what I have to live with, and it's more agonizing than anything the damned courts could have thrown at me.

I clench my hands into fists and roll onto my back. The hard mattress in my tiny cell feels like concrete. The days here have become one monotonous never-ending haze. I've been moved to a permanent prison within the fae lands. I'm no longer confined to a cage, but that's only because they have cells here strong enough to contain rogues.

Considering I'm no longer a rogue, the irony streaks a bitter smile across my face.

The other supernaturals in my prison block are from all walks of life. Werewolves, vampires, witches, sorcerers, sirens, and fairies prowl around their cells. The close contact with the other wolves means I won't turn rogue again, but none of that matters now.

My mate is gone.

I hurt her intentionally.

I hurt her *unforgivingly*, all so she would leave me and make a life of her own.

But the pain of losing her has ripped me in two.

I mechanically go about my daily existence now and do what's expected of me. I follow the rules, keep to myself, and go through the motions. This is my life now. My choices led me to this, and I deserve nothing less. I have the rest of my days to regret the murders my wolf committed and the rest of my life to mourn the woman I love.

∼

"Ward! You have a visitor." The fairy guard taps his magically-infused baton against my cell's bars. Sparks emit from it. "Turn around. Hands behind your back."

"Who's my visitor?" I ask and stand from my bed.

He doesn't answer as he waits for me to turn and accept my cuffs.

My parents have visited me several times in the past month, each time promising to find a way to set me free so I won't be "unjustly" imprisoned for crimes I "didn't" commit. Even though I've told them on numerous occasions that my wolf *did* commit all of those murders, they don't believe me. As always, their blinders remain in place.

But my parents always visit on weekends, and today's a weekday.

My heart lurches as I realize who it could be.

The guard finishes and opens my cell door. My guards have begun treating me like the other prisoners lately, not keeping the designated distance between us like they do for other rogues. They heard about Brianna's testimony and how the SF confirmed I didn't kill any innocents in the time she was with me. I've found them watching me on some days, their confused expressions letting me know they find my non-rogue behavior perplexing.

"Can you tell me who it is?" I ask again when we begin walking.

The guard tugs me down the hall. "A woman, and a very beautiful one."

My stomach plummets. *Brianna.*

The other week I finally broke down and asked the guards to tell me Brianna's history. In court it was revealed she was half-werewolf, but nobody ever told me how that was possible during my trial.

But here, one of the guards finally took pity on me and told me the whole story, about her mother, her fake death, and Brianna's werewolf origins. Her story has spread like wildfire throughout the packs, so everyone knows about her.

Looking back, it makes so much sense that Brianna's a wolf. My mind floods with an image of her kneeling on all fours, her pussy dripping and ready for me, as she looks over her shoulder and begs me to enter her.

Fuck. Remembering those times with her is enough to

make me crazy again. I'll never be able to be with her, see her, touch her, smell her, fuck her.

But I *won't* subject her to a life with me trapped behind bars, so I growl and say, "She's not supposed to be here."

The guard shrugs. "I'll visit with her if you don't want to."

I snarl as rage tears from me and my wolf.

The guard laughs. "Just messing with you, Ward. I know how possessive you wolves are about your women."

But Brianna isn't my woman anymore. Every time I realize that, it feels as though my chest has been crushed all over again.

I haven't seen my mate since that godawful day I cut her from my life. Every night I lie in bed wondering what she's doing, dreaming of the life we could have had, and cursing myself for hurting her like I did.

But it was the only way. I knew she wouldn't leave me. I knew she wouldn't move on unless I convinced her that I never loved her, which means that I can't see her now.

My footsteps slow. "Can you make an excuse and say I'm busy?"

The guard stops and eyes me. "Are you really telling me you don't want to see that petite blond bombshell in there?"

Petite? My head cocks. Even if Brianna dyed her hair, she wouldn't fit the "petite" part of that description. Curious, I continue following the guard and the woman I see seated at the table in the visitor's room has me grounding to a halt.

"Daria?"

The healer stands from the table as the guard secures my restraints to the magical bolts on the floor. "Hi, Collin."

She's thin again, her pregnant belly gone. When she sees me eyeing her stomach, she laughs and pats her tummy. "She was born four weeks ago, the day after your trial ended actually."

"You're a mom now? Congratulations." I sit on my chair, stunned that she's here. Daria and I have never been friends, but I owe her my life.

She sits again while the guard moves to stand watch by the wall. "Thanks. Logan's smitten. He's become a very protective and doting papa, and her arrival is also the reason I didn't come sooner. Giving birth and breastfeeding around the clock have been quite time consuming."

"I can only imagine." I take a deep breath and before I can stop myself, I ask, "How's Brianna? Have you seen her? Do you know if she got safely back to Quintin Valley and school?"

Daria's lips part. "Oh my. You don't know."

My stomach drops. "Don't know what?"

"She never went back to Quintin Valley. She's living in Crescent Crossing now so she can be close to her grandparents and her mom's family. In fact, she's transferred to the University of Montana and is now looking at apartments in Crescent Crossing because she plans to permanently stay there."

My mouth slackens. "She's now *living* in her pack's town?" Coming to terms with Brianna being a werewolf is one thing, but to know she's surrounded by horny single werewolves?

My hands curl into fists.

"Collin?" Daria says softly, as if sensing what I'm thinking.

I force my fingers to uncurl. "Sorry."

"I imagine this news can be upsetting, but she's adjusting well to her new life. She fits in as if she was born there."

I smile sadly. "I bet she does."

I'm happy that she's doing well and now has a family that supports her. I really am. But it also tears me apart. Living in the community also means she'll probably marry in the community. *Fuck me.* I don't know if I can stomach hearing that she's found another wolf. Knowing that she could find another human would be bad enough, but a wolf?

I feel sick.

But I still want to know how she's doing, as much as Daria can tell me. "How is she?"

Daria's expression turns pensive. "For someone who acted indifferent and cruel to his fated mate in court, you're now certainly singing a different tune."

And in her eyes, I see it. *She knows.* She knows that Brianna is my true fated mate. I sigh and rake a hand through my hair. "I didn't fool you, huh?"

"You did. Until I felt your mind when I healed you in that courtroom. That's when I saw it."

I abruptly lean forward, my cuffs rattling, but Daria doesn't flinch. "She can't know, Daria. You *can't* tell her. If she knows, Brianna will never make a life for herself. She'll come back to me, and I can't do that to her. I can't chain her to a man imprisoned. That's not fair to her."

Daria's turquoise eyes dim. "Are you sure this is what you want?"

I nod curtly. It's all I can manage.

"Okay."

A moment passes, and I ask hesitantly, "Have you seen her?"

"Once. And to answer your earlier question, from what I've heard she's doing okay and is adjusting. She's even waitressing now in Crescent Crossing, and she's apparently really good at it."

"I bet she is." I work my jaw and against my better judgment can't stop my next question. "Is she seeing anyone?" My stomach tightens. *Fucking hell, when did I become such a masochist?* I hold my breath as I wait for her answer.

But Daria only shakes her head. "I don't know."

The anxiety that's built up inside me at just the thought of Brianna with someone else deflates. "Right. It's probably best not to know." I drop my head, but I now know what my new obsession will be.

If Brianna's with another wolf.

As if sensing my downward spiral, Daria leans forward, her turquoise eyes bright again. "Anyway, the reason I'm here, Collin, isn't to fill you in on Brianna. It's to see if I can help you."

I frown and look back up at her. "Help me?"

She nods emphatically. "Not only did I see how you feel about Brianna when I healed your cut, but I also learned that you're not a rogue anymore. I felt it in your mind."

"You did?"

"Yes. I did that healing very intentionally. On the first day of your trial, Brianna came to me and explained that you'd changed, but I needed to know if it was true, which is why I jumped at the chance to heal you in court. I needed to dip my light into you to confirm it, so in a way, it was fortuitous that you banged your head."

My jaw drops. "So you really believe that I'm not a rogue?"

"I do."

I shake my head. "Well, thanks, Daria. It's nice to know not everyone believes I'm evil, but I don't know how that helps me. My beast still committed the crimes they accused me of. I'm not off the hook for that even though I'm no longer a rogue."

"No, that's true, but you *are* the first rogue to ever return from insanity, the very first in history if you want to know the truth. I even had the gargoyle scholars look into it. The history books confirm that it hasn't happened before, and since you're the first rogue to return from insanity that also means the courts have never seen a case like yours. That magistrate may have convinced the queen justice that you're still a rogue given how you told all of those women you were their fated mate, but I think she may listen to me if I talk to her. And if I can convince her that you're truly no longer a rogue and no longer bear a threat to the community, your sentencing may change."

For a moment, I sit in stunned silence. "Do you really think that's possible?"

She shrugs. "I don't know, but I know the queen justice who presided over your case—I healed her husband once. She's a fair woman. She may consider it."

I want to believe there's hope for me, but I'm also a realist. "Daria, even if she believes I've changed, it doesn't stop what I did. I still have to pay for my crimes."

"You're right, it doesn't change what you did, but as you're probably aware, the courts have become more interested in reform versus punishment. If we can convince the courts that you're capable of being *fully* reformed, there may be hope for you."

I'm silent for a long moment before saying, "So what do I need to do?"

"I don't know yet, but I'll be in touch."

∾

ANOTHER WEEK PASSES before I hear from Daria. The queen justice listened to her. She's open to believing that I truly am a healed rogue, but she needs proof. Daria's word isn't enough.

So I'm subjected to numerous psychological evaluations

by the community's leading health experts. And after weeks of testing, they all come to the same conclusion: I'm not insane and my wolf isn't either.

But that revelation brings more complications. Never before has a rogue come back from insanity, and nobody's quite sure how to handle it. So meetings begin taking place between the queen justice and the judges. Following that, they pull my pack's leaders into the meetings as they work out my reform plan.

It's January by the time I'm told the queen justice has reached a decision, and it's been two months since I've seen Brianna.

I sit in front of the queen justice in her quarters at the courthouse. She steeples her hands from behind her grand desk and eyes me through her black-rimmed spectacles.

"This has been quite the interesting case, I have to say." She breaks her composure to take a sip from her mug. Blood lines her upper lip when she sets it down before her tongue slips out to discreetly wipe it away. "It's truly astounding to know that it's possible for a rogue to return from insanity."

I picture Brianna's long brown hair, the way her eyes light up when I pull her into my arms, and how she looks when I plunge my length deep inside her.

I swallow the lump in my throat. "I can thank my fated mate for that. She saved me."

"Ah, yes, your mate." The queen justice eyes me with interest. "I'm assuming you mean your *true* fated mate, not the fake ones?" Her eyes twinkle in amusement, but I still feel shame at what an ass I was to all of those women. "Speaking of mates, I took it upon myself to convene with both the Wyoming and Montana packs. After much deliberation and negotiating, either is willing to accept you for your community sentencing. Do you have a preference or shall I choose?"

My heart pounds. *The Montana pack? I can really serve in the Montana pack?*

I somehow manage to say, "I prefer my mate's pack."

She nods. "The Montana pack it is. Now, you're clear that your new sentencing involves the gargoyles leeching fifty years off your life and that you'll be committed to a life of servitude? Since you chose the Montana pack, you're to report to Mr. Jennings every Monday, and you'll report to him every week for the next five years. We'll re-evaluate at that time to see how you've progressed, and should you digress or show any indication of returning to a life of crime, you will return to prison immediately to fulfill your life sentence. Is that clear?"

"Yes. Yes, it's clear." My mouth is dry, and my stomach's twisting. Brianna lives with the Montana pack. I'll see my mate again if the queen justice goes through with this new sentencing.

Oblivious to my physical response, the queen justice continues. "Positions have already been lined up for your work. You'll spend the rest of your life serving the packs and humanity. That will never change regardless of how well you behave. Are you sure you're ready to accept that sentence? It's very different from the way you grew up, or so I'm told."

I think of the lavish home, designer clothes, and credit card I was giving at the age of fifteen that didn't have a limit. Am I ready to give that up?

I grin, unable to help myself. "Hell yeah, I'm more than ready for that."

The queen justice nods. "Very well. In that case, Collin Jared Ward, I hereby alter your life-long prison sentence and grant you a life of eternal community servitude bar the fifty years taken from your life in punishment for your crimes." She picks up her gavel and makes a show of slamming it down.

Its loud sound rings, and magical sparks fly as my fate is sealed. I sit in stunned silence. Slowly, I come to a stand, unable to believe how my life has changed. The guard who's been standing in the corner steps forward to remove my shackles.

I rub my wrists when they're off.

I'm free.

I'm truly free.

I've been granted the blessing of a new life that begins today. I've been given a second chance, which no rogue in history has ever been awarded. And even though that means I'll never be rich, I'll never be able to choose my line of work or decide where I live, it's still a life in the community—a life where Brianna resides.

Now, I just have to find her and hope she'll forgive me when I don't deserve forgiveness.

CHAPTER FORTY-TWO
BRIANNA

"Is there anything else I can get you?" I ask the patron as I whisk his plate away.

He smiles at me, and I know what's coming. It's the werewolf's third visit this week to the diner I work at, and despite the block of ice surrounding my heart, I can't fault him for trying.

"Your number?" His smile stretches. "I'd love to take you out."

I fiddle with my apron. He's young, probably late twenties, and according to my grandmother is quite the catch, but his dark eyes and raven-black hair don't make my heart flutter.

Nothing makes it flutter anymore.

The bell jingles above the diner's front door just as I open my mouth to respond, but nothing comes out.

His smile widens. "How about dinner? Or a movie? What would you be interested in?"

"I don't know. I haven't been on a date in a while."

"We can keep it casual." He lowers his voice. "Or not."

I sigh. Even though I have zero interest in this guy,

maybe he's right. Maybe a date will help me forget Collin. "Well, I suppose—" But then the hairs on the back of my neck stand on end.

The raven-haired werewolf slips his number across the table, his eyes never leaving mine. "You're gorgeous, Brianna, and I would love nothing more than to take you out and show you a good time. What do you say?"

I'm about to respond when a deep voice growls from behind me, "She's already taken."

I gasp, and the plate I'm holding slips from my hand and hits the floor. It shatters into a hundred pieces, drawing startled looks from the other diners. I turn around, unable to believe whose voice I just heard as I come face to face with the werewolf who broke my heart.

"You." It's all I can say.

I'm losing it, clearly, since I'm apparently hallucinating that Collin just walked into my diner and looks as breathtakingly gorgeous as he always did. Everything about him is as I remember—the broad shoulders, the messy dark-blond hair, the sparkling blue eyes, and his chiseled features. He's wearing jeans, boots, and a thin jacket over his flannel. Fuck, my hallucination is even *sexy*.

"Brianna," he replies. His gaze travels over my face, soaking up every detail.

He takes a step closer, but I shake my head furiously and back up. I run into the table where the dining werewolf sits, which makes his coffee slosh over the rim.

This isn't possible.

Collin's imprisoned, and he doesn't love me.

He's not here. None of this is real. I'm hallucinating.

Fuck, I'm a mess.

I reach down to mop up the coffee, then clean up the shattered plate from the floor. But the man-who-looks-just-like-Collin beats me to it. My fingers are trembling while his are steady. He picks up the jagged shards, and when he stands with the fragments in his palms, his eyes are pleading.

The werewolf who's been hitting on me frowns as I stand there staring at my hallucination. "Brianna?" the dining werewolf asks. "Are you okay?"

An angry snarl comes from the Collin lookalike. He gives the dining werewolf a sharp look as a push of alpha power radiates off him. "She's mine, wolf, and she's not interested. Got it?"

The dining werewolf's jaw tightens, but he turns his head submitting his neck. "Right." Without another word, he stands rigidly from the table and strides toward the door, but he shoots my hallucination a nasty glare before he steps outside.

My heart is beating so fast now that I can barely breathe. *What the hell's happening? My hallucination has alpha power?*

The man-who-looks-just-like-Collin returns his attention to me. I stare into his eyes. They're so blue that I could drown in them. I don't know what kind of mean joke Mother Nature is playing on me, but it's not funny.

"Brianna?" Collin's lookalike says softly. He dumps the broken plate on the table before reaching for me. "Baby, I'm back."

I ball my hands into fists and press them to my eyes. "This isn't real."

My hallucination pries my hands away. Pain, love, and loss distort the features of the man-who-looks-just-like-Collin. "It is real. It's me."

And just like that, my pain comes back with a vengeance, searing across my soul like a meteor blazing through the sky. I slap him viciously across the face.

He takes the blow, his head barely moving, but a handprint is left on his cheek. A few of the diners gasp, reminding me that we have an audience, but I don't care.

I don't know how it's possible that Collin is standing in front of me, but the cheek that just grazed across my palm felt like Collin. It has the same rough stubble and smooth skin underneath it that I'd grown to love, and the cedar scent wafting from him smells exactly like the man who stole my heart.

Tears threaten to fill my eyes, but fuck no, that's not happening. For the past two months, I've learned to live without the man in front of me, and I'm not about to lose that ability.

"You bastard! What do you want?"

His jaw tightens as a regretful expression fills his face. His gaze roams over my features again, as if memorizing how I look. "They changed my sentencing. I'm free now, kind of, and I chose your pack as the place for my rehabilitation."

Rehabilitation? He's free now?

My chest is rising and falling too fast. I can't take it anymore. I whirl away from him and hurry to clean up my other tables. The patrons remaining in the restaurant are all watching us avidly. I'm sure this is the best show they've seen all year.

At least it's already mid-afternoon. The lunch rush has ended and the slow part of the day has begun. My shift ends in ten minutes, but I don't know how I'm going to finish with Collin Ward standing at my back.

The diner's owner comes out from the kitchen. She's frowning, so I'm guessing she witnessed most of what happened. She approaches me slowly, a wary look on her face when she eyes Collin. "Brianna? Sweety, are you okay?"

I nod quickly. "Yeah. I'm fine. Sorry that I caused a commotion."

"No, it's okay." She pries the washrag from my hands. "Why don't you head out and I'll finish. Your shift is almost done anyway."

When I begin to protest, she gives me a firm squeeze. "It's okay. Go."

I give her a grateful smile and manage to collect my things without causing further fuss. Collin waits by the door the entire time, as if I'm going to walk out with him.

I snort. If that's what he thinks is happening, he's in for a rude awakening.

After I slip on my jacket and shoulder my purse, I ignore the remaining diners who all watch me with interest, as if waiting for the dramafest between Collin and me to continue.

But instead of embarrassing myself further, I push through the front door. I practically hear the diners' collective sigh of disappointment.

On the sidewalk, I pull the collar of my jacket up higher. A cold January breeze stings my cheeks. Winter here is a bitch. My grandmother warned me that I was in for a shock since I'm from the southwest, and she wasn't kidding. It's fucking freezing in this state.

Footsteps sound behind me, and I know Collin's following me. I also know that he *wants* me to know he's following, because I can hear him.

But I ignore him and hurry my pace. My car's parked on the next block. Only a few more steps until I reach it.

"Brianna," Collin calls when I cross the intersection. He increases his pace until he's striding beside me. "Please. Can I talk to you?"

I don't respond and instead pull my keys out. My car, a gift from my grandparents, is parked ahead. It's a cute little bright-blue SUV with all-wheel drive and heated seats. It's by far the nicest vehicle I've ever owned.

I click my key fob and the doors unlock.

"Brianna," Collin says, his tone exasperated.

When I reach my car, I go to open the door, but he places his hand on it and blocks me.

Bastard! I finally give him my attention, but I'm seething. "Let. Me. In. My. Car."

His jaw works, the muscle ticking. "Not until you've let me say a few things."

"I don't have to let you say anything." I wrench at the door handle, but he doesn't budge.

I'm contemplating slapping him again when he says in a rush, "Will you please just listen to me? Please? Can we go somewhere and talk?"

"What? Talk? You've got to be kidding me. Do you seriously think I'm going to listen to anything you have to say? You lied to me and used me. Now move!"

"Brianna," he pleads, but at least he respects that I asked him to move as he inches away.

I yank my door open.

His nostrils flare, but I refuse to meet his eyes. Instead, I slip into my seat and drive away.

CHAPTER FORTY-THREE
BRIANNA

"You'll never guess who's standing outside your building even though it's snowing out." Macy snorts in disgust before letting the blinds fall back into place. She strolls across my room to plop on my bed. "You would think that after you left him standing on the street three days ago and have refused to talk to him since that he'd get the picture."

"I know, right?"

She gives me a worried look. "It's starting to border on obsessive, Bri. You sure he's not a psycho?"

If you only knew. But I shake my head. "He's not. He's just persistent. He'll lose interest eventually." *It's probably just his bruised ego that's keeping him out there anyway, but that'll pass.*

"Well his persistent ass can kiss my ass." She laughs, and I try to join in, but it's hard.

Even though it's been three days since my run-in with Collin, my nerves haven't calmed in the slightest. It doesn't help that he's been following me.

On Friday morning when I had class on campus, he was

waiting for me by my building's door. I bolted across the snowy lawn when I saw him and snuck in the back.

But only a few hours later, he was waiting outside the diner before my shift started. I entered through the maintenance door and had my co-workers serve Collin when he tried to sit in my section.

Thank the lord baby Cheez-its Macy flew in Friday night. And in a few weeks I'll fly back to Arizona to see her and finally clean out my apartment. I need these distractions right now because Collin's return has completely fried my composure.

For whatever reason, Collin seems determined to talk to me. I just hope that sooner or later he'll give up. After all, I'm not actually his fated mate as Cali helped me learn, so I don't know what the hell he wants from me.

I pause briefly, thinking of Cali. I haven't seen her since the trial, but my grandparents tell me she returned to her pack in Wyoming. I did a bit of asking around about her and from everything I could find, she's a decent person.

If only I'd listened to her.

The only blessing in this mess is that Macy's here. She flew in Friday night for a weekend visit, and I've never been so happy to have her around. It's only the second time she's come to visit me since I moved to Montana, but the timing couldn't have been better. Having her with me for the past two days has kept me occupied, especially when Collin's been lurking around every corner trying to speak with me.

Macy toys with her dark hair, curling a strand around her finger. "You know, leaving him out in the cold serves him right. That fucker. What did he think? That he could use you, ignore you for months, and then come strolling back like nothing happened?"

I take a deep breath and shake my head, but I keep my

gaze averted. Macy knows about Collin, but she doesn't know *about* him. She knows that he's the reason I left Arizona and that he helped me find my mom's family. But beyond that, she doesn't know the details.

She has no idea that I'm half-werewolf, or that Collin was in prison in the fae lands until apparently this week. She has no idea that I thought he was my fated mate or that the thought of life without him still leaves a gaping hole in my chest.

But she *does* know that he lied to me and broke my heart. And when it comes to girl-code that tells her everything important.

"Should we go out tonight?" Macy asks. She inches closer to the edge of my bed. "I mean, don't get me wrong. It's been fun hanging in your apartment watching all these movies and getting fat on chocolate, but I didn't bring my stilettos along for nothing."

I groan. "Girl. I'm sorry. You've been so amazing this weekend, and I've been such a downer."

"No, not at all. But seriously, woman, the best way to get over a guy is to go out and find another one."

She waggles her eyebrows, which gets a genuine giggle out of me. I haven't been able to fathom dating again, but maybe she's right. Maybe hooking up with some random dude for a casual one-night stand is exactly what I need right now.

"Is he still there?" I nod toward the window. I'm too anxious to get up and look. Even seeing him makes my heart hurt.

Macy returns to the window. "Yep, but if we go out the back stairwell, he won't see us, and the bar's only four blocks away, right? We can walk it."

I raise my eyebrows. "Icy sidewalks in stilettos? Are you sure that's a good idea?"

She waves off my concerns. "I'll just grab onto you if I start to go down."

Another giggle escapes me. "You know what, you're right. Get those boots on, babe, cause we're going out!"

Macy whoops and bounces off the bed. "Let's get a move on, girl. My red-eye is in five hours, which means we can tear it up for a few hours before I have to leave."

I laugh. "Do you think they'll let you on the plane if you're drunk?"

"Only one way to find out."

I shake my head and rummage through my closet for something to wear. When I grab jeans and a sweater, Macy *tsks* and pulls out a tight skirt and sequined top.

"If we're going out, we're going *out*."

I roll my eyes but oblige her.

Thirty minutes later, we're dressed to the nines with styled hair and skillfully applied makeup—thanks to Macy, that's totally her department.

"Ready?" Macy's standing at the door. She's wearing skin-tight leather pants, stiletto boots, and a thin cotton sweater that clings to her round curves. Even though she's six inches shorter than me, the boots give her extra height. She's almost at eye-level with me. Almost.

"Yeah, let's go."

∽

WE MANAGE to slide our way down the sidewalk as snow falls around us. Macy shrieks a few times when we hit patches of ice, but after many giggles and close-calls, we make it to the bar.

A blast of warm air runs over us when we step inside. The bar isn't overly crowded since it's a Sunday night, but at least a dozen guys stand around drinking beer while half a dozen women idle in small groups around them. Being a pack town, everyone's tall and built, and everyone knows everyone as I've come to learn in the past few weeks.

A few of the women and men nod in my direction, and I incline my head in greeting. I'm still learning who's who, but I know that everybody knows my story. How couldn't they? The Drummond granddaughter who only just learned she's a wolf after falling in love with a rogue who was sent away to supernatural prison.

Yep, you can't make that shit up.

I was the talk of the town when I first arrived, and that talk had only just started to die down, but then Collin shows up. Now, of course, it's back in full swing.

Thanks mate, I think sarcastically.

Macy lets out a low whistle as she appraises the guys. She grabs my hand and hisses under her breath, "Girl, look at this meat! These guys are freakin' built!"

Joel, an early twenty-something wolf is standing near the bar's corner. His lips curve up after Macy's admission, but he doesn't look at us. I work frantically to keep my blush under control. Of course he heard her, but Macy doesn't know that werewolf hearing is a gazillion times better than human hearing is.

I clear my throat and pull my puffy jacket closer around me. Most of the wolves in here are wearing ranching wear versus the city stuff Macy and I are dressed in. We're going to stick out like a sore thumb that's for sure.

But when I try to hide myself, Macy grabs my jacket and basically forces it off. "Nuh-uh. That is *not* how tonight is going to go. We're flaunting what we got and hopefully finding some hot dudes who will buy us drinks all night. And I'm telling you that covering that bod of yours isn't going to get us free shots."

She's already flung her coat on the bench in the empty corner table. A second later, mine lands on top of hers.

I do my best to stand tall, but when half the guys—the ones without dates—all turn in my direction, the blush I've been working frantically to control comes roaring back.

Their gazes rake us up and down, and their sly smiles follow.

A burst of anxiety pulses through me. I've never been self-conscious about my looks, but I haven't been with a man since Collin. It's been over two months and it feels as if my girly bits have dried up. The thought of another guy doing to me what Collin did . . . well, it's enough to make me want to swallow nails.

But then I remember that I'm trying to get over Collin and maybe having drunk sex with a random stranger is a step in the right direction.

Macy certainly seems to think so.

She pulls me toward the bar and has no qualms about sliding right up to one of the locals. Devon's around six-three, with a broad nose, dark hair, and a square jaw.

Macy smiles sweetly at him and gives him a cute pout.

Devon grins crookedly. "I don't think I've seen you around here before."

Macy pulls me to her side before replying. "Nope, just visiting my friend here for the weekend. She recently moved to Crescent Crossing, and since we're besties, I plan to come back regularly."

He seems to catch her meaning since his eyelids grow hooded. Two of the guys standing around him, Joel and another guy I haven't met, all step closer.

"Would you ladies like a drink?" Joel glances my way as Macy runs a finger up Devon's chest.

Macy is nothing if not bold, and I can tell that she's ensnared Devon's attention. My friend is dwarfed by every man here, but even though she carries an extra twenty pounds on her small frame, she carries it in all the right places.

Devon's gaze continually dips to her full breasts and round hips while Joel and the other guy drift my way.

"It's Brianna, right?" the guy by Joel says. He has strawberry blond hair and five o'clock shadow. He's at least six-four with block slabs for pecs and a sexy smile.

"That's right. Have we met?" I plant a hand on my waist and cock my hip.

His eyes drop for the merest second before he forces them up. The glitzy top Macy made me wear is low cut, and my cleavage is on full display. "No, but I've been wanting to meet you. Name's Tanner."

The bar's door opens behind Tanner, and a rush of cold air enters. A chill runs over me, but that's nothing compared to the ice that settles in my stomach when I see who the newcomer is.

Collin steps inside the bar before closing the door after him. A frightening-looking scowl covers his face. His gaze immediately finds mine, and when he sees me surrounded by a group of wolves, his jaw clenches so hard I swear his teeth crack.

"Are you fucking kidding me?" Macy hisses. She jabs me in the side. "That fucker is not ruining our night." She thrusts a shot in my hand. "Bottoms up, girl."

I throw back the shot, wincing when it burns the back of my throat, but I need alcohol *now*. "Good God what was that?" I grimace when I set the empty shot glass back on the bar.

Tanner laughs. "That was whiskey. Want another?"

He inches toward me. His hand brushes my arm, then his chest presses against my side when he leans closer to the bar to grab another round of drinks.

A swell of power barrels off Collin, but I try to ignore it when it hits me. It's hard, though. The urge to cower grows so strong I can barely resist it. The other wolves notice it, too, given their abrupt tenseness, but I imagine magical pulses from the men in this town are par for the course because they all ignore my ex.

I eye Collin again. He's stalked to the end of the bar and has planted himself on a stool. Rage shines in his eyes, and his hands are fisted. He's still staring at me and looking as if he wants to murder Tanner, Joel, Devon, and every other male within three feet of me.

I take one look at my enraged ex and turn a desperate smile up at Tanner. "Yes, please."

∼

I'M MORE than tipsy by the time someone puts money in the old-fashioned jukebox. Music blasts from the speakers, and Macy grabs Devon's hand before pulling him toward the dance floor. A few of the other couples join in, and I can't help but wonder if this is the liveliest night the local bar has seen in a while.

Whatever the case, I'm enjoying myself. Or trying to.

At least an hour has passed since Collin entered the bar. His brother, Pete, is here now too. I'd heard at work that Pete was in town, and I figured somebody called him when they realized his brother was about to go mental.

Several times, Pete's stopped Collin from vaulting across the bar when Tanner's touched me. I don't know why Collin's acting like this when I'm just another ex of his, but my stomach is so tight at the tension strumming off him that I've been downing shots left and right.

The alcohol is helping my anxiety, and hopefully Pete will stop Collin from kicking the shit out of everyone.

Cause I'm guessing if Collin hurts anyone, it will violate his parole, which probably means he'll get a one-way ticket back to prison in the fae lands.

My forehead scrunches up as alcohol swims through my veins. I don't actually know if felons in the supernatural community have parole or not.

Whatever the case, Pete now sits beside Collin at the bar. The fury pouring from my ex-boyfriend is enough to make my teeth chatter, but I imagine the only reason he hasn't gone alpha on anyone is because so far all I've done is drink.

Either that . . . or, you know . . . parole.

But I don't know if even Pete will be able to contain Collin if I leave with one of these guys. For whatever reason, my ex-boyfriend is acting as possessive as ever, which makes zero sense since we're not together anymore.

"Want another?" Tanner asks. Without waiting for my reply, he slips a shot between my fingers.

My grip closes around the cool glass as a snarl comes from where Collin sits.

Tanner's gotten a bit familiar with his hands, but every time his fingers have worked their way up my back or brushed too close to my breast, I've moved away.

I tell myself it's to keep Collin from beating him to a pulp, but I would be lying to myself if I said that was the only reason.

The truth is that my heart still aches for Collin, and as much as that irritates me to no end, I can't help how I feel.

But then I remind myself that those feelings are exactly why I'm here. However, going home with a dude with the intention of having drunk sex with him while your enraged ex watches from the sidelines is awkward with a capital A.

At least Macy's enjoying herself. I have no idea what

time it is, and I hope she's keeping track. If not, she's going to miss her flight.

"Want to dance?" Tanner asks. His eyes are glassy from the alcohol, and his touches are growing emboldened. He leans closer, and his lips brush against my ear. "Just one?"

I don't have to look up to know that Collin's just launched himself from his stool. Pete's got his hands wrapped around my ex's shoulders, but his expression's strained as Collin tries to push him off.

"You know what? Yes, let's dance!" I grab Tanner's hand and pull him toward the dance floor.

Tanner grins, not seeming to care that touching me has put a target on his back, but again, I'm guessing this kind of stuff is normal in the werewolf world so Tanner probably doesn't care.

His hands slide around my waist as I begin to sway to the beat. I close my eyes, and try to enjoy the moment, but when his head comes down and his scent washes around me, it feels . . .

Wrong.

I don't have to pull away though. A roar breaks through the music, and in the next instant, Tanner is ripped away from me.

"Seriously!" Macy screams. She jumps out of the way as Tanner slides across the floor. "What the fuck, dude!" She pushes away from Devon just as I come face to face with my ex.

Collin's seething and staring down at me. Veins pulse in his neck, and fury contorts his features.

He doesn't even glance in Macy's direction when she begins berating him for being a psycho ex-boyfriend and for throwing Tanner across the bar.

"Brianna," he says tightly. "Enough of this game. I need to talk to you, and I'm not taking no for an answer anymore." He grabs a hold of my arm and pulls me from the dance floor. A thrill runs through me at the feel of his skin touching mine, and I want to hit myself over the head.

How can I still react to him after what he's done? *I'm so fucking pathetic!*

Macy claws at his hand, but I give her a reassuring glance and let Collin pull me away. She glowers at him but stops when she sees he's not trying to take me out of the building.

Instead, he pulls me to the back corner where it's dark and less crowded.

Fury still emanates from him in scorching waves. My breathing kicks up. I can't help it. Already, my panties have grown damp from the sight and smell of him. Seeing him so worked up and jealous only makes it worse.

So fucked up, Drummond. This is seriously fucked up.

But when Collin snakes an arm around my waist and hauls me right against his chest, I can see that I'm not the only one influenced by our close contact. His pupils are dilated, and steady waves of alpha power roll off him. He pushes my back against the wall and places his other hand beside my cheek. He's effectively pinned me, and my nerves electrify.

"You are *mine*," he growls. He leans closer and dips his mouth toward my neck. "Mine and mine only. Don't you get that?"

Despite it feeling like my knees are going to give out, I shove at his chest. He doesn't budge, not even an inch, and anger swells inside me that he still has the audacity to act like we're anything after what he did.

"No, I'm not. Remember? Or have you forgotten about what a fool you made of me?"

Pain flashes in his eyes. "I know. I hate myself for doing that to you, but Bri, I lied to you. I never used you as a cover and I didn't make up that we're fated mates. I said all of that so you would leave me. I couldn't stomach the thought of you throwing your life away on me. Even though the thought of you moving on killed me, I chose that so you could have a life. With me imprisoned, you would have had no life at all. I couldn't do that to you."

My lips part. *He lied? He didn't use me?* But then I remember Cali's testimony.

"I'm sorry," I say sarcastically. "Did you say fated mates? Were you referring to me or the dozen other women before me? It seems you're fated to quite a few women. Perhaps you're getting us mixed up?"

His nostrils flare, but his lips quirk up. "Damn, I love your fire."

"Is that right? Does that mean you want me to slap you again?" I hiss.

"If that's the only way you'll touch me, you can slap me all you want."

I manage to work my arm free and raise my hand, but he grabs my wrist and pushes it against the wall. He sinks more into me, and the feel of his hard chest and stomach make my head spin.

Lowering his mouth to my ear, he says quietly, "You damn well know that you're the only true fated mated I've ever had. I told you I used to be an ass—"

"Used to?"

He releases my wrist and presses his finger to my lips. I'm tempted to bite it.

"Yes, I used to be an asshole. I didn't care about women. I didn't care about who I hurt. I was a complete dick to every female I dated, but then I met my mate, and everything changed. She made me want to be a better man, and I became one because of her."

He rubs against me, and dammit, my stomach dips

when his scent floods me. I seethe at my body. *Whose side are you on?*

Of course, a tingle runs down my spine when he leans down to inhale my scent. "I've missed you. I've thought about you every day and dreamed about you every night. All I wanted was to see you and touch you again, but I couldn't allow that. It wouldn't be fair to you."

I shake my head furiously. I try to cross my arms but once again, I fail miserably. He's got me completely pinned. I settle with, "Why should I believe anything you say?"

His eyes begin to glow. "Because you're my mate, and you belong with me."

I snort. "Yeah, I've heard that before and look how that turned out."

His lips quirk up before he grazes his fingers across my cheek. Despite trying to stop it, another shiver runs down my spine.

The music continues back by the bar, and I know Macy's going to come looking for me soon if I don't make an appearance, but for the life of me . . . fuck . . . for the life of me, I don't want the feel of him pressing against me to end.

The glow in Collin's eyes intensifies. "You are *mine*, Brianna Keller Drummond. You were from the first moment I laid eyes on you." He dips his head and whispers, "And I'm sorry. I'm so very sorry that I hurt you. I didn't want to, but I didn't know how else to make you leave and have your own life. I hate what I did to you, but I *will* make it up to you. Please forgive me."

And in those words, I *know*. I know that we truly are fated mates and that he lied to me to keep me away.

I beat a fist against his chest. I want to hate him. I want to push him off me and tell him to fuck off, but everything inside of me wants to be with him even though I'm still desperately mad at him.

"You shouldn't have done that," I say. "You shouldn't have lied to me! You should have let *me* make my own decisions about what *I* wanted. You shouldn't have made that decision for me!"

He cups my face between his hands, his palms warm and rough. "I thought it was for the best. With me imprisoned, you wouldn't ever have children or a husband to come home to. You would barely see me."

"That would have been better than you leaving me." To my horror, tears form in my eyes. "You destroyed me."

He sighs, a deep shuddering sound. "My love. My mate. I will spend the rest of my life making it up to you. I will die a thousand slow deaths if it makes you happy. I will do anything to make this right. Please, my love. Please forgive me."

I roll my eyes, and he cocks his head. "A thousand slow deaths? Really? You're being a bit melodramatic, don't you think?"

He smiles, then chuckles deeply. "Ah, right. My mate, the non-romantic. In that case, I won't die a thousand deaths, but would you settle for me apologizing to you every day and doing whatever you need from me to make you forgive me?"

I frown, the pain of the past two months still needling at my heart, but already the ice encasing it is melting. Inside, my soul is awakening, and I know I'm helpless to resist him. This man has the power not only to destroy me but to resurrect me. He holds my heart in his hands, and knowing he has that much power is unsettling.

"What is it?" he asks.

I shake my head. "You played so easily with my

emotions, and I fell apart because of that. No man has ever done that to me before. I hate that."

The music pulses more in the background as the song switches, and I can feel Macy's anxious glances my way, but I can't tear my attention from the virile werewolf pinning me to the wall.

"I know," Collin replies. "It wasn't okay what I did, but if it's any consolation, you hold the same power over me. You could break me with just a look, and right now, you hold my heart in your hands. If you reject me, I'll spend the rest of my life alone. No woman will ever come after you, and I'm not being melodramatic. I'm being honest. You're my mate, my *fated* mate. Don't you understand what that means? There can only ever be you now. There will only *ever* be you."

I shiver when he moves his arm from around my waist to cup my hip. "Can I take you home?"

"Macy's still here."

"Isn't she leaving soon?"

"How did you know that?" I roll my eyes before he can respond. "Oh wait, you've been stalking me again. Of course you know."

He chuckles before leaning down to press his lips against my neck. Desire floods my core, and I arch against him.

He growls in approval, but I somehow manage to ask, "How is it that you're here anyway?" I've heard bits and pieces in the past few days, but I tried to shut out everything floating in the air around this town that pertained to Collin, so I still don't fully know how he got out of prison.

"It all started with Daria, that healer." He launches into an unbelievable tale of how the courts are allowing him to serve his sentence outside prison after the gargoyles leeched fifty years of his life. When I gasp at that, Collin only smiles.

"Now our lifetimes are equal," he says. When I give him a quizzical look, he explains. "Werewolves live longer than humans, but you're a half-breed as I've come to learn. You would never have lived as long as me, but now that the gargoyles have taken years off my life, we should die around the same time."

"They took years from your life?" I screech.

But he just nods calmly. "It's what gargoyles do. Leeching is how they come alive and why the courts use them."

I shake my head. Even though I've been living with other supernaturals for over two months, there's still so much I don't know. "But I still don't understand how any of this is possible. You never would have been allowed to live outside of prison in the human world."

"I know, but things are different in the community. And ultimately, it was Daria convincing the queen justice that my wolf had healed, that he was no longer insane, that ultimately led to my rehabilitation program." He goes on to explain how Daria had felt his healed wolf when she touched him in the courtroom. She had dipped her healing magic into his brain and was able to see a thoroughly sane and clean mind.

"So they truly believe that you're no longer a rogue?"

He nods.

"And instead of prison, they said you could serve your sentence in a life of servitude?"

He nods again but then his jaw locks. "It's important that you understand what that means. I won't be able to work on my family's ranch, which means I won't be earning the Ward money. My income comes from the community courts now and is modest at best. I'll take a second job so I can provide better for you, but we'll never live like my parents." His brow furrows. "I won't be able to give you the life I envisioned. You'll most likely have to work, too, to make ends me."

Devastation crosses his features, and his eyes glow more. And in that moment, any remaining ice around my heart melts away. I lay a hand tenderly across his cheek. "I always intended to work, my love. I'm not one to sit at home, so if that's your biggest concern, you can rest easy." A look of such relief washes over his face that I laugh.

"So you forgive me and you're okay with the life that I have to offer you?" he asks.

I push away from the wall and pull him toward the dance floor. Quite suddenly, I want to laugh, dance, and be merry, and the only man I want to do it with is him.

In a cheeky tone, I reply, "I suppose so, and since I won't be left barefoot and pregnant in the kitchen, you better know that you're on dish duty four nights a week."

A grin stretches across his face, then he laughs before grabbing my hand and twirling me around.

Suddenly, the future feels so much brighter.

EPILOGUE
COLLIN

I survey the bedroom, making sure all of the details are right. Our king-size bed is surrounded by a sea of candles. I've changed the sheets, fluffed the pillows, and have soft music playing in the background. In our bathroom, a scalding bubble bath awaits. It should cool to the perfect temperature by the time I place my mate in it.

Brianna's due home from work soon, and I want tonight to be perfect. It's only our second night together in our new apartment, and she's not expecting me to be here, but my parole officer let me have the night off so I decided to surprise her with what I've been dreaming of since I arrived in Crescent Crossing.

Initially, I had wanted to rent a remote cabin for what I had planned tonight. A little dwelling hidden away in the woods would have been perfect—a romantic getaway that would make this night even more special—but then I remembered who my mate is. Brianna would no doubt cross her arms at the frivolous use of money and tell me that such romantic accommodations weren't needed. She would be just as happy to stay in a tent.

I chuckle. Fuck, I love my mate. She suits me perfectly and keeps me in check when I need it.

I take one last look to make sure everything's perfect. Snow flies outside, and the full moon calls to my wolf. He whines in anticipation, more than ready for what's to come since tonight is the night he's been waiting for.

The sound of a key entering the front door's lock kicks me into action. I whiz out of the bedroom and to the kitchen where the sauce is bubbling on the stove. Red wine is airing in a carafe on the counter. Dinner first. My mate's always hungry after work.

I'm shirtless, wearing only jeans, and am waiting with a glass of wine for her when she opens the door.

Her eyes pop when she sees me. "Collin! What are you doing here? I thought you were working at the community center tonight?"

I take her jacket, then hand her the glass of wine. She gives me a surprised look but readily takes it. Fatigue fills her eyes, but I've learned not to say anything. Brianna's a hard worker, she always has been, and she would rather work every day and come home tired every night than be a pampered well-rested housewife who sits at home watching soap operas day in and day out.

She's so fucking perfect.

"I got the night off," I tell her.

A smile parts her lips, and she takes a sip of the wine. "Lucky me, and mmm, this is good. Where did you buy it?"

My parents' cellar. "Just a place I know that has good wine." My mom had been more than happy to give me a bottle when I last saw her. My parents are still so ecstatic to have me out of prison—even if they're still in denial that I was ever a rogue—that they would give me anything I asked for.

But I don't take advantage of that. There are only two

things I've taken from them: the wine for my mate, and a thirty-thousand dollar advance on my inheritance. After learning the name of the hatchback's owner—the car I stole all of those months ago—I repaid him via an anonymous cash donation. He probably has no idea it was for his stolen vehicle, and he probably got an insurance payout, too, but when I told my mate what I'd done, the beaming smile across her face told me I'd done the right thing.

I also paid back my brother the three grand I stole from him during my second ATM withdrawal when I'd been on the run. Pete had been understanding, just like I thought he would be, but my guilt lessened after I repaid that debt.

And the last thing I used the money for was to pay for Brianna's final year of school at the University of Montana now that she's transferred. Just like I promised her back in the California desert, I repaid her for the semester of classes she lost in Arizona when she chose to stay with me. And paying for that final semester? Well, I meant it when I told my mate I wanted to take care of her.

But besides those two things, I haven't accepted anything else from my parents. One thing I'm sure of, after twenty-eight years of life, is that I'm not a spoiled child anymore, and I'm not the man I used to be. I've learned how to stand on my own two feet since going rogue. I've also learned that money and having nice things aren't everything, and I've realized that kindness will get me further in life than darkness and revenge.

My mate helped me see that, and I'm a better man because of it.

Brianna kicks her shoes off and pulls her hair out of her ponytail. Her long dark hair tumbles down her back, and for a moment, my breath stops. *So beautiful.* My mate is more stunning than any woman on earth.

She tilts her head and sniffs. "Did you cook dinner too?"

"I did." I give her a wicked grin before guiding her to the kitchen. Tall candles flicker on the table that's already set.

Her eyes widen when she takes in the display. "Are we celebrating something?"

"We will be."

I feel her curiosity growing, but I don't tell her anything more. Instead, I serve her a dinner of braised short ribs with a cabernet reduction, potato puree and heirloom vegetables. We spend the dinner talking about our day and our upcoming plans for the spring.

When we finish, I pull her chair out and lift her in my arms. She lets out a little laugh. "Collin! What is going on?"

I don't reply. I take her to the bathroom and strip every piece of clothing from her glorious body. Her breathing grows shallow when I kneel in front of her and peel off her panties. I press a kiss to her womanly mound and inhale. Already, my mate is aroused.

"Collin?" she whispers breathlessly.

But I leave the curious tone of her question unanswered and proceed to lift her once more before setting her in the warm bath. She moans in delight when the hot liquid eases into her muscles. I wash her from head to toe, massaging her the entire time.

Desire grows in her eyes. I'm toying with her and loving it even though my dick strains against my jeans. I keep my attention on my mate, though, and use my fingers to arouse her even more. By the time I finish bathing and caressing her, she's panting.

"Collin," she moans. Her eyelids are hooded, and she feels like jelly in my arms.

Good. My mate is ready.

"I want to claim you tonight, my love," I say when I lift her from the tub.

For the briefest moment, her eyes widen. I've only been back a few weeks, and I'm not sure if it's enough time for my mate to understand what her life will be like with me. I can only hope that it is.

"Will you let me?" I ask uncertainly.

She flings her arms around my neck and presses her lips to mine. Relief floods me, and I pull her tighter against me. I dip my tongue into her mouth. In response, she moans and threads her fingers through my hair.

I carry her to the bedroom, our lips locked together. She's breathless when she pulls back then gasps when she sees our bedroom.

A little giggle escapes her. "My love. You truly are a romantic."

I chuckle and toss her on the bed. She bounces once and laughs again, but when I peel my jeans off all laughter dies from her eyes. She spreads her legs and bares her neck, and the sight has a primal longing igniting in me to make this woman mine.

I sink between her legs, my hard length long and ready.

She strokes me, then positions me at her entrance. I prod against her swollen lips and stifle a groan. She's so wet for me.

"Make me yours, my fated mate," she whispers.

I don't need any more encouragement. I plunge into her in one long movement, and she screams in pleasure. For a moment, I can't move. She's so hot and tight. Every night I slide inside her, but each time, I marvel at how fucking perfect she feels.

She wraps her legs around me, and I pick up a steady rhythm. I got her so aroused in the bath that her eyes are already rolling back in her head. She's close to coming, which makes my dick even harder.

"Are you ready?" I ask her.

She nods and rakes her fingers down my back. I groan. My mate is a true werewolf, all hotness and fire.

I pull up my alpha magic and let it wash over her. "Open your eyes," I command, using my alpha power. She can't resist.

Her lids flash open, her mouth making a surprised O at my dominance, but her arousal grows higher, the scent of her core flooding the room. She loves when I dominate her.

"You're mine forever, mate."

"Yes," she pants. "Yes."

I let my wolf out more, just enough to make my eyes glow and my teeth elongate. She tilts her head, exposing her neck while I relentlessly pump into her.

I pick up the pace, fucking her hard just as I bite down. She gasps in pain when I break the skin, but she's so lost in the feel of me pounding her that she moans in pleasure again.

I thrust harder as my magic flows into her veins and groan when I feel the claiming begin to take root. It flows in steady rivers through her limbs, heating her body while sealing us as one. She cries out when my magic fully engulfs her. At its height, she can feel all of my power, arousal, and possessive desire to make her mine. Its strength scorches her nerves.

"Fuck yes!" she screams.

I pound her harder as the claiming molds us as one. "You're *mine*," I command.

"Yes!" Her channel spasms out of control when an orgasm explodes in her body.

I groan in pleasure when her slick walls tighten around

my cock. It sends me over the edge, and I shout my release just as my magic fully seals our bond.

Love, possession, dominance, submission—it all rolls into one as our mating engraves into our souls.

We stay locked together, my magic ebbing and flowing. Her orgasm peaks, gripping my length in never ending waves.

It lasts for minutes yet feels like hours. Pure pleasure that can only be caused by a claiming while fucking consumes us.

And finally, when it subsides, I'm panting from the exertion. Sweat coats our skin, and Brianna's arms tremble around my neck.

Working my jaw, I detach from her neck, licking where I bit her. My saliva heals the puncture wounds, and I smile smugly when I see the crescent moon mark where I bit.

Brianna's still trembling beneath me. I long to know what she's feeling, and all I have to do is open the channel that connects us.

Balancing my weight above her, I open myself.

Her lips part when all of my love, protectiveness, and fierce loyalty that I feel for her strums through our bond.

Tears moisten her eyes. "We really do have a connection."

I laugh. "Did you think I was making it up?"

She giggles, and her emotions flow into me. I feel all of it, everything inside her: happiness, awe, humility, and love.

My stomach tightens when I feel her undying love. It's as bright as the sun and as powerful as a tsunami. I swallow the thick emotion that forms in my throat, and I tenderly brush a strand of hair from her cheek.

"You saved me, my love. Without you, I was lost, and it was only a matter of time before my life ended. But you stayed with me and made me believe in myself again. I'm a better man because of you, and now with you at my side, my life is complete."

She pulls me down until our lips meet. I kiss her softly as a single tear leaks from her eye.

"No," she replies. "We saved each other, and now I'm yours and you're mine—forever."

ABOUT THE AUTHOR

Krista Street loves writing in multiple genres: fantasy, sci-fi, romance, and dystopian. Her books are cross-genre and often feature complex characters, plenty of supernatural twists, and romance in every story. She loves writing about coming-of-age characters who fight to find their place in this world while also finding their one true mate.

Krista Street is a Minnesota native but has lived throughout the U.S. and in another country or two. She loves to travel, read, and spend time in the great outdoors. When not writing, Krista is either chasing her children, spending time with her husband and friends, sipping a cup of tea, or enjoying the hidden gems of beauty that Minnesota has to offer.

THANK YOU

Thank you for reading *Beast of Shadows*.

If you enjoy Krista Street's writing, make sure you visit her website to learn about her new release text alerts, newsletter, and other series.

www.kristastreet.com

Links to all of her social media sites are available on every page.

∼

And if you enjoyed reading *Beast of Shadows*, please consider logging onto the retailer you purchased this book from to post a review. Authors rely heavily on readers reviewing their work. Even one sentence helps a lot. Thank you so much if you do!

Printed in Great Britain
by Amazon